# TO PLAY WITH FIRE

BY
TINA BECKETT

MILLS &
BOON®

Published in Great Britain 2014
by Mills & Boon, an imprint of Harlequin (UK) Limited,
Eton House, 18-24 Paradise Road, Richmond, Surrey, TW9 1SR

© 2014 Tina Beckett

ISBN: 978 0 263 90752 0

Harlequin (UK) Limited's policy is to use papers that are natural,
renewable and recyclable products and made from wood grown in
sustainable forests. The logging and manufacturing processes conform
to the legal environmental regulations of the country of origin.

Printed and bound in Spain
by Blackprint CPI, Barcelona

**Dear Reader**

I'm sure all of you have read stories about long-lost relatives somehow finding each other after years apart. Whether that reunion takes place as a result of social media, an ad in the newspaper, or through the efforts of family and friends, that first meeting is often an emotional, heart-wrenching time. Depending on how many years—or decades—have elapsed, those people might even feel like strangers when they finally come together.

This kind of story provided the basis for Marcos's and Lucas's books, only their tale has an added twist. The brothers grew up on two separate continents, one having been adopted while the other grew up in an orphanage in his home country. Now adults, with different last names, one thing binds them together: a promise they made many years earlier—one they each fulfilled in his own special way. I freely admit to shedding a tear or two as these characters struggled through some heartbreaking memories and reforged their connections to each other and their past.

Thank you for joining these strong men as they learn about love and loss, and as they work their way towards a happy ending with a couple of very special women. I hope you enjoy their journey as much as I enjoyed writing about it!

Much love!

*Tina Beckett*

Born to a family that was always on the move, **Tina Beckett** learned to pack a suitcase almost before she knew how to tie her shoes. Fortunately she met a man who also loved to travel, and she snapped him right up. Married for over twenty years, Tina has three wonderful children and has lived in gorgeous places such as Portugal and Brazil.

Living where English reading material is difficult to find has its drawbacks, however. Tina had to come up with creative ways to satisfy her love for romance novels, so she picked up her pen and tried writing one. After her tenth book she realised she was hooked. She was officially a writer.

A three-time Golden Heart finalist, and fluent in Portuguese, Tina now divides her time between the United States and Brazil. She loves to use exotic locales as the backdrop for many of her stories. When she's not writing you can find her either on horseback or soldering stained glass panels for her home.

Tina loves to hear from readers. You can contact her through her website or 'friend' her on Facebook.

**Recent titles by Tina Beckett:**

HER HARD TO RESIST HUSBAND
THE LONE WOLF'S CRAVING**
NYC ANGELS: FLIRTING WITH DANGER*
ONE NIGHT THAT CHANGED EVERYTHING
THE MAN WHO WOULDN'T MARRY
DOCTOR'S MILE-HIGH FLING
DOCTOR'S GUIDE TO DATING IN THE JUNGLE

*NYC Angels*
***Men of Honour* duet with Anne Fraser

# PROLOGUE

MARCOS HADN'T WANTED his father to go. But he'd gone anyway...just like he did every day.

Sitting in the dust outside their house, Marcos carefully sorted through the load his dad had brought home yesterday. Plastics here. Metals here... *Careful, don't get cut.* A rusty cabinet he and his brother had to drag over to the pile. Marcos had already snuck the screwdriver out of his father's backpack, so he could try to take the cabinet apart.

He had to do as much as possible before Papai came home, because it made something in Marcos's chest hurt to see his dad's hands shake as he tried to fit the tool into the screws— and the scared look he'd gotten on his face when he hadn't been able to.

"Watch your brother." His father's words had rung in his ears that morning, just as they had every morning since he'd seen his mom in that funny box. His dad had looked real scared that day, too. Marcos had just felt sad and hungry.

So he kept watching Lucas, while moving things from one stack to another. His brother was dragging a stick through the dirt, his feet almost black. Marcos frowned. Where were his flip-flops? There were lots of sharp things out here. But Lucas never listened. No matter how many times Marcos told him. He stomped over to his brother and kicked off his own shoes and pointed at them.

Lucas's lips got skinny, but he stuck his feet into the shoes.

He was mad. Marcos didn't care. It was his job to make sure Lucas didn't get hurt.

And now he had to make sure his dad didn't get hurt, either.

"We have to hurry." He glanced at the sun, which wasn't as bright any more. "Papai will be home soon."

"I don't care."

"Yes, you do. I heard you today. You said the same thing I did."

"Did not!" Lucas picked up a plastic drink bottle and threw it as hard as he could across the yard.

Marcos didn't argue with him. But before his dad had left this morning Marcos had told him he was going to be a doctor when he grew up, so he could make him all better.

Lucas's head had bobbed up and down. "Me, too. I'm going to be the best doctor in the whole world."

Papai had blinked his eyes several times and then turned away like he didn't believe them. But he would see. Marcos would make himself smart. Then his dad would stop shaking, and that scared look would go away.

The sound of hands clapping three times outside made them both freeze. Papai never clapped to get in. Only visitors did that.

Marcos snuck over to the tall fence and peeked between the cracks in the boards. It wasn't Papai. It was a man in a grey uniform. *"Polícia,"* he whispered.

He started to shake. Just like his dad.

Then the policeman squatted down and peered through the fence, staring right at him…

# CHAPTER ONE

HE COULD HAVE heard a pin drop.

Dr. Marcos Pinheiro began the slow, rhythmic countdown in his head as he waited for the patient on the other side of his desk to react.

Her hands slowly tightened on the armrests of the white leather chair.

*One...two...three...four...fi—*

"N-no more tumor? Are you sure?"

He nodded. "Your latest CT scan came back all clear. No signs of regrowth on your pituitary, *graças a Deus*. And your hormone levels are back within the normal range."

He kept his voice low and soothing, knowing she'd braced herself for bad news and was now struggling to process the fact that her worst fears were not going to be realized.

*"Graças a Deus,"* she repeated, making a quick sign of the cross over her chest.

Fifty-nine years old, with two children and three grandchildren, Graciela Abrigo might have been any number of patients he'd seen over the last several weeks. But she wasn't. And his little invocation of thanking God wasn't one he often made—especially not when talking to his patients.

But Graciela was special. She'd worked in the orphanage where Marcos had grown up—had put up with a lot of crap and acting out from him when his brother had been ripped from his side and adopted by some nameless family. He could still see the flash of fear in Lucas's young eyes.

*"Watch your brother."*

Bile rose, and he swallowed hard to rid himself of the taste.

He still didn't know what had happened to Lucas. No one by that name had shown up on any of Brazil's registries that he could find—then again, he probably had a new last name now.

But Graciela had assured him that the couple who had come for his brother had been nice. Kind. She'd seen it in their eyes. Lucas would have had a good home. *"Graças a Deus,"* she'd murmured, in a voice much like the one she'd just used.

As kind as this mysterious couple had supposedly been, they hadn't wanted Marcos. Hadn't seemed to care that they'd separated brothers who had still been reeling from their father's death six months after the fact.

He shook himself free of the anger that still had the power to wind around his gut and jettison him twenty-nine years into the past.

It was over. Those years were long gone.

Forcing a smile, he stood and rounded the desk. Graciela had been there for him when no one else had. And he was glad he'd been able to play a small part in doing something for her in return.

Because Marcos Pinheiro always repaid his debts.

And he always kept his promises.

Graciela stood as well and embraced him, cupping his cheeks and kissing his right one in customary São Paulo fashion.

The click of the door opening behind him sounded just as she said, "I have to get back to the home. Thank you, Markinho. For everything."

His smile this time was genuine, even as he tried not to wince at her use of his childhood nickname. "I haven't heard that in ages."

"Then it is time. You will always be little Markinho to me."

Turning to walk her to the door, the smile died on his lips when he saw who'd come into his office.

*Ah, hell.*

His mind blanked out all thoughts of Lucas and the past. Hopefully she hadn't heard Graciela's parting shot.

Because Markinho was not the image he wanted to project to those working under him. Especially not to a certain fiery-haired American who'd been "under" him in more ways than one. Actually, she'd been on top, if he wanted to get really technical about it.

Which he didn't. All he wanted to do was forget it had ever happened.

He saw his patient out and then slowly shut the door, turning to lean against it.

Dr. Maggie Pfeiffer. All long legs, luscious curves...and cool, collected efficiency.

*"Posso te ajudar?"* Marcos spoke English fluently, having made it a point to drill it ruthlessly into his head as he'd attended med school, knowing it was a necessity in today's medical fields. But he chose to address Maggie in Portuguese—though she still struggled at times with the language, even after six months at the hospital.

"Oh...um." After a moment's hesitation, she worked through her answer. "Yes. I have a question about one of our patients's treatment."

*Our.*

He'd been slowly letting out the reins and giving Maggie more responsibility, especially with international patients. Which served as a blessing, since it gave him some breathing space—time when he wasn't constantly aware of her scent... of the soft, sexy accent when she spoke his language.

The memory of her straddling his hips in the cramped confines of his car as they'd hammered out all the reasons she should be careful about using certain hand gestures caused a visceral reaction low in his gut. One that came on so fast he had to grit his teeth to fight his way through it. Beads of sweat broke out on his upper lip as the images of that day swept over him.

*Get past it, Marcos.*

Forcing his thoughts back to the here and now, he focused on a safer subject: her language abilities.

She was doing well, but there were still treatment methods she wasn't familiar with...words she struggled to translate in her head. And hearing her refer to his patient in a joint sense made something in his stomach shift. His eyes followed suit, moving lower for a split second to where Maggie's fingers were unconsciously fiddling with one of the buttons on her silky green blouse. Just below the swell of her breasts. Breasts that had filled his hands to perfection.

*Hell.*

He dragged his gaze back to her face. "Which patient are you referring to?"

"Ana Leandro."

"What's the question?" He pushed away from the door and took a step closer, his eyes narrowing when Maggie moved back a pace, her bottom hitting the edge of his desk. She glanced down at the wooden surface in surprise then reached back and gripped it with both hands, sending all kinds of images ricocheting through his skull.

Very bad images. Of him. And her...

And that desk.

"You have her physical therapy scheduled for once a week. But she's handling it well. Should we bump it up a bit and be a little more aggressive?"

He struggled to remember the patient's diagnosis, closing his eyes to pull up a physical description of the young woman. Marcos had always been a visual learner, committing things to memory in a way that most people couldn't. There'd been no books at their house, so he and his brother had both become adept at memorizing images and then trying to outdo the other.

He wondered if Lucas could still…

It didn't matter. Nothing did, except keeping his mind trained on the task at hand.

"Where's her chart?" She'd come into the room empty-handed, which was unusual. The woman was nothing if not meticulously efficient. Even the way she'd made love had been a study in efficiency—not a movement wasted. Not a sound made. Only the reflexive closing of her eyes as she'd lowered herself onto him one final time, the tightening of her hands on his shoulders and the sudden soft convulsions of her body telling him that she'd climaxed.

And her *frieza,* that cool, aloof manner that seemed so at odds with someone who had hair the color of burning embers had made the experience even hotter. Made him want to break through that icy wall and make her lose all control.

His body reacted again, and he took a steadying breath as he waited for her answer.

"Ana is in PT right now. I thought we might go and see her together."

"Together…" His brow lifted. "Right now?" Why he felt the need to goad her was a mystery. Maybe it was irritation at the reaction she seemed to draw from him every time she was near.

Maggie's lips parted, her teeth sinking deep into the lower one.

Okay, so maybe his thoughts weren't the only ones edging toward a very dangerous cliff. Although that might not be a good thing because he might just be tempted to leap over the edge, and take her with him.

"I would like us to go and see her. Together." Said as if she needed to clarify what she wanted to do with him.

Pity.

"Graciela was my last patient until after lunch, so…" He put a hand on the doorknob and pulled, the normal chaotic sounds of the hospital slipping through the opening and grounding him.

Just like they always did.

Silence was not his friend. Marcos was used to sound. Lots of it. His earliest memories were of his home in the *favela*, where the thin walls and corrugated metal roof had done nothing to dampen the sounds of life…and death. And afterwards, the orphanage where he'd been raised had been a boiling caldron of activity, the noise levels sometimes rising to the point where his ears had rung.

Which made Maggie's quiet manner and even quieter lovemaking seem otherworldly…as if a cool marble statue carved by some gifted sculptor had come to life. What would she think of his world? His background?

Not something he wanted to dwell on.

"After you." He motioned toward the open door.

"Oh. So you'll see her?"

"That is what you were asking me to do." He allowed the corners of his mouth to lift as his gaze trailed across her pale skin. "Isn't it?"

She colored, right on cue. His lips edged higher. At least that was one reaction he could wring from her. There were things that even Maggie Pfeiffer couldn't hide. The pucker of her nipples as he'd unbuttoned her blouse and let his fingers trail over her skin. The moist heat he'd discovered at the apex of those lean thighs as he'd pushed deep inside her.

"Yes. Of course it was." She let go of the desk and slid her palms down the fabric of her grey pencil skirt, drawing his attention once again to areas he should avoid. At all costs.

She swished by him, the economy of her steps matching everything else he knew of her. Maggie didn't waste her time on things that weren't important.

Like her own wants and needs?

Maybe that's why she'd fascinated him from the time he'd laid eyes on her all those months ago.

Brazilians were a hot people. And he'd grown up in an atmosphere where that heat had been fanned by the winds of desperation. People in the *favelas* clawed out happiness wherever they found it and devoured it whole. You didn't wait to be asked. You took. Eased whatever pain you had...whether it was in your belly or in your loins.

And right now that pain was definitely south of his stomach.

But he'd sworn to himself that Maggie was off-limits from now on. He'd had her once.

And that had been more than enough.

Maggie's legs were a quivering mass of nerves, but she forced them to keep moving down the long hospital corridor...to keep her body in motion. If she didn't stop, he wouldn't see her shake.

What the hell was it about the man that intimidated her? What was it about those brown eyes that made her insides heat?

Just because he reminded her of the dark knight from her dreams who came to rescue her from those horrible nights that seemed to never end—the ones where she tried so hard to keep quiet—was no excuse. Which was probably why she'd fallen prey to Marcos in the first place.

No. Prey was the wrong term. It had been nothing like that. Nothing like those nights from her past.

How she'd ended up kissing Marcos as they'd discussed a cultural mistake she'd made was still foggy in her head. Maybe it was some strange, unknown effect of embarrassment. One minute they'd been in his car in the staff parking garage, getting ready to drive to the apartment the hospital had secured for her. Nervous, she'd dropped her water bottle, and it had rolled into the well by his feet.

As they'd both leaned down to retrieve it, their cheeks had brushed, and heat had bloomed inside her. Marcos's head had come up as if he'd sensed her reaction, his brown eyes staring deep into hers. The rest had been a blur of movement. A hot, fast shifting of clothes. His hands on her hips, lifting her up and over him, undoing the buttons of her blouse—she swallowed hard—sliding into her. Her body's instant response.

The whole thing had probably been over in less than five minutes.

The repercussions, though, were still with her a month later.

The only thing she knew with certainty about that day was that it had been a mistake.

A lapse that could never happen again. He was a doctor. Her boss, for all practical purposes, even though she carried the same title he did.

Why had she been so bewitched by him? She should be used to Brazilians by now. Her hospital in New Jersey had had a high concentration of them, so many that she'd often grown frustrated by the language barrier and had struggled to understand cultural norms so different from her own. When a chance had opened up to come to Brazil to intern under a world-renowned neurosurgeon, she'd fought to be included in the program. And had won the coveted spot.

All she needed was to ruin it by letting the man's deadly good looks get beneath her skin.

Like she'd already done a month ago?

She quickened her pace, trying to outrun the memories.

That had been a moment of weakness. She'd been insecure in the language and had used a hand gesture with a patient that had sexual connotations. Marcos had shot her a look, eyes narrowed in speculation before swooping in and correcting her faux pas. And later that day, in the darkened interior of his car, he'd shown her exactly what that misused signal meant.

And he'd been loud. So loud.

*Heavens!*

She swallowed, her stomach quaking at the memory.

But just because she'd made one mistake, that didn't mean she should follow it up with another. She was a smart woman, not a shrinking, naive teenager—at least, not any more. She'd already seen what Dr. Markinho wanted from her.

And it certainly wasn't her expertise in the exam room.

Which was why she needed to keep that cold shoulder aimed squarely at the man following behind her. Except, judging from the way her butt was growing warmer by the second, she had a feeling the good doctor was looking anywhere but at her shoulder.

"Here we are."

Thank God. She turned to face him at the glass door of the physical therapy room. Damn. Maybe she'd been wrong. He looked perfectly in control, just like he always did—not a dark hair out of place, although a few streaks of grey had gathered at his temples, like clouds before a storm. And the man's gaze was definitely glued to her face, not the slightest twitch of eyes wandering to other places.

Maybe she'd been imagining things.

Or worse…wishing.

## CHAPTER TWO

"Marcos! Earth to Marcos!"

Cool fingers covered his eyes, and someone gave him a quick peck on top of the head, which almost caused him to lose his grip on his first real cup of coffee of the day. For a split second he thought it was Maggie who'd kissed him.

It wasn't.

He gave a soft curse, then twisted his head sideways to dislodge the person's hands. "Sophia, this is not the place."

"*Nossa Senhora.* You're so grouchy nowadays."

His childhood friend dropped into one of the hospital cafeteria's tan upholstered chairs and crinkled her nose in irritation.

Almost as slender as she'd been during their days at the orphanage, Sophia Limeira had looked Marcos straight in the eye when he'd arrived at the state-run home, plopped her thumb out of her mouth and offered the wet digit up to him. He'd just stood there staring at her, trying not to cry in front of his little brother, who kept asking where Papai was...when they were going home. Marcos had already grasped the truth of their situation from the moment he'd seen the policeman on the other side of the fence: they weren't going home. Not ever.

Sophia, as if recognizing a lost soul when she saw one—had stuck to his side like glue from that moment on. Had even followed him into the medical field. Marcos, in turn, had protected her when she'd been little—still felt the need to protect her now that she was an adult. And even though she griped about it constantly, he had a feeling she secretly liked the fact that someone cared.

He took a tentative sip of his coffee as he tried to formulate a response to her declaration. "I'm not grouchy. I'm busy."

With a flourish of her fingers, four rectangular slips of paper appeared, splayed apart like a hand of cards. "Too busy to go with me to the ballet? I won four tickets from a promotion they were having at Printemps."

"Printemps? What the hell is that?"

"Wow, Marcos. Such language." She sighed and stuffed the tickets back in her bag. "It's a department store down on 25 de Março. I know you've seen it."

A bargain-hunter's paradise, the huge shopping district in the center of São Paulo was a chaotic beehive of activity on the best of days...and the last place Marcos ever ventured, if he could help it. The area could also be dangerous. "You went down there by yourself?"

Sophia rolled her eyes. "I'm not a kid any more, remember? We've talked about this."

"We did. And you agreed to take someone with you when you shopped."

"I did. I took the American girl you have working for you. She'd never been." Her brows came together in rebuke. "After six months, can you believe it? You should have at least offered to show it to her."

Yeah, right. He could just see that happening. Maybe he'd ask her tomorrow, in fact. Marcos pinched the bridge of his nose, feeling a headache coming on.

Maggie was the last person he wanted Sophia hanging around with. His friend might take it on herself to do something crazy.

"Anyway," she continued, "Maggie said she'd go to the ballet with me, but that leaves two tickets. She said she was sure you'd want to go as well."

Something crazy. Like that.

His hand dropped back to the table, eyes narrowing. Somehow he doubted it had been Maggie's suggestion that he go. "Sorry. Can't make it."

"You don't even know what the dates are yet."

It didn't matter. No way was he going to the ballet with Sophia and her new BFF.

He tried to pry the truth out of her. "Did Dr. Pfeiffer actually mention me by name?"

"She did." Sophia drew an X across her chest with her index finger. "*Juro.*"

*I swear.* Fitting, since he'd like to do a little swearing himself.

"What did she say, exactly?"

"Well, I said I might ask you to go along with us, and Maggie said, 'Do that.'"

He gave a short laugh, relief washing through him. "It's called sarcasm, Soph. Americans use it a lot."

Okay, well, that cleared up that little mystery.

Undaunted by his lack of enthusiasm, she leaned forward. "Did you know Americans also use this…" she made a circle of her thumb and forefinger, shielding the sign with her other hand to keep it hidden from fellow diners "…to mean that something is good? Maggie said she accidentally used it with a patient a while ago."

"Yes. I know." Marcos pushed her hand down with a frown and held onto it. "That doesn't mean *you* should go around flashing it."

He remembered exactly when Maggie had used that sign. Seventy-nine-year-old Guilherme Lima had come in to ask about his test results, and before Marcos had realized what her intentions were, out had come the finger circle accompanied by an emphatic shake or two of her hand. He'd thought the poor man—whose test results really had been A-okay—had been going to die of a stroke right there in his office. Marcos had thought he might just follow his patient over the edge. But for an entirely different reason. Maggie's innocent demeanor, accompanied by that obscene gesture, had set off a firestorm in his belly that had lasted the rest of the day.

When he'd offered to drive her home with the idea of setting her straight in private so she wouldn't be embarrassed, things hadn't gone exactly as planned. He'd explained why she shouldn't use that sign, and her eyes had gone wide as she'd licked her lips. Another deadly combination he hadn't been able to resist—and hadn't bothered trying. Then she'd dropped that water bottle and leaned forward…

Something he was better off not thinking about right now.

As if he'd summoned her, a flash of red to the side caught his attention, and he swiveled his head to look. Maggie was in line with a tray, but her eyes were on him, following the line of his arm to where his hand still held Sophia's. A frown marred her brow, and something about it made Marcos let go of Sophia in a rush.

A second later, he thought better of it. Had his friend even explained their relationship to her? That he'd been Sophia's sidekick at the orphanage?

Why did it matter? In fact, it might not be a bad thing if Maggie thought there was a little something going on between them.

Which would make him look like a first-class jerk, after those passion-filled moments they'd shared.

As if realizing she was still staring, Maggie yanked her glance back to the tray in her hand and continued through the line, perusing the items behind the glass window at the counter as if they fascinated her.

Unfortunately, Sophia had also spotted her and waved her over.

*Meu Deus*. Why had he ever thought coffee was a good idea?

With a sense of impending doom, he watched as Maggie

made her selection, hunched her shoulders and headed their way, looking very much like she was facing a slow and painful death.

Well, join the club, *querida*. You're not the only one.

Maggie had wanted a simple fruit cup, hoping to make up for the fact that she'd skipped breakfast that morning. What she *hadn't* wanted, however, was to witness her boss holding hands with her new friend, Sophia, who was everything Maggie wasn't: curvy, with flawless tanned skin and silky black hair that shimmered with every movement. The girl also seemed to have cornered the market on flirty smiles, except she did it with a total lack of guile about how that sultry flash of teeth affected the opposite sex. And judging from Marcos's reaction, he'd definitely been affected.

It might even explain why Sophia had been so quick to mention inviting him to the ballet.

Did she have any idea what he and Maggie had done in the parking garage? No, of course she didn't. She had the feeling Marcos wasn't the kind of man to kiss and tell.

But he might be the kind of person who played the field. And there *was* something between these two. She could tell by the way they leaned into each other as they talked, by their easy smiles and casual manner.

Past lovers?

Present?

That thought made having to sit with them that much worse. Because, if the two of them were involved, the last thing her boss would want was for Sophia to discover what they'd been up to a month ago. From the uneasy look on his face, he was thinking much the same thing.

Before she could veer away to another table, however, Sophia leaped up and took her tray, setting it next to hers and then kissing her cheek. Maggie still hadn't gotten used to that aspect of their culture: the kissing—whether it was the casual Brazilian kissing that went on between friends and relatives or, worse, the crazy intense style she'd experienced with the Brazilian seated across from her. Yep, that style of kissing was still kind of foreign to her, since the encounters she'd had in her past life had almost never involved mouth-to-mouth contact.

She sucked down a quick breath as an unwanted memory pushed its way in. She shook it off, her fingertips curving and pressing deeply into the sides of her thighs.

*He's dead. The past is dead. Get over it.*

Slumping into her seat and wishing she could be anywhere else, she forced a smile. "I didn't realize you'd be here." She gave the offhand remark in such a way that neither party would know who she referred to.

"I come here every morning." The faint amusement that tinged his words made her bristle. She wasn't stalking him, for heaven's sake.

"Really? I only come when my boss asks me to show up at a ridiculously early hour," she retorted.

He glanced at his watch, one side of his mouth quirking. "Six o'clock is hardly early."

"Hmm." The vague noise was meant to be noncommittal, but it caused Marcos to lean back, arms crossing over his chest.

Sophia, seemingly unaware of the tension in the air, spoke up. "I was just telling Marcos about the ballet. And that you were going, too."

Oh, no! She'd hoped any drama involving those tickets would happen out of her earshot.

"When is it again?" Marcos asked, his eyes trained on her face, which was growing hotter by the second.

Sophia glanced at her. "Two weeks from Wednesday."

Lifting his phone off the tabletop, he used a finger to scroll across the screens, probably looking at his calendar. "We have a medical conference starting this Monday."

Something she was trying her best to forget. They were supposed to sit together, since part of the conference dealt with advances in neurosurgery. Marcos said he'd probably need to translate portions of it for her.

The last thing she wanted him doing was whispering in her ear. She'd had that experience once already and didn't need any reminders of what a heady thing it was.

"That's perfect," Sophia said. "Those things never go past five in the afternoon, and the ballet doesn't start until eight."

Maggie wasn't sure what she was supposed to say to that. She'd already promised Sophia that she'd go. But that had been before she'd found out she'd be a third wheel. She wanted to back out more than anything, but didn't want to offend her friend in the process.

"Will it be at the Municipal Theater?" Marcos asked.

"Of course."

Now was her chance to try to wriggle out of it. "Maybe I should just let you guys go and enjoy it on your own."

"What are you talking about? Of course you must go." Sophia laid her hand on Marcos's arm. "He wants you to come as well, don't you, Marcos?"

"Definitely. I want you to come."

The smooth words were said without the slightest twitch of an eyebrow, but she felt her face flaming back to life. He'd used that phrasing on purpose…knew it would bring up memories of her—with him—as he'd told her he wanted her to do exactly that.

And she had.

She wished she could think of something equally witty and sophisticated to lob back at him, but she couldn't come up with anything that wouldn't be obvious to everyone. Which made her feel like a royal dork.

Besides, how could she refuse to go after her friend had been so excited about winning the tickets in the first place?

Nope. She couldn't bring herself to say the words. So she gritted out a smile instead. "Well, I guess that's settled, then."

Sophia gave an audible sigh, then leaned back with a grin. "Exactly."

## CHAPTER THREE

"Do they have to shave all my hair off?"

Teresa Allen's big blue eyes looked up at her with a pleading expression. The seven-year-old had come in to have her ventriculoperitoneal shunt checked. She'd been having headaches for the last couple of days, and Marcos wanted her in his office right away to make sure the device was draining off the excess cerebrospinal fluid the way it should.

It wasn't. And now Maggie's task was to keep their young American patient and her mother calm while Marcos prepared for the emergency surgery. Once Teresa was anesthetized, however, she'd be able to scrub up and join the surgical team.

Maggie smiled. "No, they won't shave all your hair, only this little spot right here." She drew a U-shaped figure with her fingertip behind the little girl's right ear. "You can comb the rest of your hair so that it covers it once you're out of surgery. But it'll all grow back before you know it."

Her mom, seated beside her daughter, smiled. "Thank you for speaking to us in English. I really need to learn Portuguese, but there are so many ex-pats here I haven't needed to. Your English is excellent, by the way. Congratulations."

Maggie grinned back. "That's because I'm an American, too. And believe me, once I open my mouth, no one would mistake me for a Brazilian, even when I'm speaking Portuguese."

It felt so good to speak her own language. It was also the reason Marcos had left her here with the mother and daughter. And although she knew she deserved to be in that operating room every bit as much as he did, she didn't resent being here. She could remember the times her own mother had held her hand when she'd gone to the doctor to have her inoculations...or when she'd been sick. It was important to feel safe.

And Maggie could remember, down to the minute, when she'd no longer felt that way. It had taken her a long, long time to recover. Even now she wondered if she was functioning one hundred percent normally.

Her ex-boyfriend certainly hadn't given her much reassurance on that front.

But Marcos hadn't seemed to sense anything weird during their brief interlude. Then again, she hadn't been paying attention to much outside of how he was making her feel.

One of the nurses came into the room with a pair of hair clippers. "Are we ready?"

"I think so." Maggie stroked Teresa's head. "What do you think? Are you ready for those headaches to go away?"

Teresa nodded. "I'm really scared, though."

Meeting her mother's eyes, she could see it was taking every ounce of willpower for the woman not to burst into tears in front of her daughter.

Maggie smiled. "I'm going to be with you the whole time. I promise."

"Even during the operation?"

She nodded. "Even then."

Her mom's chin wobbled even more as she mouthed, "Thank you."

Forty-five minutes later, Maggie stood beside Marcos as he carefully examined the shunt valve he'd removed from Teresa's head. "The problem's in here. We'll need to replace it with a new one." Setting the device aside, his fingers followed the path of the tubing down the child's neck and chest, feeling it through her skin. "Everything else seems okay, and she's got plenty of room left for growth. So let's get in and get out."

Maggie busied herself with retrieving the replacement valve and carrying it over to the table.

Marcos took a step back. "Why don't you connect it?"

Surprised, she glanced at him for a second, before moving closer. Taking hold of the lower section of the catheter tubing, she carefully worked it into the connecting port, and then did the same with the upper end. She checked the seals. Hooking it up took less than ten minutes, but it felt good to be doing actual surgery, instead of feeling like a useless hanger-on.

She also realized that she hadn't needed to translate Marcos's words in her head when he'd spoken but had automatically processed and understood them. She gave him a huge smile, only realizing a second later that her mask kept him from seeing it. But evidently he'd seen something in her eyes because he said, "Good job."

It had taken almost seven months, but maybe she was finally getting the hang of this crazy language.

And maybe even gaining the trust of her fellow neurosurgeon?

They finished up the surgery, each of them moving forward and then back to allow the other person to have a turn securing everything in place and then finally closing the incision. Marcos examined the site with a critical eye. "I think that about does it. Let's bring her out of anesthesia while I clean her up."

Marcos gently swabbed the blood from the side of the child's head as the anesthesiologist began lightening the sedation and removed the tape from her eyelids. Within minutes, Teresa's eyelids fluttered.

Leaning over her, Maggie smiled and said, "Can you hear me, pumpkin?"

Teresa nodded her head, her gaze still unfocused.

"That's wonderful." It suddenly didn't matter that she was standing in the middle of a team of Brazilian doctors and nurses speaking English. All that mattered was that this child understood her. "See, I promised you I'd be right here with you every step of the way, and here I am. I've never left your side."

She glanced up to see Marcos staring at her with an enigmatic look. "Pumpkin?"

"It's an endearment." She couldn't help raising her brows in challenge. "Kind of like Markinho."

The whole room went silent for a second or two, and she realized she'd made some kind of serious gaffe.

In a low voice he gritted, "I'd rather you didn't call me that."

Oh! She hadn't meant to insult him, had just been trying to explain why she'd addressed their patient using the name of a vegetable. "Sorry. It won't happen again."

"Thank you." With that, he stripped off his gloves and headed out the door without a word to anyone.

*What was with him?*

She could no more imagine Marcos being embarrassed by her playful comment than she could imagine herself being. Then again, she didn't know the man at all.

And probably never would.


No one called him that.

No one except his father and his brother. And Graciela, who'd begun using it after hearing Lucas do so. Once his brother had left with his adoptive family, her use of the diminutive form of his name had made him feel cared for—and a little less lonely.

But hearing Maggie say it had made his gut do a slow burn. He knew she wasn't trying to be unprofessional, and hadn't actually been calling him Markinho. But that soft accented voice murmuring his childhood name had made those same sensations go through him that he'd had as a child. Only Maggie wasn't interested in making him feel cared for.

And he certainly wasn't lonely. Not with all the noise and activity of the hospital going on around him.

He'd overreacted. Had stormed out of that operating room like a child.

Like Markinho might have done, once upon a time?

No, he wasn't a child. He was temperamental. He'd heard the nurses use that term to excuse his lack of social interaction.

Because as much as Marcos liked to be surrounded by noise, it was more as an observer than a participant. Except with Maggie, evidently. He found he had to fill the silence that was her with talking...or, worse, groaning.

Like in his car?

The tinted windows had been dark enough to block out everything that happened inside, cocooning them in a private world where anything could happen. And it had. His eyes had been locked on Maggie's face while her eyelids had fluttered closed the second he'd moved her panties aside and found her wet and ready. Her tight heat had massaged his flesh again and again, his words of encouragement every bit as suggestive as the hand sign she'd used with his patient.

And when she'd come...

Hell, she'd exploded within minutes, the sensation taking his body by storm and forcing an audible reaction from him that had left him shaken.

They'd been lucky none of the security guards had been around.

Maggie, on the other hand, had been totally silent. Because of the fear of discovery?

The urge to find out—to have her under him in more private circumstances—swept through his system like wildfire.

He rolled his eyes as he forced himself back to the present and stepped into the staff washroom. He scrubbed his hands and splashed his face, staring at himself in the mirror—and trying not to see Markinho reflected back at him.

Why had she gotten under his skin? Even during the surgery he'd been aware of her every move. Her every word. And when she'd used his name his senses had churned to life.

He had a feeling it wasn't her use of his nickname that bothered him so much. It was what she'd said to the little girl in the operating room.

Marcos had a personal rule that pretty much governed everything he did. He never made promises he couldn't keep. Rarely made them at all, in fact. Not after what had happened with his father. Hearing Maggie toss that word around with such ease—and to a child—without thinking of the repercussions had struck him as irresponsible.

He was being ridiculous. It was only surgery…a period of an hour and a half.

And if his patient had regained consciousness and found Maggie hadn't kept her word?

He switched off the water and turned away from the mirror. Time to go talk to his patient's family, although he had no doubt Maggie had already accompanied the girl to the recovery room and made sure she was settled in. If he knew her—which he didn't, not at all—she'd also spoken with the mother and assured her everything was going to be okay.

Another promise that was impossible to keep.

What was wrong with him today? He didn't normally brood on the past.

Maybe something about his new colleague brought it out in him—or perhaps it was those flashes of something that appeared behind her blue eyes periodically.

Sadness?

He'd thought it was fear the first time he'd kissed her. The look had taken him aback, made him wonder if he was acting like a brute.

Probably.

It was why he didn't get involved with staff or any of the nurses. He didn't want tales of his exploits making the rounds.

In fact, he would have stopped with a kiss that day in the car if Maggie hadn't accepted his challenge to kiss him back and awoken something raw and primitive inside him. After that, neither of them had seemed able to halt what had happened.

Marcos huffed out a breath and left the restroom, irritated once again. He had to stop thinking about her. It was becoming almost an obsession. And he didn't obsess about anything…or anyone.

Arriving at the waiting room and finding it empty, he stopped at the nurses' desk. "My patient. Where is she?"

"Wh-which patient?"

The stuttered words drew him up short, making him think about Maggie's reaction to him. Did he engender fear in everyone he came across?

Forcing a softer tone to his voice, he clarified, "Teresa Allen."

The nurse tapped the keys of her computer and said, "Recovery room three."

He strode away before stopping again with a frown. Turning back to the desk, he said, "Thank you."

"You're welcome."

There. At least she hadn't stuttered that time.

Arriving at the recovery room, he found Maggie was indeed there, along with Teresa's mother. He ignored her for the moment, going over to shake hands with the mom and saying in English, "I'm Dr. Pinheiro."

"You're the one who did the surgery?"

He glanced at where Maggie stood, chin elevated as if bracing herself for whatever he might say. He cursed his careless words in the operating room. "Actually, Dr. Pfeiffer and I both had a part in it. She's already explained what we did?"

"Yes. The new shunt should be okay for a while?"

"For a long while, we hope." He smiled at his patient, who'd drifted back to sleep. "Teresa has to lie flat for the next twenty-four hours, so she'll need to stay here for another day or two."

"Can I stay with her?"

"I don't see why not. It might make her feel more secure to have you here. I can have a cot brought in."

"Thank you." They shook hands once again, and Maggie came over this time.

"You'll let her know I was here?" she asked the mother.

"Yes. She'll be happy to know that. Can you visit her tomorrow?"

Maggie reached out and hugged her. "Absolutely. I'll see you later."

With that she was out the door without a backwards glance at him.

Dammit.

He went after her, catching up to her within a few strides. "Hey. *Espere.*"

Maggie stopped in her tracks, the sudden halt not making the slightest sound on the polished linoleum floor. She stayed put but didn't look at him. He rounded her still form until he stood in front of her, ignoring everything around him as he stared down at her. When she finally glanced up, the cool indifference in the clear blue depths of her eyes was unmistakable, even to him.

An act? Or was she really not bothered by what he'd said to her? Either way, he owed her an apology.

"I'm sorry." He touched the line of her jaw with his index finger, forcing it not to linger for more than a second on the softness he found there. "I overreacted a little while ago. Markinho is a childhood name. No one uses it."

"One of your patients did." Her soft voice spoke volumes.

He'd forgotten she'd overheard Graciela call him that a few days ago.

"She's different." He tried to think of a way to explain it that didn't involve talking about his past. "I've known that particular patient for a very long time."

She studied him for a second or two, as if trying to decide whether or not she was going to accept his explanation.

"I'm sorry if I embarrassed you. I was trying to explain why I called Teresa 'pumpkin.'"

"No harm done."

*Really, Marcos? Are you certain of that?*

He wasn't sure of anything, when it came to her.

He forced himself to continue. "The medical conference starts Monday. I'd like us to drive over there together, if possible."

What the hell? Did he really want her back in his car after what had happened? He'd talked about them sitting together during the seminars, nothing more.

*She might need help finding the place.*

Nothing like having an argument inside your own damn head.

"I think catching a taxi from the hospital might be a safer bet...for everyone."

He couldn't hold back a smile. "Point taken. Tell you what. Why don't we meet here in the lobby at seven and we'll take the subway instead. It stops close to the convention center and we can walk over there together." He glanced at her shoes. Swallowed hard. "Wear something comfortable."

And on that note—trying not to dwell on the fact that her shiny black pumps looked exactly like the pair she'd been wearing that day in his car, or the fact that one of them had fallen off some time during their maneuvering, forcing him to retrieve it from the floor afterwards—he stalked away to get his fifth cup of coffee.

And to hopefully locate his damned sanity.

# CHAPTER FOUR

MARCOS MURMURED SOMETHING to the woman seated behind the registration desk at the conference center, but Maggie couldn't hear what it was.

He hadn't said anything else about what had happened during the surgery two days ago—when she'd mistakenly used his nickname in front of a roomful of medical staff. In fact, Maggie hadn't seen much of him since then. But he had left a note at the nurses' station confirming he'd meet her in the hospital lobby this morning.

Riding on the São Paulo subway had been a new experience for her as she rarely traveled downtown, but it had been a fairly simple trip. They'd even found seats next to each other—which Marcos had indicated wasn't always an easy feat. Not that it mattered. He'd been glued to the screen of his phone the whole time, evidently checking and responding to emails.

Despite the quick ride over, they were still a few minutes late for the opening of the convention. Marcos didn't seem overly concerned. These things never started on time, he'd said.

He'd been right. The line behind them grew longer by the second, and she didn't hear anything coming from behind the closed doors to their right.

Maggie was used to punctuality, so the laid-back atmosphere she'd found in Brazil was another thing that was hard to get used to, but it all seemed to work out in some weird way. And the hospital was top notch, up on the latest treatment methods and as spotless as they came. Teresa Allen's impeccable surgery was the norm, rather than the exception. As for the doctors… She glanced at Marcos from beneath her lashes, a shiver going over her. Well, that was something she shouldn't think about right now.

What she *did* know was how fortunate she was to have gotten this internship.

The receptionist handed Marcos two lanyards, along with a couple of printed name tags, and he paused at the table to slide the paper tags into the holders. They'd put an "a" at the end of her name, instead of an "e". Marcos sent her a grim smile as she slipped the cord around her neck. "It seems they think you're magic."

"I'm sorry?"

He lifted the plastic holder from her chest and nodded at it. "*Maggia*…or *magía*, in Portuguese. Magic."

Another shiver went over her as he let the tag fall back into place and donned his own lanyard. She licked her lips, not sure if she dared joke about it. "Well, at least they didn't make the same mistake I did by using your nickname. What does it mean, anyway?"

"Markinho? It means little Marcos." He steered her toward the doorway, which was being pushed open by a couple of dark-suited ushers. "Although I might take exception to being called 'little'. Do you want to weigh in on that?"

Heat flashed up her neck. Oh! He was in quite a mood today. Maybe because Sophia wasn't here to witness his antics. She switched to English. "Don't you think you should be a little more discreet?"

He stopped in front of the doors and turned to face her, ignoring the clipboard-wielding attendant who was tilting his head to try to catch sight of their names.

"Discreet? In what way?"

"Does Sophia know about…what happened?"

Realizing there were people waiting to get in, he held his badge up to the man, who flipped through the sheets and checked something off. Then Marcos moved through the door, leaving her to catch up.

"Do you mean between us?" He narrowed his eyes as he glanced sideways at her, making his way up the tiers of blue-upholstered chairs in the main room of the conference center. "No, and there's no need to tell her."

Outrage flashed up her back and made her blink. What kind of man was he? "You often do that sort of thing?"

He gave her a strange look. "It depends on what you mean by 'that sort of thing' and your definition of 'often'. But what does any of this have to do with Sophia?"

No one could be that dense. Unless he truly didn't care about the other woman's feelings. "If you two are, um…*seeing* each other, surely she wouldn't appreciate—"

*"Seeing?"* His brows drew together, and he switched back to Portuguese. "As in *transar*?"

More heat poured into her face, joining the simmering flood that was already at work there. That was one verb she knew. But did he have to be so blunt? She glanced around to make sure no one had heard. "If you want to put it so crudely, yes."

"Sophia and I aren't…" His furrows eased, and he actually laughed, taking her elbow and leading her to a seat in the middle of the auditorium. "She's like a sister to me. We've known each other since we were…young children."

Despite the puzzling pause at the end of his words, a wave of pure relief washed over her, rinsing away the heat that had collected in her cheeks. Okay, so he and Sophia weren't lovers. Although why she should care one way or the other, she had no idea. Except that she didn't want to hurt the other woman.

Maggie knew first hand what it felt like to be racked with guilt over the consequences of someone else's actions. Only her aunt had never found out the truth about her husband—and never would now.

Thank God. It would have killed her to know what he was really like.

Fingers slid across the small of her back, sending a zing of electricity through her. "How about here?"

For a split second she thought he was asking her where she liked to be touched, then realized he was nodding to the chairs in front of them.

Sitting next to him for the next several hours was going to be pure torture if she didn't get her head on straight. She was going to try very, very hard not to ask him to translate anything during the conference. Which meant she'd have to concentrate. A good thing, in this case.

"It's fine. It doesn't matter where we sit."

People were now moving through the auditorium in clusters, talking shop as they went by. Why couldn't she and Marcos be like that? Simply focus on their jobs and leave their personal baggage at home.

Maybe because most coworkers didn't engage in car sex…a fact that sent a worrying tingle through her fingers every time she thought about it. It was the guilt that was causing it. She'd done something she shouldn't have. She glanced down at her hands, checking the length of her nails, just in case.

It was normal for things to be awkward. How could they not be?

She dropped into her seat, staring doggedly at her program. Their unexpected kiss that day had been an almost violent encounter. So much so that the suddenness of it—his hand curling around her nape and then the harsh, desperate press of his mouth against hers—had stormed her senses. The momentary sense of shock at her reaction had rendered her immobile, unable to do anything except let the wash of need sweep over her.

He'd pulled away at that second and stared into her eyes. "*Meu Deus.* You're frightened."

She'd shaken her head, realizing she wasn't. "No."

"Then kiss me back, *querida*…"

A hand touched hers, yanking her back to the present with a start. "I'm sorry, what did you say?"

"I asked which of the seminars you wished to attend. The only one I'd like to sit in on is called 'Sublabial versus Endonasal Surgical Options for Patients with Pituitary Adenomas.'"

She stared at her program, trying to make sense of the words. Not easy with Marcos looking over her shoulder, his warm, mellow scent carried to her on subtle air currents. "I'm here for the language more than anything so whatever you choose is fine."

"Are you interested in any of the other specialties?" He fanned through his book to find the directory. "They've got endocrinology, plastic surgery, oncology, pediatrics..." Reaching over to flip her program to the right page, his fingers brushed hers, causing her to freeze for a second.

She inched her hand away from his, hoping it wasn't as obvious as it felt. "I'm good."

A masculine throat cleared above her, and they both glanced up. Marcos smiled and rose to his feet in response to the newcomer. She tried to shrink into her seat as the two men talked above her, but she was painfully aware that Marcos's brown leather belt with its elegant silver buckle was right at her eye level. Her fingers tingled again, and she forced her gaze to move higher.

Marcos set a hand on her shoulder. "Maggie, this is Dr. Silvano Mendoso, head of pediatrics at our hospital. Silvano, meet Dr. Maggie Pfeiffer. She's here from the States to do a year's internship in my department."

They must get tired of using a title for every single person they came across.

She craned her neck up to smile at the other doctor. Almost as tall as Marcos and with dark curly hair, he gazed down at her. She squirmed in her seat. Standing was out of the question at this point, as she'd be pancaked between the two men if she tried. She settled for lifting her hand to shake Dr. Mendoso's. "Pleased to meet you."

"I haven't seen you around the hospital," he said, gripping her fingers for a fraction longer than necessary.

Up went Marcos's brows. "That's because I keep her quite busy, learning new things."

It had to be the language that made everything sound exotic...and slightly suggestive.

The lights dimmed and then came back up. Dr. Mendoso gave her an apologetic smile and then slapped Marcos on the back. "I'd better get back to my seat before someone decides to steal it. Nice to meet you...Maggie, wasn't it?"

"Yes. Thank you. You as well."

She tried to settle in to listen to the opening speech, not daring to ask Marcos to translate missed words here and there. She caught the gist of the instructions: the explanation of the layout of the building; where to find the refreshment tables between sessions; and who to ask if you got lost.

Lost? She was all that and then some.

Surprisingly, she understood a good deal more than she'd expected to. Several hours later, though, she revised that thought. Her mind felt like Swiss cheese, the gaps in comprehension growing with each change of subject matter. The temptation to lay her head on Marcos's shoulder and drift off was strong.

Too strong.

She fought the urge by holding herself rigid in her chair as they went from one seminar to another and listened to various speakers lecture on the latest advances in this or that.

"You're doing well." Marcos glanced up from the notes he'd been jotting on his program during a lull. "You haven't asked for my help. Not even once."

No. Thank God.

"This isn't life or death like at the hospital. If I don't understand a word or two, it won't hurt anything."

"No. I suppose not." He tapped the end of his pen against the program. "But the challenge to understand what's happening around you does make things interesting, yes? What does your family think of you living in another country?"

The sudden change in subject threw her. "They've always encouraged me to think for myself."

The only person who hadn't was gone now. Her fingers curved reflexively into the tops of her legs before she forced them to relax. To lie absolutely flat.

Not wanting to think about her family, she followed his lead. "What about you? Anyone else in your family go into medicine?"

There was a pause, and Maggie thought for a second that her phrasing was off. But then he answered. "My family is a complicated subject. Best left for another time."

Wow. So it was okay for him to ask about her family, but not the other way around. Well, great. The man burned hot and cold, and she could never predict which one he might be at any given moment. If she felt this way after almost seven months of working with him, she doubted if the next few would bring any serious changes.

He glanced at his watch and swore softly. "It's almost five. Do you mind missing the last session? We need to catch the subway—rush hour in São Paulo is best avoided if at all possible."

"Oh, no, of course not." In actuality, it was a relief to get away. She wasn't sure she understood his hurry, though, since they *had* taken the subway, rather than his car. How would rush hour matter one way or the other if you weren't actually driving?

She soon found out. People getting off work streamed through the turnstiles at the metro station and swarmed down the escalators to reach the lower levels. A faint sense of claustrophobia began to press in around her, and Marcos stopped to take her hand after five or six people came between them, threatening to make her lose sight of him all together.

"You have to be aggressive," he murmured, gripping her fingers and towing her along. "It only gets worse from now until about eight at night."

"Worse?"

He grinned down at her. "Hard to believe, isn't it? But it's exhilarating, no? The life, the movement...the noise."

The noise? No, she found it kind of unsettling. Chaotic. Her instinct was to cling to the railing on the side of the wall and hang on for dear life as the crowds swept around her. She clung to Marcos's hand instead.

And prayed she'd live to see another day.

# CHAPTER FIVE

DAMN. HE'D MEANT to leave the conference earlier.

He knew how crowded the *metró* could get at rush hour. Despite how calm she'd seemed during the trip this morning, he could tell Maggie was not enjoying how tightly packed the station was now. Looking at it through the eyes of a foreigner, he could see how it might seem frightening—dangerous even.

Keeping a tight hold on her hand, he forced her to keep up, knowing if he didn't they'd get pushed further and further back, and the conditions behind them would grow worse as rush hour shifted into full swing.

They finally reached the platform, and Marcos eyed the lines, calculating exactly which one would give them the best chance of getting on the next train. Briefcases and purses the size of small suitcases were the norm with passengers. As were boxes and shopping bags. People from all walks of life—and from all socioeconomic levels—relied on public transport, especially on the one day of the week when they were prohibited from driving. His day was Monday. When he'd explained the traffic rotation system to Maggie, she'd stared at him in disbelief. "You mean you're only allowed to drive downtown on four of the five business days? How do people get to work on their off day?"

You made do. Just like he'd done as a kid, when his family hadn't had a car at all…or a game console or even a computer. Just a two-roomed shack in the middle of a *favela*.

And without the license-plate restrictions, what were already snarled traffic conditions in São Paulo would grow even worse.

But it also meant that public transport was busy every single day of the week, because those who couldn't drive rode the bus and subway.

A train whooshed past them, leaving a warm breeze in its wake before pulling to a stop with a drawn-out screech. Gripping her hand once again, Marcos hauled her after him the second the doors opened. They were six stops from their destination, so he headed for the far side of the car to let others board, not even bothering to look for a seat. There would be none at this hour.

And the commuters kept coming—people jamming in all around them. Marcos saw someone jostle Maggie and push past her. She seemed to cringe into herself, edging closer to him. "Come here," he said.

He shifted, turning Maggie around until she gripped the metal pole in front of her, then he bracketed her in, his arms going around her to hold on to the same pole. He then widened his stance a bit to shield her legs with his own. He figured between the solid bar in front of her and him at her back, she would be relatively protected, and he could give her a bit more breathing space than some of the other passengers had.

What he hadn't expected, however, was to feel as if he were holding her in his arms, or the way the back of her head rested against his chest, doing strange things to his insides. She wasn't doing it on purpose, there just wasn't anywhere else for her to go. It also meant her rounded bottom was pressed against his upper thighs.

The doors slid closed and things went from merely uncomfortable to nightmare proportions as the sudden motion of the train pulling away from the platform threw Maggie against him, her body snugging to his in a way that had him spiraling down a dark rabbit hole and putting him on high alert.

"Sorry," she gasped. But every bump and curve in the track had that delectable ass sliding over and into him time and time again.

He'd been trying to protect her. What about protecting himself? Because by the time they got off this train, his situation was going to be very noticeable.

The train began slowing rapidly as it reached its first stop, and Marcos braced one arm on the pole while sliding his other around her waist to keep her anchored against him, and to prevent the people behind him from squeezing Maggie further against the metal bar.

People shifted…some getting off, new passengers crowding closer. Things should get better after the third or fourth stop when they moved further away from the downtown district.

Maggie twisted her head to the side and looked up at him. "Sé Station…isn't this the shopping district? Where I came with Sophia?"

"It is."

The train pulled out again, preventing any further talk as he concentrated on keeping his body under control as the sweet assault from hers continued to grind away at his senses. The clean scent of her hair rose around him, cutting through the other less agreeable smells on the subway, and without realizing what he was doing he pulled it deep into his lungs, leaning closer…until all he smelled was Maggie.

And that's all he felt as well as he leaned into the turns, his arm still wrapped around her, still holding her in place.

*Had she just pressed closer?*

It had to be his deranged imagination that had her butt nestled between his legs, the small of her back pressing on a very sensitive—and very dangerous—area of his anatomy. And up that area came, right on cue.

Damn.

It was too late to do anything about it now, other than grit his teeth and enjoy the ride.

Except this was one ride that wouldn't be made to completion but would just leave him hungry for more.

Third stop. Three more to go.

If he survived this, he'd need to do some serious penance afterwards. Because his body was howling at him now, and he couldn't help using the momentum of the train to his advantage. He could have sworn that Maggie answered every bump and grind with one of her own.

Marcos closed his eyes. *Just let me make it through this alive.*

Fourth stop.

Maggie's shuddered breath was not his imagination this time. Neither did she move away from him as more people filtered out and fewer people packed on. This should be their cue to start edging away from each other.

He would, when she did. And the woman hadn't budged an inch.

No longer was he praying to make it out alive. He was praying to be dragged down to hell and be done with it.

The train exited the station, and Marcos's hand tightened on her waist once again, his thumb doing an experimental strum down her side. Maggie's knuckles turned white as they gripped the pole in front of her, but there was no hint of struggle or of wanting to get away.

He was doomed.

Fifth stop.

Maggie's blouse had edged up during the trip, and when he shifted his hand, his pinky finger met bare skin. His hard-on was now a raging inferno that showed no hint of subsiding any time soon. And that warm, silky sliver of flesh tempted him to move his hand a little lower, to widen that gap between her trousers and shirt.

He didn't. But his little finger did explore as much as it was able, dragging backwards and then retracing its steps time and time again. He swore he could hear her breath, shallow and rapid above the churning sounds of the train.

Kind of like the churning going on in his gut.

And then the nightmare came to a crashing halt as the train began to slow for the last time...way before he was ready.

He ducked his head low, until his lips almost touched her ear. "This is our stop."

"Is—is it?"

"Yes." Her earlobe was close—a tiny diamond glittering in the delicate flesh. All he had to do was open his mouth and draw it in, stroke his tongue across it.

The subway doors opened with an ugly hissing sound.

Marcos blinked back to awareness as folks around them began moving, exiting with quick, jerky steps, in a hurry to reach their destinations. The fire still burning strong in his belly, he forced himself to take a step back, to unwind his arm from Maggie's waist, pinky making one last desperate pass across her skin before withdrawing completely.

Maggie's shoulders lifted as she let go of the pole. "Ready?"

Not by any stretch of the imagination. But he would take the steps necessary to get off this train.

Both the physical one...and the mental one.

No matter how much he longed to stay.

Except the second he let Maggie move through the open door and followed her off the train, he couldn't draw his eyes away from the soft ass in front of him, or banish the memory of it swishing against him time and time again. And a certain throbbing part of his body made sure that memory stayed painfully alive.

They rounded a corner of the station and exited near a darkened stand of trees. He needed to stop for a second and catch his breath, because if he didn't get control of himself—right now—then the second they reached the parking lot and got into his car, he was going to do something extremely stupid. Like haul her onto his lap, unzip, and put an end to this torture once and for all. He'd done it once before—could remember every second of the time they'd spent doing just that.

Forcing the thoughts back down with a soft curse, he snagged Maggie's hand, tugging her off the sidewalk. People continued to stream by them, oblivious to anything but getting home.

"What—?"

"Shh."

He moved deeper into the bushes, stopping behind a large oak tree. The dark shadows played a tantalizing game of hide and seek with her features.

She blinked at him. "Is something wrong?"

Was she serious?

"Yes, Maggie. Something is terribly wrong." Even as he said it, his back connected with the tree behind him. Taking her other hand in his, he bent his elbows to shift her a few inches closer.

Her tongue came out to dampen her lips, eyes still on his.

She knew. She *had* to know.

Just to make sure, he slid his hands up either side of her neck until his thumbs rested just beneath her chin, applying the barest amount of pressure to tilt her head up. "Can you guess what it is, *querida*?"

"I—I don't…"

"Yes. I think you do." He stared down at her, a strange sense of resignation sliding through him as he realized no place was safe with her. Not a subway, not a car…not even behind a tree. "Come here."

There was a pause then she took one step toward him, then two. Something inside him twisted with a mixture of lust and exultation.

"Do you want me to show you what it is?" he continued, his thumbs caressing the edges of her jawline.

She nodded, then seemed to need to back up the gesture with her voice. "Yes."

The whispered word seemed to unleash something primal in him, and he lowered his head, almost touching her lips. He felt the warmth of her breath as it slid from her lungs in a quick, steady stream in preparation for his kiss. But he wasn't interested in taking her mouth in a rush, like he had in the car. If he was going to kiss her, he was going to make it count—draw it out as long as humanly possible—because Marcos had no idea how long it would be before he tasted those sweet lips again. If ever.

Why wasn't he kissing her? Was he going to back out?

She sensed him close. Had actually shut her eyes in anticipation, but he didn't completely close the gap between them. Parting her eyelids again, she saw he'd stopped less than an inch away, his head tilted at the perfect angle, hovering so close she could have licked his lips if she'd wanted to.

*Could have licked his lips...*

Before she could think better of it, her tongue came out and touched his full lower lip, then darted back inside her own mouth, quick as a bunny.

Marcos let out a quiet groan that sounded painful. Her heart pounded in her chest as she waited for him to recoil. He didn't. Instead, he muttered something that sounded suspiciously like "Again."

But she wasn't sure. What if he—?

"Again, Maggie." This time there was no mistaking those words.

Slowly, her tongue edged forward and touched him again, this time sliding across that same lip, her eyes closing as the textures she admired each and every day came alive in a completely different way.

His hand slid deep into her hair and held her in place as she explored him. Tracing first his bottom lip, and then moving up to taste the top.

He lifted his head a fraction of an inch until she was at the seam of his mouth, and he opened, his lips surrounding the very tip of her tongue, kissing it softly. The act made her legs wobble beneath her.

She pulled back to swallow and try to catch her breath. She couldn't. The air was long gone from her lungs. Maybe he was some kind of alien creature, and this was his way of sucking the life force out of her. She'd be long dead before she realized what hit her.

Only he made it seem like it was the other way around. That what she was doing was the most exquisite sensation imaginable. He wasn't the only one—touching him gave her chills and heated her up all at the same time.

"Again." His voice was a little hoarser than it had been. "Just once more. And then I'll let you go home."

Let her go home?

She didn't want to go home. Not now. Maybe not ever.

This time when she edged forward, she licked across his lips in a single long swipe, hoping the action came across as sensual and not like a puppy lapping crumbs from his master's hand.

The fingers in her hair tightened just a bit, as if he didn't want to let her go quite yet, despite his words to the contrary. The move emboldened her, and she again approached the seam of his mouth, nudging a bit this time.

It worked. He opened, allowing entry, but her victory was short-lived when he dragged her forward in a rush until she was fully splayed against him—fully aware of every hard inch of his body against hers. His lips finally found hers and all thoughts of coaxing him fled as he swept aside her timid attempts at seduction and replaced them with something that was far removed from anything she could have thought or attempted.

His free hand went to the small of her back and fisted in her shirt, his knuckles grazing bare skin. She gulped back a wave of raw heat when his erection nudged at her belly, just like her tongue had done at his lips seconds earlier. Only this wasn't a request. It was a command. One that she readily answered with a slight tilt of her pelvis—and an inner plea for more of the same. So much more.

*"Meu Deus."* He dragged his lips from hers, ignoring her squeak of protest and her gripping fingers. "You really are magic—*magía*. You take my noblest intentions and turn them on their head." Pressing his cheek against hers, he drew in a deep breath. "I need to get you home before I forget all the reasons I pulled you back here in the first place."

As he reached for her hand and dragged her back to the realm of reality, rejoining the next wave of travelers as they exited the subway, she couldn't form a single coherent thought or response to what had happened between them.

All she knew was that he'd called her magic. And for a few brief moments…she'd almost believed him.

# CHAPTER SIX

*"BUT IN THE STATES—"*

*"You're no longer in the States, Maggie." He made a circle of his forefinger and his thumb as they sat in his car. "And, in my country, this sign is not something you use."*

*There was a note in his voice—the accented English gruff and bold—that made her shiver. But then again she'd been shivering in his presence for months now. "Why?"*

*"You don't want to know."*

*She licked her lips. She did want to know. Desperately. Especially as he'd just shifted his body toward her in his seat, pupils dilating.*

*"Tell me." The breathy quality to her voice tugged at her, sending a warning that told her to make her way up to the surface. Now. Because danger lay in the direction she was headed.*

*Not yet. Please. Not yet.*

*Her water bottle, wet with condensation, slid from her hand and dropped to the console before rolling to the floor by his feet. They both swooped to get it. Cheeks met...slid against each other.*

*"That sign means something very bad,* querida.*" One hand went to the nape of her neck, holding her in place as his words continued to whisper past her ear. "So bad, you should never flash it at a patient. Or a man. Unless you want something equally bad to happen to you."*

*She swallowed. "Like what?"*

*He pulled back just far enough that she could see his eyes. The heat swimming in them was sensual. And just a little bit terrifying.*

*"Like this." His head came down until his lips were inches away, his warm breath washing across her face.*

Why did this scene feel so familiar? Like it had already been played out?

*His thumb traced a path across the sensitive skin of her neck. "Can you guess what it means now?"*

*"No." Her breath swept into her lungs, readying itself even before her brain was fully cognizant of what was about to happen.*

*"Then I must show you, Maggie." His fingers tightened, mouth suddenly sliding across hers with a low groan.*

*For a split second she couldn't move, couldn't breathe, an unexpected wave of desire spiraling through her. She froze, eyes blinking wide.*

*Marcos eased back, a frown on his face. "Meu Deus. You're frightened."*

She'd definitely lived through this before. Had heard these exact words—could anticipate his every move. In a past life?

*"No. I'm not frightened." It was the truth, because the second his mouth left hers the only thing she was afraid of was that he might not kiss her again.*

*He stared at her for a long time, before murmuring, "No? Then kiss me back, querida. And I'll show you exactly what that symbol means."*

Maggie jerked to awareness, her fingers crushing something. His shirt?

She glanced around. No. This wasn't Marcos's car. It was her apartment.

Her bed.

And Marcos had definitely never spent the night in it.

She'd been dreaming. No wonder everything had felt so familiar. Releasing her death grip on the covers, she dragged one of her palms across her face, horrified to find her hand was shaking like a leaf.

He'd shown her what that sign meant all right.

And no matter how much she might deny it during her waking moments, her dreams told a different story. And it was something she was going to have to acknowledge sooner or later.

Far from being over what had happened, she was fixated on it. Enthralled by the memory of his touch.

She'd wanted it on a crowded subway, she'd wanted it as they'd kissed behind that tree.

And she still wanted it—even in her sleep.

She wanted Marcos Pinheiro to show her exactly what "A-okay" meant. Again.

Marcos's phone buzzed in the middle of the seminar, making her jump. A few people seated nearby gave them knowing smiles. Whenever a group of doctors got together, being called away was one of the unavoidable realities of the job. They'd all had it happen at some time or other.

Pulling his smartphone from the holder on his belt, he glanced down at the screen then leaned closer to her. "We need to slide out. There's been a traffic accident."

Following his cue, she got up from her seat, crouching as she tried not to disturb her fellow attendees. By the time she made it to the aisle, Marcos was halfway to the door, and she had to hurry to catch up.

Not that she wanted to. She'd been struggling to act normally all morning long after waking up swamped by the memory of them together in his car. His scent. His husky words.

The feel of his hands on her hips as he'd directed her movements.

*You have a patient. Get it together, Maggie!*

Marcos had been his same stoic self, never mentioning what had happened on the subway—or afterwards—although she knew for a fact he was as affected as she was. She'd felt a definite ridge of interest as they'd kissed.

*Patient. P-a-t-i-e-n-t.* She spelled the word out in her head, using a slow, robotic monotone that she hoped would pop whatever bubble of craziness was floating around inside her.

She caught up with Marcos in the lobby. "What happened?"

"Head trauma. Sixteen-year-old female." A muscle worked in his jaw. "She was a passenger on a motorcycle."

"Oh, no."

The motorcyclists in Brazil took their lives in their hands each and every day, darting back and forth on the heavily traveled roadways and wedging themselves into the most minuscule spaces, or flying down the center line between rows of vehicles with tiny warning beeps of their horns. She'd read somewhere that the average life expectancy of a *motoboy* in São Paulo was thirty-odd years.

"How bad is it?"

Marcos kept walking. "Skull fracture. The driver tried to avoid a man pulling a handcart and plowed into a bus in the neighboring lane. He was killed instantly. The passenger was thrown into one of the concrete road dividers."

Maggie shuddered at the image. "Those handcarts should be outlawed."

His steps faltered for a second before recovering. "People do what they have to do to survive."

"Even if it kills or maims someone else?"

"Have you seen the way those motorcycles drive?" A thread of anger had entered his voice.

"Yes, I've also seen those carts." Piled high with what looked like sacks of garbage, she'd seen men and sometimes boys struggle to keep the rickety contraptions moving, even in rush-hour traffic. Cars were forced to go around them, sometimes having to swerve into the next lane if they came upon one suddenly. Most of the people who pulled those carts lived in the slums that dotted the landscape of São Paulo, a lifestyle so far removed from what she'd known in the States it was hard to fathom.

As if he'd read her thoughts, he said, "It's difficult for the wealthy to understand how the other side lives."

*The wealthy?* He said it like it was some kind of plague. She'd seen Marcos's car—intimately, in fact—had ridden in it today. He wasn't exactly scraping the bottom of the barrel. And if that "wealthy" crack had been aimed at her, he was sadly mistaken. Her family might have money, but she was still paying her school loans and would be for a long time. It had been a sacrifice to come to Brazil in the first place.

She decided to strike a conciliatory tone. "You're right. It's hard for an outsider like me to understand."

He stopped and turned to face her in the parking lot. "I didn't mean it that way."

Then how *had* he meant it? He acted like he knew from personal experience what it was like to pull one of those carts.

She shook off the thought. Maybe he thought she was insulting his country. If so, she could understand why he might be upset. "It's okay. Do you know anything more about our patient?"

"No. One of my colleagues has ordered a CT scan. I'll know more once he calls with the results."

As soon as they got in the car, his phone buzzed again. He answered and spoke for a minute or two, before disconnecting and putting the car into gear.

Marcos drove with a surety and confidence that came from years of training, much like the skill with which he performed delicate surgeries that saved lives.

And the skill with which he made love.

A fresh wave of guilt washed over her, and her fingers clutched at the sides of her seat, nails digging into the soft leather. "Was that the other doctor on the phone? What did he say?"

"It doesn't look good. There's bleeding on the patient's brain. They've already had to put her on a ventilator."

Maggie tried to think of the young life that might be tragically altered for ever or, worse, cut short. "Is there any hope?"

"I like to think there's always hope." He slid a glance at her. "It's why I went into medicine."

Interesting. She'd heard so many stories of people becoming doctors for a specific reason, whereas she'd just kind of drifted into it. She'd wanted to help people, but she could have gone in any number of directions to do that. Medicine was just a means to an end.

What she'd really wanted to do was help those who couldn't help themselves.

Because she'd been helpless herself once upon a time?

Probably.

"So that's why you became a doctor? Because you believe in hope?"

"No. Because I believe in keeping my promises."

She looked at him in surprise. "Promises? I don't understand."

"It doesn't matter." He shrugged. "I love what I do. Bottom line, as you would say."

That was his bottom line. He'd become a doctor because of a promise? To whom? His parents? Someone who'd been ill?

"And you became a neurosurgeon because…"

He didn't say anything for a moment or two. "It's hard to verbalize. Let's just say it was something I needed to do. What about you?"

What had made her think she could ask a question like that without him lobbing a similar one back at her? And why did she expect *him* to have an answer when she didn't have one herself?

"I became a doctor to help people. And a neurosurgeon?

Maybe to understand how the brain works," she said slowly,
wondering if that really might be part of the reason. She'd
thought about going into psychiatry before deciding that dealing with emotionally damaged minds might not be the best
choice for someone like her. But dealing with physically damaged ones...yes, that she could handle. It was a type of damage she could see. Feel. Do something about without being
touched by it herself.

*Really?*

And what about patients like Teresa Allen? Hadn't the little
girl touched her in a way that cut right to her heart?

Maybe, but at least a shunt replacement was something
that would definitively fix the child's problem. Unlike her
own problem, which even after a couple of years of private
counseling—counseling that not even her parents were aware
she'd undergone—had still lingered on the fringes of her life,
bringing with it the tendency to blame herself for things that
were out of her control. Although she was learning to tune
out that negative voice.

Like when Marcos had kissed her that first time? Oh, yes.
That voice had tried to re-emerge—only to be beaten back. At
least she hoped so. Even as she thought it, she became aware
of her nails digging into Marcos's expensive leather uphol-
stery again. Appalled, she released her grip on the seat, hoping she hadn't left any permanent marks.

"We're almost there. Do you want to assist? Or would you
rather take a taxi back to your apartment?"

"I'm here to learn. I can't do that from my apartment."

He sent her a look that bordered on approval. But something else was mixed in with it. "You sure? Motorcycle acci-
dents aren't pleasant."

"I'm not here for 'pleasant' either."

He pursed his lips. "No. But surely it's not always so bad,
is it?"

There was something beneath his words that made her wonder if he was talking about this case or something else. "No. Of course it's not."

He pulled into the parking lot of the hospital and swung around to the underground lot used by staff members, sliding his card into the holder and waiting for the automatic arm to go up. He glanced at his watch as he pulled into the nearest spot. "It's almost five. I have no idea how long this will take."

"It doesn't matter. I'm here until it's finished."

He reached over and squeezed her hand before popping the handle to his door. "Good. Let's go."

Marcos kept his eye trained on the craniotome as it inched along the bony surface of his patient's skull, the saw's eerie whine overriding the saxophone solo from his favorite jazz album each time he engaged the footplate. The background noises around him seeped into his subconscious from time to time, but they didn't distract him. He wasn't sure why it was, but the ebb and flow against his eardrums sharpened his concentration somehow. Some surgeons worked best in a quiet, controlled atmosphere, others—like Marcos—preferred noise. He glanced at Maggie as she studied the images of Stácia Lauro's brain, wondering which type of surgeon she was.

Did she like absolute silence, like when she made love? Were the sounds around her slowly eating away at her composure this very second?

He finished the cut, preparing to lift the section of skull to give the patient's still swelling brain a place to go without herniating through her brainstem. The growing pressure over the past half-hour had thwarted every effort to stall its progress, forcing them to make a life-or-death decision.

"Is the music bothering you?" he asked.

Her gaze still locked on the images in front of her, it took a quarter of a turn of Maggie's head before her eyes shifted to meet his. "I'm sorry?"

"The music. Is it bothering you?" He examined the creamy

white section of the patient's exposed dura, frowning at the darkened area where blood had collected beneath the brain's protective cover. Exactly how large was that clot?

"It's fine." She moved toward him to peer down into the open portion of Stácia's brain. "Her motorcycle helmet cracked in half. Her father showed it to me when I talked to him. He's beside himself."

"I know." He closed his eyes for a second. "If the craniectomy does its job and the swelling slows, maybe she'll have a chance. If not…"

He left the words unsaid, but Maggie would know what he meant. They'd have to talk to her devastated parents about organ donation. It was one of the hardest things about his job, even worse than death itself because it involved decisions like artificially keeping someone's body—i.e., their organs—alive, even after there was no hope of regaining brain function. What was a tragedy for one family became a ray of hope for another.

But Marcos wasn't ready to give up on Stácia just yet… as long as she remained stable, they had a shot at preserving cognitive function. And like he'd told Maggie, he wanted to believe there was always hope.

Two hours later, he'd removed the clotted material and did another scan to make sure the brain wasn't bleeding anywhere else.

Suturing the dura and the scalp closed once again, he made a surgical pocket in the patient's abdomen and placed the portion of the skull they'd removed within it. Doing this would keep the bone flap viable for months to come, if necessary—although he hoped it would only be a matter of weeks. If Stácia survived, the bone would be reset in its original spot.

"All we can do at this point is wait." Sweat had collected beneath his surgical gown, despite the chilly temperature in the operating room.

Maggie nodded. "She's lucky to live near a hospital like this one."

He remembered his father, who'd lived not so very far away from this part of the city. "Living near a hospital doesn't always mean much. Some very deserving people never see a doctor."

She blinked at him as if surprised by his answer.

"No. You're right," she said, stripping her gloves off. "And sometimes undeserving people get anything they want."

This time he was the one surprised. "What kinds of things do they get?"

Some dark emotion flashed across her face, and Marcos tilted his head, trying to figure out if she was still talking about medical care or if—like him—she'd shifted to something much more personal.

"Nothing." She gave an almost visible headshake. "I was just thinking out loud. Do you need me for anything else?"

"I think we're about done here. I'm going to stick around the hospital for a couple more hours to see if her condition changes."

"Do you think it will? I could stay as well."

"It's up to you." He wanted to probe a little bit more about those undeserving people, but if it was something she wanted to tell him then she would.

Just like he'd chosen not to say anything about his father.

"I'll keep my cellphone on. Will you give me a call if something happens?"

"If you'd like."

"Thanks. I really would." She tugged her mask up and over her head and discarded it in one of the waste bins. "If not, I'll see you tomorrow. Do you plan to do rounds before the convention?"

"Yes. Around seven-ish."

"Great. I'll see you then."

With that, Maggie reached up to tighten her ponytail and pushed through the door.

And all he could wonder was who those undeserving people Maggie spoke of were…and exactly what they'd gotten.

# CHAPTER SEVEN

MAGGIE WAS TALKING to someone.

After stepping outside the convention hall to call the hospital to check on Stácia's condition, Marcos had returned to the lobby to find Maggie engaged in conversation—her animated hand gestures the liveliest he'd seen from her since she'd started working at the hospital. The man she was with nodded at whatever she'd said.

A spike of something strange went through his chest, and he debated whether to let her finish her conversation or make his way over to them.

Stácia was holding her own, the craniectomy finally lowering her intracranial pressure. So there was no immediate danger of her brain herniating. They wouldn't know her long-term prognosis until the swelling went down, however. For now he wanted to keep her in a medically induced coma until she was a little more stable.

Maggie's red hair was a beacon in a sea of dark heads—so he'd spotted her immediately by the counter where water and coffee were being served. And Marcos was tall enough that he was able to see over the crush of people to tell that she was doing a lot of the talking, her face changing with each shift in emotion. She was speaking English. Her mouth movements were quick enough that she was very familiar with her subject matter…wasn't hesitant about choosing her words. He knew a lot of people here, but he didn't know this particular man—although he seemed vaguely familiar. But the smile the guy gave as she responded to something he said was full of interest, his intent eyes never leaving Maggie's face. The man laughed, his hand going up to touch her arm.

That made his decision for him. Marcos veered to the right, rather than heading back through the double doors across the room. By the time he reached her, however, the stranger had handed her something and moved away, but Maggie's eyes followed his progress for another moment or two before swinging around to meet his gaze.

A flash of guilt went through the blue depths before she smiled. Only the smile looked forced, nothing like the carefree grin she'd just bestowed on the good-looking stranger.

And why the hell was he suddenly noticing what other men looked like?

"Who was that?" he found himself asking.

"Oh…um." She licked her lips. "He's a doctor."

He feigned surprise. "No. *Verdade?*"

"Of course it's the truth." Then, as if realizing he was teasing, she added, "He's from my home state."

"He's an American?" Not that people from other nationalities didn't come to these conventions, but it was usually only for specialties in which Brazil excelled.

"Kind of."

His brows went up. "He's *kind of* an American?"

"You know what I mean."

"I really don't." This woman had the power to send his head spinning in all different directions.

"He was born in Brazil but raised in New Jersey. He knows the hospital where I used to work." She seemed to rethink her words. "The hospital where I still work."

The spike that had jabbed his chest pushed a little deeper. "He works at your hospital?"

"No. He practices in California now. But his parents still live in New Jersey. He gave me his card." She handed it to him.

Marcos glanced at the words.

*Dr. L. Carvalho. MD FACS*
*Facial and Reconstructive Surgery*
*Appointments: 555-555-2389*
*Cell: 555-555-1930*

"He's a plastic surgeon?"

She nodded. "He's here for the conference."

Brazil was a pioneer in that particular area, which explained his presence.

He glanced at Maggie, studying the lines of her face. He could see why a plastic surgeon would gravitate toward someone like her. Her flawless skin and delicate bone structure drew the eye—the dusting of freckles across her nose only adding to her charm. He happened to know from experience those freckles extended to her shoulders. His tongue had nudged aside her shirt as he'd followed the trail a month ago.

Right on cue, his body reacted. On impulse he flipped the card over to the reverse side and saw an email address as well as another phone number scrawled in a messy hand across the back.

"He gave you his private number?"

Maggie's face flushed scarlet. "I came out to the lobby to call my parents—I've been too busy lately to talk with them much. He heard me speaking English and thought we might like to get together for drinks."

*I'll bet he did.*

He wouldn't ask whether or not she'd agreed to meet him. He settled for something a little less obvious. "You realize there are areas of São Paulo that you shouldn't venture into alone."

"I'm not stupid. I wouldn't knowingly put myself in a dangerous situation."

"No? You don't know this man at all. He could be something other than what he appears."

The tightening of her jaw said she was remembering something. "Sometimes it's not just strangers who aren't what they appear."

Was she talking about him?

He started to respond, just as the doors to the conference hall were pushed closed by two ushers. Maggie nodded in that direction. "I think they're getting ready to begin."

When he started to slide the business card into the pocket of his sports coat, Maggie plucked it out of his hand with an enigmatic smile and dropped it into her purse instead.

Did she really mean to call the man?

It was none of his business. She was probably homesick and hungry for a native English speaker.

He immediately flinched away from the word hungry, as it called up all kinds of images he'd rather not see. Of Maggie and the dark stranger getting it on in some hotel room—or worse a motel, notorious in Brazil for their hourly rates and clandestine sexual encounters. Maggie might not even know the difference between the two types of establishments.

And that thought made an entirely different image rear its head. Of him—and Maggie—in one of those very motel rooms.

Just before they reached the entrance to the lecture hall, he put his hand on her arm to stop her. "Be careful, okay?"

Marcos wasn't sure if he was warning her off the stranger or off himself.

"Of course I will."

"You don't know anything about this country or what can happen here."

Maggie gave a visible swallow. "You're right. I don't. But I'm quickly finding out."

* * *

She'd spoken the truth. She was quickly finding out exactly how dangerous Brazil could be. Not in terms of crime or assaults but in feeling completely out of her league most of the time with her boss.

She'd been so grateful to find someone to talk to who was open...whose body language she could read without second-guessing every little nuance. Unlike the brooding doctor who sat beside her—who she couldn't read if her life depended on it.

He was gorgeous...just as handsome as the doctor she'd spoken to in the lobby. But whereas she found herself overthinking everything Marcos said or did, the stranger she'd met was easy to decipher—his face withholding nothing and revealing everything. Even the hint of interest, which had given her a surge of confidence.

It would serve Marcos right if she did call him.

Really? Other than warning her of potential danger, he didn't act like it would matter one way or the other to him.

They'd slept together, and he'd kissed her behind the trees at the subway station...so he found her physically attractive, but then again she'd been in that kind of situation before. Someone had found her attractive in the past and had taken what he'd wanted.

No, that wasn't fair.

Marcos hadn't taken anything she hadn't freely given. In fact, she felt safer with him than she had with any other man, even the casual boyfriend she'd had a couple of years ago. While she'd finally learned that sex could be an enjoyable experience, rather than something to be dreaded, her body's reaction to Marcos had been completely unexpected—shattering her lukewarm expectations and haunting her dreams. She wanted more of the same, even though it was out of the question. Those cravings—for her boss, of all things—had reawakened a guilt she'd thought long gone.

But it was obvious he wasn't interested in anything other than her body. To all appearances, he'd taken what had happened between them in his stride, never missing a beat. Neither had he apologized for what had happened in his car or on the subway. Maybe it wasn't as out of the ordinary for him as it was for her.

Did she really want him to apologize? Wouldn't that be the ultimate slap in the face?

She had no idea.

She only knew that if you could have too much of a good thing, then a few days of a not-so-good thing could quickly turn into pure torture.

Seated next to Marcos, she'd finally decided that was the best term to describe her current situation: torture. It had taken her four days to realize that what she'd hoped would be a reprieve in their uneasy working relationship was actually the opposite. No, they hadn't ridden the subway again—and Maggie honestly didn't know what she was going to do when Monday rolled around and they found themselves back on it. Because, even sitting quietly in the convention hall, she was aware of exactly how many millimeters separated her knee from Marcos's, and it was driving her crazy.

Because the space was always way too small.

She whispered a question about their patient, and Marcos leaned over to fill her in, his breath smelling of coffee and the mint he'd evidently consumed some time afterwards. Goose bumps rose along the side of her neck, and Marcos must have noticed because he pulled back a few inches to tell her the rest.

Which sent a stream of crushing humiliation pumping through her veins. Why did her body have to be so obvious about sending out signals? Why couldn't she be more like her boss…cool, calm, and supremely unflappable.

Except on the subway, and then again afterwards when she'd felt the very obvious reaction to their proximity.

But surely that had been a guy-mashed-against-girl thing.

Her response hadn't been any better, but she could blame it on the same thing. He was an attractive man, and he'd wanted her. For a few minutes anyway.

The only reprieve to their time at the conference lay in the fact that their patient was still not out of the woods, and Marcos had been cutting their days shorter in order to go back to check on her.

None of that helped.

Because she swore Marcos could see inside of her. Like when she'd talked about people not always being who they appeared to be.

The words had come out before she'd really thought about them.

The situation with her uncle wasn't something she wanted Marcos to discover. It had been a soul-crushing time in her life that she didn't like revisiting. Looking back on it now, she knew it was wrong not to have told her parents or her aunt… she would never in a million years counsel another child to remain silent in the face of something so horrific.

But she'd been a child herself. If someone had asked her outright what was going on behind their backs, would she have spoken up?

Maybe. But no one would have ever guessed Uncle Ted was not a loving, kind husband who'd lavished affection on everyone in the family.

And especially on his "favorite" niece.

She'd avoided him when she'd been able to.

And when she hadn't, she'd paid the price.

It made her realize Marcos was right about trusting strangers. She needed to be smart. Careful. Maybe she should chuck Dr. Carvalho's business card in the trash when she got home. Except she'd also given him her Brazilian cellphone number. That had been stupid of her. What if he actually called and asked her to go out?

She could just say no. Tell him she was busy.

After all she was, most days. And she'd learned not to let anyone walk all over her again. *Stop means stop*, as her therapist had been so fond of saying.

So why hadn't she said it to Marcos that day in the car? Because the last thing she'd wanted had been for him to stop.

"Are you okay?" His voice pulled her from her thoughts, a thread of worry in his tone.

She blinked and glanced down to where her fingernails were digging into the soft flesh of her thighs through her slacks—the pain both old and familiar. The urge to welcome it back slid over her.

*Do it. You'll feel better. You know you will.*

She released the pressure instead. Her therapist had said the compulsion—forged over many years—wouldn't magically disappear. It would lurk, like an addiction, hoping to tempt her back into old habits. The trick was to avoid anything that could act like a trigger.

Did that mean Marcos?

Speaking of Marcos, she realized he was still waiting for an answer. "I'm fine. Just a little tired."

Tired of being on edge. Tired of this hyperawareness of each breath the man beside her drew. Tired of second-guessing every decision she made.

"We can leave after this seminar, if you want."

Relief poured over her in a flood. "Would you mind terribly?" she whispered back.

He shook his head. "I want to check on our patient anyway."

Perfect. That would give her a chance to clear her head and figure out exactly what she needed to do to get through the next four months—until her time in Brazil was over and done.

She stared down at her splayed hands, where thin crescents of white showed above the tops of her nail beds. She could start by cropping those back to their customary nubs so there was no opportunity to revert to destructive behaviors of the past.

Then she could stay far, far away from any kind of temptation, both new and old.

She avoided glancing at the man next to her.

And maybe this time she could actually stick to that plan.

# CHAPTER EIGHT

WHAT THE HELL had she been doing to herself?

He pressed the button on the water cooler in his apartment, letting the icy liquid fill his glass. He downed it with several long gulps, the chill hitting his stomach and helping to ground him back in reality.

Because what he'd witnessed this afternoon had been a study in the surreal.

For the last fifteen minutes of the conference he'd watched as Maggie had methodically pressed her nails deep into her thighs and then pulled them back, the action reminding him of a cat extending and retracting its claws. But this had a strange quality to it—the sight casting a shadow of uneasiness over him that had been hard to dispel.

He'd wondered if she'd been in pain for a minute or two—a headache, menstrual cramps, or something like that.

The second he'd asked if she was all right, however, she'd given a violent start and stared down at her lap as if horrified. She'd carefully uncurled her fingers and laid her palms across her legs, keeping them perfectly flat. She'd gone back to being the still, silent figure he'd grown accustomed to.

But below the surface?

If he could peek at the pale skin beneath her slacks, he knew exactly what he'd find. Ugly red welts dotting the surface of her flesh.

It suddenly made him wonder what other parts of Maggie

were covered in welts. Not the areas you could see, but the parts you couldn't.

He set his glass down on the marble countertop and wandered aimlessly around his living room as he tried to think through the possibilities. He should have been asleep hours ago, but he couldn't shake the feeling that something was wrong—and hoping he wasn't the cause.

He'd been domineering when he'd crushed her mouth at the subway station. Maybe she really was afraid of him. But she'd seemed to want his kiss just as badly as he'd wanted hers.

Making his way over to a cabinet against the wall, he stopped in front of a large flatscreen television. A small ornate frame was propped next to it, the sizes between the two a study in contrasts. He picked up the picture and stared at the faded, ragged image beneath the glass. It was the only picture he had of his family. His mother held Lucas, who was still a baby, as she sat on the empty handcart at the top of their street, while his father gripped the front pull bar. He himself stood beside the cart, hands on his hips as if he were king of the world. He remembered the day. He'd been happy—so proud of their few possessions. He cringed as he thought back on it.

He couldn't imagine his parents having the money to buy a camera, so the photo had to have been taken by tourists or someone with enough resources to both take the picture and have it printed.

He was glad whoever had snapped the shot had given them a copy. It was the only physical thing he had of all of them together.

For the millionth time he wondered what had happened to his brother. It was possible that he himself was the only surviving member of his family.

The loneliness that swept over him seemed to amplify the silence around him. Setting the picture down, he scooped up the remote to his television and switched it on, turning the sound up enough to drown out whatever stupid emotions were welling up within him.

All because of Maggie and that blank, desolate stare as she'd dug her nails into her legs time and time again. What kind of pain made a person act like that?

He stared at the remote in his hand as the sounds of raucous, canned laughter from a pre-recorded show surrounded him and he wondered if maybe he and Maggie weren't so very different after all.

Twice.

The number of times Maggie had seen the handsome stranger loitering in the lobby of the conference center since their initial meeting. And the number of times she'd ducked through another set of doors undetected.

They'd just started their second week of the conference, but they'd had to skip out of today's sessions. The swelling in Stácia's brain was subsiding, a mere six days after the accident—which was almost unheard of. Marcos wanted to reattach the bone flap they'd removed as soon as it was feasible to reduce the risk of infection.

She pulled her hands from beneath the faucet, having already scrubbed up for the surgery.

As she prepared to slide her fingers into the gloves, she glanced at her nails, which were now chopped back to nothing, just the way she liked them. Even if they misbehaved the next time she was at the conference—or, worse, at the ballet two days from now—they'd find themselves without traction.

*As if they had minds of their own.*

No. It was all her. It always had been.

Her nails—long and sharp during those terrible days— had been one way to maintain rigid silence. A way to scream without anyone hearing. The searing pain she'd inflicted on herself had also provided a way to focus on something of *her* choosing. Not his.

And he'd wanted her full attention.

His death of a heart attack during a business trip had put an end to the abuse, but it hadn't put an end to her compulsion. The endorphins released every time she hurt herself brought about a wave of calm during stressful times. But it had also been destructive to both body and soul.

Her therapist had helped her find positive strategies to cope with her fears and frustrations when they came up. It had been several years since she'd actively scratched herself, the sunken white scars the only reminder of what she'd once done.

So why was that familiar tingle raising its ugly head again?

Maybe it was Marcos's comments about not everyone being safe…or that vague warning about what could happen in São Paulo. It made things from the past rush back to mind.

Or maybe it was guilt over her growing feelings for Marcos, and how little control she seemed to have over them. Was her subconscious trying to block out the attraction by shifting her focus to something else?

That had to be it.

Finally ready to join the surgical team, she exited the scrub room and pushed through the doors of the operating room, where she found Marcos examining the area on Stácia's abdomen where he'd stored the bone flap.

She kept her fingers flexed and relaxed as she approached the table. "I'm here."

He glanced to the side, eyes searching her face for a second or two. "Just getting ready to make the incision. The EEG shows an increase in brain activity, so that's an encouraging sign."

"I hope so."

"The plan is to start weaning her off some of the meds and let her slowly regain consciousness. We're not out of the woods yet, though."

No they weren't. Because that strange sensation that happened whenever she was around Marcos was still there. As strong as ever.

He made the cut just above the incision from the last surgery, and retrieved the bone, examining it carefully through his surgical loupes as a second doctor closed the incision. He glanced at her over the tops of the magnifying lenses. "Looks good. I don't see any areas of bone resorption, although I didn't expect any after this short length of time."

"I'm surprised the swelling went down so quickly."

"I am as well, but I'm not about to complain." He sluiced the bone flap with sterile saline solution and moved up to Stácia's head, where a tray of tools was already in place. "Have you done one of these before?"

"I have. Twice. Decompressive craniectomies at my hospital back home are usually reserved for cases where there's an imminent threat of death, though."

"Yes, they are here as well." His movements were deft as he reopened the site on Stácia's head and then matched the edges of the bone flap, using a combination of wire and screws to secure it in place. Even through the latex gloves, his fingers were lean and strong as they reconstructed the patient's skull. Cosmetically, the work would be undetectable once everything healed. Maggie could only pray the damage to the soft tissues of the brain would be just as unnoticeable.

Unlike the damage once inflicted on her own body and mind?

But just like their patient, the damage couldn't be seen on the outside—for the most part anyway.

Except for what she'd done to herself.

No, she looked like any other woman who'd had a healthy and happy childhood. But deep inside, there were scars that would never disappear. Just like those blemishes on the outsides of her thighs, where she'd gouged at her own flesh. Those tiny marks were just the tip of the iceberg, warning anyone she might get involved with that there were worse things hidden under the surface.

*Danger! Keep away!*

Her boyfriend had been repelled by them, although he'd done his best to hide his reaction. If Maggie was honest, he'd probably been more horrified by what they represented—although she'd never told him everything that had happened. His subtle avoidance of the tops of her legs when they'd made love had made her feel self-conscious, the feeling growing over the months they'd been together. When she'd finally broken things off, he'd seemed more relieved than anything.

She'd been leery of opening herself up like that again. Marcos hadn't been able to see the scars when they'd come together, and for that she was grateful. The last thing she wanted to do was to explain them to him and watch his eyes grow dark with disgust over what had happened to her. Over what she'd done as a result of it.

For some reason, what he thought about her mattered. A lot.

The rest of the surgery was uneventful, and Maggie was relieved to get out of there. She had a date with Sophia this afternoon to choose their dresses for the ballet. The outing would give her some time to decompress and get away from Marcos.

Physically away, that was. Because it was much harder to flee her thoughts. Thoughts that, for some reason, all seemed to revolve around the one person she needed to forget.

"This is the one. You have to get it!" Sophia made her turn around one more time before pulling her over to the mirror on the side wall of the tiny boutique. Standing behind her, her friend draped her arms around Maggie's neck, her impish face appearing just over her shoulder. "Just look at yourself. You're gorgeous."

Maggie twisted her lips in amusement over the other woman's enthusiasm, but did as Sophia asked. Silky green fabric shimmered as it floated down her figure until it reached her hips, where side gathers emphasized her narrow curves, making them appear more generous than they actually were. There were no shoulder straps to the thing, and Maggie tugged the bodice up with a worried frown. "Are you sure this won't fall down in the middle of the ballet?"

Sophia let go of her and moved around to the front to look.

The salesperson, who was hovering nearby, stepped forward and took hold of the back of the dress, doing something that snugged it tight against Maggie's breasts, making the tops of them spill slightly over the upper edge of the dress. "Better, yes?"

Better if you were intent on putting your assets on full display—which was something she never did. But Maggie had to admit the floaty fabric and jeweled tone did make her look better than she normally did. But wasn't that considered false advertising?

No, because she wasn't advertising anything. To anyone.

"Yes, but I don't sew," she said, hoping that would be that and that they'd put her in something beige with long sleeves and a high neckline. Something that would make her invisible.

"No need. Our seamstress can alter it to fit." The woman smiled at her, obviously not deterred in the least.

Maggie tried again. "You have a *costureira* here at the store?"

Sophia laughed. "Of course they do. Most dress shops do alterations. And you must get this dress. Marcos will love it. His jaw will hit the floor when he sees you."

The last thing she wanted was for anyone's jaw to drop, or for her friend to get the wrong idea. "Marcos isn't interested in how I dress."

"*Verdade?* I've seen the way he looks at you from time to time. He likes you. I can tell."

*Like* was not the right word. They'd had sex *once*, for heaven's sake—it was called lust. Or insanity. Besides, what Sophia'd probably seen had been embarrassment. Or annoyance that the Master of Control had deigned to give in to a momentary rush of hormones. Maggie was just as guilty of giving in to her urges. Her follicle-stimulating hormone was obviously functioning at optimal levels.

None of that meant she or Marcos liked each other.

*Liar. What about the bump and grind on the subway? That crazy kiss afterwards?*

They'd been caught up in the moment. It still meant nothing. And all it had done was make things more awkward than ever.

The salesperson, probably knowing when it was smart to slide away, murmured something about going to get the seamstress and that she'd be right back.

"Sophia, he doesn't look at me any differently than he does any other member of the staff. Or you, for that matter."

"Me?" She laughed. "Oh, no. Marcos and I are like brother and sister. The orphanage was so big we learned to stick together at an early age. I kind of adopted him."

Only one word in Sophia's entire speech stood out.

"Orphanage?" she asked.

"Well, yes. That's where we lived." Sophia's brows arched. "He didn't tell you?"

"That he grew up in an orphanage? No."

Her friend bit the corner of her lip, obviously trying to figure out how to say something. "Marcos, his brother and I lived there together. Only Marcos's brother..." She paused. "I think it is better if he tells you himself. I'm sorry, Maggie. I thought you already knew. This won't make you think badly of him, will it? That he was a *moleque*?"

Maggie made a pretense of casually adjusting the dress, but her mind was reeling over the word Sophia had used. Marcos Pinheiro had once been a street urchin? He'd lived in an orphanage? She could have sworn he'd come from a wealthy background. He was urbane, self-confident and practically oozed sophistication. That sophistication had been part of why she'd fallen for him so hard—he knew exactly what to say, what to do, to leave her panting for more. Nothing like she'd expect of someone who'd lost the people he'd loved most. And he had a brother!

She stopped fiddling and laid her hand on Sophia's arm, glancing to make sure the salesperson was still out of earshot. "Of course it won't make me think badly of him."

It actually made her admire him even more. Maybe he wasn't as impervious as he seemed. Maybe he had vulnerabilities he hid from the world, just like she did. Her fingers curled in for a second, her nails touching her palms before she forced her hands back open. Had he ever had anything precious ripped from him?

His parents, obviously—although Sophia didn't mention them at all. And he'd never mentioned a brother. It was on the tip of her tongue to ask, but it didn't feel right to do so. Especially as Sophia had pulled back suddenly, as if she'd said something she hadn't intended to. Even now her hands were twined together, knuckles white.

Time to put her mind at ease. And what would it hurt if Marcos's jaw really did hit the floor? Not that it would. But the slight prodding inside her to try made her decision.

"Well, I think I'm in love with this dress. Are you sure you don't need one?"

Sophia's shoulders relaxed, and she shook her head. "I've been a bridesmaid often enough that I have more than my share of formalwear." Something about the way she said it sounded wistful. But before Maggie had time to dwell on it, her friend went on, "Let's have them put a rush on the alterations and then go and make our nail and hair appointments."

Nails and hair? Maggie winced. Her nails had practically been hacked off to the quick—out of necessity, rather than efficiency. Besides, getting dolled up wasn't one of those things she particularly relished. But Sophia was on a roll. And knowing she'd been an orphan made her friend's happy enthusiasm over the smallest of things seem that much more understandable. It was also why she seemed younger than she probably was.

And Maggie had a feeling that not much deterred the other woman when she had her mind set on something.

But as long as those ideas didn't have anything to do with her and Marcos, she should be just fine.

# CHAPTER NINE

MARCOS PRESSED THE intercom on Maggie's apartment building, sending a quick glare at the car on the other side of the street.

Why was Sophia being so stubborn? He would have preferred her to sit in the front seat with him, but she'd insisted that Maggie was a guest.

She was no guest. What she was was an enigma, an expert at getting under his skin and staying there, before proceeding to drive him crazy with need.

Magic.

More like a voodoo sorceress who chanted incantations every night in an effort to make his blood boil and his gut ache. Whatever it was, it worked. He was under her spell, the last place he wanted to be.

The doorman answered, and he glanced at the paper in his hand. "Apartment 203."

A minute later Maggie's voice floated through the speaker. "I'm almost...um..." A weird pause. "Is Sophia there, by any chance?"

He rubbed the back of his neck. "She's waiting in the car."

"I'm having a slight problem. Could you ask her to come up?"

His regrets about agreeing to go with them grew. Why hadn't he just booked a patient for tonight and played the forgetfulness card? He slid a finger behind the constricting band of his bow-tie and tried to ease the growing pressure. "Maggie, she's in the parking lot across the street. Is it something I can help with?"

He glanced at the steady row of traffic between him and the car lot. It had taken for ever for the light to change when he'd crossed over here. He spied Sophia looking at him, and he held up a finger to let her know it would be another minute.

"No... I mean, that's okay. I'll ask my doorman to help."

Visions of Maggie with a zipper stuck halfway up that creamy back made him swallow hard. No way in hell did he want a doorman helping her with anything.

Although why it mattered was still beyond him. "Let me come up."

She didn't say anything, and he thought for a moment she might refuse, but then the sound of the front-door buzzer had him pushing through the entrance. The *porteiro* turned a guestbook toward him, and Marcos scribbled his name, the time, and Maggie's apartment number in the appropriate spaces. At least she'd chosen a secure building.

He got into the elevator, punching the button for her floor. He'd been counting on facing Maggie with Sophia in tow. Maybe he should have just gone back to get her.

Too late now.

The elevator doors opened, and he exited, crossing to ring the bell at the appropriate apartment. Before he could do so, the door swung open, and Maggie stood there, a pair of silver shoes in her hands.

"Hi."

For a few seconds his mind refused to function, and he gathered from the fact that he was breathing through his mouth that it was hanging wide open.

He snapped it shut. "Hi."

Maggie had on a dress that should have been illegal. There wasn't a damn thing covering her naked shoulders, and as his eyes trailed down to where the dress hugged her torso, he could see the tops of her breasts. Also naked.

Not her whole breasts…but enough to set loose a series of X-rated images in his skull.

Yes, Brazilian women dressed like this all the time. And, yes, it was part of his culture, he should be used to it.

But something about seeing Maggie—who'd always covered up everything except those fantastic calves—standing there like that caused those voodoo-doll pricking sensations to erupt over his entire body. "You have a problem?"

Mouth-breathing again. Hell. He ground his teeth together and locked his jaws tight.

She held out the shoes. "Sophia loaned me these, but…" she licked her lips. "All the straps… Every time I try to stick my foot in, it's the wrong way."

He saw immediately what the problem was. There was a tangled crisscrossing of thin silver bands on the top of the shoe. So many that it wasn't at all obvious where her foot should slide through. And the buckle and latch were set on opposing diagonals, one at the top, the other at the bottom. She was right. It was a mess.

"Maybe I should just walk to the car barefoot and have Sophia show me how it's done."

Like Cinderella fleeing from the ball? He didn't think so.

The ludicrousness of the situation hit him as they both stood there staring at the sandals, and he couldn't hold back a soft chuckle. "We're both brain surgeons, Maggie. How hard could it be?"

She grinned back. "Pretty hard. I think whoever designed these had a degree in engineering."

"Sit down for a minute, and let me see if I can figure it out."

"I've already tried, and Sophia is probably wondering where we are."

"She knows I've come up." His brows lifted in question. "Afraid I'll be able to figure it out when you couldn't?"

"Of course not." She spun around to walk toward the living room, and Marcos thought his eyes might bug out of his head. He'd assumed the dress wrapped tightly around her entire body, kind of like a towel, with a single panel of green fabric. No. That would be far too easy.

This monstrosity had two wide satin straps that crossed at the back, running from where they were attached at the top of the dress to a point on the opposite side about six inches down. It held the dress up in front, but the straps formed a wide V at the back. And below those straps? Nothing. Not until you reached the small of her back—where the slinky fabric cupped her bottom in a way that made his mouth water. The same butt he'd lusted over since that day on the subway.

This was just great.

She glanced over her shoulder. "Coming?" He swore there was the slightest hint of a smile on her lips.

"Not yet. But I'm close." He muttered the words to himself, hoping she hadn't heard him.

Once she sat down, he'd be fine, right?

Maggie perched on the edge of a brown leather sofa and a slender foot appeared from beneath the dress. She handed him one of the shoes.

Cinderella, part two. Wasn't this what he'd been trying to avoid? Images of her in that role with him kneeling beside her as Prince Charming?

Except he was much more likely to be cast in the role of pauper with Maggie as the royal princess, considering their respective backgrounds.

He knelt beside her, and she frowned.

"No, wait. I just wanted you to help me figure out where I'm supposed to shove my foot."

He couldn't hold back another smile. "I'm sure you could think of a few places."

Her lips twisted as if she was fighting her own smile. "Here, give it to me. I'll do it."

Keeping hold of it, he glanced up at her. "I thought you already tried."

"I have."

"Then let me see if I can figure it out. Sometimes it just takes a fresh pair of eyes."

How hard could it be? He'd done this in reverse many times in the past. Yes, but he'd never actually helped a woman get back *into* her shoes before.

Then again, he and Maggie seemed to do everything backwards.

"See why I wanted Sophia? They're her shoes."

He didn't answer, setting the object on the floor and studying it. He matched up straps with the proper side of the shoe, just like he'd do when piecing together a bone flap, like the one he'd reattached to Stácia Lauro.

There were four points where the straps crossed in the middle. He set those together. A tiny diamond buckle sat at the lower right hand side of the shoe, while the strap with the holes was at the top left, so it had to go over the whole mass like so. He slid the end through the buckle just to keep it straight. And this last loop with elastic at the back... He tested the length. Too short for her foot to fit through it, so it must go around the back of her heel.

He undid the buckle then carefully turned the shoe around, lifting the crazy bunch of straps up and away to create a pocket, while leaving the back loop alone. "Okay, slide your foot underneath my hand and see if this works."

Maggie held her foot up and tilted it forward. It whispered into the shoe on the first try—glittery silver toenails winking up at him as they passed through the labyrinth and came to a stop at the end of the shoe.

Success!

He tugged the back loop up over the curve of her heel until it settled in the tiny arch where the back of her foot met her ankle. "I think we got it."

Taking the loose strap, he inserted it into the buckle and pulled it snug. "How's that?"

"Wow. You're quite the expert when it comes to women's shoes."

The words had a strange sound to them, and he eyed her, wondering if she was referring to he and Sophia being more than friends. But he didn't think that was it. The word *women* was plural.

He wasn't going to deny it. He'd had his share of female companionship. But they'd all been willing, and they'd all known where things had stood when the night was over. Which was nowhere.

No promises made. No promises broken. Ever.

Better to keep his responses light. "Brain surgeon. Remember?"

"I do remember."

The words were still tight-sounding. Hell, this was ridiculous. "Give me the other shoe, and I'll set it up for you."

The handoff was made in silence. Now that he'd done it once, Marcos made short work of untangling the straps and putting them in the right order. He handed the shoe back to her.

Maggie slipped it on and leaned over to buckle the thing, the front of her dress gaping a bit and giving him a nice view of pale skin and the soft creamy mounds of her... He stood to his feet in a rush.

When she straightened, holding her dress up to wiggle both her feet, she bit her lip. "People actually walk in these?"

Brazilian women loved their towering heels. They wore them with everything, including jeans. "Don't ask me how. Straps I can do. Surgery I can do. The mystery of the high heel, however, still eludes me."

She stood and drew in a deep breath, the top of her head now reaching his chin. "I couldn't get them on to practice walking in them. Good thing we don't have to take the subway."

Sudden color bloomed in her cheeks and silence filled the room as they stared at each other. Marcos remembered every painful second of that subway ride. And with those heels on, that would put her ass right on a level with a certain worrisome area of his body.

He turned away before he could dwell on that thought. "Sophia is probably wondering what's happened to us, so if you're ready…"

"I am." He heard a clinking sound behind him and glanced back in time to see her pick up a silver purse with metallic links making up the shoulder strap. She followed him to the door.

"Don't you need a sweater…" he gestured in the general direction of her top "…or something?"

"Nope. No sweater."

Just bare shoulders. And shoes that he now knew how to operate.

A deadly combination that he was going to regret at some point this evening.

His only salvation was that Sophia was serving as chaperone. And right now he could bow down at the woman's feet and worship the ground she walked on. Because she was going to save him a whole lot of grief.

# CHAPTER TEN

"I DON'T FEEL WELL."

Maggie turned to glance at her friend in concern as they stood in the lobby during intermission. Sophia had been fanning herself almost nonstop during the entire first half of the ballet. It was freezing in the arts center, but that hadn't stopped the other woman from swishing her program back and forth near her face.

In reality, the rhythmic movement had helped keep Maggie's mind busy and off the tuxedo-clad man who'd been seated beside her.

Marcos had taken her breath away when she'd opened the door to find him standing there, his black suit and impeccable white shirt setting off the tanned skin just above his collar. His hair had still been damp, and he'd smelled of soap with a hint of spicy aftershave, which had swirled around her senses, rendering her speechless. He'd seemed pretty shocked himself, although his jaw hadn't quite hit the floor, like Sophia had promised it would. When she'd turned around, though, she had heard his breath hissing in through his teeth.

Right now, he was off talking to another suited man, who'd waved him over almost as soon as they'd come through the doors. Marcos seemed to know pretty much everyone. Considering how huge São Paulo was, that was saying a lot.

Her eyes fastened on Sophia's face. "Do you want to go home?"

"I think I do. Would you mind terribly?"

"Of course not. I'll just tell Marcos we need to leave."

She shook her head. "No. You should both stay and enjoy the rest of the ballet."

*What? No!*

"If you think I'm going to let you go home by yourself, you're wrong. What if you pass out or something?"

"It's just a headache. I get them sometimes. I'll be fine as soon as I get home and take a cool shower."

"Marcos won't—"

"*Pfft*. He's like an old man. He worries all the time." She touched Maggie's hand. "The subway is right across the street. I'll text you the second I get on the train and when I get back to my apartment, okay? There are *policía* right outside the door, see?"

She motioned at the open door, where there were indeed two uniformed officers, one on either side of the street. And Maggie could see the subway station not two hundred yards away, with people going to and from the well-lit entrance.

"I'll text you," Sophia repeated. "If you don't get one when I get on the train, you can send Marcos to the rescue. It's his favorite role, you know: protector. He drove me crazy when we were kids."

Maggie bit her lip, still unsure. She glanced out the door again and saw the same officers. "Text me."

"I will. Promise." Then with a quick smile that looked suspiciously headache-free, she flounced through the doors and headed toward the street, pausing to toss her program into the trash can at the edge of the sidewalk. She waved to one of the officers as he stopped traffic to let her pass.

Turning back around, Maggie squeaked when she met dark brown eyes, double furrows marring the space between his brows. "Where's Sophia?"

"She…um…" She blinked, wondering what exactly she could say. "She left."

He cocked his head. "Left to go where, exactly?"

She wished she could smirk at him and say the other woman had just gone to the restroom and that he should cool it. Instead, she found herself wondering if she was about to become the object of his wrath. "She had a headache. She went home."

"And you just let her go?" Each word came across as an accusation, although Maggie had a feeling it was more out of worry for Sophia's safety than anything.

"No, of course not. I tried to tell her I would get you, but she called you an old man." She turned her head. "There are policemen right there, see?" She parroted Sophia's words, knowing she was babbling, but she couldn't seem to stop herself.

Just then her purse vibrated. She clicked it open with shaking fingers and pulled out her phone.

On train. see? safe & sound. txt u when arrv.

She turned the screen to face Marcos. "She's on the train. She's promised to let me know when she gets home."

"So I see." One side of his mouth lifted in something resembling a smile, although she supposed if she tilted her head just right, it might look more like a snarl. "Did you two cook this up?"

Okay, maybe it wasn't a smile… "Cook what up?"

"This…" He swirled his hand around, sweeping it from her face to about hip level. "This whole evening, with the shoes, and dress, and Sophia's sudden departure."

Her eyes widened as she realized where this was headed. He thought she and Sophia had gotten together and planned some kind of seduction scene? Right. He'd already seen how good she was at that. If anyone was the expert, it was him.

"No. We didn't." Her mouth tightened as a wash of anger went over her. The nerve of the man. "And I'd be just as happy to skip the rest of the evening, if it's all the same to you."

Her phone buzzed again. She peered at the screen. "'Sé

station.' She knew you'd be worried, so she's probably going to count down every single stop along the way."

A slow infusion of color went up his neck, making the stiff collar of his shirt seem even whiter. "I know firsthand how much good that does."

"I'm sorry?"

"Nothing." He smiled, the furrows easing just as suddenly as they'd come. "How are your feet?"

"Killing me." She risked a smile in return. "Any other questions?"

He nodded. "How interested are you in seeing this particular ballet? Because I know a little place where we could get a bite to eat, and you could lose those shoes."

"This is so beautiful." Maggie dug her bare toes into the still warm sand beneath her chair and took a sip of her wine.

Moonlight glimmered off the water, casting a crescent of light that seemed to go on for ever. And every time she drew a breath, the heavy scent of the sea rushed in to fill her lungs before drifting away again. Just like the waves.

Marcos swirled the wine in his own glass and looked off into the distance. "I thought you might like it."

"I love it. Thank you for suggesting it." She sighed. "It's hard to believe it's winter in the States right now. But the water is chilly in New Jersey, even in the summer."

"You've lived there your whole life?"

"Yes. My parents were from there, as were their families." Everyone except her uncle, who'd found little things to complain about constantly—even while laughing his words off as jokes. Like the time he'd made fun of her haircut when she was ten, saying it made her look like a boy. He'd chuckled and nudged her arm as if he'd found the whole thing hilarious. Four years later, the joke had been on her. If she'd known when she was ten what she'd learned as a teenager, she'd have kept her hair cropped short—tried to really make herself look like a boy rather than a girl who'd developed earlier than everyone else in her class. And had gained her uncle's attention in an entirely different way.

A deep sliver of pain went through her right thigh, calming her almost instantly. She closed her eyes and took it in.

"Why do you do that?"

Maggie turned her head to glance at him. "Do what?"

He nodded at her lap, drawing her attention to the nails she'd dug into the top of her leg.

Her breath whooshed out of her lungs as she tried to stem the panic and desperation that raced through her veins. She'd stupidly let Sophia talk her into getting acrylic nails for the event—not long ones, but long enough evidently to score some points with her subconscious. Sophia had tsked and clucked over the terrible state of her natural nails, having no idea that she cut them down to nubs on purpose.

Smoothing her dress back down over her thighs, she tried to wipe away the visible imprints she'd left on the shiny fabric. "It's nothing. Just a nervous habit. An *old* nervous habit."

"Talking about your family makes you nervous?" His lips thinned. "Or is it me?"

She tried to evade the question. "I'm not used to having long nails. I keep them cut short because of my job."

"But they used to be long. Or the habit would not have developed." He set down his wineglass and picked up her free hand, examining it. "Very pretty. This is Sophia's doing, I take it."

The man was more intuitive than she gave him credit for. On more than one level. And that meant she needed to be very careful. She tugged her hand back, took a quick slug of wine and decided to address his second statement while ignoring the first. "Sophia's very persistent."

"She is. That persistence used to get her into trouble at times." He ran his thumb over his lower lip as if thinking, an act that reminded her that she'd swept her tongue across that very same lip not that long ago. "So, if it's an *old* habit, and you keep those nails short now, something must have triggered it. I wonder what."

The word "trigger" made her freeze for a couple of seconds before she realized he was using it in a general sense and not as a psychological term. It had been one of her therapist's favorite words.

And the man was right. Of course he was. Ginny had told her long ago that most addicts had a trigger, something that could kick in and tempt you to revert to destructive patterns long after you thought that behavior had been conquered.

It hadn't been talking about her family that had done it. It had been remembering her uncle and what they'd done together.

No. Not what *they'd* done. What *he'd* done.

*What happened is not your fault. It never was.* Her therapist's words came through loud and clear.

"Like I said, it's an old habit."

He studied her for several long seconds. "Fair enough. We all have our secrets."

Hardly. She doubted Marcos had a whopper like she did. Sophia had said they'd been raised in an orphanage, but that was hardly something to be ashamed of. Lots of kids grew up under difficult conditions and came out just fine.

*Like you did?*

Her situation was different. Marcos had probably never felt the urge to gouge himself to the point of drawing blood over being raised in a group home.

Maggie lifted her glass and took a slow, careful sip. If she didn't ease up on herself, she was going to ruin what had been a pleasant evening. She decided to try to get that easy camaraderie back.

"Who knew these kiosks were open at night?" She crinkled her nose and stared at the now-empty plate, where a tasty seafood paella had been. "Okay, you obviously did or you wouldn't have suggested coming here."

"I come here when I need to get away. Get back to the raw, untamed elements of life. The sound of the waves and the constant shift of the tides seem about as untamed as you can get."

She agreed. And something about the rhythmic crash of the surf was soothing. One type of noise she didn't find jarring and chaotic. She was curious about what else he liked. "What other things do you find raw and untamed?"

"What a deep question for such a beautiful night."

"I'm sorry, I was just—"

"No, don't apologize." He held up a hand. "It's an interesting question. What else do I find raw and untamed?"

He stared back out at the ocean for a moment or two before returning his attention to her. "An eagle soaring high above the earth maybe. A big cat as it takes down its prey." Maggie swallowed hard as his voice got softer, and his eyes trailed over her. "The passion that goes on between a man and a woman."

Holy cow. He didn't believe in beating around the bush, did he? Then again, she'd been the one to ask the question, and if she thought about it, her words had lent themselves to a suggestive answer.

He smiled. "At least I haven't made those nails go back to work. Yet, anyway."

Nails go back to… Oh! She glanced down at her lap where her hand was still and unmoving, fingers relaxed. He was right. Because she felt safe being with him, maybe? Then again, maybe it was the wine.

As if reading her thoughts, he nodded at her empty glass. "Would you like another one?"

She'd only had one. Why not? "Only if you'll join me."

"I can't, Maggie. I have to—how do you say it?—keep my head on straight."

Keep his head on straight.

Or what? He'd let himself fall back into bed with her? Regret it with every fiber of his being the next day? She rubbed her hands on her thighs.

His narrowed eyes were on her again. "What are you thinking? You are so closed—so hidden."

Because she was smarter than she used to be. At least, she hoped she was. "I was thinking about the wine, that's all."

"My reasons for not wanting another?" His fingers skimmed her forearm. "Because I have to drive us home very soon. That's all."

How did he seem to know exactly what she was thinking? She evidently wasn't as closed as he seemed to think she was. Because he nailed her thoughts more often than not.

And his statement sent a pang of longing through her chest. *I have to drive* us *home...*

She wanted there to be an "us" someday. Oh, not with Marcos, but with someone. She wanted a husband who would love her unconditionally, scars and all. She wanted children she could protect without fail.

His hand was still on her arm, his skin warm against hers, and she shivered.

"You're cold. You should have said something. São Paulo cools off at night, even on the hottest days." He shrugged out of his jacket and stood to drape it over her shoulders.

Her little tremor had nothing to do with being cold, but Maggie wasn't about to tell him that his touch made her insides jiggle like Jell-O. That would just be too embarrassing.

She reached up and tugged his jacket closer, his warm scent surrounding her.

"Would you like to walk along the beach for a few minutes?" He held out a hand.

Without thinking about the consequences, she placed her fingers in his and allowed him to draw her to her feet.

# CHAPTER ELEVEN

MARCOS SCOOPED UP her shoes, letting them dangle off his index and middle fingers, while Maggie slid her arms into the sleeves of his tuxedo jacket, holding the edges closed. He struggled not to smile. The thing swallowed her whole, coming down almost to her knees.

Good. Because the last thing he wanted was any of the men on the beach ogling what was...

*Not* his.

What was wrong with him? She wasn't his. She would never be. They were from two very different worlds.

It had to be the combination of the moonlight and being in a place that he loved. In fact, he'd never brought a woman here before. Maybe for this very reason.

He swallowed as they walked further away from the crowded kiosk and into the dark night, feeling like a huge ball of emotion was trapped just behind his bow-tie—the second time that had happened to him tonight.

Still moving across the sand, he reached up with his free hand and tried to tug the loops on his tie, his fingers getting hung up.

"Here. Let me." Maggie came around to the front, forcing him to stop. She took hold of the tie and deftly unfastened it, her hair gleaming like burnished copper in the moonlight.

"You're good at that."

She shrugged. "My mom taught me. I used to tie these for

all the men in our family." Her fingers paused for a second before finishing up, letting the loose ends dangle around his neck.

"Thanks. I hate these things." They reminded him of everything he hadn't had as a child. And re-emphasized all the ways he and Maggie were different. She'd been to enough fancy dinners and events that she knew how to knot a man's tie. Had done it on multiple occasions. Had she done it for anyone outside her immediate family?

Blue eyes came up to meet his. "You look good in one, by the way."

That bubble of emotion made its way back to his throat and his fingers tightened around the straps of her shoes. She thought he looked good?

Marcos started walking again, his dress shoes sinking into the sand—he vaguely wondered if he'd end up ruining them. He tended to do jeans and bare feet when he came here. "I have to wear tuxes periodically to go to fundraisers for the hospital. And now the ballet."

"I'm glad Sophia made it home safely."

"Hmm…" He couldn't help but think that Sophia had somehow orchestrated this whole night—except she really had won the tickets in a game of chance. Maggie had said she'd been with her when her name had been drawn. But she sure hadn't worked very hard to find someone to fill that fourth ticket.

Which was probably a good thing. Because if she'd brought a man as a date for either herself or for Maggie, there might have been trouble. Good thing Sophia hadn't heard about that business card the Carvalho man had handed Maggie.

Speaking of which…

"Did you ever meet up with your fellow American again?"

Maggie frowned. "Who?"

"The plastic surgeon from the conference. The one from your home state."

"Oh, um…" She ducked her head, and Marcos could have

sworn her cheeks were tinged with red, although it was hard to tell because the lights from the kiosks were far behind them now. "No. I never called him."

Something about the way she'd said that... "Did he call you?"

"Once or twice. I was always busy at the time."

The tension in his muscles eased, and Marcos allowed the steady sound of the ocean to soothe the wreckage his nerves had become over the course of the evening. If she'd been interested in the guy, she would have either picked up the calls or returned them, neither of which she seemed to have done. Although maybe it was better if he didn't know one way or the other.

He made a decision. He wasn't going to ask about the other doctor again. It was her business. Surely she was smart enough to play it safe.

A gust of sea air blew some loose tendrils of Maggie's hair, and she lifted her face to the wind, giving a soft sigh. "I haven't walked along a beach in ages. So long that I'd forgotten what it's like." She smiled and glanced over at him, her fingers tangling in another strand of hair that sifted across her face. "And I don't think I've ever come to the beach in a long dress."

"You should do it more often. You look beautiful standing here." He didn't know why he'd said the words, they'd come out of their own volition, but they were true. The woman looked stunning, the bottom of her dress tugged by the breeze, the outline of her legs visible beneath his jacket.

Somehow seeing her standing there with his jacket wrapped around her made his chest tighten. He took hold of the lapels and drew her forward, the high heels still dangling from his fingertips.

Her eyes were wide and serious as she peered up at him. "You think I look beautiful?"

"Isn't it obvious?"

She shook her head. "Not to me."

"Then you don't know how to read men very well."

"No. I'm afraid I don't. I never have."

There was such a sad note to her voice that the tightness in his chest turned to a band of steel. "You're pretty good at reading me. Can you guess what I want to do this very second?"

Still gripping the lapels to his coat, he tugged her a few inches closer. "Guess, *querida*."

They were all alone, the night wrapping around them and shielding them from prying eyes.

Her teeth sank into her lip. "Kiss me?"

"Mmm. Yes. Definitely kiss you." He leaned down and slid his lips softly across hers, before retreating. He'd berated himself for crushing her to him behind the trees of the subway station when she'd been timidly exploring him. He was too impatient. Too rough. This time it would be different. "Nice. So very nice."

His lips found hers again, and he applied a little more pressure, his heart pounding out a dangerous rhythm when she responded in kind. Softly. Quietly. But even that had the power to slice right through him.

He kissed along her cheekbone, tasting the slight saltiness of the sea on her skin. "See? You're very good at reading me. Now it's my turn. Should I guess what you want to do?"

"You can try."

He smiled. "Maybe I should rephrase that to say, what I *hope* you want to do."

"And what is that?"

"Kiss me back?"

She glanced down at her toes and several beats went by before she answered. "I'd be lying if I said I didn't want to."

"I'm very glad you're an honest woman, then, Maggie." He released his hold on one side of the jacket and slid his hand into her hair, tilting her head back up. When he lowered his lips this time, he let Maggie take the lead. Let her kiss him however she wanted to.

And it was a heady experience. Her lips nibbled his lower one, slowly kissing her way across his mouth from one side all the way to the other, seeming to take an eternity to finish. The sweetness of it almost overwhelmed him.

The need he'd forced down time and time again over the past month came boiling to the surface, spilling over as he tried to hold himself in check—to keep from grabbing at whatever crumbs she offered him.

"Maggie," he whispered, dragging the back of his knuckles across the hollow beneath her cheek, the velvety texture threatening to unravel him. "I think I want more."

More than kisses. More than petting. He wanted to lay her down in the sand and have her moan beneath him. Just once. He wanted to hear her.

"What do you mean, 'more'?" Her voice was just as soft.

He cupped her face. "Guess."

He was playing a dangerous game. One that could have her bolting at any second. "I—I don't know."

"I think you do." He wasn't sure why he was insisting. Maybe he needed to be certain the wanting went both ways this time—although her body had given up all its secrets as soon as he'd touched her. But he wanted her to openly acknowledge that she felt the same way. That she wanted to be here with *him* and not with the American doctor she'd met.

"You want more than kissing," she whispered.

He nodded.

She moistened her lips. "You want…" She slowly lifted her hand and touched her forefinger to her thumb, making the forbidden sign.

His breath hissed in through his teeth as she stood there.

*"You should never flash it at a patient. Or at a man. Unless you want something bad to happen to you."*

Had she remembered those words? Remembered what had happened afterwards?

He took hold of her hand, and brought it to his mouth, his

eyes holding hers as he kissed the circle she'd formed with her fingers. "Yes. That's what I want. I want it very badly. But only if you do, too."

"I do."

He didn't want to offer her an escape, but he knew his conscience wouldn't let him take the easy way out. Not this time. "I want there to be no misunderstandings, Maggie. I want you. Right now, with the waves pounding behind us. The night all around us." He undid her fingers and twined his through hers. "Say that's what you want, too."

"It's what I want." There was no hesitation as she said the words.

He kissed her again. Firmer this time, letting her feel some of what was coursing through him. She twined her arms around his neck in answer, and she must have gone up on tiptoe because suddenly she was higher, closer to his mouth, closer to the center of his desire.

Marcos forgot about everything other than the feel of this woman against him. Her scent. His hands going beneath the jacket to the bare skin of her back.

He planned to enjoy this night. To make it last. To take her home afterwards and make love to her again in his bed. To wake up with her beside him.

Deep inside, a flicker of fear came to life as he wondered if one night would be enough. Or if he'd be left wanting much, much more.

More than she was willing to give.

Or, worse, more than he was willing to receive.

He drew her backwards, drugging her with a chaotic blend of kisses until she found herself near a lifeguard shack—unmanned at this time of night. She vaguely wondered how often this scene had been played out in Marcos's past. How many times he'd made love to someone on this very beach.

The thought didn't last long because as soon as her back

pressed against the wooden wall of the structure he was kissing her again, sliding both hands into her hair and muttering his disapproval at her tight chignon. Lips still against hers, he murmured, "Why do women torture us with these hairstyles? Turn around."

He took hold of her shoulders and turned her toward the building, where a tiny window gave a dim reflection of her flushed features. He pulled out one hairpin, allowing a winding lock of hair to fall free, which he twirled around his finger. "Much better, yes?"

Leaning forward, he pressed his cheek against hers, chin nudging aside his jacket to rest on her bare shoulder, the prickles of stubble sending shivers through her. "I could stare at you all night." He laid a kiss on the side of her neck. "And I will."

Another shudder gripped her as a wave of raw desire went over her. He planned to keep her here the entire night?

Yes. She wanted that…wanted this man with a desperation that was unmatched by anything she'd felt before.

He lifted his head and plucked more pins from her hair, letting strand after strand fall in soft waves around her shoulders.

"Can anyone see us?"

He smiled. "No. This is a long way from the nearest kiosk." Pulling the very last hairpin, he slid them all into the pocket of his tuxedo trousers then reached up to comb his fingers through the locks. "That's better. I wish you could see yourself, *querida*. You look as wild and untamed as the sea."

The last thing she was interested in was looking at herself, not when he was standing just behind her like some dark Adonis. Not when the back of his hand was trailing across her cheekbone, down the side of her neck, along her shoulder, the jacket almost falling free.

"Marcos." Her voice was breathless. "You're driving me crazy."

"I want you crazy." His fingertips whispered down her arms until he reached her hands, threading his fingers through the backs of hers. Lifting them, he placed her palms on the warm wood in front of her, holding them there as his body crowded hers from behind. She felt the hard ridge of flesh against the base of her spine, even through his suit coat.

She didn't get a chance to enjoy it, though, because Marcos spun her back into his arms as gracefully as if they were dancing. He then scooped her into his arms and carried her through the open doorway of the shack, kicking it closed behind them.

"Just in case," he whispered. "I want you all to myself."

Oh, Lord. This was actually going to happen. She was in Marcos's arms, and he wanted her.

He went to his knees, before lowering her gently onto the wooden planks, his jacket cushioning her back. He followed her down, his lips covering hers in a flurry of light kisses that had her arching up for more, all thoughts of their location lost in the rush of sensation.

She bit back a gasp as he leaned up and peeled the top of her dress down, revealing a lack of hardware beneath it. The cool night air brushed across her nipples, bringing them to stiff peaks.

"*Meu Deus*. I was afraid of this. I've wondered all night long what you could possibly have on under this dress." He gave her a pained smile. "Thank God I didn't know until now."

He hadn't bothered taking off the tuxedo jacket, so she lay with the coat spread open, her dress pulled down and her breasts on full display. It seemed obscene somehow, and incredibly erotic. Especially when he leaned down and licked the very tip of one of them, sending a shaft of ecstasy shooting through her. Suddenly she just wanted him to hike up her dress and be done with it. Who needed to get undressed anyway?

As he continued to lap across her nipple with wet strokes of his tongue, her eyes fluttered shut and she pressed closer, unable to stop herself. He rewarded her by closing his mouth around her and sucking hard. Gritting her teeth, she struggled not to moan, the sound going through the inside of her head instead.

Just when she thought he was going to drive her insane, he sat up, pulling her up with him. "Let's get these clothes off, shall we?"

*Yes. Please.*

Suddenly, their location didn't matter. All she wanted was to be as close to him as humanly possible.

He tugged off the jacket, one arm at a time, before folding it into a makeshift pallet on the floor. Drawing a line across the top edge of the dress where it lay beneath her breasts, he followed it around to the back. "And this little beauty, does it have a *zipper*?"

The word, the same in English and Brazilian Portuguese, slid from his mouth with that peculiar accent she found so damned hot.

"No. It has hooks on the straps."

"Ah, I've found them." Wrapping his arms around her, he held the dress with one hand, while the other undid the fasteners on either side. When he let go, the fabric fell around her hips. She watched his Adam's apple dip beneath his shirt collar then come back up. "You're so incredibly lovely. I'm glad the moon is out tonight."

The ends of his bow-tie still dangled around his neck, and Maggie chanced tugging it free of his collar. She let it drop to the floor beside her.

Marcos unbuttoned his shirt and then stood to pull it loose from his trousers.

Oh, Lord. She was right on a level with his...

And what he wanted was so very obvious.

It was what she wanted, too.

She pulled in a careful breath then started to shimmy out of the rest of her clothes, only to have Marcos stop her. "I want to do that. I've been dreaming of easing that dress over your body all night long. I couldn't even concentrate on the ballet."

So she sat there as he slowly slid his elegant black belt from his trousers one loop at a time, then rolled it around his hand a time or two in a way that made her eyes widen. He gave her a wicked grin. "Worried I'll use this? Or are you hoping, *querida*?"

Use it how?

He waited a beat or two. "All you have to do is say the word, Maggie. I can make it happen."

Was that what she wanted?

*Yes! No!*

She had no idea what this man was going to do next. Or how far he would go. Suddenly, she wanted it all. Everything he had to give. But she couldn't get the words out of her throat.

He lifted a brow then coiled the belt the rest of the way and set it on the windowsill beside him. Still in plain view. Her mouth went dry.

"Next time, maybe," he murmured.

*Next time.*

The man wound her up in a way that went beyond comprehension. Just with a word. A touch of his hand.

But right now all she really wanted him to do was hurry.

As if he read her mind, he unfastened his pants then unzipped them.

When he knelt again and reached for the bottom of her dress, she started to lift her hips to help him take it off, but he tunneled up underneath it instead, his hands gliding up her bare thighs until he found her panties. He made a sound as he hooked his fingers around the upper elastic. "I wondered about this as well. You're willing to go bare on top, but not on bottom. So many secrets to unravel. But you won't be needing these." As soon as he said it, he yanked her underwear down her legs and tossed them to the side.

His hands went back to her dress, but instead of pushing it up or taking it off, he lifted the green fabric away from her thighs, like a surgical drape and then ducked beneath it. Too late, she realized what he was going to do, and she reflexively tried to close her legs, but she couldn't, because he was braced on his arms, holding them apart.

*Oh, Lord.*

Anticipation gripped her, and suddenly she was trapped in a swift-moving current of desire she was powerless to fight. She struggled to find something to hang onto, but all she could do was hold perfectly still and wait.

The heat of his breath was the first thing she felt as it washed across her most sensitive area. Her eyes closed, stomach muscles clenching and unclenching as his hands wrapped around her upper thighs, thumbs strumming across the flesh a time or two before he pushed them wider.

He said something, the words low and unfamiliar, but his tone made her think he was invoking some higher power. Maybe she needed to do the same.

*Do it! Oh, please, do it.*

The litany went through her brain, repeating again and again, until she thought she would scream.

When that first touch came, his tongue was as soft as the words he'd just whispered, but it didn't matter. Her reaction was immediate. She was so ready, wanted him so badly that she went off like a shot, the air sawing in and out of her lungs as she silently bucked beneath him, struggling to process the torrent of sensations pouring through her. Not even that little device she'd bought at one of the naughtier shops had prepared her for the force of being back under Marcos's spell, having him touch her again.

When he finally came out from beneath her dress, he sat back on his heels for a second or two. "You take my breath away."

He wasn't the only one. She could barely breathe. And, crazily, she still wanted him just as badly as she had a second ago.

His hands went to her dress and tugged it over her hips and laid it beside her. Out came his wallet, the little packet inside.

And then he was free of his clothing, nudging her thighs back apart and covering her body with his—flesh to flesh, this time.

This was right. So very right.

"*Deus*, I want you. Want...this." His hips jerked forward, pushing into her with a single thrust that knocked the wind from her lungs a second time. For a moment she lay still, trying to absorb it all, then her arms went around him as she drew him closer. Letting him fill her.

He started to move. Too slowly.

She didn't want slow—had waited far too long for this. She wanted deep. Hard. Fast.

Heart pounding and blood rushing through her ears, she used her hips to tell him what she wanted. He responded instantly, his body and hands urging hers to fly again—muttering gritty, nonsensical things in Portuguese, the sounds amplified tenfold as he pressed his lips against her ear. Instead of grating on her nerves, the whispers made her feel cherished, as he told her exactly how being with her made him feel. With every thrust the words grew more heated, his groans rougher. Half of the sounds meant nothing to her, the other half...

Marcos used the other half to rush her toward the edge of a steep cliff and then didn't hesitate to shove her over the side, gripping her hands as he followed her, flying into space and falling...falling, the ground rising up to meet her at a frightening rate.

Shattered, she lay there, eyes closed as his weight settled on top of her, his gusting breath taking the place of his groans. Then she was moving. Onto her side, his hand on her hip as he steadied her on his jacket, before sliding into her hair. His lips pressed against her forehead, feathering back down to her ear.

"*Tu és perfeita. Magía.*"

She wasn't magic. Neither was she perfect. Not by a long shot. But it was nice to hear him say it.

Smiling, she tried to gather her thoughts into something

coherent. But they had been flung far and wide, never settling into place. Just like a shell tossed about by the waves.

Marcos leaned up on one elbow on the rough boards, his palm skimming over the curves of her side before cupping her hip.

He'd said she was perfect. *He* was the one who was perfect.

Thick stubble lined his jaw, even though he'd been clean-shaven at the beginning of the evening. His dark eyes roved over her as if he couldn't get enough.

She could lie here for ever.

Then he found the first of her scars.

His fingertips slid down her outer thigh, pausing as if noticing the difference in texture there. His eyes followed, narrowing in the dim light as he leaned up a little further. Before she could reach for her dress and yank it over the marks, a low curse broke the silence between them.

Then he was back. His gaze glued to hers.

"What are these?"

# CHAPTER TWELVE

THOSE SCARS WERE more than skin-deep, but Maggie had refused to talk about them last night, saying they were in her past.

But the way she'd dug her nails into her skin back at the kiosk—her so-called bad habit—made him think the two were related. That the marks were self-inflicted. The way she'd slapped his hand away and tried to hide them with her own had set alarm bells off in his skull. But there were too many of them, her hand couldn't even begin to cover them.

They weren't just in her past.

Because he'd seen her. At the conference. At the beach.

And when she'd grabbed her panties and tugged them up her legs, he'd seen scars marring her other thigh as well, cementing his theory. Either she'd hurt herself or someone else had done it to her.

He was supposed to be at the conference with her right now, but he'd left a note with her doorman, begging off, saying he needed to check in on Stácia, which he did. But the reality was he didn't want to face her. Not only because of what had happened between them last night but because he wasn't sure what to say to her.

He'd stood there staring at her in that little shack as she'd hauled her dress up and over her hips, breasts—holding it in place when he'd made no move to help her fasten it in back.

The thought of taking her back to his place and making love

to her for the rest of the night had imploded right in front of him. He'd dressed in silence, sliding his belt back through the loops of his slacks and wondering what she'd been thinking as he'd stood there and teased her with it earlier. No wonder she hadn't responded to his words. The joke suddenly tasted sour on his tongue.

Had someone actually hurt her? Burned her? Or had she done it all herself?

The questions had gone round and round in his skull as Maggie had sat stiff and unyielding in the passenger seat on the ride back to her apartment And now she was at the conference. Alone.

*And if Dr. Carvalho is there as well?*

He pressed his thumb and forefinger to the bridge of his nose. That wasn't something he could control. In fact, there wasn't much he *could* control right now.

Except his job. Which was what he should be doing. He picked up the first patient's folder from his desk and flipped it open, then reached for a pen.

A quick knock came at the door, and Sophia popped her head in with a smile. "Hey, are you busy?"

Great. Just what he needed. A question-and-answer session with the world's nosiest nurse.

"I'm about to be. What do you need?" He allowed a portion of his frustration to show through in his voice before regretting it and softening his words. "How's your headache this morning, by the way?"

"I've been taking ibuprofen for it. I think my allergies are acting up." She stepped inside and shut the door behind her. "Sorry for leaving you in the lurch last night. I know you really didn't want to go to the ballet in the first place. You went because I pushed you into going."

He leaned back. Interesting. He'd assumed Sophia's enthusiasm for life had just gotten the better of her. He was getting a hint that this had been more than that. "So why did you?"

"Because you've turned into a stuffy old man."

Old man.

The term Maggie had quoted her as saying last night.

Marcos's brows went up. "I hardly think thirty-five qualifies as elderly in today's society."

"You know what I mean."

She dropped into the chair across from him, and he sighed. This didn't bode well for a quick exit on her part. "You never go out and have fun," she said.

"You know this for a fact, do you?" He had plenty of fun. Besides, he loved his job. Maybe that was the only diversion he needed. The nightlife had never really appealed to Marcos—the discos, the bars, the excesses of Carnival.

He was fine spending a quiet night on the beach. Alone.

At least, he had been fine with that, until last night. The result of that lapse was exactly the reason he didn't take women out there. Making an exception to that particular rule had just complicated his life—and his job—as there was no getting around working with Maggie for the next four months. Unless he turned her over to another doctor. Which he wouldn't do. Maggie was a good neurosurgeon. She deserved to do what she'd come here to do. Serve out her internship under him.

And that did not include her being *under* him in the baser sense.

He shifted in his chair, trying not to wonder about the ethics of what had happened between them on the beach. It wasn't as if she were a twenty-one-year-old virgin he'd seduced.

And it definitely hadn't been him who'd flashed that hand signal last night.

Sophia picked up a paperclip from his desk and fiddled with it. "I worry about you. I always have."

He couldn't hold back a smile. Yes, she had. Even though she'd been a few years younger than him, she'd taken him under her wing at the orphanage, pulling him by the hand from place to place to show him where the cafeteria was, where the place to pick up his clothes was, where the best spots to be alone were. Marcos had always imagined himself Sophia's self-appointed guardian, but maybe it had been the other way around.

"I know you worry, but I'm a big boy now."

She crinkled her nose with an answering smile. "And I'm a big girl. But that didn't stop you from calling me this morning and chewing me out for taking the subway by myself. I texted Maggie every step of the way."

"If you'd let me know you weren't feeling well, we could have all left together." Only then he wouldn't have gotten to spend the rest of the evening in Maggie's company. And despite how it had ended, it had been one of the most incredible nights of his life.

*Because she's a foreigner. She's exotic. Mysterious.*

He swallowed hard. *Magic.*

Hell, he had to stop thinking of her like that. There was nothing magic about animal lust between two human beings. Nothing magic about those scars riddling her pale flesh.

They'd had sex, and now it was over. They'd go about their business just like every other member of the animal kingdom.

*It was more than that, and you know it.*

"I didn't want you to go home just because of me," Sophia said. "I wanted you to enjoy yourself."

She dropped the paperclip back on his desk, and the click as it landed echoed through the room. "How was the rest of the ballet?"

How did he tell her that he and Maggie hadn't stayed for the rest of the performance? They'd left almost as soon as Sophia had. "I don't know much about that kind of thing. I guess it was okay."

There, not exactly a lie. More like an evasion. He glanced at his watch, hoping to call a halt to this interview pretty soon. "Are you off duty?"

"Nope, just on a break. I wanted to stop in and check on…"

Her hand suddenly went to the back of her head, and she leaned forward for a second or two before straightening back up in her seat.

"Sophia? What's wrong?"

She started to shake her head, then gasped. "Nothing, my head just feels a little…" Sitting very still, she pulled in air with slow, careful breaths.

Marcos came around the desk. "Is your headache worse?"

"I don't know what's wrong. I took some medicine for it. The pills don't normally wear off this quickly." She got up suddenly, her face turning pasty white. "Oh, I think I'm going to be…"

She rushed over to the trashcan beside his desk and dropped to her knees. She vomited. Then again.

Marcos knelt beside her as she clutched the sides of the plastic container and retched over and over. He held her shoulders to steady her. "Hell, you're burning up, Soph. I want to get some bloodwork. And maybe a spinal tap."

"No. It's probably just a migraine."

"You said it was allergies a minute ago."

"I thought it…" The sentence died as her stomach heaved again, but there was nothing left to come up this time. She moaned, her hands covering her face as she breathed in and out as if trying to get her body back under control.

"Where does it hurt, exactly?"

She didn't try to answer him, just laid a hand across the back of her neck where it connected with her skull.

"Don't move." He went around to his desk and hit the button to his secretary. "I need a wheelchair in here. And clear my calendar. Also, I need you to page Dr. Pfeiffer and get her out of that convention and back to the hospital as soon as possible. Tell her it's urgent."

"Yes, sir."

He went back to Sophia, ruing that he'd ever doubted her

story last night. She'd finally let go of the wastebin but it was obvious something was very wrong.

"I'm sorry about that, Marcos."

Brushing off her apology, he went down on his haunches beside her. "That's the least of my worries right now. Was your headache this bad at the ballet?"

"No, it was just nagging. It was a little worse when I woke up, but the medicine did help, or I wouldn't have come to work this morning."

"Of course not." His door opened, and an orderly appeared with a wheelchair. He stood then lifted Sophia and placed her gently in it. "We're going to get you into a room and draw some blood."

"I feel so silly. It's probably nothing."

"Probably. But we're going to make sure." From the way his insides were knotting and releasing, he wasn't as sure as she was. And Maggie was probably a half-hour out, even if she got the message and left the conference immediately. Thank God he'd needed some breathing space this morning and had sent her on without him. Or he wouldn't have been here for Sophia.

Following the wheelchair from his office to the bank of elevators, he punched the floor into the main keypad and waited as it flashed the letter of the next available elevator. The orderly pushed her over to it just as it pinged its arrival. Once in it, Marcos took her hand as she leaned her head against the back of the wheelchair, eyes closed. Every once in a while he could see her wince as a wave of pain went through her.

Hell, he hoped it wasn't a brain bleed. "Still hurt?"

"Shh. I'm concentrating on not throwing up right now."

He set a hand on her shoulder and gave a soft squeeze. "Don't worry about anything, *querida*. We're going to figure this out."

This time Sophia didn't argue or say that he was overreacting. From the temperature of her skin through her blouse, her fever had to be approaching thirty-nine degrees, high under any circumstances. But it helped put the brain-bleed theory to rest. There was an infection of some sort in her body. Meningitis, maybe, like he'd originally suspected. Or it could even be a cerebral abscess. "Have you had a sinus infection or dental problems recently, Soph?"

Her eyes fluttered open, and she fixed him with a glare. Okay, she wasn't going to be a good patient. Not many healthcare workers were. "Allergies, remember? My sinuses have been backed up for weeks."

The pollution in São Paulo tended to aggravate allergies and make them worse on days when the haze hung low over the city. If her sinuses really had been full for a while, an infection could have settled in, which in turn could have traveled to her brain and formed a pocket. Not a common occurrence, and definitely not good.

The elevator opened on the third floor, and Marcos walked ahead, motioning for the orderly to follow him. He checked in at the nurses' station and glanced at the chart, noting there was an empty room just around the corner.

The nurse did a double take when she saw who was in the chair. "Sophia, what happened?"

Sophia waved off her colleague's concern and closed her eyes once again. Her bubbly personality had suddenly gone dark, which was another sign that things were not as they should be.

They got her settled into the room, and Marcos handed her an emesis basin, smiling faintly when she sent him another weak glare, but she took it. One of the other nurses came in, and Marcos gave her a list of instructions. Once she'd had her blood drawn, he wanted a sample of her spinal fluid. "We're going to do some poking and prodding. You know the routine."

"I hate needles."

He blinked. "You're a nurse, for God's sake."

"Exactly. I'm the one who does the jabbing." Her hand went to her head again, despite the playful words.

At least she could joke. He'd thought for a minute or two she might go down in his office. And the thought of the world without Sophia if she'd caught something really serious...

No, he'd already lost too many people: his father and mother...and Lucas. He wasn't about to lose Sophia as well.

"Maybe I have dengue."

Marcos shook his head. "I haven't heard of any cases in the last month or so. Let's just do some tests and see what we've got."

Leaving the room as the nurse prepared to draw blood, he spied Maggie coming down the hall, her heels clicking on the linoleum floor as she hurried to the nurses' station, beige skirt snug around her hips. That was fast. She still had the lanyard from the conference around her neck.

"Maggie."

Whirling around, she stared at him for a second before squaring her shoulders and walking toward him. Good, she was going to face him head on, rather than try to avoid him.

"The message said something was wrong with Sophia. What happened?"

"She collapsed in my office. Severe headache, vomiting, fever."

"Oh, no." Her eyes focused somewhere below his chin. "Meningitis? Encephalitis?"

He could almost see the wheels working in her head. "If it's meningitis, it would be viral as she's been vaccinated against the bacterial version, just like the rest of our staff."

"Could it be something tropical? It has to be infectious."

"Unless it's two separate agents at work." He glanced back at the door of the room. "I'm taking her to the imaging department, just in case."

Maggie frowned. "You need to call someone else in on the case. You know that, right?"

"Yes. That's why you're here."

Her brows went up. "What?"

"I want you to take her case. You're not related to her."

"Sophia and I are friends. We went shopping together. I shouldn't be treating her any more than you should. If something is going on with her brain, you need to call in another neurologist, someone impartial. Surely you could ask a colleague you trust to take this on."

"I thought I was, actually." His mouth tightened, even though he knew he wasn't being fair. In reality, he'd hoped to keep the letter of the law by having Maggie listed as her attending, while still calling all the shots himself.

Her fingers went to his arm. "Marcos, I would if I could, but I care about her too much to trust my own judgment."

"Fine. I'll call Dr. Romildo."

She didn't back down, like he'd hoped she might. Instead, she said, "You're doing the right thing."

He hoped so. Because he sure hadn't been making the best decisions lately—not about letting the night go by without checking on Sophia. And not about taking Maggie to the beach.

But from here on out he was going to be smart. Just like he'd promised his father he'd be.

# CHAPTER THIRTEEN

"Thank God."

Maggie sank into the chair across from Marcos's desk when the results came back in. Viral meningitis, just as he'd predicted. Seven to ten days' recuperation time and Sophia should be as good as new.

"They're going to discharge her today, but I'm taking her home with me. Which means you'll have to go to the conference without me for a couple of days."

The thought should have dismayed her, but it didn't. It had actually been a relief not to have to face him this morning after what they'd done. And the thought of extending that reprieve was an even bigger relief. Their interactions had been a train wreck from almost day one. And she didn't seem to have the will to say no.

And to flash that sign at him at a public beach? What kind of craziness was that?

The kind of craziness that had her hormones jumping like mad when he'd slowly brought her hand to his mouth and kissed her fingers.

Lord. And here she was thinking about it all over again. She sat up straight, curling her fingers in her lap and twining them together in a knot.

"That's fine. I've understood the seminars for the most part. There are a couple other ones I'd like to attend tomorrow. Do you need me at the hospital for anything?"

"No. You go and enjoy." He rubbed the back of his neck. "Which seminars are they?"

"I'll have to look at the program, but I thought I'd go to the 'Innovations in Cranioplasty' one, especially after observing Stácia's surgery."

"Cranioplasty? Is that part of the neurology track?"

"I think it's listed as a dual-track seminar. Neurology and plastic surgery, as it deals with cosmetic elements of skull reconstruction as well as the functional ones."

One brow went up. "Maybe you'll run into the plastic surgeon from New Jersey there."

Maggie couldn't tell whether he was hoping to deflect her attention away from himself or if he was just making idle conversation. Either way, the offhand remark stuck in her craw. "Maybe I will. That would be lucky, wouldn't it?"

"If you do, make sure you pick up a business card for me. I might just have to look him up."

She went from irritation to shock in the space of a nanosecond. Was that a veiled threat? No. Of course not. He just meant because the man was Brazilian by birth, that's all. Maybe he wanted to discuss treatment differences between the States and Brazil.

Unsure if he expected her to answer him, she decided to prevaricate. "I'll do that. I'll let him know you're interested in speaking with him."

He gave her a slow smile. "Or I could just make a copy of the card he gave you instead."

A second wave of panic went through her when she thought he actually meant to call the surgeon and say something about last night. She immediately squashed that idea. Why on earth would he do that? It wasn't like last night had been special in any way. To either of them.

But just in case… "Sorry. I left it by the phone at my apartment."

The coolness in his eyes dropped another twenty degrees.

Great. The last thing she wanted to do was start a war with the doctor she was supposed to be working with—or to make things more awkward than they already were.

*Dumb move, Maggie.*

She didn't want Marcos thinking she played the field, jumping from one bed to another. Although surely he could tell by her behavior that she wasn't the most experienced woman on the planet when it came to intimate relations. And she could have died when he'd asked her about those marks on her legs, his fingers tracking over them one by one.

Suppressing a shiver at the memory, she stood. "I want to go up and check on Sophia, and then I think I'll go home. It was a long night last…"

Her voice trailed away when she realized exactly why she felt so tired and sluggish today. And exactly where she'd spent a good part of her evening.

"Yes, Maggie. It was a long night." He stood and placed his hands flat on his desk, leaning forward slightly as he looked her in the eye. "I expect you to remember each and every minute of it as you attend those seminars."

Shifting in her chair for the fifth time, Maggie closed her eyes and cursed Marcos Pinheiro for what he'd done to her. Dr. Carvalho had waved at her from across the conference room before getting up and moving to the chair next to hers. "Hi. I wondered if I'd see you again before the conference was over."

She'd given him a half-hearted greeting and slid a little lower in her chair. Of course the cranioplasty lecture would be the last seminar of the day. And of course Marcos had said she might see the other doctor there.

If Marcos had been here with her, this probably wouldn't have happened because he'd be occupying the chair the plastic surgeon was in. And she was also more than a little irritated at her boss for that last loaded statement he'd lobbed at her before she'd left his office.

*"I expect you to remember each and every minute of it as you attend those seminars."*

She did. She remembered it all. And those memories were doing awful things to her equilibrium.

Luckily, by the time she'd arrived the lecture had been getting under way, so there hadn't been a lot of time for chit-chat before the speaker had got up to the podium, but now that it was almost over? Was she going to have to stand around and talk to her fellow American—or, worse, turn down that offer of drinks he'd made last week?

After what had happened with Marcos, she didn't see herself wanting any more casual outings with men. She obviously was not to be trusted to keep things at a superficial level. *Only when it came to Marcos.* Maybe her subconscious was right. Because there was no heart-flipping or quivery feelings low in her belly from Dr. Carvalho's proximity. But he also wasn't leaning into her and forcing himself into her personal space. He was being a perfect gentleman. He seemed genuinely happy to talk to someone who spoke English.

She turned her head during a lull at the end of the seminar as the lecturer paused so audience members could jot down information from several of the slides he'd presented earlier. "Didn't any other doctors from your hospital come to the conference?"

He glanced back at her with a friendly smile. "No one else at our practice understands Portuguese. I told them I'd take notes and let them know if I learned anything interesting."

"And have you? Learned anything interesting?" She found herself smiling back, unable to resist his easy charm. There was nothing threatening about his demeanor in the least. Marcos had been wrong about him.

"I have, actually."

"Really? What?" She relaxed into her chair, leaning her chin on the palm of her hand as she looked at him. She was actually grateful to have something to take her mind off the turmoil of the past week.

"For one thing, I learned that staring daggers at someone is not just an expression."

Her chin slipped off her hand. "I'm sorry?"

He inclined his head toward the far wall without actually looking in that direction. "Isn't that the doctor you were with when we met the first time? He looked at me exactly the same way when I handed you my card."

Oh, God. Her glance skated toward the other side of the room and she spotted Marcos, who was leaning against the wall, his strong arms crossed over his chest.

And, yes. Those were daggers. Aimed not at the man beside her but at her.

"Um. Yes, I'm actually doing an internship under him at the hospital. I hope nothing's wrong."

He gave a soft laugh. "Oh, I think something is wrong all right. If you could assure him I only have the purest of motives, I'd appreciate it. I'm not looking to go home and asking one of my colleagues to put my nose back in its correct location."

"Oh, I'm sure he's just..." What could she say, really? She and Marcos weren't a couple, and they never would be.

They'd had a one-night stand. Okay, two, if you counted that day in his car. But she had no intention of hanging around Brazil and starting something with a man she found dangerous on so many levels. "We have a friend who contracted meningitis. I'm sure he's just here to give me an update on her condition."

"I'm sure that must be what it is." His dubious look said he wasn't buying her explanation.

Well, neither was she. But there was no way she was going to cringe down in her chair and let Marcos make her nervous.

Instead, she gave the other doctor a brilliant smile, the brightest one she could dredge up, even though a strange sense of excitement and foreboding was beginning to pump through her veins. "Don't worry. He's harmless."

*Really? Really, Maggie? That's not what you thought to yourself a few minutes ago.*

The screen went dark and the lecturer thanked everyone for their attention, moving away so the conference co-ordinator could get up and give instruction about the next day's events.

"I have to tell you, he looks like a regular bastard to me."

She couldn't hold back a laugh. "Do you think so? He's not as bad as all that."

Although she had to admit he did look like one, glowering at her from across the room like he was.

"Seriously. You aren't letting him bully you, are you?" He glanced back at Marcos, a challenging glare marring his rugged face this time. "I could hang around for a while if you want me to."

She drew in a deep breath, her laughter drying up. "No, I'll be fine. I'd let you know if there was a problem."

Maggie realized she was telling the truth. Gone were the days when she'd silently accept someone forcing her to do something she didn't want without the slightest murmur of protest.

Dr. Carvalho touched her arm then stood. "If you're sure, I'm going to slide out, then. My email address and phone number are on the back of that card I gave you. Get in touch with me when you get back to the States, okay?"

"I will." Suddenly she knew she would contact him. There was something about the other doctor that struck her as vaguely familiar, though she wasn't sure why. Maybe it was because he was nothing like Marcos, whose hard, haughty attitude kept everyone at a distance.

Didn't she have barriers that did the same?

Probably. But knowing that didn't magically make them disappear. But maybe she could work on it. Start trusting men again, little by little. Maybe even beginning with Dr. Carvalho.

And Marcos?

Possibly. If he'd let her.

She watched as the plastic surgeon made his way between the chairs to the exit on the opposite side of the room from where Marcos was perched. She guessed he didn't want a confrontation if none was needed.

A whisper of air drew her attention to the fact that she was still seated, and someone had just dropped into the chair next to hers.

She swallowed then willed herself to turn and face the inevitable. Marcos crossed a foot over his knee and studied her for a moment. Dressed in a black button-down shirt and equally dark dress slacks, he looked as elegant in business clothes as he had in that tuxedo.

"Enjoying yourself?" he murmured.

"As a matter of fact, I am." Her chin popped just a bit higher as she dared him to say anything about the other doctor's presence.

"I thought you might like an update on Sophia's condition." He glanced around the emptying room. "And I wanted to offer you a ride back to the hospital—unless you're planning to take the subway."

At rush hour? She wasn't interested in doing that again. She'd planned to catch a cab instead. "Oh. You didn't have to do that."

His eyes softened a fraction. "I know. I wanted to. And I did want to let you know that Sophia is better, in case you went straight back to your apartment, rather than stopping by the hospital."

"Has she been released?"

"Yes. She's at my house."

"Good, I'm glad she won't be alone."

His lips curved slightly. "Sophia tends to worry about other people being alone, rather than her. She always has."

Something about the way he said it made her chest ache.

Was he talking about himself as a boy at the orphanage... something he'd still not mentioned?

She decided to steer clear of that subject. "Thank you for coming to tell me in person. It was thoughtful."

"Thoughtful." He seemed to mull over that word. "I wouldn't exactly call it that."

Had he really been worried she might hook up with the plastic surgeon? If so, he must have been surprised when he'd found her sitting beside the man. "Just so you know. He sat with me, rather than the other way around. And he was a perfect gentleman. He wants to keep in touch after he gets back to the States."

The stiff set of Marcos's shoulders seemed to soften further. "He's going back soon, then."

"I don't know. He didn't say, but I imagine so. There are only a couple more days left of the conference, and I don't think I'll see him again."

"So, will you? Keep in touch with him?"

No reason not to be honest. "Yes, I think so. We're from the same state. He probably comes home to visit from time to time."

"I see."

Maggie's emotions were all tangled up inside her right now. She didn't know how Marcos could see, when she herself couldn't make heads or tails of anything.

She only knew that her stomach had that quivery sensation she'd been missing while Dr. Carvalho had sat beside her.

And her fingers were tingling with the old familiar pins and needles that had plagued her on and off for the past month. Why?

She stared down at them, trying to figure out what was happening to her.

Marcos wasn't a threat to her so she didn't understand what was causing it, or why she...

The realization came to her in a flash, and the blood drained from her head, making her feel dizzy.

She knew why her fingers were tingling and what the warning sensation meant.

Marcos had the power to hurt her—really hurt her—if she wasn't careful. Not physically, like her uncle had done. But emotionally. Not because of anything he did but because of her own stupidity in not protecting herself.

If she fell for this man, Maggie knew beyond a shadow of a doubt it would not end well for her. And she knew that was not a chance she wanted to take.

So from here on out she was going to have to be very, very careful and keep her distance. Just like Marcos did on a daily basis.

Maybe the best way to do that was to tell him about her past. It had seemed to destroy what she'd had with her ex-boyfriend, even though she'd kept some parts to herself. Why would it be any different with Marcos? As soon as he knew the truth about her, about what she'd done to herself, he'd go running for the hills.

When to do it, that was the question.

How about on the ride to the hospital?

Yes. The sooner the better.

Now all she had to do was actually work up the courage to pull the switch and put an end to things once and for all.

# CHAPTER FOURTEEN

MAGGIE WAS QUIET as they got into his car to ride back to the hospital.

*Why wouldn't she be? You glared at her from across the room like a jealous lover for a good fifteen minutes before either of them noticed you were there.*

She was probably furious.

He was pretty damned angry with himself, for that matter. The other doctor hadn't tried anything. Hadn't slid his arm around the back of her chair, or even touched her, other than that one quick finger-to-the-forearm gesture as he'd said goodbye.

But ever since Maggie had walked out his office yesterday, he'd been eaten up by some type of tension he could only attribute to jealousy. All because she'd said she was going to the cranioplasty seminar.

His attitude infuriated him. He had no hold over Maggie. No right to ask or expect anything from her.

And he'd never promised her a thing.

She was here for a few more months and that was it. Dr. Carvalho was from her home state. Of course they'd keep in touch.

And he himself? Would he keep in touch with her once she was gone?

He swallowed down the wash of stomach acid that bubbled up his esophagus. There'd be no reason to contact her ever again.

And he knew he wanted to. He wished he could casually suggest they get drinks or say, "Hey, let's stay in touch once you get back to the States."

But he knew he wouldn't. He'd never been the type of person who formed strong attachments.

A hopeful part of his subconscious perked up. *What about Sophia?*

That wasn't the same thing at all. Sophia had attached herself to him, not the other way around. He'd formed no lasting relationships since his brother had been adopted by another family.

*Maybe it's time you changed that.*

With a girl who was only here for a short period of time?

No, thanks. He wasn't into that kind of masochism.

His lips curved up. No, he was into the kind that provided the most powerful physical rush of pleasure he'd ever experienced, while supplying him with enough mental torture to last quite a few years.

"What's so funny?"

He glanced to the side to see Maggie frowning at him in much the same way as he'd frowned at her in that lecture hall. "Nothing much. Just thinking of joining the BDSM movement."

Maggie's eyes widened. "I'm sorry?"

"Nothing. Bad attempt at a joke."

One that was totally on him.

His thumb rubbed along the steering-wheel as he braked for a red light. "So how was the conference?"

"Fine. How was your day at the hospital?"

"Pretty typical. No surgeries, though, which was good. We did have a teenager come in with a severe concussion."

"What happened? Car accident?"

"Yes. She should be fine, though. No lasting effects."

"No lasting effects." The words were soft. Sad.

He turned and glanced at her. "Maggie, are you okay?"

She licked her lips. "Can we stop somewhere for a minute?"

An alarm went off somewhere in his head, similar to the one he'd heard when Sophia had almost collapsed in his office, although Maggie seemed perfectly composed. Too composed, if anything. Almost plastic.

"Sure. Just let me find a spot."

He pulled off the highway and found the only spot he could, in the no-parking zone near the city park. They wouldn't be here long enough for it to matter.

Turning the car off, he shifted to face her. "What's going on?"

Maggie sucked down a long, deep breath then released it on a sigh. "You asked me about those marks on my legs."

He nodded, his stomach tightening. After all that coaxing and demanding, why had she suddenly decided to tell him now?

Lifting her hands so that the backs of them faced him, she wiggled her fingertips. "I made them with these."

He'd been right. Despite his suspicions, a thread of nausea wound through his stomach at the matter-of-fact way she'd said it. She'd scratched herself hard enough to leave scars, and she acted like it was nothing. "Why?"

There was a short pause, as if she was trying to figure out exactly what to say. "Because my uncle hurt me. More than once."

Marcos was having trouble keeping up. She'd said she'd made the marks herself, but that it had been her *uncle* who'd hurt her. That didn't make any sense. "You scratched yourself because your uncle hurt..." The dots rearranged themselves in his head, forming a picture he suddenly didn't want to see. But he had no choice. He'd asked Maggie to tell him—had demanded to know what those scars were. What kind of man would he be if he told her to stop now?

He braced himself to hear the worst. Every last terrible word of it. "What did he do, Maggie?"

She twisted her hands in her lap, not sure if she could go through with this after all. She'd thought telling him would be the perfect solution, but she'd never actually shared the whole story with anyone before, except for her therapist. She'd told her ex-boyfriend bits and pieces, but not the worst of it.

It was for the best. Once Marcos knew, it would be all over.

"My uncle abused me. Sexually. For almost two years."

*"Meu Deus."* Instead of recoiling, like she expected him to do, he gently slid his knuckles along her cheekbone. "How long ago was this?"

"It started just before I turned fifteen."

"You hurt yourself because of what he did?"

She swallowed, knowing she had to continue now that she'd started down this path. "No. I did it to force myself to stay quiet. To concentrate on something other than what he was doing to me. To prove that I could hurt myself more than he ever could."

*"Shh...you have to be very, very quiet, Maggie. Don't make a single sound."*

The memory of the terrible excitement in Uncle Tom's voice as he'd pressed her into her childhood bed crawled up her spine and lodged in her head, along with all the things that had come afterwards: the feel of her nails tearing at her skin as she'd fought to not make a sound; the control she'd felt when she'd inflicted more pain on herself than he had; the sense of release as endorphins had flooded her system, allowing her mind to override the humiliating things her uncle had forced her to do to him—the things he'd done to her.

The vicious cycle had been set into motion with a single act. A cycle that had lasted for years after the abuse had stopped.

"He raped you?" Marcos's eyes were filled with outrage, but not disgust.

A niggling worry sprouted. This was not going the way she'd expected it to.

"Yes. He did."

"And your parents did nothing to stop him?"

"I never told them." She'd been going to. Then her uncle had died suddenly. And as she'd looked into her aunt's grieving face, she hadn't been able to bring herself to say anything. What good would it have done? Her uncle couldn't hurt her or anyone else ever again.

"Maggie...why? Why didn't you ask for help? Tell someone?" His fingers withdrew from her cheek, and she heard the faint tinge of anger in his voice.

"Because I was a kid. I felt powerless. My uncle was an adult and I was a child—I'd been taught to respect my elders." How could she really explain what had been going through her head back then? The sense of shame she'd felt for what her uncle had done—somehow feeling she'd brought it on herself. He'd accused her of that very thing, in fact, taking her hand and putting it on him, telling her to feel what *she* made him do.

Should she have known better than to give in to his subtle threats and demands? Probably. But she'd been grappling with her own feelings of sexuality toward a couple of boys in her class. And things had seemed so mixed up. So twisted out of context.

"I didn't say anything because my uncle died suddenly."

"I hope it was a horrible, painful death. In a dark prison."

His face was a tight mask of fury and Maggie realized it wasn't directed at her but at what her uncle had done.

Relief went through her system, the feeling in direct opposition to what she should be feeling at this moment. She'd told him the truth in order to push him away. Instead, he was drawing closer, and she welcomed it—tears springing to her eyes.

She touched his hand, starting when Marcos captured her fingers with his own.

Taking a deep breath, she continued. "He never went to prison. He had a heart attack. He was only fifty-nine at the time."

"*Only* fifty-nine." He pulled in a deep breath then released it. "He lived fifty-nine years too long. My God, Maggie, why didn't you say something that day in the car? Or at the beach?"

She shrugged. "I never told my parents. Or my aunt. Why would I tell *you*?"

The second she said it she knew she'd made a mistake. A quick flash of hurt went through his dark eyes, followed by his hand opening to release hers. She reached over with both of her own to capture it again. "I didn't mean that the way it sounded. It's just that I'd never told anyone about what happened, other than a therapist I talked to years later, when I couldn't stop hurting myself even after my uncle passed away. It threatened to destroy my dreams of becoming a doctor. Of helping those who can't help themselves."

Her fingers went up and trailed across the planes of his face, his fierce cheekbones, strong autocratic nose. Traced across his lips. "I should have told you, but I was afraid." It was the truth. And she'd told him today for the very same reason. Because she was afraid. Marcos's throat moved with a quick, jerky swallow. "You said you hurt yourself in order to stay quiet. Is that why you're so quiet now? Why you seem uncomfortable with noise, like at the subway?"

"Yes. My uncle didn't want anyone to hear us." He knew the worst of it. Why try to hide the other stuff? "I'm okay most of the time. It's just when I read something in the paper or come across a patient at the hospital who's been abused that it hits me—the realization that there are other kids out there just like me. Who are suffering the very thing I once suffered. And knowing there's nothing I can do to help them."

She paused to take a breath. "You've seen me curl my fingers into my legs. The temptation to self-injure is still there just beneath the surface. It's something I think I'll always struggle with. It's why I keep these so short." She held up one of her hands to display ugly, stubby nails—the acrylics from the ballet already long gone. "Good thing I'm a doctor, right? No one expects me to have long elegant fingernails."

Marcos tugged her hand toward him, his index fingers sliding along hers. "You have long elegant fingers instead." He kissed each of her fingertips.

There was something painfully sweet about seeing him do that after what she'd just shared. As was the fact that he wasn't gripping the steering-wheel, knuckles white, as he waited for the first available opportunity to tear out of that parking space. To slowly withdraw, like her ex-boyfriend had done. Or, worse, dump her off at home with a relieved goodbye, never to see her outside the hospital ever again.

Because she realized, despite all her reasons for telling him about her past, she did want to see him, despite the risks. He made her feel safe. Wanted.

*Normal.*

Even if what they had was only temporary.

She'd never meet anyone like Marcos again. No one made her heart pound quite as hard, made her stomach wind up in anticipation of his touch.

"You're not running away," she murmured, half-afraid she was dreaming all of this.

"No. Why would I?"

She pulled her hand back down to her lap. "It's not every day you run across someone like me."

"No. It's not." He laid a finger across her lips, shushing her before she could assign a meaning to his words. "And it has nothing to do with your uncle or what happened to you. Do you think you're the only one who feels shame or regret about their past?"

"No, of course not."

"I have things I hide from people too. You asked about Sophia, once, about how we met…" Marcos glanced to the side as a police officer drove by their car then slowed down. "I think we should move before they decide to send for a tow truck."

"Do you want to go back to my apartment and talk?"

His lips quirked. "I was thinking along those same lines, but for an entirely different reason. But only if you want to."

"I do." Maggie smiled back, relief singing through her system, the delicious quivery feeling in her stomach returning with a vengeance at the look he gave her. "Maybe there's time for both. Talking...*and* the other."

He leaned over and gave her a soft kiss. "Maybe there is at that."

# CHAPTER FIFTEEN

MARCOS PACED AS Maggie brewed coffee.

He'd made a quick call to Sophia, who'd assured him all she wanted to do was sleep. Her head still ached, but the pills he'd prescribed her were dulling it enough to let her rest. He promised to be back before bedtime.

Which meant time was at a premium. No overnight stays. Besides, he was having second thoughts about sharing the gory details of his own past. No, he'd never been abused. He'd been well loved, in fact. But to tell her he'd started out life as a garbage picker who'd lived in a squalid shack on the side of a hill?

He shuddered, remembering what she'd said about those handcarts needing to be outlawed. To tell her his father had thrown his weight against the front bar of one of those very carts, struggling to get it up one hill after another? About how their very survival had depended on every member of the family pitching in to help? How he'd ridden on one of those very carts many times?

If they were at his apartment, he could simply hand her the worn photograph on his television stand and let her see the evidence for herself. But they weren't, and Marcos wasn't sure if his courage was going to hold out. No one at the hospital besides Sophia knew his secret.

Maggie came out with a tray that held a thermal pitcher, a couple of mugs, sugar and milk. There was also a plate of cookies on the side. He took the tray from her, raising his brow in question.

"Just put it on the coffee table, please."

He carried it over to a low table made out of worn slats of wood. Some of the slats were painted pale blue and sanded to give them a rustic appearance, while other boards were stained a dark walnut. Others had been left in their natural state, alternating with the other two finishes. The table was then burnished to a warm sheen. He gave a half-smile. It was always interesting that the very things the poor used out of necessity could be found in high-end homes and bore equally high-end price tags. He vaguely remembered a dining room table his father had put together out of multi-colored slats of wood he'd dug out of the garbage.

Marcos was drawn to sleek modern furniture for that exact reason. It looked nothing like what he'd grown up with. Rustic furniture of any kind made him feel uneasy—reminded him too much of his past.

"What?" Maggie's voice brought him back to reality, and made him realize he was hovering over the table without actually setting the tray down.

"Just wondering where you bought your table." He couldn't think of anything tactful to say.

"I bought it at one of those *moveis rústicos* booths at the hippie fair. Do you like it?"

Tension made his lips curl into something that resembled a smile but which felt a whole lot different on the inside. The hippie fair—so called because it was an artsy outdoor collection of vendors who sold everything from crafts to jewelry to furniture—just like the piece of furniture in Maggie's living room. The second part of her comment was much harder.

Did he like it?

He set the tray down, trying to think of an answer. He could appreciate the creativity that had gone into the making of the table, just as he could appreciate the ingenuity behind a lot of hand-crafted items here: Christmas trees made out of the bottoms of two-liter soda bottles; paper swans fashioned from hundreds of painstakingly folded sections of magazines; purses made from the pull tabs of soda cans and crocheted together. But that didn't mean he wanted to have any of those items in his house.

Maybe it was like Maggie and her fear of going back to hurting herself. She kept her nails cut ultra-short to prevent any temptation. Well, he didn't keep around many reminders of his past.

"It looks similar to something my family used to have." There. He'd said it without giving an opinion one way or the other.

"I thought you grew up in an orph…" She dropped on the sofa, hands in her lap, while Marcos slowly deciphered her words.

When he did, he rolled his eyes. "Sophia?"

"I'm sorry, Marcos. She thought I already knew. It just kind of slipped out."

"Kind of like now."

"Please sit down. You're making me nervous." She waited until he sat next to her before continuing. "Don't be mad at her. I wasn't supposed to say anything unless you told me."

Sophia had never made that kind of slip before, so he had no doubt that what Maggie said was true. But he couldn't help the little spurt of acid that pooled in his stomach. What else did Maggie know? "What exactly did Sophia say?"

"Just that you grew up together in an orphanage. Did you go there as a baby?" She poured coffee into both of the mugs. "Milk and sugar?"

"Black is fine." He accepted the cup from her, fingertips brushing hers as she handed it over. She pulled back quickly, and he found himself frowning. "No, I was six when I wound up at the orphanage."

So she didn't know that he'd spent the first years of his life in a *favela*.

"You said your family had a table like this one? You have siblings?"

Why had he not thought about where this would lead when he'd agreed to come back here? For one thing, he'd thought they'd end up in bed pretty quickly. For another, he'd been full of bravado back at the park, but when it came down to sharing the nitty-gritty details of his own past, he was having a hard time making himself tell her.

"I have—or was it had?—a brother. He was adopted six months after we arrived at the home."

"And you weren't?"

"No. It's one of those things. It happens. He was cuter than I was, evidently." Somehow saying that made it sound trite, like they had all been puppies at a pound, every child vying for a chance to be taken home first. He knew that wasn't really how things worked. He was grateful for every adoptive family that gave a kid a chance at a normal life.

Maggie took a slow sip of coffee as if thinking about what to say. "It's sad to separate brothers, especially at such a young age."

"Maybe they thought it would be easier because we were younger."

"But it wasn't." She curled her fingers around her cup. "Do you still keep in touch with him?"

"I haven't seen him since the day he left." The little prick of pain was just as acute now as it had been back then.

"Oh, no! Surely the orphanage would know something about where he went."

"They tried looking into it once I turned eighteen, but the records were sealed. I don't even know the adoptive parents' names." The ache from those frustrating days never quite went away. "Graciela—the patient who called me Markinho—said she knew the couple was kind and that they would be good to him." But none of that made up for not knowing what had become of him.

Marcos took a big gulp of his coffee, welcoming the liquid heat as it burned its way down his esophagus.

"Was this the secret you were talking about? That you were raised in an orphanage? That's nothing to be ashamed of, you know." She set her half-empty cup back on the tray. "After all, look at you now."

The temptation to make light of her words came and then went. Because, really, it was dishonest. Especially after the bombshell she'd dropped about her own past.

"No. That's not the secret."

Maggie touched his forearm, the light pressure of her hand reassuring. "You don't have to tell me if you don't want to. I'll understand."

That was the problem. A part of him did want to, while another part desperately wanted to keep the truth compartmentalized in the tiny area of his brain reserved for this very thing.

Maybe it was time to set the record straight.

He set his cup down and then ran his fingers across Maggie's coffee table. "We really did have something like this. Only it was a dining-room table. And my father made it. Out of wood scraps he collected over a period of a couple of weeks."

Maggie nodded but didn't comment, maybe realizing that wasn't the point he wanted to make.

"We had one like this because we couldn't afford a real dining-room table."

"I don't understand."

He decided to just get it out there. "My dad pushed one of those handcarts you see around the city. He picked up recycling items and delivered them to a man who bought them for pennies. My brother and I helped him sort the things he collected." He swallowed hard. "Then one day my father didn't come home. He'd been sick for a while before that. I think he had some form of Parkinson's from the tremors he had."

"You mean he died on the street?"

"I don't know. We were never told exactly how it happened. We just knew he died and that we had to live at the orphanage. They wouldn't even let us bring anything from our old house—although I snuck a picture out." He pulled in another breath. "We lived in a *favela* not so very far from the hospital."

"A *favela*?"

"The slum down the road." He forced the words out. "I'm sure you've seen it."

She nodded. "And your father… How awful. What about your mother?"

"She died when I was very young. The picture I have includes her, but I don't remember much about her."

"You went to the orphanage after your father died, then."

"Yes. A police officer came to the house…told us to come with him. That was the last time I ever saw our home. My father never even had a funeral, as far as I know. I don't know if he has a grave."

"I can't imagine what that must have been like. How terrifying for a young child to be carted away not knowing where he's going." She'd withdrawn her hand a few moments earlier, but now reached over and threaded her fingers through his. "You said the slum was close to the hospital."

He nodded, not sure what she was getting at. "It's about a quarter of a mile down the hill. I do volunteer work there from time to time."

"Your father lived within walking distance of the hospital and never went in to be diagnosed?"

"No, he never did. That's what I meant when I said sometimes deserving people never get to see a doctor. He could have been treated had he gone somewhere. We do have public hospitals, but the waits can be interminable, and there's a certain social stigma involved with being a *favela* dweller."

She gave him a smile. "And yet look at you now, Marcos. You're a well-known neurosurgeon."

"Some people took an interest in me along the way, when I was a kid. Gave me a hand up." And he was paying that back the best he could every Tuesday morning, when he volunteered at the orphanage and did free healthcare clinics in the *favela*. "And I made a promise to my dad."

"A promise?"

"I told him I'd grow up and become a really good doctor." His heart gave a hard thump as he remembered Lucas whispering the very same thing.

Maggie kicked off her shoes and tucked her feet up under her on the couch. She then laid her head on his shoulder. "You kept that promise. Your dad would be very proud of you."

"Thank you." Too bad his success had come too late to be of any benefit to his father. He decided to bring this conversation back around to Maggie. "You've made a successful life for yourself as well, Dr. Pfeiffer."

"I still have a few scars, unfortunately."

He reached up to stroke her hair, liking the feel of her head on his shoulder, the easy way she curled against his side.

It felt like home.

Maybe a little too much so. But he wasn't about to dislodge her. Not yet. He wanted to soak up as much of this feeling as he could, knowing it would have to last him for a long time to come.

But the hours he'd spent with her gave him hope that maybe he'd be able to have a real relationship at some point in the future. Maybe even have kids. Maggie hadn't leapt away when he'd talked about his background. But, then, she wasn't Brazilian. Americans still held that romantic notion that anyone could succeed if only they worked hard enough.

*Didn't you do that very thing? Succeed through hard work?*

Yes, but he was the exception rather than the rule. Which was why he felt it was so important to help at the *favela*. Maybe he could someday help another child the way he'd been helped.

"Do you think you'll ever tell your parents about what happened?" He murmured the question in a soft voice, not wanting her to stiffen and pull away. Just in case, he slid his fingers into the hair at her nape and rubbed in slow, soothing circles.

"What purpose would it serve? They'd only torture themselves for not seeing the signs, for not stopping it. And my aunt...I don't think I could bear to see the look in her eyes, knowing that the person she'd trusted, that she should have felt safe leaving her niece with, hadn't really existed."

"Do you feel safe with me?"

She lifted her head to look at him. "I do. You're nothing like him."

"And yet there were those who thought he was kind and gentle."

"True." She blinked. "If you're trying to scare me, it's not working."

He eased her head back onto his shoulder. "No, *querida,* I'm not. That's the last thing I want to do right now. I want you to know you're safe with me. No matter what happens."

There was a short pause then her voice came back. "What if I don't want you to be safe? At least, not right now."

"What do you mean?" His pulse quickened just a touch as all kinds of thoughts went through him, most of them decidedly *un*safe.

"I didn't invite you back here just to talk, you know."

He smiled, even though he knew she couldn't see it. "No? And here I had these visions of trading secrets and painting our toenails. The skeletons in our closets could rattle their bones and dance a *quadril.*"

She gave a laugh that sounded free and maybe even a little happy. "A *quadril*? What's that?"

"It's like that dance that Americans do in a square. Couples prance around together. It's very popular with the Brazilian *gaúchos*—what you would call cowboys."

"Oh, a square dance." She wrapped her hands around his upper arm. "I didn't bring you here to do that either."

Yep, his heart rate was definitely off and running and funneling blood down to a certain part of his body. "So you don't want to dance. And you don't want to play it safe. I admit, I'm a bit stumped."

Maggie's head shifted and something warm brushed across the underside of his jaw.

Her lips?

It happened again. A butterfly-soft press of something against his skin.

Yes. Definitely her lips. And being alone in her apartment was sending his thoughts sliding down that little hallway to his right, where he suspected her bedroom lay. "You're treading on dangerous ground here, Maggie."

"Am I?" Her husky voice slid across his senses like the barest touch of silk. But it was as if she sent a message right to the heart of him. She wanted him. Despite her uncle's monstrous actions. Despite his life in the slums. This beautiful, brave woman was sending a quiet request. One he wasn't about to turn down.

"You are." He tilted her head back and looked down at her for a long moment. "And if you're going to stop, you'd better do so now."

"What if I don't want to?"

"Then I'll have to do this." With his own muttered growl still vibrating in his chest, he lowered his head—did what he'd wanted to do to her since he'd found her sitting next to another man in that conference room.

He kissed her.

# CHAPTER SIXTEEN

THE SECOND HIS lips touched hers she was lost.

No, that wasn't true. She'd been lost ever since that day in his car, when he'd taken her with a passion that had rocked her world. Far from being afraid, she'd gloried in the roughness of his touch, in the harsh press of his body against hers.

He shifted the angle of his lips as if knowing her thoughts weren't centered fully on him and calling them back.

And, oh...

His tongue nudged against her, asking permission.

She granted it without hesitation, opening her mouth.

Only he didn't thrust home, the way she'd expected. Instead, he pulled back just a bit. Kissed along her lower lip with slow, methodical touches of his mouth that made her shiver. "I want you to feel safe, Maggie. Always. Tell me you do."

He kissed the corner of her mouth, then trailed across her cheek until he was at her ear. "I need to know you're here with *me*. At this very moment."

"I... I..." His teeth closed over her earlobe, robbing her of words and wrenching a low moan out of her that shocked her.

"Yes. That's it, *querida*."

His mouth moved back to hers, but again the pressure was light. Undemanding.

She wanted more. Didn't want him to be worried about hurting her.

More than anything, she wanted him to make her feel...

not safe but fiercely alive. Like he had before he'd found out her secret.

Her fingers went to his hair and sifted through the dark strands. The bubble inside her popped, and the words swelled inside her. "I don't want to feel safe. At least, not in the way you mean. I don't want you to treat me with kid gloves."

He paused at her mouth. "What do you want?"

"I…" *You can do it, Maggie. Tell him.* "I want you to make me feel the way you did before. No holds barred."

He pulled back to stare down at her, a strange heat appearing in her eyes. "None?"

She shook her head.

"Oh, sweetheart, you may be very sorry you said that."

"I won't. I promise."

He pressed his cheek to hers, his right hand going to the back of her head and holding her in place as his breath feathered along the side of her face. "You make promises so very easily, Maggie. But this is one I intend to hold you to."

With that he moved, the suddenness of the act startling her, and she found herself flat on her back on the sofa, with Marcos leaning over her, his cheekbones tight with what looked like desire. Or lust.

Whatever it was, the change in his demeanor was like quicksilver, washing over her in a heated stream.

He'd been willing to do safe. To hold back. Just for her. But that's not what she wanted. Not what she needed. She wanted Marcos in all of his fierce glory. She had from the day she'd met him.

What did that mean?

She didn't have time to wonder, because the press of his body drove everything from her head except his presence. His mouth slanted over hers with a pressure that was just as sharp and sweet as it had been on previous occasions. His tongue finally slid home—no hesitation this time, only a hard, needy drive that set her heart pounding in her chest. She wrapped her lips around him and stroked herself against him.

He gave a muttered oath and shifted his weight, one knee sliding between hers, as he settled into place. Maggie's body had twisted sideways on the couch, her legs hanging over the side, but Marcos somehow fitted himself to her, mirroring her position. He was hard against the yielding flesh of her inner thigh. And what she wanted more than anything was for him to slide higher and close the six-inch gap and take her.

No holds barred.

Only her clothes were still on. And so were his.

She gave a soft whimper of disapproval mixed with need. As his tongue continued to invade her mouth, setting up a rhythm that made her quake inside, her hands went to his dress shirt, trying to wedge her fingers between their bodies so she could undo the buttons. Instead of helping her, his hands found her wrists and tugged them away, lifting them over her head and holding them there. Her fingers clenched and unclenched; she still felt no fear, only a sense of desperate frustration.

"I want to go slow, *querida*. We've done fast, in my car. We've done greedy, at the beach. I want to feel every inch as I sink into you, until there's nothing left between us."

His bald words made moist heat gather between her thighs, and she shifted, trying to ease the ache. There was nothing wrong with greedy, as far as she was concerned. Couldn't he see that?

Greedy was her middle name.

"I want to force sexy little sounds from you that you can't hold back. Sounds that are all mine."

All his? Something swirled around the periphery of her mind. Something important. Something that warned her that what she was doing was dangerous in more ways than one. But right now she wanted nothing more than to stamp out that irritating little voice.

She was made for this one moment in time. For what he was doing to her.

He leaned down and nudged aside the collar of her shirt, the breath huffing in through his nose as if he was trying to capture her scent. The sensation drove her wild and her hips lifted in response.

So caught up was she in trying to find some relief for the growing discomfort at the juncture of her thighs that she wasn't prepared for his teeth nipping hard at the joint between her shoulder and her neck.

"Mmm…" The sudden rush of sound exiting her throat was almost shrill with need.

His tongue licked over the bite with a steady rhythm that matched what he'd done inside her mouth. And she suddenly wanted that tongue everywhere: back in her mouth; behind her ear; on her breasts.

"I love it when you sing to me, Maggie."

She had no idea what he meant and didn't want to bother working it out. But those little whimpers she could still hear were somehow coming from her. She wanted to make them stop, but she couldn't. It was as if Marcos was drawing them to the surface and teasing them out of her one by one.

"Please. I want you."

He'd talked about her being magic. That couldn't be right, because *he* was the one who was manipulating her like a puppet, forcing her to do his bidding.

No, not forcing. Coaxing. Cajoling. Enticing.

She wanted to grab his head and make him return to her mouth, but her hands were still imprisoned above her head. She tried to yank them free, but the effort was half-hearted. She'd wanted dangerous. He was giving her all that and more.

Suddenly, he levered himself off her, leaving her sprawled on the couch unable to move. She blinked up at him in confusion.

"You have no idea how much I want to take you right here. Right now."

"It's okay," she whispered. "I want it. All of it. Want you."

A muscle worked in his cheek as he stood there.

Without another word he hauled her off the sofa and into his arms, striding down the hallway with her.

Wait! He didn't know where her bedroom was.

As if he had an internal radar, though, he seemed to sense exactly where it was. Maybe her bed was giving off the same needy vibes as she was.

He set her down on the bed, head on her pillow, but didn't join her. She held out her arms in silent supplication.

"I wanted slow."

"It's okay, Marcos." Barely aware that she was talking, she only knew that he seemed to need some kind of reassurance that it really was okay. That she was fine with fast. Wanted it, in fact.

Maybe she could do more than simply tell him. Sitting up, her fingers—although shaking slightly—somehow found the buttons on her shirt and undid them one after the other, until it hung free on either side of her. Feeling wanton and, yes, *greedy*, the word he'd mentioned earlier, she took hold of either side of her shirt, shimmied it down her shoulders and pulled her arms free, until she was just in her bra and slacks.

How brave was she? Especially when Marcos's breath was growing more ragged by the minute, in a very audible display of need.

She was brave enough, evidently, because her fingers went to the clasp in the middle of her back and unclipped it. Not quite brave enough to fling the strapless bra from her body, however, because her hands went up and held it over her breasts.

Marcos gave a slow smile then unbuttoned his own shirt and let it fall to the floor. Unlike her, however, there was nothing that stopped her eyes from trailing over his firm chest, licking across his nipples, her tongue unconsciously swiping across her lips as various thoughts went through her mind.

Then his fingers went to the belt on his pants and all brain activity ceased, as with slow—and enviably steady—hands he threaded the tab back through the buckle, then pulled the whole length from the belt loops through which it exited with a soft hiss of sound. He laid it on the bed, then toed off his dress shoes and peeled down his socks, his eyes never leaving hers. Maybe she was supposed to finish undressing too, but she couldn't seem to move. Not even when he came over to kneel on the bed in front of her, still in his trousers.

"Finish me."

Her breath swept into her lungs as the double meaning took hold. Did he really mean her to use her hands? Her mouth? To make him lose control? Or was he asking her to finish undressing him? A fresh flood of moisture hit both her palms and the pulsing spot between her legs.

She started to reach for him, only to realize that in order to do anything, she'd have to let go of her bra, and it would fall, baring her to his eyes.

He'd seen her before, but this was in broad daylight.

"Do it."

The low intense tone made her muscles quiver and her nipples draw to hard peaks. He knew exactly what she was thinking. Instead of complying, she laid her forearm across her chest, and used it to hold up her bra, while slowly reaching for the button on his slacks with her other hand.

He reached down and gripped her wrist, drawing it up to his mouth and planting a warm kiss on her palm, before whispering against her skin, "You're going to need both hands for what I have in mind, Maggie."

Another hard shiver went over her. She'd never met a man as absolutely comfortable with his own sensuality as Marcos was. It was earthy and organic—and focused on her with an intensity she found unnerving.

Continuing to hold her hand, he crooked a finger for her to give him the other one.

She licked her lips, held her position for another couple of seconds then reached out for him, feeling the fabric of her bra whisper across her breasts as it fell onto the bed beside her knees. She ignored it, kept her attention on him as if by not looking down she could pretend that what had happened really hadn't.

Marcos met her hand halfway and gripped it with strong, confident fingers, carrying it up to his mouth and gently kissing it, just as he'd done with the other one. Then he joined her wrists together and gathered them in one hand, easing her back to the bed as he retrieved his belt.

What? She'd thought he said she'd need both hands to...

"Wait. Didn't you want me to—?"

"No. Not yet."

Her head landed on the pillow. "Then why did you need my hands?"

"So I could do this." He lowered his head and caught one of her aching nipples in his mouth, tongue brushing over the tip in haunting, gentle touches that made her back arch off the bed. She didn't notice until it was too late that the leather of his belt had wound around and around her hands until they were fastened together, the end safely looped through the buckle once again. Her heart rate took off as she realized he'd planned this all along. She was trapped. At his mercy. And she loved it.

Through it all, he continued teasing and tormenting her breasts.

She bit her lip as the sounds in her head careened wildly, seeking the nearest exit. They found it. Her breath came out on a stuttered moan that had his head coming up to look at her.

"*Deus.* I love to hear you, *querida.* That soft, sexy voice wraps around my gut like a vice. It makes me want to take you in a rush."

"Then do it." Maggie could not believe she'd just said that. Heat splashed into her face, but Marcos seemed not to notice.

"*Esta vez não*. I promised myself I wouldn't. And I always keep my word." The fingers of his left hand tightened as he lifted her bound hands over her head and pressed them into the pillow above her head. "It's why I don't want you free. You'll take me over the edge far too quickly."

The idea was heady. Did she really have that kind of power over a man like this?

Before she could let the sense of wonder wash over her fully, Marcos had lowered his head again, planting a single kiss on her other nipple. Then he shifted his attention to her slacks, and Maggie felt the button give way with a quick flick of his fingers. Down went the zipper.

"This is where things get tricky, Maggie." He insinuated himself between her legs, using his body to part them. "This is where you need to co-operate. Can you do that?"

She'd do just about anything at this point to have him inside her as quickly as possible. "Yes."

"I'm going to let go of your hands. But you need to keep them right where they are. Or it'll take me twice as long to finish undressing you."

She didn't want it to take twice as long, so she nodded her agreement.

Her fingers curled as he let go of her wrists, but she held very still, as if the slightest move could dislodge him from his task. Not that she could do much with her hands the way they were.

A quick tug at her waist had her pants and underwear over her hips and down to the tops of her thighs. He put a knee on either side of hers, pressing them back together so he could slide the clothing down to her calves. Standing, he removed them the rest of the way and let them drop to the floor.

"You are *lindissima*, stretched out like that." He gave her a smile. "Maybe I'll just stand here and enjoy the scenery for a while."

He wouldn't. Would he? As heady as it was to have a man like this call her beautiful, she wanted him on the bed. Now. "You wouldn't dare."

"Ah, but I would." His hands went to his trousers and undid the button. Slid down the zipper. Shoved everything down around his ankles and then kicked them away. When he stood, he was hard. Just as he'd been when pressed against her thigh moments earlier. "But I can do other things while I admire the lines of your body."

Still standing, he leaned over the bed and trailed his fingers along the underside of her arm, over the slope of her shoulder, down between her breasts. He made a complete turn around her belly button before slowly veering to the side and tracing the bone of her hip…her thigh until he'd made it all the way down to her foot. He'd hit nothing vital, and yet her body thrummed as if he'd stroked every erogenous zone she possessed.

When he made a leisurely return trip back the way he'd come, she could contain herself no longer. She reached down with both hands and gripped his wrist, bringing it up to her mouth the way he'd done with hers a few moments earlier. She kissed his palm, traced the lines with her tongue before deciding enough was enough. She wrapped her lips around his index finger and sucked lightly, her tongue stroking along the digit as she held him in place.

*"Feiticeira."*

Sorceress.

The muttered word was hot. Thick. And it messed with everything that was female inside her. Suddenly she felt wild and abandoned. Reckless. Because he'd shown that the tiniest attempts on her part could crack that iron will of his in half.

She released her hold and sat up, deciding to go for broke.

But the second she leaned toward him, meaning to try the very same thing on his flesh, he backed away with a hissed breath.

"Not this time, *querida*."

*Like that.* The hint that her touch was as dangerous to him as his was to her.

Raw emotion bloomed inside her, flooding every nook and cranny. A deep sense of…something. Something she couldn't quite put her finger on but that was beyond anything she'd ever experienced before.

Marcos came down on the bed, erasing all thoughts of anything but his body against hers as he rolled onto his back, hauling her up and over him in the same movement—until she was seated on his hips, his rigid length pressed along all those sensitive areas that were squirming for attention.

"Do you have anything in this little table beside the bed? Otherwise we'll have to retrieve my wallet." He shifted, his hips lifting to slide himself along her, hitting the spot at the very top of her thighs and causing everything to clench down hard. Only there was nothing to clench onto. "And the last thing I want to do is leave this spot."

"The top drawer," she whispered, even as her face burned red hot at the fact that she'd gone out after their first encounter in his car and bought some supplies. She'd told herself she was being smart. Protecting herself.

He reached over and opened the drawer, his hand feeling around inside.

"What is this?" His eyes met hers as he held up something other than a package of condoms. Something she'd never meant him or anyone else to see.

"Oh, no!" She reached forward to grab at it, but her hands were still trapped together. Horror flooded her chest. How could she have forgotten?

That particular purchase had everything to do with the man who was now studying the object with blatant interest. She started to knock it from his hands but he stopped her in mid-swing, holding her wrists in one hand as he'd done earlier.

"Maybe I should have tied your hands behind your back instead." Still holding her wrists, he ran the hard plastic tip of her so-called "personal" vibrator along the underside of her chin. Down her throat. Over one of her nipples. Her eyelids fluttered closed in reaction. "You continue to surprise me, Maggie. I never would have guessed. Where is the on button, I wonder?"

Her eyes popped back open. "No. Don't." The conviction behind that demand was feeble, even to her own ears.

"But I will. You told me no holds barred, remember?" He glanced at the bottom of the vibrator, and his thumb flicked something. The low, warning hum seemed to fill the room. "What do you do with this little treasure, *querida*? Do you use it here?" He skimmed the object over the tops of her breasts.

"Here?" He slid the side of it up the length of her neck and trailed it across her lower lip, continuing to talk to her in low, gravelly tones. "Do you know what I thought about as your lips were wrapped around my finger?"

She could guess, but there was no way in hell she was going to answer that question. Because to do so she'd have to open her mouth...and that suddenly seemed like a very dangerous proposition.

"Do you want me to use this on you?"

She shook her head, even as she felt his erection jerk against her as if he were thinking about doing that very thing.

"Oh, Maggie...I think you do."

"No." The word came out on a breath of desperation, but she realized her mistake too late when he was right there between her lips, turning off the vibrations even as her teeth clenched in reaction.

"Let me. Just a little."

What was wrong with her? Moist heat was flooding her insides, and she recognized she was as excited by what he was doing as she was embarrassed. Would he really use it on her? Watch her reaction?

He would. She knew it as surely as she knew she was going to open her mouth. And the anticipation wound up inside her until it reached unbearable proportions.

Her teeth parted an inch, then two.

"That's it, *querida*," he said as he slid the vibrator just past her lips and watched them close around it. "You have such a beautiful mouth. So soft. If you only knew how much I want it on me."

He slowly withdrew and dragged the moisture across one nipple and then the other, turning on the mechanism again.

She moaned as he continued to draw tiny circles around her breasts for another minute or two. Trailing the device down her stomach, the vibrations spread through her as he moved lower and lower, drawing it all out with torturous slowness. He let go of her wrists, but she had no desire to stop what he was doing at this point, even though she knew with a certainty where he was headed, and that the second he arrived she was going to come unglued.

Reaching the spot where their bodies were joined, he didn't put the vibrator directly on her; instead, he put it on himself—on those couple of inches that extended past her body. And she felt the vibrations all along her most intimate parts in a long glorious line. She couldn't stop herself from grinding down on him to increase the pressure, even as she noted the muscle working furiously in his jaw.

"*Faça*, Maggie. *Tem que voar. Por mim.*"

Do it, Maggie. You have to fly. For me.

The raw need she heard in his voice melded with the vibrations and the motions from her own body, until they all rushed toward her in a single red-hot ball of fire. Her back arched, every muscle in her body heating as the flames carried her higher.

An explosion went off somewhere inside her, rolling up her spine until it came out of her throat in a long keening sound. *"Isso!"*

Before she even had time to fully feel the effects of her orgasm, Marcos had tossed aside the vibrator, rolled the condom down his length and sheathed himself in her body with a shout that made her tighten up all over again.

Again and again, he guided her, hands at her waist as he drove into her, each time seating her deeper, the sensation of utter fullness completing the act in a way nothing else could and heightening the pleasure.

Grabbing her bound hands with his, he pulled her down onto him as far as she would go, holding her there as he groaned and strained upward with his hips several more times as he climaxed. He remained that way for a moment or two, before letting go of her hands to cup her face, his breathing rough, a sheen of perspiration across his upper lip.

He gently eased her down to lie across his chest, undoing his belt and setting her free. Then his hands slid up and down her back in soft, slow strokes. *"Meu Deus.* What I've done... are you okay?"

The gruff concern in his voice made moisture gather in her eyes. Pressing her face to his shoulder, and letting his warm scent surround her, she did her best to blink it away while trying to gather the splintered fragments of her composure. In reality, there was no way she could appear untouched by what had happened. So she didn't even try.

"I'm okay." Her arms lifted to cradle his head as best she could from her position. "I'm more than okay."

It was true. She'd never experienced such deep satisfaction in her life. Or felt such a profound sense of despair. Because along with the physical release came the knowledge her heart would never be the same again.

Because she loved him.

# CHAPTER SEVENTEEN

MAGGIE DID NOT want to face him today.

She walked across the parking lot of the hospital with slow, measured steps, adjusting her purse on her shoulder as she went. Every move was geared to take as much time as possible to reach the front doors. Her nerves were stretched to breaking point, since last night had gone from wonderful to terrifying with a single awful revelation.

The realization that she loved him had struck like a lightning bolt, seeming to come out of nowhere, along with the threat of waterworks. There'd been no way to stop the flood so she'd pulled away and run to the bathroom. She'd switched on the faucet as hard as it would go and let the silent tears flow for as long as she dared. But even a cold washcloth pressed to her eyes after she'd gotten control of herself had been unable to mask the puffy lids and pink nose. Winding a huge green towel that came down to her knees around her body, she'd exited the bathroom to find him already dressed.

He'd taken hold of her shoulders and gazed down at her for a long moment, while she looked anywhere but at him. Then he'd pulled her to him, wrapped his arms around her and squeezed. And then he'd left with a quiet goodbye.

Goodbye had never sounded so final.

She'd let him out, gone back to her bedroom and removed every trace of what they'd done together.

Well, every physical trace. Because the emotional one was

still stamped across her heart. And she feared it would be for a long time to come.

A sense of melancholy had compelled her to pull on some running shorts and a light sweater, then she went out to her balcony where she leaned against the railing. Rubbing her arms and staring out at the lights of the neighboring buildings for what seemed like hours, she tried to figure out what to do about Marcos. Nothing came to her. The mosquitoes finally drove her back inside, reminding her she'd forgotten to put repellent on her bare legs. Her reward was several fresh bites that kept her company during the lonely night that followed.

*Well you're here now. So it's time to face the music.*

Maggie paused outside the doors to the hospital, closed her eyes and sent up a quick prayer for strength. Then she strode through the entrance, forcing a confidence she didn't feel in every clickety-clack of the high-heeled leather boots she'd put on to give her as much physical height as possible. Her feet would pay the price by the end of the day, but she didn't care. She needed to appear sophisticated, worldly, and able to brush off what had happened with a careless shrug of her shoulders. Just like she was sure Marcos did on a regular basis with whoever his latest conquest was.

She guessed that would be her.

The thought made her feel unbearably sad.

Making her way to the circular bank of elevators, she punched in the floor number on the central keypad and waited for it to spit out the number of her elevator, then she stood in front of the correct one, absently scratching at one of the mosquito bites on her leg. It was still early, so she was the only one in the area at the moment.

The elevator pinged within a few seconds and she boarded, resolute about one thing. No one would ever know that she'd stared down at her scars last night for a long, long time in front of the mirror and decided no man would ever make her do that to herself again.

That included Marcos.

She clasped her hands in front of her. He'd never made her any promises, and she'd never asked for any. No matter how she felt, she was leaving in a matter of months. Then she'd be home, where everything was familiar, and where there were no sexy Brazilian neurosurgeons waiting to turn her world— and her heart—upside down.

The elevator doors opened and Maggie got out to see the neurology floor gearing up for a new wave of patients. She made her way to Marcos's office and knocked on the door, figuring he'd already be there. He always beat her to the hospital. Silence greeted her knock. Was he already doing rounds?

She went over to the nurses' station and found one of the early morning crew tapping on the computer and pulling up the day's scheduled exams. "Have you seen Dr. Pinheiro? He's not in his office."

She checked her screen. "I don't see any appointments for him, and he usually takes Tuesday mornings off."

That's right, he did. How could she have forgotten that? Maybe because she wasn't thinking straight these days.

"Oh, okay. Thanks. What have you got for me today?"

As the nurse went over the layout for the day Maggie sagged, half in relief and half in disappointment.

All that worry and procrastinating for nothing. The man wasn't even here.

"Tia Graciela tells me your ear doesn't feel well." Marcos lifted six-year-old José Sousa onto the portable massage table he used for giving examinations at the *favela*. Brazilian children often used the terms "aunt" and "uncle" to refer to adults who were in authority, even their schoolteachers. He could remember calling Graciela "Tia" from the moment he'd arrived at the orphanage.

She was retired now. But despite her brush with the pituitary tumor, she still showed up week after week, whether it was at the orphanage or at the *favela*, to help him provide much-needed health care to those who were often shunned by society. It was one way he kept his promise to his father. José nodded, his bare feet swinging back and forth as Graciela moved over to the child's side and allowed him to grip her hand.

"Does it hurt all the time?" Marcos asked.

Another nod.

"How about when I do this?" He gently tugged the child's earlobe downwards, watching for a reaction. The child winced, right on cue, his palm coming up to cover the affected ear.

"Sorry. I know it's no fun to have someone poke and prod at you. But we're going to try to make you all better."

This time it was Marcos who gave an internal wince as he remembered saying that very thing to his dad, that he was going to "make him all better."

Well, he hadn't been able to help his father, but he could help as many of these kids as he could. The fact that he'd been born here gave him an "in" with the folks who still lived here. Not many people had the courage to venture down the dirt road that led to the heart of the slum, where drugs and police shootouts were common, and where HIV and STDs ran rampant. Electricity was siphoned to makeshift homes via clandestine lines strung in the dead of night. More than one person had been electrocuted trying to tap into overhead power lines with little or no experience. No one worried whether it was legal or illegal. Laws were for those who could afford to pay for what they wanted.

As hard as it was to come back here, Tuesdays provided Marcos with a way to remember his past, and he often heard stories about his parents from those who remembered them.

In a place where outsiders of any type were viewed with suspicion, he was lucky to be able to drive in without anyone saying a word. Despite his medical license and his expensive car he was still accepted by most who lived here. He was "one

of the lucky ones" who'd made it out and who cared enough
to come back for those who hadn't. Part of the responsibility
he'd taken on included awarding anonymous scholarships to
kids who worked hard. He hoped that would one day include
little José, who he saw almost every week.

Marcos gave the boy's shoulder a light squeeze then un-
rolled his instruments. Slipping a protective sleeve over the
tip of the otoscope, he showed it to him. "Do you remember
what this is?"

*"O—"* José squinted, deep in thought. *"Oto-scóp-scóp..."*

*"Otoscópio.* You almost had it. It's a funny word, isn't it?"
Part of Marcos's goal was to teach these kids about his profession, including what tools he used and why. He could remember being fascinated the first time he'd seen a doctor's
roll of instruments, only to have the man brush off his questions. He'd vowed never to do that.

For these kids, soccer was often seen as the only ticket out
of the *favela*—and they spent hours and hours honing their
skills, hoping it would one day pay off. Marcos wanted to
show them there was more than one path. Education was just
as—no, *more*—important than soccer, since few kids actually made it to the pros.

The boy chanced a smile. "You will look in my ears with
your *otoscópio*?"

"Yes. To see if there's an infection." He switched on the
light. "I'll have to pull on your ear just a little bit, like I did
before."

The technique helped straighten the ear canal and gave
him a clearer view. He leaned down and peered inside. Red,
inflamed tissue dotted by pustular material appeared, just as
he'd expected. There was also a build-up of fluid inside the
canal. He clicked the instrument off and released José's ear.
"How about your other one? Does it hurt as well?"

"Only a little."

Marcos could feel the heat of a low-grade fever radiating

off the boy's body. He glanced at Graciela. "How many of these infections has he had?"

She flipped through the papers on the table, finger skimming down the list of names. "Three so far this year."

"We might need to check in with a pediatrician about putting tubes in his ears."

Graciela winced. "You know how tight funds are for these families. It was the same way at the orphanage."

Jaw clenching, he nodded. He could remember how tight things had been when he'd been there. Beans and rice might be ubiquitous Brazilian fare, but when there was little else to go with them, even if the combination had been manna from Heaven, it still got a little old. "Let me talk to a specialist I know and see if we can get him in."

Marcos had pressed his colleagues for favors over the years. Most of them just gave a good-hearted eye-roll when they saw him coming, but he'd rarely had one turn him down. Most of them knew that they might one day need a favor from him in return.

And what about Maggie? Would he one day ask her for a favor?

*What did she have to do with anything?*

Hell, just when he thought he might get by without thinking about her for a couple of hours, there she was, her image hovering in the background just like the music he played in the operating room. Only, unlike that music, he found her anything but soothing.

In fact, he'd been careful not to bring her with him on these forays into the *favela*...into his past. Why?

Because she was only here for a couple more months, that's why. She wasn't a permanent fixture in his life—he'd never allowed her to be.

His teeth clenched even tighter. It seemed that anyone he lov—no, he didn't love Maggie. He changed the thought to something closer to reality. It seemed like anyone he *grew to care for*—there, that was better—anyone he grew to care for left. Whether it was through death or through adoption, there had been very little he was certain of in his life. He'd known from the beginning that Maggie wasn't here for good, so why had he slept with the woman? Held her in his arms and thought about what might have been?

Because it seemed like he was destined to make one stupid decision after another. Which might also explain why he'd had sex with her not once, not twice, but three damn times.

And that last time he'd upset her. Somehow. He'd seen it when she'd come out of the bathroom.

He'd pressed her too hard. Had gone beyond what she was willing to give. He'd even reminded her that she'd said "no holds barred" when she'd started to balk. And yet he hadn't stopped—hadn't paused to think about anyone but himself. Swallowing, he pulled his thoughts back to José, continuing his exam while trying to banish the pair of tragic blue eyes that had stared hopelessly back into his own. The ones that had followed him into his dreams and had dogged his steps all morning long.

Had she gouged herself after he'd left?

*Deus.* A muscle in his jaw spasmed, the pain welcome. That only made things worse, because it reminded him of Maggie's comments about what she used to do. About what he'd *seen* her do with those nails.

If he'd sent her reeling back to the past, he'd never forgive himself.

Well, that would be nothing new.

He'd never quite forgiven himself for his father's death either. Or for Lucas being taken from his side. He knew he couldn't have stopped either event from happening—knew it had probably only been a matter of time before his father had collapsed, even at home, setting in motion the same chain of events.

But just like Maggie scratching at those creamy white

thighs because of things that had been out of her control, he still tore at himself emotionally for much the same thing.

And he had a feeling Maggie battled the very same demons.

At least she'd conquered hers.

Unless what he'd done last night had opened old wounds and tempted her to make fresh new ones. Physical ones.

How would he even know? Maybe he could talk to her, make sure she really was okay. Apologize, if necessary.

And if she refused to discuss it?

Then he'd have to find out the truth some other way. Because he needed to know how she was doing. If not for his own sake then for hers.

Because if she'd gone back to past habits, he might have to make one of the hardest decisions he would ever have to make.

He'd have to revoke Maggie's internship. And send her home to the United States.

# CHAPTER EIGHTEEN

MAGGIE SAT PROPPED up against the headboard of Sophia's bed, thumbing through a magazine, while her friend ate lunch. She'd come to check on her after calling and hearing the other woman's pitiful voice. Thankfully Marcos was still at the *favela*, which was where Sophia had said he'd be. Her friend insisted she was fine, just bored. And she was planning on returning home within the next day or so.

Marcos's housekeeper was safely in the kitchen right now and well out of earshot as Sophia griped about the woman fussing over her ad nauseam. "I don't know how he can stand to have someone else in his house all the time. It would drive me insane."

Raising her brows, Maggie glanced over at her. "Are you talking about yourself or about Maria?"

"Hmph. I'm family. That's different."

Maggie grinned then settled into the pillow a little more. "So he volunteers every week."

"Without fail. He's even teaching any of the kids who are interested about different medical specialties. I'm surprised he hasn't asked you to come in and talk to them."

"Well, I'm an American, for one thing." She didn't say it, but for another thing she had no doubt that Marcos was avoiding her. Even when he'd come back to the hospital he'd managed not to come within fifty feet of her. She'd caught a couple of quick glimpses of him, but they'd exchanged no words.

So he was upset about what had happened between them. He'd get over it. They'd slept together before, and things had gone back to normal after a few days.

*It hasn't been a few days yet.*

She sighed and scrubbed at the side of her thigh with the tippy tops of her nails, grunting in frustration as it did little to stem the itching.

"What's wrong?" Sophia asked, glancing at her.

"I stood out on my balcony last night in shorts and forgot it's the height of mosquito season. I have bites all over my legs. And, uh...elsewhere." Those little suckers could evidently bite right through shorts, because she even had a couple of quarter-sized welts on her behind. Invariably, the spots would turn into grotesque bruised-looking areas. Not to mention the itching.

God, the *itching*. It drove her crazy. And she'd forgotten to take an antihistamine before leaving the house this morning.

She scratched again, for the first time wishing her nails were just a little bit longer.

Sophia giggled then grew serious and laid her magazine down over her lap. "Marcos warned you about dengue, right? You can get it even here in the city. You should put some repellent plug-ins in your apartment." She nodded toward the device in the electrical socket across the room.

"I have some—and I know about dengue. I thought maybe your headache had been caused by it." She drew her knees up and wrapped her arms around them to keep her fingers occupied. "How is it, by the way? Your head? I probably should leave so you can get some more sleep."

Besides, the last thing she wanted to do was have Marcos come home and find her invading his space—especially after he'd gone to so much trouble to avoid her.

"And leave me to Maria's nagging? Please stay for a while longer. Besides, my head is better today. And my neck isn't nearly as stiff."

"What time is Marcos due home?"

"I'm surprised he isn't already here." Sophia laid her head back against the pillows with a sigh. "At least Maria will have someone else to hover over once he gets home."

"Then I definitely should go."

"Why?" She frowned, then her eyes grew round. "Is there something going on between the two of you? I noticed he's been acting a little strangely."

Her brain kicked into high gear. She didn't want Sophia to start asking pointed questions. Ones that could quickly become embarrassing, especially if Marcos found out she'd spilled the beans without meaning to.

"Nothing's going on. We're just colleagues, which means I shouldn't pop in unannounced like this."

"You called me before you came."

Yes, to make sure Mr. High and Mighty himself wasn't home. "I didn't want to wake you up."

Just then the sound of a door opening and closing caught her attention. Her voice dropped to a whisper. "What was that? Maria?"

*Please, oh, please, let it be Maria.*

Sophia tilted her head to listen. "No, I think it was—"

Footsteps sounded on the tile floor of the entryway, along with the sound of low murmured voices. Then those same steps headed their way. The doorknob turned and the door opened.

She and Sophia glanced at each other.

"Hello, ladies. Having a party?" The lazy voice from the doorway made Maggie squeak in alarm.

She unwrapped her arms and straightened her legs. Damn. She knew she should have left.

The worst of the mosquito bites burned and she pressed her hand over the right side of her thigh, knowing the sensation was probably caused by nerves more than anything.

"Maggie felt sorry for me, so she came to visit."

Actually, Sophia had been the one to ultimately convince

her to come, saying Marcos had given Maria strict orders to keep her there in the bedroom—by whatever means necessary.

"Did you, Maggie?" The low, husky voice called her eyes up to meet with his. After a tense couple of seconds his gaze finally moved, sweeping down over her body and coming to rest on something near her waist.

He didn't give her a chance to answer his question but pinned her with a look. "What are you doing?"

Oh! She'd known things would be awkward between them once they came face-to-face, but she hadn't expected the accusation in his voice over her visit. Did he think she was using Sophia to get to him? That she'd be so desperate to talk to him that she'd use any means necessary? The thought stung and for a second or two she couldn't think of a response at all, just sat there like a lump.

The itching became scratching.

"I don't know what you mean."

Sophia spoke up. "She has mosquito bites."

Huh? Why on earth would her friend bring that up?

Then she realized what he'd been looking at a second or two ago. She was clawing at her leg, without realizing it. She immediately stopped and forced her hand into her lap. "Yes. I've got a ton of bites. From my balcony last night."

Something flashed through his eyes. Suspicion, mixed with some deep emotion she couldn't decipher.

"Let me see them."

"What?" Both she and Sophia spoke at once, then her friend continued. "What on earth is wrong with you, Marcos?"

He shook his head. "Sorry. It's been a long day."

"I guess so."

Maggie was still too shocked by the demand to take part in the exchange. He wanted to look at her mosquito bites? Why? Not to mention the fact that she didn't want Sophia to know what had gone on between the two of them. She had a hard time believing that Marcos would be any less anxious than she was for others to not know the truth.

So he had to have been talking about something else. "They aren't from the mosquitoes that carry dengue. No white marks on their legs. Just the garden variety pests."

"Yes, those white marks serve as a warning." Again there was some strange intensity behind the words. Almost as if he'd meant them in an entirely different way.

"Can I see you outside for a minute?" he asked.

Sophia scooted up in bed. "What's going on, Marcos? You've been acting all *maluco* lately."

*Maluco* was a good way to put it. Maggie was feeling a little crazy herself right now.

"Nothing's going on. I'd just like to talk to Maggie about a patient."

"Aren't you even going to ask how I'm feeling?"

He quirked a brow at her. "I think that's pretty obvious. Besides, I called Maria a couple of times. She told me you'd been cranky."

"Cranky?"

She wondered for a second if Sophia was going to come off that bed and let him have it.

"I think she used a stronger word than that, actually." The thread of humor was still there in his voice. More than anything, Maggie wished he would use that tone when he talked to her. Instead, their conversations were like high-tension lines— full of dangerous electricity that could cut through body parts like a knife through butter if one wasn't careful.

"Well, you can tell Maria to kiss my—"

He held up a finger and cut her off. "I'd like to still have a housekeeper tomorrow, so if you could try not to insult her, I'd appreciate it." He nodded at Maggie. "If you can do without your friend for a minute or two, I'd also appreciate it."

She found herself rubbing at her bites again and having to

stop before he saw her. He'd called Sophia cranky. Well, he was the *king* of crankiness.

Sliding off the bed, she leaned over and kissed her friend on the cheek. "I think I'm going to leave once I speak with him, okay? I'll check in on you again tomorrow."

Sophia glared at Marcos. "And maybe I'll be at my own home when you do."

He came over and gave Sophia a kiss on the head. "Let's discuss this once we've both had a few minutes to cool off."

So he was admitting he was a bit hot under the collar. Not that it helped her anxiety level at all.

He ushered her out with a sweeping gesture of his hand, and Maggie stalked through the doorway and headed for the living room, only to have him take hold of her upper arm and pull her down the hallway instead.

What the...?

Surely he didn't mean for them to have sex while Sophia and his housekeeper were in the house?

With the mood he was in, that hardly seemed likely. On either side.

He hauled her through the doorway of his bedroom and slammed the door shut.

"What are you doing?"

"Show me the bites." One hand went to the wall beside her, caging her in. His voice was low enough that no one could hear but them.

Still thinking this was some kind of excuse to get her out of her clothes, she drew herself as tall as she could. "I don't think this is the time or place for...whatever you're thinking about doing."

He frowned, his eyes raking over her face. "You think this is about sex?" His hand came off the wall, and he took a step back. "That's the furthest thing from my mind right now."

"Then why do you want to see my mosquito bites?"

"Because I don't think they're bites." He dragged a hand

through his hair. "Damn it, Maggie. I'd apologize for last night, but I wouldn't even know where to begin."

Apologize? Oh, Lord. He was sorry it had happened?

Well, hadn't she told herself the very same thing? Yes, but only because she'd realized she was in love with him. But that still didn't explain...

Her brain latched onto something.

"What do you mean, you don't believe they're bites?"

He didn't say anything, just propped his hands on his hips and stared at her.

If they weren't mosquito bites, what did he think they were?

*Those white marks serve as a warning.*

It hit her. He thought she was self-injuring again. Because of what they'd done?

"Marcos, they're mosquito bites. And there's no need to apologize for last night. We're both adults. We both wanted what happened."

"I...went beyond what I'd meant to do." The hesitation in his voice clawed at her heart. It explained his words from the previous night as well, when he'd asked her if she was okay. He thought he'd hurt her somehow. Emotionally?

She took a step forward to close the space he'd opened up and lifted a hand to his face. "I wanted what happened as much as you did. You have nothing to apologize for. I promise."

"Then show me your legs."

He was absolutely serious—he wasn't going to accept her word that they were what she said they were. A deep slash of pain went through her, and she let her hand drop back to her side. Then she backed up. "All right."

If he made her do this, nothing would ever be the same between them.

But as she lifted the hem of her shirt, fingers going to the button on her pants and undoing it, she waited for him to stop her. To say he believed her. That he didn't need proof to back up what she'd said.

Of course, he didn't say a word, so she unzipped her slacks and hooked her thumbs into her waistband. "Don't do this. Please."

"I need to know."

*Have it your way.* She yanked her trousers down to mid-thigh, then stood up straight and proud.

"*Meu Deus.*" A litany of Portuguese words followed that low exclamation, the bulk of which she was sure were not meant for public consumption.

Puzzled, she glanced down at her thighs, and her eyes widened in horror. The three bites that had dotted her upper right leg were now angry, purple marks, crusted over with dried blood that had oozed repeatedly with each new batch of frenzied scratching during the day. Looking at her beige slacks, she saw the blood had actually seeped into the fabric. She'd had no idea she'd dug at herself that much. She'd have seen it, if not for the long tunic top she was wearing.

In fact, those scratches looked suspiciously like the ones she used to…

Her glance flew up to his. "Marcos, I swear to you, they're mosquito bites. I didn't do this."

Of course she had. She'd scratched them until they'd bled. But what she really meant was that she hadn't gouged her nails into herself to blot out other—deeper—pain. Had she?

No, they were bites. She knew they were. She'd noticed them last night as she'd scratched them in the shower. "I tend to have an allergic—"

"I've seen enough, Maggie, you can pull your clothes back up." His eyes closed for several long seconds as she did just that. When his voice came again, it was so low she almost couldn't hear it, and it sounded like it was filled with a wealth of pain. "I'm sorry, but you've given me no choice. I'm going to have to send you home."

"Home?"

"I won't mention this to anyone. We'll just say the internship was mutually terminated."

His words sank in and her stomach sank too, right through the floor where she stood.

"You're sending me back to the States?"

"Yes."

"But why?" Even as she asked the question she knew. It was because he didn't believe her. He thought she was like an alcoholic who'd fallen off the wagon. Hadn't her therapist told her it was possible? Why would Marcos believe her?

"Isn't it obvious?"

"They're mosquito bites."

The words shook, tinged with a desperation that was swarming in her chest and buzzing in her ears. She'd thought she'd have the next four months to prepare her heart for leaving Brazil. For leaving Marcos.

She'd been wrong. Her time was up. And the last thing she was…was ready.

# CHAPTER NINETEEN

ONE WEEK.

No. One week, two days, fourteen hours and... He glanced at his watch... Twenty-two minutes since the last time he'd seen Maggie.

And yet the ache in his chest still hadn't subsided.

He'd handled things stupidly, but the sight of those ugly marks on her thigh had brought all his fears home to roost.

Mosquito bites.

They hadn't looked like the kind he got. But then again, he didn't scratch at them until they bled. But Maggie had sworn to him that's what they were.

He'd reacted without thinking, jumping to the worst possible conclusion and blaming himself. In fact, he'd had second thoughts during the night about what he'd said. But the next morning when he tried to call her apartment, the doorman had said she'd left unexpectedly.

"Left?"

"Yes, said she was called home due to a situation out of her control."

He'd repeated those words to Sophia later that day when she'd asked where Maggie was.

She'd given him an accusing look. "*You* did this. I don't know how or why, but you did."

Yes, he had. But he didn't know how else he could have handled the situation. If those marks were a result of her relapsing, then the best place she could be was at home where she could get some help—go to her own therapist. And if he'd somehow brought it on, then she needed to be as far away from him as she could get, because he didn't see how he'd be able to stay away from her if she remained in Brazil.

He took a half-turn in his chair and leaned his head against the back. She was like a feather drawn over his skin again and again—soft and gentle at first but becoming torturous if ignored for too long.

And he didn't want to ignore her. He wanted her in his arms. Night after night. He wanted to do things to her that…

That was the problem. She drove him crazy. Excited him like no other woman ever had.

He wanted…

Turning back around, he brought both palms down onto the top of his desk with a thud. He wanted her. For ever. That's what it boiled down to.

He loved her. Could finally admit to the emotions that had been festering inside him—maybe now he could lance them and drain the poison so the wound could heal.

Only it didn't feel like poison.

But if he was damaging her by being with her, he had to learn to live without her. Somehow. Although how the hell he was going to do that, he had no idea.

He'd done it before. He'd survived the loss of his father and his brother.

Hell, this wasn't doing anyone any good.

Just as he got ready to haul himself out of his chair, his phone rang. He swallowed, a tiny seed of hope struggling to burst free of its prison, just as it did every time someone called.

It was never her.

Pulling in a deep breath, he picked up the receiver. "Pinheiro here."

"Dr. Pinheiro, we've got a patient down here we think you should see."

He carefully crushed the seed beneath the sole of his shoe, before answering. "Head trauma?"

"No, shooting victim. Chest and leg."

"You need an emergency-room doctor."

"He's asking to see Dr. Pfeiffer. Says he met her at some medical conference you attended. I tried to tell him she no longer worked here, but he won't listen. He's kind of in and out of consciousness. We need to get him into surgery, but I promised I would try to reach you before we took him back." She paused. "Besides—and this is a bit strange—well, I know you're busy, but would you mind coming down here for a minute?"

The man had met her at the medical conference? Ah, hell. It had to be that Carvalho guy. The plastic surgeon who'd practically hit on Maggie. The last thing he wanted to do was see him. And how in God's name had he been shot? Probably wandering in places he shouldn't have been, like rich tourists who didn't realize what could happen.

The least he could do was go and see him. And he could have the satisfaction of telling him in person that Maggie was no longer here—and good luck in finding her.

"I'm on my way."

"Thank you, Doctor."

Just as the nurse had said, the patient was in one of the triage bays lying on a gurney, already hooked up to an IV and a unit of blood. Nurse…Anabela Coelho, according to her tag, was taking his vitals.

She glanced up. "Oh, good, Doctor. You're here."

The man in question turned his head, his eyes glazed over a bit, but it was definitely the man from the conference. The stranger's mouth moved, and he grunted out, "Great. Just what I need. The bastard doctor. I asked for Maggie."

*Bastard* doctor. Had Maggie called him that behind his back?

If so, she'd spoken the truth.

Marcos held his hand out for the chart, ignoring the stranger's words.

Giving a quick glance at the vitals, his lips twisted. Bullet wounds to shoulder and lower left quadrant of abdomen, moderate blood loss—two pints given so far. The patient had a compression bandage across his left shoulder, just above a tattoo of some type.

He moved over to the bed, taking a look at the name on the chart. He frowned and blinked a couple of times, his heart rate beginning to climb. "Are you sure of this name?" he asked the nurse.

"That's what was so strange. It's what was listed on his passport and his Brazilian ID. He says he knows Dr. Pfeiffer."

It couldn't be. It had to be a coincidence. All the same his mouth went dry, his heart still pounding in his chest.

Lucas Elias *Pinheiro* Carvalho. His brother's name…all except the Carvalho. He cleared his throat. "Dr. Carvalho? Do you remember me from the conference?"

The man lifted his hand partially off the bed and then dropped it. "Yes. You're the bastard. Where's Maggie?" the man continued. "What did you do to her?"

What *hadn't* he done?

He shook off the thought. "Is your last name Pinheiro or Carvalho?"

"Adopted name. Carvalho."

*Adopted.* His brain began swirling in crazy directions. Maybe Sophia was right. He really was *maluco*. Because nothing about this made sense.

His eyes went to the man's tattoo, and his breath seized in his chest. He recognized the rod of Asclepius with its serpent twining around a staff. Above the medical symbol were the English words "Promises Kept" and below it... *Deus Santo!* Below it was the name of his father: Carlos Rodriguez Mateus Pinheiro.

He felt the blood drain from his head and the world around him spun in and out of focus for a few seconds, so much so that he had to grab onto the side of the bed to steady himself. "Dr. Pinheiro, are you all right?" asked the nurse.

The man's voice cut through the fog. "Pinheiro. Your name. That was my name."

Marcos swallowed hard, a rush of tears flooding his eyes and blurring his vision. "My name is Marcos Almeira Pinheiro. And I think..." His throat clogged, and he had to try again. "I think you might be my brother."

A hand reached out and grabbed his wrist, and the man twisted his own arm—the tattooed one—gasping as the movement pulled on his wounded shoulder. "Is...?" He drew in an audible breath. "Is this your father?"

Marcos couldn't manage anything more than a quick nod, his insides all wadded up in a ball of spinning emotion and stunned disbelief.

The other man's fingers tightened. "Marcos? My God. It's true. I'm Lucas. Y-your brother." And with that the man promptly passed out cold.

Three hours later Lucas was still in surgery, and Marcos paced the waiting room, still in shock. He hadn't sorted through all his twisted emotions. He felt like his abdomen had been slashed open, his innards spilled out for all to see. The nurse at Lucas's bedside had discreetly handed him a tissue as he'd stood there, staring at his brother's form as they'd prepared him for emergency surgery.

Only then had he realized his face had been wet with tears. Sophia, recovered from her meningitis, had come down to join him as he'd waited. "I can't believe he's back, after all these years."

"He's not back. I'm sure he'll be heading back to America as soon as he can."

"But you're glad to have found him again, right?" Sophia grabbed his arm as he walked by and dragged him down to sit beside her. "Stop pacing. You're making me nervous. Don't forget I haven't even gotten to see him yet. Not that he'll remember me."

Marcos gave her a dim smile. "How could anyone forget you?"

"Well, how could you have let Maggie go without even a goodbye?" she countered.

Oh, hell, not that again.

He'd gotten nothing but grief from Sophia about what had happened with Maggie. Not that he'd told her anything except Maggie had decided to leave suddenly—no explanations. It was true. Technically. But his friend still believed he'd had something to do with the decision.

He had. And as much as he regretted jumping to conclusions without giving himself a couple of days to think it over— something totally unlike him—there wasn't a damned thing he could do about it now. Besides, he'd just about convinced himself it was all for the best.

At least, until his brother had appeared and he had started getting all kinds of weird ideas.

"Sophia, it'll do no good to keep rehashing this. Email her, if you want to know her reasons for leaving."

And he prayed Maggie would stick to the "mutually terminated" story he'd foolishly suggested. Because if she told Sophia the truth, his childhood friend would never speak to him again.

An hour later, Sophia had to go back on duty and Marcos was left by himself in the waiting room.

One of the surgeons appeared in the doorway. "Marcos? Dr. Carvalho is out of surgery, if you want to come on back."

He stood. "Is he okay?"

"Yes. We had to patch up an area of his liver, but we were able to retrieve both bullets with minimal damage. We've handed the slugs over to the police, but you know how things are in the *favelas*. No one ever sees anything."

He couldn't have heard correctly. "He was in a *favela*?"

The other doctor nodded. "The big one down the hill. He evidently got caught in some kind of shootout between the police and drug runners. Not the best place to stop for pictures."

That was *his favela*. The one he and Lucas had been born in.

Lucas had been there? Why? Could he have remembered it after all this time? Their old house wasn't even standing any more, so Lucas wouldn't have found it even if he'd tried. But he had tried, evidently. His chest tightened. "Thanks. Which room is he in?"

"Three-oh-one B. Don't stay too long. He's still a little groggy, so he may not remember much about what happened." The doctor shrugged. "The police will want to interview him as well, once he's stronger."

Marcos went through the doors and made his way down the surgical corridor until he found the right room. Sucking down a deep breath, he went in and found Lucas awake, staring vacantly at the television.

He pulled up a chair. "Hello, Lucas. Would you feel more comfortable speaking in Portuguese or English?"

He had no idea if Lucas even remembered his native tongue. He'd spoken to him in English, when he'd first been admitted, just as he'd done with Maggie many times in the past.

But Lucas answered him in Portuguese, surprisingly alert, although his voice was gritty from the surgery and tinged with an American accent. "Either is fine."

Marcos sat by his bed, fifteen minutes turning to thirty

as they talked about what Lucas remembered of their child-hood—and about what had happened to him today. He didn't remember much. Just that he'd been in a taxi when he'd spot-ted a familiar area. The next thing he remembered, he'd been on the ground, his arm and side feeling as if they were on fire. That was it, until he'd woken up in the hospital.

Then came the question he'd dreaded. "I thought Maggie still had four months to go in Brazil. What happened?"

Marcos shrugged. "We both felt it wasn't working out."

"I'd just seen her not long ago. She never said anything about being unhappy."

For someone who was still supposed to be groggy from an-esthesia, his brother was pretty quick on his feet. Then again, they'd been talking for a while.

His jaw tightening and molars aching even more, he gave another quick shrug. "Things change."

"I see."

"What do you mean?" Great. First Sophia. Now Lucas.

"I wondered if there was something between the two of you at the conference."

"There's not." He paused, knowing that just barely missed being a lie. "At least, not any more."

"I thought so. She seemed nervous about seeing you at the conference. In the way that a woman who's interested in a man might be."

"It was complicated." Guilt roared through his chest. Yes, it was complicated, but that didn't excuse what he'd done. Even his brother—a man he hadn't seen in almost thirty years—seemed to be able to see the truth for what it was.

As if to confirm his thoughts, Lucas gave a tired chuckle. "Complicated? No, Marcos. *We're* complicated. Did she break things off?"

"No. I sent her home. And she went."

"Why?"

The word echoed in his skull. It was a question to which

there was no answer other than fear. Fear that he could some-how hurt her. Fear that she might disappear from his life just like his father and Lucas had done.

He gave an internal snort. Well, hadn't she? One day she'd been here and the next she'd been on a plane back to the States.

*Because you put her there.*

He'd been worried about her scratching at herself again, but when he got down to it, this had been mostly about him. About him not trusting her enough to accept what she'd said at face value. For not believing she would stay with him, if he asked her to.

Lucas's voice poked at him again. "Why, Marcos?"

"Because…" Hell, was he really going to do this with his brother lying there in a hospital bed? "Because I think I might be in love with her. And I knew she was going to leave, even-tually. So I forced her out before she left on her own."

"You always were an overbearing ass. Even as a kid. *'Put these shoes on, Lucas, your feet might get cut… Do your home-work before Papai gets home.'*"

Marcos couldn't hold back a laugh. "You remember that?"

"Yes." He closed his eyes with a sigh before looking at him again. "You can't control what happens in life, Marcos. You, more than anyone, should realize that. You just do the best you can, and keep your promises, no matter what. Looks like we both did that, at least."

"Looks like we did." They'd both kept their promises de-spite the odds against them. Two *favela* boys who'd made something of themselves.

Lucas grimaced. "I'd like to continue this conversation, but I'm beat. Getting shot evidently takes it out of a man. Besides, don't you have a phone call to make, an apology to offer…or, better yet, a plane to catch?"

"What?"

"This is probably the drugs talking, but if you love her, go.

Make whatever you did right. After all, there's no guarantee you'll get two miracles in a row."

"Miracles?"

He nodded. "Us. Fate brought us back together at the perfect time. Don't count on it happening twice. This time you need to go out and hunt Fate down and make her do exactly what you want."

# CHAPTER TWENTY

"Approaching the site of the malformation."

Maggie kept up an oral commentary of the surgery as she went. She'd transcribe the recording and put the notes into her patient's medical chart as soon as she was finished.

Keeping the catheter steady, she focused on the screen that showed the snarled network of veins that comprised the aterio-venous malformation located deep in Clara Gerard's cerebellum—a place where her scalpel couldn't reach safely. Creating an embolus in just the right spot was tricky, but by blocking the defective vessels they'd divert the flow of blood into the parts of the brain that were now being deprived. Hopefully that would alleviate the patient's seizures, which had been increasing in severity over the past several months.

She moved the catheter forward another couple of millimeters and studied the image again.

Maggie knew they might have to follow this procedure up with a blast of radiation to close the vessels permanently, but for now she was crossing her fingers that the blockage she was creating would do the trick.

Just like filling her days with work was creating a blockage in her own heart—one that prevented the pain from all that had happened in Brazil from reaching vital areas of her soul. But like her patient's embolus, it was a temporary solution to a very real problem. Right now, though, she couldn't think of a better way to deal with it. After two weeks she was still too raw to think straight.

"Preparing to inject the embolic material."

She could hear the faint rustle of clothing in the background as people moved from one place to another as they did their jobs but, unlike Marcos, she preferred to have a totally silent surgical suite. No music. Not much talking other than her own voice recording the procedure or asking for instruments. The vague thought went through her head that people must think her cold and unfeeling, although no one had ever said anything.

If they only knew just how cold she felt right now.

But unfeeling? If only she could be.

Holding her breath, she squeezed the plunger on the syringe, watching the screen as the glue-like liquid flowed into the offending vessel. The material was designed to harden quickly, so she should start seeing results right about...

Now.

The blood-flow pattern changed abruptly as the rogue vessels that had been siphoning off precious amounts of oxygen went dark. Careful murmurs went up around the room as others saw the same thing she did, but didn't want to disturb her.

Suddenly, she missed the open cheers that heralded success in Marcos's operating room. The slaps on the back, the loud congratulations. Marcos's proud smile as he saved a life that had hung in the balance—and when he'd aimed that smile at her...

She closed her eyes for a brief second as pain overwhelmed her.

Shaking it off, she concentrated on the job at hand. She still had to withdraw the catheter and finish her surgery. She owed it to her patient to give her the best she had. Several minutes later there was still no sign of blood leaking around the embolus. She withdrew the catheter and applied pressure to the entry site as she nodded to the anesthesiologist, who lightened the sedation.

Once her patient was awake enough to respond to questions, she gave the woman's shoulder a gentle squeeze and left to talk to the family.

The waiting room was crowded with Clara's relatives. Maggie smiled as she saw how loved the woman was. When they realized who Maggie was, everyone went quiet, and she gave a thumbs-up sign before she realized where she was. The A-okay gesture was perfectly fine to use here. But she couldn't bring herself to. Not yet. Maybe not ever.

She spoke with them for a few minutes longer, then gave a quick wave as she turned to go. She still needed to change out of her surgical scrubs and get cleaned up. She rounded a corner, her mind on what she needed to do that night, when she heard something behind her.

*"Magía."*

Her steps faltered as the quiet word wound around her with tantalizing familiarity.

She stood there for a second, uncertain what to do but unwilling to turn around and prove herself wrong. She had to have misheard. He wasn't here—had made it plain he didn't want her. And he certainly didn't think she was magic. Not any more.

She took another two steps before the voice came again, a little clearer this time. "Maggie."

A moment of indecision gripped her before she finally forced herself to make a half-turn.

Oh, God. It *was* him. Marcos stood in the corridor, hands shoved into the pockets of his beige chinos, a black Polo shirt hugging the hard lines of his chest. And those eyes. There was no mistaking those warm chocolaty eyes, the corners just barely crinkling as he watched her.

For a terrifying moment she thought he'd come here to talk to the hospital administration about what he *thought* he'd seen back at his apartment. Those mosquito bites he'd jumped to conclusions over. Could he get her fired? Surely he wouldn't be that vindictive.

Unless he thought he was helping her by ratting her out.

There was nothing *to* rat out, she reminded herself. Because she hadn't done what he thought she had.

"Why are you here?"

His hands came out of his pockets, and he took a couple of steps forward, stopping within three feet of her. Even though he hadn't invaded her private space, Maggie had to force herself not to back away.

"I came to apologize."

"Really? I thought you were here to ask me to drop my pants again." She stood straight and tall. "It's a little late for apologies."

"I know. But that doesn't mean I shouldn't offer one." He dragged a hand through his hair. "Can we go somewhere quiet for a few minutes and talk?"

*Don't do it.*

She knew her subconscious was probably wise, but she wanted to hear him out. Especially after the horrific two weeks she'd just had. It might be pathetic, but she wanted to be near him, even if just for a half-hour. There were so many things she didn't understand about what had gone wrong between them. Not to mention why he'd flown hundreds of miles to see her.

"Follow me." Conscious that her modest hospital was nothing like the huge one Marcos worked at, she led him back to one of the little-used exam rooms off the main corridor. Once inside, she shut the door with a quiet click. "Okay. I'm listening."

"I thought you might have started...hurting yourself again, because of something I did."

She frowned. "I'm not sure what you mean."

Leaning against the counter, while Maggie sat in one of the two chairs, he said, "I was feeling a tremendous amount of guilt after the last time we were together. I know there were things I did that made you…uncomfortable. But I pushed you to do them anyway. I worried that I could have brought back some bad memories."

"Bad memories?"

"You had one man who made you do things you didn't want. You don't need another one doing the same thing."

Maggie had had no idea that someone's jaw could actually drop, but hers did. "Are you talking about my uncle?"

"Yes. I was afraid you might think I was like—"

"No." She came up out of her chair and couldn't stop herself from going to him. "You're nothing like him. I can't believe that thought would ever cross your mind."

"It did." He closed his eyes for a second before opening them again. "And when I saw those marks, *Meu Deus*, Maggie, I thought I'd caused it all to come back. I was terrified. Stupid. I didn't want what I'd done to add to whatever scars you're carrying inside."

"You haven't. I loved every minute of the time we spent together." She offered a small tremulous smile. "I've grown enough over the years to say stop if I'm ever really uncomfortable with something."

He reached out and brushed a strand of hair from her cheek. "The vibrator…"

"I'm the one who bought it. After that first time we were together, in fact." She gave an embarrassed laugh. "I just never meant anyone else to find it. But I liked what you did with it, if you couldn't tell." Maggie needed him to know that she'd wanted everything he'd done to her.

"Then you don't hate me for what happened?"

"Hate you? Of course not. I was angry…no, furious that you wouldn't believe me when I told you what those marks were, but looking at it from your perspective—especially after what you've just told me—I can see how it might have appeared."

Her brows went up. "I can assure you those bites are all gone now. Or do you want me to prove that, too?"

"No. No proof." He took a deep breath then blew it out. "I came to apologize, but I also came to ask you something."

She swallowed, not daring to hope for anything more than she'd had. "What is it?"

"Would you consider coming back to Brazil with me?"

Go back? Why? To finish her internship? Wasn't that just asking for more heartache? Nothing had changed. She still loved him.

She answered slowly, "I don't think that would be wise. I have..." God, could she really do this? She had to. He had to know the truth. "I have feelings for you that would make any type of working relationship between us...awkward."

"What kind of feelings?"

Maggie could swear she saw something leap to life in his eyes. The little flicker of hope grew. "Romantic feelings."

Before she could think or react, Marcos had wrapped his arms around her and pulled her close. *"Graças a Deus,"* he breathed. He eased back to look into her face. "I have feelings too. Romantic feelings, as you put it. But it's more than that. I'm in love with you. I have been since that first month you came to work for me. I just couldn't see it at the time."

"You do? Are you sure?"

"Yes. It's why I sent you away. I couldn't bear to cause you any pain. I was also afraid you'd eventually leave me, one way or another."

The choking laugh that came out of her throat was a mixture of tears and joy. "I've known since that last night we spent together. It's why I bolted to the bathroom like I did."

"So much of this could have been avoided." The words were whispered, and Maggie wasn't sure if they were meant for her ears or not. Especially as his next ones were clearer. "I knew something was wrong afterwards. I thought I was the reason—what we'd done. I decided that was the end. I couldn't push you to sleep with me ever again."

"I was upset because I couldn't believe I'd let myself fall in love with you. I was devastated. And so very scared you didn't feel the same way."

He leaned down and kissed her softly. Maggie's arms went around his neck, and she held him tight, tears rising in her eyes again. She pulled back with a laugh and pointed at them. "These are out of happiness—just in case you get any other crazy ideas."

"I have many, many crazy ideas. And most of them involve you." He frowned. "But only if you'll come back with me."

"To finish out my internship?"

"Yes, that. But I'd like our partnership to continue long beyond that. We could use someone with your skills at the hospital. And I want to show you the place where I was born." His arms tightened around her. "I want you with me all the time. Will you come?"

"Yes." Maggie's heart filled to bursting. "I'll need a week or two to hand my patients over to another doctor."

"I'll wait. And when we get back, I have someone special I'd like you to meet." He opened the door and slung an arm around her as they trailed back down the hallway. "My brother."

Shock went through her. "Your brother—after all this time? You found him?"

Marcos shook his head. "He found me. Actually, he found *you*. And I can't tell you how grateful I am."

"I don't understand."

"Remember L. Carvalho?"

Maggie stopped and looked up at him, her eyes widening. "The plastic surgeon from the conference?"

"The same. His whole name is Lucas Elias Pinheiro Carvalho. His adopted name is Carvalho. He was shot and asked for you—"

"Shot?"

"It's a very long story, *querida*. One we'll have plenty of time to talk about."

"So you both became doctors. Just like you promised." She glanced up and tugged his head down for a quick kiss. "I think your father would be very proud of what his sons have accomplished."

Marcos didn't say anything for a long moment; in fact, he looked away, before scrubbing a hand down his face. But not before Maggie caught the glitter of moisture across one rugged cheek.

After a moment he started walking again, threading his fingers through hers. "I think he would, Maggie. I think he'd be proud of all of us."

\* \* \* \* \*

# THE DANGERS OF
# DATING DR CARVALHO

## TINA BECKETT

MILLS &
BOON

Published in Great Britain 2014
by Mills & Boon, an imprint of Harlequin (UK) Limited,
Eton House, 18-24 Paradise Road, Richmond, Surrey, TW9 1SR

© 2014 Tina Beckett

ISBN: 978 0 263 90752 0

Harlequin (UK) Limited's policy is to use papers that are natural,
renewable and recyclable products and made from wood grown in
sustainable forests. The logging and manufacturing processes conform
to the legal environmental regulations of the country of origin.

Printed and bound in Spain
by Blackprint CPI, Barcelona

To those who keep their promises.

# CHAPTER ONE

LUCAS CARVALHO WAS a lucky man.

At least, that was what his doctors told him. If only he could remember why.

It wasn't that he couldn't remember anything. He could. He knew his full name. That he was a plastic surgeon from California. That he'd come to Brazil for a medical conference.

But there were large swathes of empty space that he couldn't seem to fill with information. As if there'd been important data there at one time but it had been wiped clean with a single keystroke. Things like how he'd wound up with a sling around one arm and a surgical incision across the left side of his abdomen—or why he was now lying in a hospital bed without the foggiest notion as to how he got there.

And his brother—the person who'd been standing over him as he'd awoken from surgery three days ago, the person he hadn't seen in almost thirty years—had left the day before yesterday for the United States on important business.

Business that involved a woman.

Lucas's lips twisted. The last time he'd chased down a woman had been... His brain clicked through several files and discarded them.

Nope. Never happened. Never would.

At least he hoped he hadn't done anything crazy in that blank space where most of his recent memories should be.

The cute little nurse who'd come to visit him a couple of

times had assured him that *he* was the one who'd talked his brother into going after that particular woman.

He struggled into a sitting position, wincing as pain sliced through his shoulder, the sling that secured his arm doing little to prevent his stitches from feeling like they were tearing free from his wound.

Not wound...wounds. Two, to be exact.

That's what the police had told him...that he'd been shot. Twice. Right outside the entrance to a nearby slum. And like his doctors, the law enforcement officials insisted he was lucky to be alive.

Today he didn't feel quite so thrilled about that fact. Actually, he didn't feel thrilled about much of anything. The aches and pains, dulled by strong doses of medication a couple of days ago, now bit into his flesh with every movement.

He eyed the IV stand to his left and noted the wheels at its base. They'd had him up and walking soon after his surgery—he remembered the same warm-eyed nurse had hovered in the background, hands twisting as he'd taken his first painful, curse-filled steps. He didn't think she was assigned to his case because she hadn't helped in any way, but he couldn't shake the feeling that she'd wanted to say something to him.

But she hadn't.

Shifting to the side of the bed where his IV bag hung, he let his legs dangle over the edge, hands gripping the mattress as he thought about his best course of action—the first being a much-needed trip to the john.

Which he could manage on his own.

He hoped.

His feet hit the floor, and the world spun for several nauseating seconds, causing him to clutch the pole beside him with a low curse.

Three days.

Surely he should be more ambulatory than this by now. The wave of dizziness passed and he stayed in place another minute or two to get his bearings. Then he leaned on the IV stand as he wheeled it toward the bathroom.

Doing the deed was a marvel in logistics co-ordination, but he somehow made it to the finish line without doing a face plant, and even washed and dried his uninjured hand afterwards.

There. He felt more independent already.

Right.

Judging from the pale face staring at him in the mirror, he might *feel* independent but he could use a big infusion of some kind of miracle drug. He jabbed his fingers through his hair, pushing it back off his forehead, not that it helped much.

Now that he was up, though, there was no way he was climbing back in that bed and staring at the dull white ceiling for hours on end. He'd done enough of that. So if walking would get him out of this place any faster, he would do just that. In fact, he'd jog if he had to.

All by himself.

He ignored the remote control dangling by its cord off the side of the bed and slogged his way toward the door, feeling like he was pushing through a huge vat of Jell-O. He refused to call for a nurse who would fuss over him like he vaguely remembered his brother doing when they'd been kids. At least until he and Marcos had been separated and grown up on two completely different continents.

His birth country had evidently missed him as much as he'd missed it, judging from the two slugs the doctors had dug out of him. His mouth twisted. Maybe he should have just stayed in the States.

Taking a deep breath and hoping he wouldn't live to regret the move, he pulled the heavy metal lever on the door and stepped into the hallway.

As a testament to how utterly fantastic his last couple of days had been, the door hit him squarely on the ass as it closed, almost sending him and his IV pole spinning to the floor.

He bit back a whole string of English cuss words that could get him into trouble, even here in Brazil, and pulled himself upright.

*It's a beautiful day in the neighborhood...*

With a heavy sigh of resignation he started down the long corridor in search of some answers. Or a good stiff drink. Whichever he came across first.

*Nossa Senhora do céu!*

Sophia Limeira's eyes nearly popped out of their sockets.

As head nurse, she should probably show a little more dignity but, *Deus*, she couldn't help but stare in awe as every female head—patients and visitors alike—turned in graceful synchronization to watch Lucas Carvalho make his way down the hall.

Long legs showed off the beautiful lithe movements of someone who knew the effect he had on those around him. Even with his left arm in a sling and dragging an IV stand along with him, he could have crooked a finger at any woman in the place and she'd have rushed toward him, snarling and snapping at anyone who dared get in her way. Even eighty-seven-year-old Marta Silva, who was parked in a wheelchair against the south wall, looked like she might slither from her seat and land in a heap at his feet.

Thankfully, Sophia was firmly anchored in her office chair—behind the desk that sat directly in Lucas's path.

It was then she noticed he wasn't making the slightest effort to hold his hospital gown closed at the back.

Maybe that was why all the women were ogling him.

It wasn't entirely his fault, as both his hands were occupied with other things but, still, she was really, *really* glad he was facing her.

Although that was ridiculous. She was a nurse, for heaven's sake. She'd seen plenty of bare masculine butts over the last ten years.

But none of their owners had looked like Lucas.

She touched the flesh above the right side of her lip with her index finger, self-conscious all of a sudden, although she knew she didn't need to be. The scar was barely visible—the lip margins perfectly aligned. A dot of concealer on a sponge and the flaw almost blended away into nothingness.

Almost.

But Lucas was a plastic surgeon. His knowing eye could cut right through the thin layer of make-up and see the scar for what it was. A remnant from her childhood. She wondered if he ran across many cases like hers in his practice.

Probably not. He was from California, the land of beautiful bouncing breasts and perfect spray-on tans.

She gulped as his eyes met hers, then narrowed slightly, as if trying to place her.

He didn't remember her. Even when she'd slid into his room that first day and introduced herself, there'd been no hint of recognition. Even when she'd stood nearby as he'd taken his first steps.

Marcos had once said no one could forget her.

Ha! Well, someone could. And someone had.

Not that it mattered. It had been ages since she'd seen Lucas. And they'd both been children at the time.

And he'd been so very sad that first week at the orphanage. Within a month, however, they'd become inseparable— the dynamic trio, the workers had dubbed them.

Only Lucas had been one of the lucky ones who'd been adopted, leaving Marcos and her behind for ever.

*Deus!* He was still headed her way. And the bony hollows of the boy she'd once known were now filled in with muscle and sinew that rippled with every step he took.

Fully man. Fully dangerous.

She knew she should be on her feet, scolding him for getting out of bed and walking unassisted, but she couldn't seem to make her body obey the normal commands. Casting a quick glance around her, she saw there wasn't another nurse in sight. Just her. And Lucas's eagle-eyed gaze was fastened directly on her.

Needing to be the first one to speak for some crazy reason, she arched a brow when he reached the desk. "You do know you're putting on quite a show for the folks behind you, don't you?"

He frowned for a second then gave her a slow smile as if realizing what she meant. "Don't worry. I eventually have to go back the way I came."

Yes, he did.

Holding tight to her impassive "nurse" demeanor when all she wanted to do was keep staring, she forced a shrug. "Don't worry," she parroted. "I'm immune."

"Ah, yes, a sad byproduct of the nursing profession."

"The same can be said of plastic surgeons," she lobbed back.

See? She could be just as suave and sophisticated as he could.

"Ah, but I could never grow immune to the wonders of the female body."

Scratch that last thought. She might be able to put on a pretty good act but she could never be as sophisticated as he was. Inside, there were still remnants of the shy little orphan she'd once been. One who'd latched onto Marcos's hand the day he'd arrived at the orphanage, while shooting his cute little brother surreptitious peeks from beneath childish lashes. She'd been bowled over by Lucas then, and as aggravating as it might be, it appeared she was still flustered by him now.

Tall, at six feet two—at least, according to his chart—with dark wavy hair that hung low on his forehead and even darker eyes, he was mesmerizingly beautiful. Kind of apt for someone in his line of work, but Sophia could swear his good looks owed nothing to plastic surgery. There were faint crinkles radiating from the corners of his eyes and a long line bracketed his left cheek, evidence of a slightly lopsided smile that she could remember even from his childhood.

The times he'd smiled, that was.

Both brothers had seemed strangely grown up, even as young children. Which made sense, considering they'd lived in one of the notorious *favelas* that dotted the landscape.

And although Lucas still spoke flawless Portuguese, an American accent threaded its way through each and every word, sending shivers over her each time he opened his mouth.

Or she could just be catching the flu.

Realizing she hadn't responded to his outrageous comment, she climbed to her feet, hoping the added height would snap her back to normal.

Mistake. Because her eyes only came up to his neck, where a pulse beat a steady tattoo against his skin.

Time to send him on his way. "Now that you've had your fun, do you need help getting back to your room?"

As nonchalant as he might appear, she couldn't forget he was less than a week out of major surgery to repair damage to his liver. And when she glanced higher, she spied a tell-tale glimmer of moisture across his upper lip, but he held her gaze with a steadiness that surprised her.

He shook his head, his eyes trailing down her face then pausing to retrace their path, a slight pucker appearing between his dark brows. She forced herself to remain still when he reached across the desk, his thumb brushing the area just below her right nostril and sliding to the bottom of her lip. Her heart rate shot through the roof, stomach quivering at the unexpected contact. She should be furious at his audacity, angry at how quickly he'd noticed what she'd done her best to hide, but the warmth of his skin somehow blotted out everything... except the sensation of flesh sliding against flesh.

She swallowed then answered his unspoken question. "I was born with a cleft lip. It was repaired when I was one."

"I'm sorry, I shouldn't have…" For the first time he looked uncomfortable.

Uncomfortable with what? The image of how she must have looked before her reconstructive surgery?

Surely not. But this was a man who sold beauty for a living…who knew perfection—or imperfection—the second he saw it.

Very few people ever spotted her scar. And she'd had enough attention from the male population to know that her curves tended to be the first thing a man noticed about her. Maybe that was a blessing.

But she couldn't count the number of times she'd wished a man would look into her eyes rather than stare down the front of her shirt.

*Yeah? Well, here was one who had, and look what he zeroed in on.*

"Don't worry about it. I'm sure in your line of work…" She let the words hang in mid-air.

His brows went up. "Why do I get the feeling the last part of that comment would have been less than flattering."

"Not unflattering, just realistic. I'm sure your training lends itself to searching for flaws and then fixing them."

"Ah, yes. Well, if that were the case, I have two pretty big flaws right now, don't I?"

She blinked in surprise. "Really? And what would those be?" Because she couldn't see the slightest hint of any defect in the man standing in front of her. In fact, she *was* kind of looking forward to the moment when he'd turn around and walk away, just so she could get a peek at what all the other people in the wing could still see.

He lifted his bandaged arm. "Bullet holes tend to announce their presence in no uncertain terms."

Yes, they did. And that was her cue to get this man back to bed where he belonged.

*Deus!* That last thought carried a few more Freudian connotations than she cared to admit.

A laugh bubbled up her throat before she could stop it, and she slapped a hand over her mouth, eyes wide.

"What?" he said.

"Nothing. We just need to get you back in...in your room before you collapse."

His glance tracked to her chest, where her nametag hung, and then back up to her face. "Sophia, right? You were in the hospital after my surgery."

The laughter dried up in a flash. "Yes."

"And when I took my first steps after the surgery."

She nodded. "I work here."

The words sounded ridiculous, even to her, but she did *not* want to explain that they'd met before. Or ask if he remembered her from when he'd been four years old. Of course he wouldn't. He'd had a brand-new life in a brand-new country. Even his last name was different now than it had been when he'd been at the orphanage.

The weird thing was that seeing him again dredged up that infantile crush she'd had on him way back when—her very first memory from her childhood days. She'd seen that beautiful face and stared at him in awe...right before she'd grabbed hold of Marcos's hand instead—too afraid to say anything to the boy standing next to him. She'd warmed up to him later but it had been a very different warmth from what she was feeling right now.

Those brown eyes touched on her scar once more and then brushed across her lips. Could he sense her thoughts? *Deus*, she hoped not. With a rough indrawn breath his gaze left her and moved to his uninjured hand, which was still hanging onto the IV pole, knuckles white as his grip tightened further. "I think you're right. I've had about all I can stand for one day. Would you mind giving me a hand?"

Sophia steadied her emotions and drew on years of training. "Sure."

Moving around the desk, she commandeered the IV stand and tucked her shoulder beneath his arm. "You ready?"

Even as he gritted out an affirmative, and they started to make their way back down the corridor, she was very aware of the warmth of his body against hers and the fact that her arm was resting across naked skin where his robe parted. Her heart shivered a couple of times then leaped into space, landing at the bottom of her abdominal cavity with a thud. It didn't quite shatter, but there was definitely a crack or two lining its tough protective surface.

*Get real, Sophia. He's just one more patient in a long list of patients. He'll be gone in a matter of days or at the most a few weeks.*

Maybe it was better if he never remembered her. If she never mentioned their time together at the orphanage.

She attempted small talk as they shuffled back down the hallway. "It's really *bacana* that you and your brother found each other after all these years."

*"Bacana?"* Lucas stopped for a second to look down at her.

She searched around for an English word that would get across the meaning. "It's um…cool. Good."

"Yes. Very cool." The way his muscles stiffened at her words made her wonder if he really did think it was. But why wouldn't he? Marcos was a great guy. Besides, now he could get to know his home country. Get to know someone he'd once been close to.

Unlike her, who had no one. Whose parents, although still alive, had left her at an orphanage when she'd been a baby because they hadn't had the money to deal with her defect—an unfortunate reality in her country.

They'd reached out to her once, when she'd moved into her teenage years, when her government-funded surgery had been but a distant memory, but things had been strained and neither her parents nor her had particularly wanted to pick up the pieces. They'd moved to another part of Brazil by the time she'd reached adulthood, and although she still had their address, she'd never bothered to get back in touch with them. And they'd never contacted her again.

Her downed heart rolled around, reminding her of its presence. Hmm...maybe those cracks in it weren't so new after all. Maybe, like her lip, they'd healed with barely a trace. Until a hard knock—or the gentle brush of a thumb—had brought back all the reasons she needed to be on guard.

Especially with a man who'd spied what lay beneath her make-up within the space of a heartbeat but hadn't been able to see beyond it. Lucas had touched her scar back then as well—when it had been fresher and more noticeable. Before she'd learned how to cover it up with the quick flick of her make-up brush.

Surely she'd be able to do the same with her heart. By the time she was done, no one—not even the plastic surgeon by her side—would be able to see through the carefully applied layers.

And that was just the way she wanted it.

# CHAPTER TWO

LUCAS HAD JUST perched on the edge of his bed when a buzzing sound came from the nurse's pocket.

"Oh, sorry. I was expecting your brother to call me this morning between rounds. He wanted to check on you."

He waved her away. "Go ahead."

His legs felt like spaghetti, despite his trash talk a few minutes ago at the nurses' station. He hated feeling helpless. Hated being at someone else's mercy.

Something about that fact tickled the back of his subconscious. A memory he couldn't quite grasp no matter how hard he tried.

Sophia pulled the phone from her pocket, her eyes still on his as she checked the readout. "It's Marcos. I'm sure he'll want to say hi."

Answering the phone, her eyes sparkled as she chatted with his brother, asking him about how things were going in the States. Something he said made her laugh. "Well, tell Maggie I send my love."

The way she said those words made a warm current flow through his chest. He hated to admit it, but being back in Brazil wasn't like he'd expected it to be. Friendships here seemed more intimate somehow, not like the superficial relationships he tended to foster. Or maybe it was because Marcos and Sophia knew each other well...maybe they'd worked together for years.

"Sure. He's right here." Sophia pressed the mouthpiece to her shoulder. "He wants to talk to you."

Lucas held out his hand, waiting as she placed the cellphone in his palm. The instrument was still warm from being in her pocket, and he hesitated before lifting it. Something about knowing she'd breathed into the receiver—had held it close to her lips, made the heat in his chest spread to his gut. It had to be the after-effects of the anesthesia and pain pills he'd had during and after his surgery. They hadn't completely cleared his system yet. He took a quick breath and held the phone close to his ear, not quite letting it touch his skin.

"Hi, Marcos. How's it going?" He spoke in English, feeling awkward talking to his brother in Portuguese. After all, he hadn't even been able to understand a simple slang term the nurse had used.

The medical conference had seemed the perfect venue to visit his home country and learn more about his culture. Unfortunately it had only served to show him how little he knew—it was just one more place he didn't belong.

His brother's amused tone brought him back to the present. "Everything's fine. I thought I'd check and see how the hospital was treating you." A female voice murmured in the background, and his brother's response came through muffled, indicating he'd turned his head to answer whoever it was.

He rolled his eyes. Surely Marcos wasn't actually in bed with his new... Searching for a word, he came up blank, as he wasn't quite sure what kind of relationship the two had. All he knew was that when he'd introduced himself to Dr. Maggie Pfeiffer at the medical conference, a glare from across the room had hit him like a fist to the jaw. He hadn't known who Marcos was at the time but he'd recognized that pointed stare. It had said *off-limits* and *mine* in no uncertain terms.

He couldn't blame his brother. Maggie was beautiful, her ready smile showing her love of life.

Not like Sophia, whose prickly attitude a few minutes ago

seemed strange, seeing as they didn't know each other. Maybe she'd had a bad day or maybe she was just that way with everyone. He glanced at her to find her busy straightening things on his bedside table, her scrubs doing nothing to detract from the generous curves beneath them.

He realized he was staring when Marcos repeated the question about the hospital.

"Everyone's been great," he said. "Thanks. The police still want to depose me in a day or two, and I should probably stick around for a couple of weeks to see if they make an arrest. So I'll take you up on your offer to stay in your apartment, if it's still okay."

"Absolutely. I told the doorman you might be coming. He has a set of keys. So does Sophia. Make yourself at home."

The thought of Sophia having a set of Marcos's house keys made him uneasy. "Thanks. I really appreciate it."

More murmurs sounded in the background, and that was definitely Marcos chuckling at something. Hand tightening on the phone, he realized he now had the thing mashed to his ear. So much for not letting it touch him any more than necessary. The fire in his gut burned just a little bit hotter when he caught a faint whiff of her scent clinging to the thing. His glance swung back to the nurse, wondering how he knew what she smelled like.

*It's your sick imagination, bud.*

As soon as he got back to the States, he was going to sink deep into the first willing woman he came across. It had obviously been far too long since he'd gotten any. Maybe he'd even find someone here in Brazil at one of the clubs, if he was here long enough.

"Well, I'll let you go." Lucas was suddenly anxious to get off the phone.

"Okay... Oh, wait. I forgot to ask. How does it feel to see Sophia again after all these years? It's hard for me not to still picture her as a little kid."

Little kid? That was the *last* thing he'd pictured when he'd looked at Sophia. But Marcos's words made a slight chill come over him, dousing the flames that had begun licking at places he'd rather were left alone.

"I don't follow."

There was a pause. "You don't remember her? I guess it was so long ago that—"

"Remember her from where?" The chill grew. When he glanced to the side, he noted Sophia had turned toward him.

Before Marcos's next words came over the line, he knew he'd somehow missed something. Something big.

"She was at the orphanage with us. Stuck to our sides like glue. *O trio dinâmico*. Ring a bell?"

The dynamic trio.

Why hadn't she said anything?

"I…" Feeling like an idiot, Lucas stared at the woman in front of him, trying to see something that rang a bell. Instead, he settled for the first lame words that popped into his brain. "I was just a kid."

"Right." The disappointment surrounding that single word cut him to the quick.

How could he be expected to remember something that had happened thirty years ago? It wasn't like he'd spent his whole life in Brazil, the way Marcos had. But it did explain why Sophia had been there each step of the way during his surgery and recovery. He suddenly felt like a first-class heel.

He tried to explain. "There've been things I haven't been able to remember since the shooting. Maybe that's why."

Sophia turned away, just as Marcos said, "Don't worry about it. Could you pass the phone back to her, please?"

"Sure."

"Take care, Lucas."

"You too."

Jiggling the phone in his hand and not sure if he should just tap her on the shoulder or say her name, he settled for clearing his throat, even though the last thing he wanted to do was face her again. "He wants to talk to you."

She turned back around and gave him a cheery smile then held out her hand, her eyes skipping away from his almost immediately.

Like a man caught in a riptide and unable to pull free of its deadly grasp, he slowly handed over the phone. Then he did the unthinkable. He took a step closer and cupped her chin, his thumb strumming over the softness of her cheek as he forced her to meet his eyes. "Why didn't you say something about the orphanage?"

She took a step back, dislodging his hand. "It didn't seem important."

Not wanting to give him a chance to respond, she put the phone to her ear. "Hello?"

And proving they were indeed brothers, the first words out of Marcos's mouth were, "You didn't tell him?"

This wasn't a conversation she wanted to have in front of Lucas. Turning on her heel, she left the room. Once outside the door, she gulped down a couple of quick breaths, leaning a shoulder against a wall. With a shaky hand she brushed her hair off her forehead. "No. Why would I? Like he said, we were just kids. It's ancient history."

But the tremor in her voice said the same thing her heart did: she'd remembered *him*. Despite their ages.

*What did it matter?*

Exactly. She was being ridiculous. Lucas was alive—that was the only important thing. He'd be able to get on with his life as if this little interlude in Brazil had never happened. It was fine.

Her friend's voice came back through. "Well, since it's ancient history, I kind of feel funny asking you to..."

As if at a loss, he didn't finish his sentence.

"Asking me to what?"

"Check in on him every once in a while at the apartment? Make sure he's okay."

She gulped. That was so not a good idea. Lucas already made her pulse race, and he didn't even know who she was. It was one thing to act the part of his nurse at the hospital... but outside of it? "I don't know."

"Please, Soph. I know it's not fair to ask you, but you're the closest thing to family I have. You were practically a sister to us, whether he remembers it or not."

"You and I grew up together. You only remember me because we were at the orphanage longer than he was. He doesn't remember anything about his life here in Brazil."

That wasn't entirely true. She'd heard Marcos talk to Lucas after his surgery, and he'd remembered some things from his childhood. He'd remembered his brother. Remembered the promise he and Marcos had made to their father—those words were tattooed on his arm, in fact, along with his father's name. Lucas even remembered the policeman who'd found the two boys sorting through a pile of garbage at their tiny shack of a house all those years ago.

Despite all that, Lucas probably didn't recall much about his father's sudden death or what had come afterwards.

She tried again. "I'm a complete stranger to him, Marcos."

"Possibly. But you're not a stranger to me."

And there it was. He was calling up the friendship card. It wasn't like she hadn't given him enough grief over the years: Getting into trouble. Nagging. Matchmaking.

The matchmaking bit had worked out pretty well, actually, since it had given him Maggie. Still, in all the years she'd known him Marcos had never really asked anything of her. How could she say no and face herself in the mirror?

Sighing, she tipped her head against the wall and stared at the ceiling. "Fine. I'll try, but only if he lets me."

She brushed off Marcos's thanks and murmured a quick

goodbye, more than ready to be done with this particular conversation. Almost as soon as she hit the "end" button, a sudden swish of air brushed her left arm, making her tense.

Her head came off the wall, and she turned to find that Lucas had silently come through the door of his room, with no warning rattle from his IV pole to alert her. She couldn't keep her gaze from tracking over him, pausing at the top of his hand, where a thin trickle of blood marred his tanned skin.

She frowned. "Where's your IV?"

That's why she hadn't heard him. He'd pulled the catheter out of his vein.

"I don't need it any more."

Right. Marcos wanted her to take care of him? Well, they were off to a great start. "That's for your doctor to decide." She motioned to the door. "I'll get you hooked back up."

He pressed the needle puncture against the fabric over his thigh, drawing her attention to the fact that he was still in his hospital gown. Still naked beneath it.

A slow breath hissed between his teeth. "I feel like I should say something here. About what Marcos said about the orphanage—"

"No need to worry about it. Like you said, we were young. You'd just had your whole life torn apart. You would have clung to the one person who was a constant in your life: Marcos."

The words made perfect sense, but they didn't take away the tiny ache that lingered inside.

"I think I've just blocked some of those memories. The day my father...when he didn't come home... Things are just a big blur. I don't remember much more than snatches of sensation here and there." He gave a lopsided smile that didn't quite reach his eyes. "I do remember the food at the orphanage leaving something to be desired. I'm still not a big fan of beans and rice."

And that should remind her, if nothing else did, that although he was Brazilian by birth, in his heart, he was just another rich man who'd left his roots far, far behind.

Her chin went up. "And I still love them."

Something touched her wrist and then slid lower, wrapping around her index finger. She glanced down in surprise to find he was no longer putting pressure on his IV site but had hooked his finger around hers. A flare of something dangerous kicked to life inside her belly.

"They're probably going to release me in a day or two. Maybe we could meet somewhere, and you could tell me what you remember from those days. Fill in some blanks. At least until Marcos gets back."

And have him discover that, unlike him, she remembered quite a bit about their time together? That while Marcos might have been his lifeline, they'd *both* been hers? "I don't think—"

"Please. I want to know."

*Deus.* As much as she wanted to turn her back on him and forget their paths had ever crossed again, she couldn't. Not only because of Marcos's request but because—despite the macho display as he'd swaggered toward her desk earlier—there was a hint of something beneath the knowing smile he'd given her. Something she couldn't quite put her finger on, but it was enough that she couldn't just brush off his request.

"Okay. But until the doctor releases you, you can't go around unhooking yourself from your IV. Deal?"

The smile he gave her was just as lazy as before, but this time it reached all the way up to his eyes, making her stomach do a back flip.

This was a big mistake. She felt it in her bones. But at least if she got him tethered back to his IV pole she could keep him in one spot. And she could remain just out of reach. Far enough away that he couldn't touch her again without warning, because her finger was painfully aware that he was still holding onto it. And the cheek he'd stroked a few minutes ago still tingled.

Yes, staying out of reach was a good thing. For her own peace of mind.

And if that meant keeping him at the other end of an IV line then the man was going to find himself pumped so full of fluids that he'd inflate like a water balloon.

And that's how he'd stay. At least until she could get herself—and her out-of-whack emotions—firmly under control.

# CHAPTER THREE

"YOU'LL NEED SOMEONE at home to help you for at least a week." Lucas's doctor glanced up from his chart. "No driving or lifting anything heavier than a comb, so someone will have to take you to your physical therapy sessions. Is Dr. Pinheiro back from his trip yet?"

*No, Dr. Pinheiro is not back yet.*

Lucas's temper flared for a second before cooling down again. He knew the standard protocol. It was just irritating to have it recited to him by another doctor. And as far as his dear brother went, who knew when he'd blow back into town. Not that he needed Marcos to run behind him and wipe his nose any more. Those days were long gone.

Lucas steadfastly refused to glance at the quiet figure waiting in the far corner of the room and tried to work through his options. If he were in the States, he could call on any number of friends, or simply ask to be moved to a rehab center for a couple of weeks. But here...

"No, he's not back, but—"

"I'll be staying with him." The soft voice made both men look up.

Lucas's jaw clenched until it became a tight ball of muscle. "There's no need."

He somehow got the words out, though he still avoided looking directly at her. He'd already racked his brain during his week of hospitalization, searching for any glimmer of memory that included the slender wraith who always seemed to be hovering nearby. But he'd come up blank, despite what Marcos had said about the three of them sticking together at the orphanage. The guilt over that ate away at him, even though Sophia acted like it didn't matter one way or the other.

Well, it mattered to him. He had very good recall when it came to women—and Sophia was not someone he would have forgotten.

Only she hadn't been a woman back then. She'd been a young girl.

"Would you rather stay at *my* apartment?"

The wry suggestion finally made his eyes light on her, and they stared at each other for a full minute. She might have been teasing but he wasn't in the mood for games right now. Especially not with the dark thoughts that careened through his head whenever he laid eyes on her. Thoughts that made him do a mental penance dance each time they arose. It had become a vicious cycle, one he'd have no hope of breaking if they were forced to shack up together.

No, it wouldn't be shacking up.

As if aware of his thoughts, Sophia's throat moved in a quick swallow. Maybe she was about to take back her offer. *Yes. Please do.*

The doctor spoke up. "Well, I'll leave you two to work out the details. Sophia, if you could free him from that IV? I'm sure he'll be glad not to be dragging it behind him any more."

Something flashed through her eyes and her teeth came down on her lip before she answered, "Of course, Doctor."

Lucas couldn't hold back a small smile. She'd been none too gentle when she'd jabbed the catheter back into his vein the other day. He could have sworn she had been trying to get a wince out of him.

For not remembering her?

There it went again. He really needed to stop dwelling on this.

TINA BECKETT 29

The doctor left the room, and he was alone with her. His smile widened just a bit. "I could always unhook myself, you know, if it makes you more comfortable. I did it once before."

"No, I'll do it." She moved to the counter with quick, precise motions, snapping on her gloves and getting a cotton ball and sticking plaster.

As soon as she was within reach, he wrapped his fingers around her wrist. "You don't have to do this, you know."

"The doctor said to undo you."

His thumb swept across her hand, grimacing when it met latex rather than the silky skin he knew lay beneath the gloves. "I'm not talking about the IV. I'm talking about you staying with me. I'm sure there are nurses I can hire. A..." He struggled to find the Portuguese equivalent of an LPN. "The kind that come to patients' homes."

Her brows went up in that indignant way he was coming to recognize. "You think I'm not qualified?"

Hell. How did he get himself into situations like this? "No, that's not it. I just know that you're busy with your job."

"I don't normally work at night. And the hospital is close to Marcos's apartment." She tugged her hand free. "Surely you can manage for a few hours here and there while I'm at work."

Why was she so insistent? They were nothing to each other, and she'd made it pretty clear she didn't want to have much to do with him. So to spend the night in the next room—at least, he figured it would be the next room. Who knew? Maybe the bedrooms were nowhere near each other. "Don't you have someone waiting for you at home?"

She sucked in a breath then released it in a slow, steady current of air. "That doesn't really have anything to do with this situation. You're Marcos's brother, and he's a special friend."

Exactly how special?

He shook his head clear of that thought. His brother had said he'd had trouble picturing Sophia as an adult so surely... Besides, Marcos and Maggie were evidently an item now. And

Sophia didn't act as if she was jealous. In fact, she seemed genuinely happy for them.

With gloved fingers she took hold of his arm. "You might want to look away."

This time Lucas was the one who lifted his brows. "I think I can handle it."

"Okay." She put the cotton ball over the catheter and slid it free of his vein, then pressed on it lightly. "Hold this for a few seconds."

He blinked at her then gave the arm in the sling a little wiggle, grimacing when it hurt more than he'd expected. "Kind of hard to do that right now."

Her face turned pink. "Oh. That's right. Sorry." She kept pressure on his wrist with her thumb for a few seconds, fingers curling around his wrist. The contact lasted long enough that Lucas began to wish he'd used his chin or something else to hold onto that cotton ball as the warmth of her skin was quickly cutting through the chill of the room.

At last she eased the compression and lifted the gauze to look. "That should do it." She dropped the cotton ball into a basin then quickly peeled apart a sticking plaster and applied it over the puncture mark.

Dragging a nearby chair to the bed, she dropped into it and regarded him with serious eyes.

"What?" For the first time he wished he actually had some real clothes on, because if a certain part of him decided to go rogue, it was going to be awfully difficult to conceal it.

"The doctor was right. We need to work out the details."

"Of?" He decided to play stupid.

"How things between us are going to work."

Okay, that rogue part was already feeling the heat.

*Think of something else.*

Should he refuse her offer of help? Or should he suck it up and decide to make the best of a bad situation? He'd asked her to tell him about their shared past, so he could look at it as a way to kill two birds with one stone. "How many bedrooms does Marcos's apartment have?"

"Two, of course." She leaned back and crossed her legs. "Otherwise I wouldn't have offered to stay."

"Right." And she'd just made everything worse because now he was picturing a single shared bed and Sophia's lush figure sprawled across the mattress.

She fiddled with the hem of her top. "Besides, you weren't worried about the number of bedrooms a few minutes ago when you were talking about hiring a nurse."

Bingo. But then again he doubted any other nurse was going to mess with his head the way this particular one did. And he had no idea why she affected him so much. He'd love to blame it on the pain meds, but as he'd refused to take anything yesterday or today, that was impossible.

"I wasn't expecting a hired nurse to actually spend the night."

"Oh. I think that's what the doctor intended, though." She smiled at him, her brow clearing. "I've taken the rest of the day off, so whenever you're ready we can get your discharge papers signed and be on our way."

Something about that rattled around in his brain for a moment or two before he realized what he was looking for. "You were already going to offer to stay with me, weren't you, even before the doctor said anything? Why?"

"Because Marcos asked me to."

Ah, yes. His brother, the saint. Sophia would never have agreed to do it on her own, evidently.

Even though he knew his waspish reaction was childish, he couldn't help it. Lucas had often felt guilty over the years, wondering if his brother had been adopted as well. Finding out he hadn't been…that he'd spent most of his childhood in that orphanage…was hard to swallow. He had no idea why his folks hadn't taken them both, and by the time he'd been old enough to have asked, he'd rarely thought of the life he'd left behind in Brazil. And what memories he'd had weren't ones that would make him proud.

And yet he'd permanently inscribed his father's name on his arm, along with a rod of Asclepius and the words "Promises Kept" written beneath it. He did remember both he and his brother promising their father they'd become doctors—that they'd make him feel better. Of course they hadn't been able to keep the last part of that promise. Their father had died, leaving them orphans.

To take his mind off those morbid thoughts, he slid off the bed and stood. "Well, since you seem determined to stay at the apartment, I do have one rule about this whole setup."

"And what's that?" Sophia stood as well.

"I don't want any help in the bathroom. So if you could leave me to my own devices when I'm in there, I'd appreciate it."

Her eyes went wide. "Tell me you don't do drugs."

What the hell?

"Of course not. Where'd you get that idea?"

"If you don't want anyone near the bathroom while you're there…"

"Because I intend to bathe and…" he shrugged "…do whatever else I need to do all by myself. I don't need your help."

A little scoffing sound came from her lips. "You might surprise yourself and actually *ask* for my help."

That rogue part of him began stirring right on cue, forcing him to shift his stance.

*She's not helping you with anything, you idiot. The doctor—and Marcos—want her there in the event you have an aneurism or something.*

Which might be now, actually, because he was desperately trying to keep his mind off the tightening sensation in his groin that just wouldn't let up.

If she didn't hurry and get him some pants, he was going to embarrass both of them. "Let's just agree to play it by ear for the next couple of days. Now, if you could send me in the general direction of my clothes…"

"Oh, about that…"

She seemed flustered all of a sudden. Or maybe it was just his imagination.

"Is there a problem?"

"Yes. Kind of." She made a production of sliding the chair back against the wall. When she faced him again, her face was back to that delicious pink color he was beginning to enjoy. "You don't actually have any clothes."

# CHAPTER FOUR

"WHAT DO YOU mean, I don't have any clothes?"

Lucas's narrowed eyes made her want to take a step back but she forced herself to hold her ground. "You were shot, remember? Twice. You were bleeding profusely when you arrived, and we had to...cut them off."

She expected him to focus in on the last part of her sentence, but instead his gaze sharpened. "*We* had to?"

Licking her lips, she tried to explain. "I don't mean we, literally. I mean the team who worked on you."

"I see."

Did he? Because he sure didn't act like it. She didn't understand why he was so upset all of a sudden. He acted like they'd done something obscene to him while he'd been lying helpless on that table. "I assure you everyone acted professionally."

"Were you there?"

"Well, no, but—"

"You weren't?" The line of his jaw relaxed so suddenly that she found her own muscles untensing as well.

"No. None of us knew who you were when you arrived." She hurried to add, "That 'us' is also figurative."

"It's okay." He gave a half-shake of his head that seemed self-deprecating, his mouth twisting into a half-smile. And just like that his mood shifted back toward that of the charmingly flippant man who'd strolled toward her desk less than a week ago. The man whose ass she'd never quite got a good look at. "But I don't think I should leave the hospital like this, do you?"

Her own lips curved. "It didn't seem to bother you before. You're lucky we didn't have any cardiac patients milling around."

Just then, the sound of some kind of commotion made its way through the heavy metal door, along with a shout. Sophia straightened, her head turning toward the noise.

*"Socorro!"*

The desperate cry for help grabbed her.

She threw a glance at Lucas. "Wait here."

Pulling the door open in a rush, she saw a man standing at the nurses' station wearing a gown just like Lucas's, only he was holding something…waving it around. She couldn't tell what it was. But what she *did* see turned her blood to ice. He'd grabbed the nurse on the other side of the desk by her wrist and looked like he was physically trying to drag her over the barrier. Then Sophia caught a glint from the thing he held in his other hand. A scalpel!

*Deus!*

She rushed forward, yelling at one of the other patients who'd peeked out of his room, "Dial 111! Tell Security we need someone up here now."

It was lunchtime and most of the doctors had already done their rounds so there weren't a lot of people on the floor at the moment. She shouted at the crazed patient, "Let her go."

Judging by the yelp that came from the other nurse, the man squeezed even tighter. "Stay back! This one's infected. I can see it in her face."

What?

Her eyes went to Paulina, whose skin was as white as a sheet, her free hand digging at the man's fingers, trying to get him off her. Luckily the scalpel was waving aimlessly in the air, the patient didn't seem to be actively trying to cut her.

Yet. Who knew what he might do next?

This man had to be disturbed...or high. In fact, there was a long line of stitches over his right eye and in spite of the clean hospital gown he wore, his socks were filthy and crusted with blood. Had he been in a fight? Was he drunk?

She took a few more steps, circling around the man, only to hear him growl low in his throat when she ventured too close. "It's okay," she said, deciding to play along. "We know all about the infection. She's taking medication for it."

"You're lying!" A few drops of spittle flew from between his lips.

Out of the corner of her eye she spied Lucas, who'd somehow come down the hallway on silent feet and was easing toward them. One turn of the crazed man's head and he'd see him as well. Sophia didn't dare gesture for him to get back. Besides, she was damned glad to see him, even though she'd told him to stay put. And although it seemed like hours, less than a minute had passed since she'd asked the patient to call for help.

Lucas was now about twenty feet away.

Trying to maintain eye contact with the patient, she eased further to the left, glad when the man's unblinking gaze followed her movement. It reminded her of a cobra, ready to strike at the first hint of weakness.

"I'm not lying," she murmured in as soothing a voice as she could manage. "Her hair has light streaks of color in it. It means the treatments are working."

*Are you insane, Sophia? What are you trying to do?*

Keep him busy. Until someone could get to them. Anything to stop that scalpel from slicing through the air and hurting Paulina.

The patient's lips thinned as his feverish gaze tripped from her to Paulina and then back again. The fingers holding the deadly weapon trembled for a second or two. "I don't see anything."

"Because you're not a doctor. You're not trained to."

Just then, Lucas succeeded in covering the last few feet that separated them and grabbed the man's knife hand. An enormous roar came up from the patient's chest. He released Paulina and pivoted with lightning speed toward Lucas. Sophia lunged forward and caught the guy's other hand to keep him from twisting the rest of the way round. The man was as strong as an ox. He threw her backwards, sending her skidding across the floor, where she flailed as she tried to maintain her balance—only to fail miserably and land on her butt.

She scrambled back up just as the sound of tinkling metal hit her ears, along with Lucas's grunt of pain when the man's fingers closed around a fistful of his hair and hung on. Before she could run toward them again, two men in uniforms stepped out of the elevator, took one look at the scene and charged, each man grabbing a gowned figure and wrestling them apart.

"Dammit! Let me go!"

The oath came from Lucas, who was now pinned securely in front of one of the guards, one elbow locked behind him, while the injured arm dangled awkwardly, the sling bunched along his forearm. Amazingly, the troublemaker had gone totally limp once subdued, moaning as if mortally wounded. He looked like the victim, rather than the guilty party.

As she put a hand to her throat and struggled to catch her breath, one of the guards glanced expectantly at her. "Which one did you call us about?"

"The one on the left."

Poor Lucas looked like he'd been through the wringer. His hair stood straight up where the other man had grabbed it and his gown had twisted sideways, revealing quite a bit of one taut thigh.

Releasing him, the guard said, "What happened?"

"That man attacked Paulina, yelling about some kind of infection."

Just then a woman exited a second elevator and rushed toward them, followed by one of the emergency room doctors.

"Please don't hurt him. I'm his sister," she said. "He's schizophrenic. I didn't realize he was off his meds until this morning when I found him covered in blood, saying someone was after him. I lost track of him in the emergency room."

The doctor nodded. "He wasn't particularly agitated when he arrived. I stepped out to call his psychiatrist, who's on his way. It'll take him about ten minutes to get here."

His sister spoke up. "I'm so sorry about all of this. My mother called and I left the room for just a second to talk to her." She glanced at Lucas and then evidently spied the scalpel on the floor. "Oh, no. Did he hurt someone?"

"No, we stopped him in time," Sophia said. The woman seemed so genuinely upset that she didn't have the heart to tell her just how serious the situation had been. And from the look of the man now, you'd never guess he'd just gone on a rampage. She could understand why they'd let their guard down.

Besides, even with all the precautions in the world, you couldn't always stop bad things from happening. She knew that for a fact. Look at Marcos and Lucas. Or even her own childhood, for that matter.

The doctor turned to the guard who'd been holding Lucas. "Could you accompany us back to the emergency wing? I'd appreciate it."

Within minutes they'd bundled the patient, whose name was evidently Ronaldo, into a wheelchair and got back into the elevator, his sister holding his hand.

Sophia sent Paulina a shaky smile. "Are you okay?"

The nurse chuckled and pressed a hand to her chest. "Other than wondering if he was going to carve out my heart and eat it, yes. Thank you for coming when you did." Her gaze went to Lucas, who leaned against the counter. "And thank you for wrestling that scalpel away from him."

Sophia realized Lucas wasn't just leaning against the nurses' station, he was propped against it as if he'd fall to the floor if he let go. "Hey. Are you hurt?"

"You mean besides my pride?"

His pride. What did that have to do with anything?

"You made him let go of the knife."

"And if those guards hadn't gotten here when they had, that's about all I would have done."

Shock whistled through her. He acted like he'd just let the opposing team score the winning goal of the season.

She moved over to him and laid a hand on his arm. "What are you talking about? You disarmed him, Lucas. You saw how he threw me across the room like a toy. If you hadn't stepped in to help, who knows what damage he could have caused?" She frowned. "Speaking of damage, how are your stitches?"

"They're not happy, but they're still there. I'll be glad when the damned things come out."

Paulina wheeled an office chair around the desk and put it behind him. "Sit, before you fall down."

"I'm fine." Despite his words, he carefully lowered himself into the chair. Was he really okay? Or just saying that for her and Paulina's benefit?

"How about your side? Did he get you?"

"No. Believe me, I was keeping everything of value as far out of the reach of that scalpel as I could."

Paulina giggled at the words, although it took Sophia a second or two to get his meaning. Then her face heated in a rush, and her glance instinctively dropped to his lap. "Oh."

"Yeah. As it was, no harm done." He dragged a hand through his hair, pausing to rub the area of his scalp where the patient had pulled his hair. "I'll give you this, Nurse Limeira, you sure do run an exciting ward here."

She laughed. "All in a day's work, Dr. Carvalho."

He sighed and leaned back in the chair, closing his eyes for a second or two.

Hmm, the man really did look a bit shaky. Maybe it was time to get him out of there. "Are you still feeling well enough to be discharged today? Or do you want to stick around for one more night?"

"And risk another scene like that one?" He shook his head. "I think I'm more than ready to leave. A nice—*quiet*—apartment is sounding better and better."

She glanced at Paulina, who seemed positively starstruck by Lucas, even going as far as to twirl a strand of her bleached-blonde hair around her index finger as she watched him.

Even injured, he had the same effect on other women that he'd had on her when she'd been little. A tiny part of her wondered if she was the only one he'd forgotten. Maybe he didn't remember any woman he'd had contact with. He was handsome enough that he could have his pick—just look at Paulina. And maybe he did just that. Maybe he went through them so fast that none of them made a lasting impression.

Her mood took a sudden nosedive. She needed to remember her earlier admonition to steer clear of him as much as possible. Not that it was going to be possible as she'd volunteered to sleep over. If it weren't for her longstanding friendship with Marcos, she wouldn't have offered in the first place. But she had, and she felt obligated to go through with it.

Well, just because she had to sleep *near* him, it didn't mean she was going to sleep *with* him.

She blinked. Why had that thought even come up?

Maybe because she'd gotten a good glimpse of rock-hard thighs and a nice tight tushie during the struggle with Ronaldo.

Yep, visions of sponge baths were now dancing through her head.

Well, there'd be none of that. Not here. Not at Marcos's apartment. She was simply there to make sure the man didn't fall and suffer a concussion.

Although if he didn't wipe that knowing smirk off his face, a concussion wasn't out of the realm of possibilities. And she'd be the one inflicting it.

She stepped in front of Paulina in an effort to snap the

woman back to reality. "Well, I guess that's settled. Before we have any more mishaps, maybe we should find you something to wear and get you out of here."

## CHAPTER FIVE

AT LEAST HE didn't have to wear his brother's clothes.

Lucas knew it was a strange thing to be thankful for, but he was borrowing his brother's apartment, sleeping in his brother's bed, and making use of his brother's friend.

No. She was *their* friend. At least, from what Marcos had told him.

Damn, if only he could remember.

Right now, Sophia was brewing coffee in his brother's kitchen as if she'd done it a million times. That thought made him uneasy and he wasn't sure why.

He should be grateful for all she was doing for him. And he was. After all, she'd gone to his hotel and arranged for his things to be taken to Marcos's place. And he hadn't had to watch her actually carry his stuff into the building while he'd trailed along behind.

Unlike her own suitcase. Which he'd been painfully aware he couldn't offer to carry. It made him feel useless, something he wasn't used to.

Perched on his brother's couch, the scent of coffee hit his nose, and he breathed deeply as he surveyed his surroundings. Modern furnishings, almost painfully so, were strategically placed, from the black leather sofa and swivel recliner to the low black cabinet where a flatscreen television sat at eye level. A photo to the left of the set caught his attention.

Struggling to his feet while trying to ignore the fierce burning in his shoulder—a direct result of the scuffle at the hospital—he moved toward the picture.

"Do you want *café com leite*? Or do you take your coffee black?" Sophia's voice came from behind him, distracting him for a second, and when he turned his head he found her peeking around the corner, a few locks of sleek black hair sliding over one bare shoulder as she leaned to the side. She flipped the strands back with a quick shake of her head, leaving a long line of tanned skin that seemed to call out to him.

Damn. He knew she had a shirt on, he'd seen it—some kind of fluttery green thing that wrapped around her just above the swell of her breasts. There were no straps, though, so right now all he could think about was how she'd look if she stood in that exact pose *without* the shirt. And, boy, could his imagination drum up a pretty good set of possibilities.

"Lucas?" she said. "What do you want in your coffee?"

Besides you?

He shook himself back to reality. "Just a couple of drops of sweetener, if Marcos has any." Artificial sweetener in Brazil came in plastic bottles, he'd found, although some of the higher-end coffee shops carried packets of the stuff, along with sugar.

"Okay, I'll be out in a minute." A quick smile accompanied the words, and she popped back into the kitchen.

Lucas braced a hand on the television stand, swearing softly. He probably should have suggested that he hole up in his hotel room for another couple of weeks. *Had* suggested it, in fact, once his discharge papers had been written up, but Sophia had held him to his promise of letting her help—compliments of his brother. Again. The tattoo on his arm was a constant reminder that he kept his word when at all possible. He hadn't been able to keep much of anything else in his life—not even his real last name—so it was the one thing he'd felt he had control over.

So he was stuck with her. For now.

Brazilian women tended to dress to accentuate their curves, and Sophia was no exception. There was no way he was going to tell her to change for his benefit. But he also hadn't expected to be knocked for a loop by seeing her out of her customary scrubs either.

The slim white jeans she wore hugged her body, cupping her curves in all the right places. Then there was that blouse, the deep green fabric snug on top before floating down around her hips, the silky fabric molding to her form whenever she moved. It was almost long enough to be a dress—a teeny-tiny one. And those heels…

*Whew.*

Despite the sexy clothes, there was a youthful innocence to Sophia, although he couldn't quite put his finger on why she gave off that vibe. It wasn't that she was a child—he shifted his aching shoulder as he turned back toward the framed photo on the television table—far from it. But there was a certain *joie de vivre* that clung to her as tightly as her narrow slacks. Strange that she would give off that kind of glow, despite growing up in a bare bones orphanage. Or after what she must have gone through with her facial surgery.

The narrow scar on her lip had made something contract inside him. Maybe because he spent almost all of his vacation time treating children in developing countries with just that type of deformity. The fact that Sophia bore the telltale mark of a surgeon's tools made his heart cramp.

There was something about the scar that struck a chord deep inside him. And touching it as she'd stood behind the desk at the nurses' station had triggered a visceral reaction that had been both foreign and familiar. Those two sensations had warred within him for several seconds. Had he remembered the scar from their time together at the orphanage?

Possibly.

It wasn't a real memory, per se, more a remembered emotion. Curiosity, maybe? It hadn't been disgust. Far from it. But it seemed to mesh with his reasons for choosing pediatric reconstructive surgeries over the more lucrative types.

Pulling his focus back to the picture, he picked it up. Two adults and two children were grouped around a rickety handcart. The image was real. Not one of those staged, stick-your-head-through-the-cardboard-figure kind of thing he saw from time to time. He narrowed his eyes and tried to see the details past the sepia tones and the midline crack where the picture had evidently been folded at one time. A man stood at the metal bar across the front of the contraption and held the cart level, while a woman and baby perched on the flat bed, and the older child with a grubby T-shirt and worn flip-flops stood with his hands on his hips, legs braced apart.

Lucas swallowed. It was them—his birth family—he knew it even without being told. His mom held him close in a protective gesture, while his brother dared the world to mess with any of them.

His father already looked broken down, even back then. Staring at the picture, he tried to sense some kind of emotional connection with the figures, but felt only a vague sense of shame, which was probably left over from days gone by. His brother's feet were the only thing that elicited a strong reaction in him. He had shoes on, while his own feet were bare. He did remember snatches of arguments he and his brother had had—with Marcos constantly railing at him for not wearing shoes in the yard.

He still preferred his feet bare, not that he got much of a chance any more with his busy lifestyle.

A soft click sounded behind him and then Sophia's voice came again. "That's you and Marcos with your parents."

The fact that Sophia didn't expect him to know what he was looking at sent another wave of shame washing over him. His adoptive parents had said they'd chosen him because the day they'd visited he'd been curled in a corner, sucking his thumb. He'd been skin and bones, and had seemed hopeless, they'd said…so much so that it had frightened them. They'd never thought about having kids of their own—although they'd worked with several children's charities—until they'd seen him.

They'd given him opportunities that few kids in his situation would have ever dreamed of having. And that just compounded his guilt, even though Marcos and Sophia seemed to be doing just fine, judging by the high-end furniture in his brother's apartment. In fact, the picture was the only shabby-looking thing in sight.

He set the frame back in its spot and turned toward her. "I'll have to ask Marcos to make a copy for me."

"Do you remember them at all?"

He hesitated. "I think I remember my father and Marcos, but not my birth mother."

"She died when you were still a baby." She reached back and bunched her long hair in her hand, then twisted it and tied it somehow so that it stayed up off her neck. "Your parents loved you very much, from what Marcos says. Your adoptive family must have as well."

"They did. I guess I was lucky."

He'd called them, in fact, after the shooting. They'd been worried sick, had wanted to come down immediately, but he'd assured them he was fine and would be back in the States soon.

Sophia turned away and walked to the glossy coffee table. "I brought the bottle of sweetener and a spoon. I wasn't sure how much you wanted."

Her words were tight, and he got the feeling he'd said something wrong. Was she upset because he'd been adopted and she hadn't? Surely not. He'd had no choice in the matter. Looking back, though, he could certainly see how hard it must've been for Marcos to be the one left behind. But he was glad his brother had been there for Sophia.

"Thank you for the coffee." Following her, he noted one of the clear glass mugs was filled almost to the brim, while the other was only half-full. He found out why when Sophia tipped a white pitcher of milk into the one with less coffee. He smiled. "When you say *café com leite*, you mean it."

"Brazilian coffee is stronger than what you serve in the States, at least from what I've heard."

A barista at a local coffee shop had jokingly referred to American coffee as "*água suja*" or dirty water. And compared to the dark, full brew that most Brazilians preferred, he could see why.

Sophia settled onto the sofa and took a sip of her drink with a sigh.

You could tell the apartment belonged to a bachelor by the lack of seating options. It was either sit beside her or try to perch on the low-slung easy chair to the right of it. And his side still bothered him enough that he chose the sofa over his sense of self-preservation. So once he'd doctored his coffee, he sat next to her, waiting for the surgical sites to settle down before he took his first slug.

The dark liquid was smooth, with a slightly bitter after-taste that lingered on his palate the way good coffee should. He closed his eyes and let the scent and taste fill his senses. "I'm glad I didn't drink the hospital's coffee before I left. This was worth the wait."

She smiled at him and bumped his uninjured shoulder with hers before kicking off her heels and curling deeper into the sofa. "I'm glad you like it. And thanks again for your help with that patient. I was worried you'd ripped your stitches."

"Does that kind of thing happen often?"

"No more than at any other hospital, I suppose. You've never had a patient go berserk on you?"

"My patients are generally a lot smaller than that one."

Her lips twisted. "That's right, most of yours are probably women who are looking for a tune-up."

"Actually, no. I work with children. I'm a pediatric plastic surgeon. I deal with..." He swallowed at what he'd been about to say and changed the words slightly. "Facial reconstructive surgery, usually after a traumatic injury."

Her finger went to her lip, the way it had a number of other times. Surely she wasn't self-conscious about it. No one but a surgeon who dealt with cleft lips on a regular basis would be aware of her scar. "Why do you do that?"

She didn't ask what he meant. "Maybe because you noticed it right away."

"I didn't. Only after you touched it that first day." He wasn't about to tell her he hadn't been looking at her lip when he'd seen her at the desk. Or that there'd been something about her that had drawn him toward her, as it did even now.

He'd thought it had been because he'd recognized her from her earlier visits, but who knew? His head had still been pretty foggy about the shooting and what had happened afterwards. Maybe he could tackle that. Get her talking so he could keep his mind off the fact that he was seated beside a beautiful woman—all alone in his brother's house. And that he couldn't seem to stop staring at her lips—not because of her scar but because they were pink and inviting and...

And he had to put a stop to this right now.

"Did the police tell you anything else about what happened?"

She shook her head. "Marcos said you were standing in front of the *favela* where you both lived as kids. The police were involved in a drug raid, and a couple of the dealers' shots hit you as they tried to evade capture."

He should remember something more about that time—like how he'd even known where he'd once lived—but it was still a blank for the most part. "That's what the police told me as well. I just can't remember."

"It happened fast, from what I understand. Didn't the doctor say your memories should come back after a while? You banged your head pretty hard on the pavement when you went down. Unfortunately the taxi driver took off once he heard the shots, so the police had to step in. Maybe they'll find the driver and you can ask him how you ended up there." She shifted on the couch so she faced him.

"Maybe." He took another sip of coffee, trying to use the strong fragrance to blot out the more subtle scents of vanilla and flowers that drifted his way whenever she moved.

Perfume or body wash?

Perfume. It was the safer option as he really didn't want to picture her hands sliding in long soapy strokes over her body.

Hell! He'd just pictured it anyway.

"At least something good came of it," she said, her hand wandering from her knee to her ankle and curling around it. "You found your brother."

There was a hint of shadow in her tone, and Lucas wished to God he could remember her. Wished he'd been around to watch her grow into the gorgeous woman she was today. Then maybe he wouldn't be so floored every time those expressive brown eyes met his. Like right now.

"There is that." He set his coffee on the table. "So you didn't know I was a pediatric plastic surgeon?"

"Nope." She laughed. "I thought you spent your days looking at…" She let go of her ankle and waved a hand in a kind of winding motion over her chest.

Yeah, well, it seemed like he'd spent an inordinate amount of time over the last couple of days looking at just that area. And her reminding him of that fact wasn't helping an increasingly uncomfortable situation that was beginning to arise.

Fast.

"Ah…no. That never appealed to me at all." His vision shrank to a pinpoint when he realized how that sounded. "Not that I'm opposed to those who might want to…I mean, I like them and all."

Her brows lifted and she laughed. "Maybe you should quit while you're ahead."

"Maybe I should." His mouth curved as well.

They smiled at each other for a second or two then she licked her lips, drawing his attention back to them once again. "You seemed to have made a fan of Paulina this afternoon."

"Paulina?"

"The nurse who helped you sit down."

"Ah." The way she'd said it bothered him, for some reason. "I didn't make a fan of you, I take it."

"You're Marcos's brother. I don't need to be your fan."

Perfect. Just what he needed, a reminder that she was only here because of his brother, not because she found him the slightest bit attractive.

His masculinity took another hit. First, he was still as weak as a kitten, having had to be carted out of the hospital in a damned wheelchair. Then he'd been unable to even help Sophia carry her things into the building when they'd arrived. She'd had to prop him up with one arm while lugging her purse and overnight case with the other.

And now this.

"So what would it take to make you a fan, Sophia?"

"I don't know what you mean."

He tilted his head and studied her. "You don't like me very much, do you?"

"Of course I do. I'm here, aren't I?" Was that genuine surprise in her voice?

"But you're only here because of Marcos."

"I... I..." She paused as if unsure of what to say. Then she set down her coffee and reached over to touch his hand. "I'd have probably offered to help, even if he hadn't asked."

He curved his fingers around hers before she could withdraw. "Would you?"

Why was it so important to him that she wanted to be here? Maybe because this country—his homeland—made him feel like a stranger. In fact, he'd heard Sophia use that very word when she'd talked to his brother.

Her eyes held his, and she made no effort to tug her hand free. "I think so."

"So would you call yourself a fan?"

"Would you call *yourself* one?"

His fingers tightened at the faint challenge he heard in her voice. "Definitely. I think you have a lot of fans, though. My brother being one of them."

"I think you have quite a few yourself. Especially after strolling down the hallway and leaving very little to the imagination. Are you always so uninhibited?"

"Uninhibited?" He cocked a brow. "It depends on the situation."

Sophia's lips parted, giving him a glimpse of straight white teeth, and she hesitated as if trying to figure out how to respond. "You were feeling uninhibited at the hospital?"

The atmosphere in the room became thick, heating quickly. "Hmm. Maybe you have that effect on me."

"I doubt that."

"You underestimate yourself, Sophia." He released her hand and brushed a loose strand of hair back over her shoulder, his palm grazing her bare skin. It was just as silky soft as he'd imagined, and her rough intake of breath at his touch made his insides ignite. "In fact, I feel like doing something a little crazy right now. Something wild and uninhibited."

He went on, "I remember you called Security on the last guy who did something like that."

"Does what you want to do involve a scalpel?"

"No. No scalpels. But it does involve lips. Yours and mine." He upped the ante a notch, letting his fingers slide along her jaw until he cupped her chin and looked deep into her eyes. "So are you going to call Security on me, Sophia? Or can I kiss you?"

She shook her head.

He smiled. "Does that mean you're not going to scream for help? Or are you saying no to me kissing you?"

There was silence for several tense seconds, and he thought at first she was going to pull away. Then she took a deep breath.

"I won't call Security," she whispered.

"Oh, honey," he said as tiny clusters of heat burst into flame throughout his body. "I was so hoping that's what you'd say."

# CHAPTER SIX

H<small>E'D</small> <small>GIVEN HER</small> plenty of warning, but nothing could have prepared her for this.

The second Lucas's lips closed over hers, her heart stumbled into a rhythm so chaotic she could swear she was going into V-tach. Any second now a monitor would start sounding an alarm and everyone would come running.

Only there was no one else here. Just her…and Lucas. And this exquisite, soul-shattering kiss. One that was nothing more than the barest touching of lips but it was more than she'd ever imagined a kiss could be.

More than it ever had been. With anyone.

His fingers sifted into her hair, the messy knot soon giving way and sending everything cascading down her back as he held her in place. But if he was worried about her moving away, he needn't be. Sophia had no intention of going anywhere.

Not yet.

Maybe not ever.

Her hands went to his shoulders and curled over them for several seconds, unsure how far he planned to take this. Testing the waters, she slid them further up until she reached his nape, then went on past, until her arms were around his neck.

He made a sound, halfway between a groan and a growl, and Sophia started to pull back in a hurry, thinking she was hurting him, only to have his fingers tighten in her hair.

His good arm suddenly snaked around her waist and hauled her closer.

Oh!

Thigh to thigh, torsos twisted towards each other, Lucas finally opened his mouth. Really opened it and swept her away on a wave of longing so strong she had trouble breathing. Or that could just be the way her body was contorted.

He pulled back, lips trailing slowly towards her ear, sending a shiver over her that turned to a shudder when he whispered, "Kiss me back, Sophia."

What? She thought she had been.

No, that wasn't really true. She'd been wallowing in the heady reality that what she'd thought was an unreachable daydream wasn't so far out of the realm of possibility after all.

He *was* attracted to her. Even if he couldn't remember who she was.

Maybe it was better that way. Because the last thing she wanted right now was for him to treat her like a child.

When his mouth landed back on hers, her thoughts were buried beneath the sudden hot pressure of his lips as he urged her to keep up with him—to give back some of what she was receiving. So she parted her own lips and buried her fingers in the thick hair at the back of his head.

It wasn't long before his tongue found hers and slid along it, edging deeper and deeper until he filled her completely. A moan worked its way up from the lowest regions of her abdomen and came out before she could stop it. Not that she wanted to.

No. She wanted this. All of it. Wanted more.

Her eyes sealed shut, trying to lock out everything but the feel of him inside her. All around her. His scent, his heat.

And, God, he was only kissing her. What would happen if they actually…?

She'd wind up on life support probably.

Lucas shifted slightly, and her eyes blinked open as he drew back with a soft curse.

"What is it?" she murmured.

"My damn side."

She pulled away. "Oh, I'm sorry."

"No, stop. Don't go anywhere." He touched one of her legs. "Here, climb on top of me so I don't have to twist to reach you."

"Excuse me?"

He grinned, a flash of white teeth. "Ready to call for that rescue team now?"

She licked her lips. Climb on top of him. Like how? Surely he didn't mean for her to lie on him. If his side hurt now, she could only imagine what it would be like if she put any pressure on it. "I'm not sure—"

Leaning back on the sofa, he took hold of her hands then his fingers slid up her arms. "Straddle me. I promise I won't go any further than a kiss."

She gulped. Maybe that life-support idea wasn't so far-fetched after all.

As if he could read her thoughts, he continued, "Just sit on my knees. I'll let you keep as much distance between us as you want. But I'm not quite ready to let you go yet. Unless you want me to."

No. She didn't.

Sophia knew she was going to sorely regret this as soon as her libido had a chance to cool down, but she wasn't ready to stop yet either. Uncurling her legs and rising to her knees, she swung one leg over his thighs and started to lower herself, only to have his hands tighten on her upper arms. She glanced down to find his smoldering eyes locked on her face. "Slowly. Let me imagine."

*Deus.* She knew exactly what he was imagining, and her face flamed with a heat that threatened to consume her. But she did as he asked and inched her way down, until the backs of her thighs grazed his legs. She allowed her weight to settle, realizing that because of the way his hips were slouched forward, she wasn't exactly sitting on his knees. But then again she was at least six inches away from any dangerous areas. And she didn't mean his injured side.

Her hands went to the back of the sofa to brace herself, and she leaned forward to kiss him again. His palms cupped her face before she could get there, his thumb traveling in a slow arc down her scar. "You're beautiful, you know. If anything, this just adds to it."

She'd never had anyone talk so openly about her lip—an area of her body she was self-conscious about. And yet Lucas hadn't hesitated either time. He'd gone right to the spot most people tried to ignore—or maybe they really didn't notice.

Something about the way he touched it wove a silky web of desire that slowly tightened around her. "Kiss me," she said, handing his own words back to him.

Pupils widened as his thumb continued to stroke over her skin with velvety passes. "I'm right here, honey."

Whether it was because of his injuries or because he was throwing down a challenge to see if she would accept it, she arched her brows and allowed herself to slide a few inches forward on his legs.

Big mistake, because the friction just made things inside her narrow their focus, a dangerous melting beginning to take place.

"Not fair, Sophia."

He wasn't kidding. Her body was saying pretty much the same thing.

Trying to hold onto her new-found bravado, she murmured, "Very fair."

What the hell was she doing? She was straddling a man she barely knew. A couple more wiggles and she'd be into lap-dance territory.

He chuckled. "I guess it is." Using the hands that were still on her face, he drew her towards him until there was only an inch of space between them. "You, young lady, are a very dangerous woman. You're also a very, very lucky one at the moment."

She could agree on the lucky part. *Now do it!*

Instead of kissing her, however, he curled an arm around her back and settled her against his good shoulder, his hand sliding up and down her spine in a slow, soothing cadence that did anything but calm her. She blinked in confusion as his breath whispered past her ear and stirred strands of her hair.

There was still some space between their bottom halves, and she was tempted to move forward again just to see what was going on. Then the hand at her back hesitated, before moving again. Slower this time. It paused again, then took longer to start back up.

When the sound of his breathing changed—deepened—she knew the awful truth even before his palm gave one last downward pass and went completely still.

The man had fallen asleep.


The smell of bacon made his nose twitch.

He opened his eyes to find he was still on the sofa, but lying on his back, shoes off, a light blanket pulled over him. And the firm, luscious bottom that he remembered resting on his thighs was nowhere to be found.

He'd conked out? Unbelievable.

He'd been in the middle of the hottest damn kiss of his life, everything had seemed to be up and working like it should, and he'd just passed out in the middle of it. He'd been planning on keeping his promise of just kissing her, but he'd hoped to enjoy it a little bit longer. In fact, that was why he'd *stopped* kissing her. He'd needed to give himself a moment or two of downtime to combat the way his senses had gone haywire as her butt had slid across his legs. That downtime had turned into hours, if the light pouring through the sliding glass door to his left was anything to go by.

He cranked himself upright with a groan as tight muscles protested the movement.

Hell. He'd probably never get the chance to take up where they'd left off. It was surprising that Sophia hadn't just left him sitting upright in a pool of his own drool. Instead, there was a pillow with a light blue pillowcase where his head had just been. She'd evidently climbed off him and, ever the dutiful nurse, had made sure he was taken care of before she went to bed.

He blinked. Well at least he remembered what had happened last night. Mostly. Up until the part where his eyelids had come together and sealed shut. He remembered his thumb brushing across Sophia's scar repeatedly, the act once again strangely familiar. Comforting in a weird kind of way.

Yes, it was weird. And she probably didn't appreciate him drawing her attention to it over and over. It was intrusive and rude.

His already foul mood headed further south.

He shook himself out of his thoughts just as she peeked around the corner, the sensation of *déjà vu* growing until he remembered she'd done the same thing yesterday.

"Oh, good," she said. "You're awake. Do you need any help?"

He scrubbed a hand through his hair. "Hell, I'm sorry about last night. I don't know what I was thinking—"

A wooden spoon appeared around the corner, waving off his words. "You've just gotten out of the hospital. I had no business getting on your... I had no business doing any of that. I hope you'll forgive me."

*Forgive* her? She was acting like she'd breached some kind of professional barrier and was struggling to get back behind it.

"You're not my nurse, Sophia."

"I'm responsible for you." Even from his perch he thought he spied a glimmer of guilt in her brown eyes.

"No. You're here to make sure I don't fall and crack my head wide open."

"Exactly."

Said as if that settled everything. It didn't. It settled nothing, and a burning in his gut was now rivaling the growing pressure in his bladder. So he hauled himself up and off the sofa, ignoring the sharp pull in his side as he did so. It took Sophia's soft gasp for him to realize—far too late—that his slacks were undone, his fly stationed at the lowermost part of its track.

He looked down, his brain struggling to process the consequences of her not bringing any briefs to the hospital when she'd brought his clothes: he was now standing here in front of her...in all his questionable morning glory.

*Damn.* Maybe his memory of the events surrounding that kiss weren't as clear as he'd thought. But surely he'd have remembered if they'd...

He quickly zipped himself back in then his glance came up, eyes narrowing. "What exactly did we do last night?"

# CHAPTER SEVEN

"WE DIDN'T DO anything!"

Sophia's face sizzled like the bacon she could hear in the background as she tried to look anywhere but below Lucas's waist.

Several large pops, followed by angry hissing and sputtering came from behind her, and she ducked back into the kitchen, more than glad to scoot away from the memory of his bare…

Okay, he hadn't exactly been sticking out of his pants when she'd undone him last night.

Rescuing the strips of bacon before they burned to a crisp, she laid them out on a paper towel as she tried to get the image of what she'd just witnessed out of her mind. She failed miserably. The shocked look in his eyes. The alarmed *zzzzip* as he'd yanked the tab of his fly back up.

She'd been trying to do him a favor last night, not wanting the tight waistband to damage the stitches in his side as he slept. She'd forgotten he didn't have on underwear, but then again…she hadn't peeled his pants apart to look. She'd just covered him up with a blanket and that had been that.

It certainly had. Because he'd *fallen asleep*!

It still stung that not only was she not memorable as a person, she wasn't even interesting enough as a potential lover to hold his attention…during a kiss that *he* had initiated. Okay, that wasn't fair, he had still been weak from the trauma of the gunshots followed by blood loss and then surgery. Of course he'd been tired.

*You'd have done the same thing, Sophia.*

She'd just about convinced herself of that when he appeared in the kitchen doorway a few minutes later, his hair damp from an apparent shower and dressed in fresh clothes. Firmly zipped, she noticed. The stiff way he held his left arm as he leaned against the doorframe said that whatever he'd done in the bathroom had cost him dearly.

"You should have waited for me to help you. That's why the doctor asked me to stay, remember?"

"I think you've helped quite enough already." His mouth tightened slightly. "I'm still waiting for what promises to be a very interesting explanation."

"No explanation needed. You fell asleep, and I didn't want to undress you all the way, so I settled for opening…"

Okay, well, that hadn't come out exactly right.

One brow went up. "I'm regretting nodding off more and more."

Despite the tension still radiating off him, the words came out with a trace of lazy humor. The last thing Sophia wanted, however, was for him to think she'd ogled him in his sleep. Or worse.

"I was only thinking about the stitches on your abdomen."

"That's not what I was thinking about at all. Especially last night."

Right. She could tell. Which was why he hadn't been able to keep his eyes open long enough to kiss her again.

She couldn't stop herself from handing back a waspish reply. "I unzipped you so that you would be more comfortable. Satisfied? So now that we have that settled, if you think you can sit upright long enough to eat your food—without falling asleep and landing face first in it—I have bacon and eggs ready."

With that, she plunked his plate onto the small dinette table, unwound the dishtowel from around her neck and dropped it onto the countertop beside her. She then stalked off to get her own shower. And to set her muddled brain back on the right track before the long day ahead of her…and to hopefully keep it off the most perfect piece of male anatomy she'd ever seen.

*Round and round and round she goes, where she stops nobody knows.*

Lucas felt like he'd been pedaling the ergometer for hours, his hands moving in slow painful circles, his shoulder catching at a certain spot with every turn of the wheel. Where the hell was that physical therapist anyway? He'd hoped to at least have a couple more days to rest before Sophia dragged him down to the rehab center to start on his recovery regimen. He had a feeling it was because she didn't want to leave him in Marcos's apartment by himself.

What exactly did she expect him to do? Pitch head first off the balcony and land on the sidewalk below?

She was taking the doctor's orders a little too seriously. Besides, she'd been tense and irritable all morning, and he had no idea why. He suspected it had something to do with what had happened between them last night, but when he'd tried to talk about it on the short drive over to the hospital, she'd shut him down before he'd got six words out.

Surely she didn't want to forget that kiss ever happened, because he sure didn't.

It had been hot and wet and erotic. And that had been before she'd even opened her mouth and let him in.

After that…

He'd been a goner, because between her lips lay the thing a man's dreams were made of. So slick and—

*"Ai, Senhor Carvalho! Cuidado!"*

The warning had come from in front of him, and he realized the whine of the machine had increased along with the speed of his strokes, and his shoulder was now a quivering mass of burning rubber.

He let go of the pedals, cradling his arm as he let the machine come to a halt on its own. "I wasn't…" He wasn't what? Able get his mind off what it would have been like to have Sophia straddle him in an entirely different way?

"This was supposed to be a warm-up, not the main event." The therapist tsked at him. "Do you wish to damage your shoulder before we even start?"

Start? As far as he was concerned, they were done here.

But Greta—from Sweden—had other ideas. She worked his butt—and every other part of him—until he swore his skin would peel back and expose the muscle fibers underneath.

When she was finally finished with him, Lucas slumped in a chair in the waiting area, wanting nothing more than to curl into a ball and block out the world.

Only he didn't want Sophia to find him like that and tell him to get with the program. Because he was more than willing to, *if* he knew what the program was.

Greta-the-Terrible must have called her, though, and let her know the session was over because Sophia came around the corner ten minutes later looking as fresh as a daisy, while his T-shirt was plastered to his skin and his hair was stiff from sweat. He was ready for his second shower of the day, although he doubted he could manage it at the moment. And somehow it galled him that Sophia was right there to see his every weakness.

Why couldn't their initial introductions have been made at the medical conference, before the shooting…when he'd still at least had a few witticisms left in him? Right now he felt drained of everything, even words.

"Ready?" The question was light and brimming with cheer—nothing like her attitude from this morning. In fact, she flashed him a smile that seemed to come way too easily.

For some reason, it rubbed him the wrong way. "You stay and work. I'll take a taxi back to Marcos's place."

"No need. I've already found someone to fill in for me for the rest of the day."

Great. The last thing he needed right now was a babysitter, when all he wanted was to be left alone to lick his wounds. "Look. I know you told the doctor you'd stay at the apartment, but I'm sure he didn't mean for you to trail after me like a puppy every second of the day."

The words came from an ugly, hurting place inside him, and even as they spewed out he knew they were a mistake. Her face confirmed it, changing in the space of a few heart-beats, her smile freezing into an icy mask.

Her chin jerked up and she met his eyes without a flinch. "Have it your way, Dr. Carvalho. This *puppy* knows when it's time to leave." She backed away.

"Wait, Sophia." He struggled to his feet. "I didn't mean it like that."

He succeeded in grabbing her wrist before she reached the door, his shoulder blaring out a warning. To his left he saw Greta throw him a frown and take a step in their direction. He let go, holding his hands away from his sides, palms facing out. "Don't leave. It's just hard for me to... I'm not used to relying on anyone."

And that was the truth.

The few childhood memories that had stuck with him had been of Marcos—a mini-warrior—who had always had to do everything just right, taking care of everyone around him. He'd been a tyrant, even kicking off his flip-flops and order-ing Lucas to put them on because he'd been worried about him cutting his bare feet. What about Marcos's feet? Who'd worried about those?

Lucas had chafed under his watchful eye, had fought back every time his brother had sacrificed something on his behalf.

He hadn't needed it. Hadn't wanted it. He could take care of himself.

That battle cry had become ingrained. Once he'd gone to live with his adoptive parents, the trend had continued. They'd tried to do things for him, had made sacrifices for him—perhaps trying to make up for the poverty of his childhood—and he'd fought against them, the need to be fiercely independent hardening into a cement-like substance that was almost impossible to break through.

It infuriated him that he couldn't get up and stroll out of the hospital—or get into a vehicle and haul his ass back to the apartment by himself. But that didn't mean he had to take his frustrations out on Sophia. Or anyone else.

He glanced back to make sure Greta wasn't going to come over and clobber him then moved forward another step. "I'm sore and tired, and I'm being extremely ungrateful. I'm sorry."

Her expression held steady for another moment before thawing around the edges. She released a small sigh, shoulders relaxing. "I'm sorry, too. I overreacted. Do you want me to drive you home?"

Home.

Lucas couldn't remember the last time he'd thought of anything by that term. He'd always been a drifter, too streetwise to put down roots, fearful they might be ripped up at any moment.

He had no home. No country—his trip to Brazil just seemed to re-emphasize that point.

He didn't know what he'd expected to find during this trip, but there'd been no burning sense of belonging. No flash of patriotic pride. No real sense of recognition, even when he'd seen Marcos for the first time in thirty years.

Maybe he was incapable of those kinds of feelings. Maybe that's why he traveled from city to city during his vacations under the guise of helping others.

No. That wasn't right, either. He got an immense amount

of satisfaction from helping children who had little more than the barest of necessities. Kids who might not get a chance for a normal life without surgery.

Kids like Sophia had once been. She was the perfect example of what cosmetic surgery could do to improve someone's quality of life.

He glanced at the woman who was waiting patiently for his answer. "Yes, I think I'm more than ready to go."

Sophia had no idea what had caused his sudden shift in attitude, but her heart felt like it had cracked in half as he'd stood there and asked her not to go.

He may not have heard the note of pleading in his voice, but she had. And it brought back memories of when he'd been taken from the home. The way he'd pleaded for the young couple to let Marcos and Sophia come too. Of course he wouldn't remember any of that. And he hadn't been there to witness his brother's raw grief afterwards.

But it had cut her to the quick back then, just as his words had done a few seconds ago.

Once back at the apartment, Lucas dropped onto the leather ottoman and tried to lean over to undo his tennis shoes, only to sit up again, pain and exhaustion etched on his face. Sophia knelt in front of him and reached for the first shoe, ignoring his attempts to brush her hands away as she untied the laces and pulled it and his sock off. She repeated the act with the other foot. When she reached for the bottom of his T-shirt the muscles in his jaw went dangerously tight, but he let her tug it over his head without a word.

*Deus.* She tried not to stare, but her eyes skipped quickly over his torso, absorbing the smooth skin, the olive coloring showing off his Brazilian heritage to perfection.

The men she'd dated in the past had had this same olive skin, but the resemblance went no deeper than that. Neither of her other two lovers had carried the dangerous undertones that this man did. They'd been gentle and kind—and had avoided her lip like the plague. There was no pretense with Lucas. She had a feeling he took exactly what he wanted—said exactly what he pleased.

And if he wanted her?

She shook off the thought, realizing he was still sitting there without a shirt. Time to finish what she'd started.

She reached toward his belt, only to have him stagger to his feet. "I can manage the rest of it myself." As if realizing his words had come out with a hard edge, he added, "Thanks. I'm just going to shower and lie down for a while."

"Do you want some pain medicine?"

"Don't need it." As he walked away, Sophia frowned after him. He'd refused to take anything the last time she asked either, even though she'd known he'd been hurting like crazy. She'd heard of doctors who wouldn't go near any type of narcotics, but his words about not relying on anyone came back to her.

Maybe it wasn't just people he wasn't used to needing, but everything. Including pain pills.

While he slept, she took the opportunity to catch up on some emails and do some dusting and light housework. She had no idea if Marcos planned on bringing Maggie back with him or what was going on with their relationship, but she had a feeling wedding bells might be ringing before very long.

Marcos had never been one to dilly-dally. When he wanted something, he went after it. And he'd wanted Maggie. As much as Maggie had wanted him.

As happy as she was for her childhood friend, she couldn't wait for him to come back to São Paulo. It would be a relief not to be alone with Lucas day after day. Once home, Marcos could take over helping his brother, and she could quietly slip out of the picture, unnoticed and unmissed.

Her chest tightened at the thought.

No more kisses. No more anything.

She glanced at the hall, tempted to tiptoe back to the bedroom to make sure he was all right while she still could—to make sure he'd managed the shower on his own. From her perch on the sofa she saw the bedroom door was open, but it felt too peeping-Tom-ish to move closer. Besides, after the scene in the kitchen this morning, she was going to let him take care of his own sleeping arrangements from now on— she wouldn't be the one to cover him up or slide a pillow under his head.

Neither would she be unzipping his pants any time in the foreseeable future.

Yeah, well, even in the *un*foreseeable future, that wasn't going to happen. If that little metal tab had proved dangerous when the man was asleep, just imagine what would happen if she touched it while he was awake.

*Deus.*

That thought was best left behind if she hoped to make it through the next week or so unscathed—a prospect that seemed less and less likely. Because right now her emotions were showing some definite signs of wear and tear. One wrong move and they could rip apart at the seams. If that happened, even a plastic surgeon as talented as Lucas might not be able to stitch her back together.

# CHAPTER EIGHT

Sophia pulled the curtain around Sílvio Airton's bed and prepared to check his vitals.

"How are you feeling today?"

Sílvio, a sweet elderly gentleman who'd joked with the staff for the last couple of days, had been battling renal failure for months. He'd been hospitalized several times in recent weeks with infections that came and went and had had a bout of pneumonia last January.

His relatives knew one of these visits would be Sílvio's last but everyone—Sophia included—hoped he would rally once again, like he'd done on previous occasions.

"I'm getting pretty tired of being poked and prodded." The words were delivered with a smile, despite the fact that dialysis wasn't a pleasant event. But without it Sílvio wouldn't have a chance.

And with a new grandbaby due in less than a week, he wasn't quite ready to throw in the towel yet.

She patted his shoulder. "I know. Just hang in there, okay?" Pushing up the sleeve on his hospital gown and wrapping the rubber tourniquet around his upper arm, she got ready to do a blood draw. "So, is Jesse having a girl or a boy?"

By now, Sophia was on a first-name basis with most of Sílvio's relatives.

"They want it to be a surprise."

His veins were fragile, and Sophia took special care to try to get the needle in on the first attempt.

There. Blood flowed into the vial, and as soon as the tube was full she popped it off and attached a second one. "Surprises can be fun."

Well, some of them anyway. She'd thrown herself into her job over the last couple of days due to just such a surprise. She hadn't quite decided if that kiss fell into the good category or the bad. What she did know was there was an awful ache of need that was steadily growing inside her.

The result of seeing Lucas all too often, because she was still spending each night at the apartment—rearranging her schedule to drive him back and forth to his therapy sessions.

In fact, untying his tennis shoes and helping him out of his shirt afterwards had become almost sacred rituals. Watching him rise from that ottoman like a god—lithe and strong—muscles pumped full of blood from his workout, made her feel weak in the knees. She tried to make sure she'd scrambled to her feet before he got up, because having that pesky zipper at eye level made her want to extend her ministrations to other areas.

Well, she wouldn't be taking off his shoes—or anything else—for much longer. As soon as he got the all-clear from his doctor, she was out of the apartment and out of his life. Why? Because it was getting harder and harder to keep her mind—and hands—off Marcos's brother.

Make that impossible. And she had no idea why.

For his part, Lucas seemed oblivious to her inner turmoil. For that she was thankful. He hadn't tried to kiss her again or given any indication that he even wanted to if the opportunity were to arise.

And it had.

Almost every time she hauled his shirt over his head, he could have reached out and had her writhing beneath him in a matter of minutes. He'd never made a move.

*Yep. Very grateful.*

Mixed in with that relief, however, was a strange sense of disappointment. She felt flat. Out of sorts.

Sonia, one of Sílvio's adult children, peered around the curtain just as she was affixing labels on the sides of the blood samples. "How's he doing?"

Sophia smiled and waved the woman in. She went straight to the bed and kissed her dad on the cheek. A lump gathered in her throat at the obvious affection between the two. This was what parent-child relationships were supposed to be like.

"He's just getting ready to head to dialysis." Sticking the vials of blood in the holder, she peeled off her gloves. "I hear Jesse is getting close to term."

The woman grinned. "Yes, we keep hoping she'll deliver just a little early." She glanced at her dad, and there was a wealth of meaning in her look. She hoped her father would live to see the birth of his grandchild.

The lump in her throat grew. "Well, you'll have to keep me posted."

An orderly appeared around the corner with a wheelchair. "You have a patient for me?"

When he saw who it was, the man grinned. "Ah, Senhor Airton. You're just the man I was hoping to see today. So, what's the newest piece of government gossip?"

Sílvio had been a politician in his younger days and had his own set of opinions on just about every subject, but he delivered them with a wit and humor that disarmed even those who weren't of the same political bent.

As usual, the two got into a good-natured discussion as the orderly helped Sílvio into the chair and took off down the hall. Sonia gave a quick roll of her eyes, before waving and hurrying after them.

As Sophia headed back to her desk, she wondered if the woman knew just how lucky she was to have a large and loving family. Or Lucas, for that matter, who'd had people who'd loved him enough to take him in and give him a home.

As if he knew she'd been thinking about him, he came strolling down the hallway much earlier than he should have and crooked a finger at her. She frowned. He didn't look tired. Or sweaty. Could he have showered before he'd left the therapy area?

Faint disappointment slashed through her, making her wince. Great. All those thoughts about being glad when this was over? Lies. She *wasn't* glad. She wanted to rip that shirt off his body just to prove her point.

She curled her fingers into her palms to stop them from getting any bright ideas then forced herself to move towards him, her shoes making almost no sound on the polished floor. "Are you done already?"

"GTT is sick today, so I'm off the hook."

Her brows went up. "GTT?"

"Greta-the-Terrible."

She laughed. "Very mature, Dr. Carvalho. I suppose you have a witty moniker for everyone."

"Of course." He leaned closer with a conspiratorial whisper. "Want to know what yours is?"

"I don't think so." Another lie. But Lucas didn't have to know that.

"It fits you to a T."

She gave a mock sigh, his woodsy masculine scent doing a number on her insides. "Oh, okay. What is it?"

"Sophia-the-Sweet."

Sarcasm. Just what she needed today. "I thought it might be Sophia-the-Slave-Driver."

"Slave-driver. Mmm. I kind of like the sound of that."

*Deus!* All kinds of images popped into her head. Bad images. "So you're not having therapy at all today?"

"I'm supposed to work on it at home." He propped a shoulder against the wall. "So I came down to ask a favor."

"You need me to drive you to the apartment? It's a little early, but I'll see if I can find—"

"No, no. I don't need you to take me home. I need you to remove my stitches."

She blinked. "What?"

"I was supposed to have them out the other day after therapy, but I had that meltdown, and then didn't want to ask you to drive me back to the hospital."

Sophia counted through the days that had passed since his surgery. How had she lost track of time? "That therapy session was three days ago."

He gave a quick shrug that said it was no big deal. "I could do the ones on my abdomen myself, but I can't get to the ones on my shoulder or snip them one-handed."

Her mouth popped open. "You are *not* going to take out your own stitches."

"Well, it's either that or…ask you to do it." He gave her a slow smile. "If Sophia-the-Sweet can come out to play, that is."

Ah, so that's where the name had come from. He was buttering her up.

Great. The last thing she wanted to do was "come out to play"—or lay her hands on his bare abdomen, for that matter. "We could call the doctor and set up another appointment. I'm sure he's going to want to have a look at it anyway."

"Come on, Sophia. It'll take maybe ten minutes at the most. If it looks like there's a problem, we'll call the doctor and have him check it. As it is, the edges of the incisions look sealed, and I'm doing my therapy without any problems."

"I'm still having to help you get undressed afterwards."

"Yes. You are. Which is why this should be no big deal. What do you say?"

She swallowed. This man was turning out to be a whole lot more work than she'd bargained for. And it had nothing to do with physical work—it was her emotions that were feeling the strain. "Fine. Let me tell someone where I'll be."

A few minutes later they were in one of the exam rooms and she had his chart out. Against his wishes, she'd made a quick phone call to his doctor to make sure it was okay for her to remove the sutures. Once she'd got the go-ahead she laid out all the items she'd need and motioned for him to take off his shirt.

Instead, he held his arms up.

Oh, Lord. That's right. He couldn't do it on his own. She glanced at the closed door.

*What have you let yourself get talked into, Sophia?*

She gingerly grabbed hold of the bottom of his shirt and pushed it up his torso. There was a quick wince as he lowered his injured arm, rotated his shoulder.

She gave her own little wince as the familiar smooth tissue and subtly defined muscle groups came into view. He didn't have the overly developed body of someone who worked out all the time, but he was firm in all the right places, his biceps curved and strong, his stomach taut and flat. The light dusting of hair narrowed once it left his chest, running down in a straight line and disappearing into his pants. But she knew first hand his zipper followed that narrow trail as well.

And that was her cue to cut her glance back to his face and get on with her job. When she did so, however, there was a glimmer of amusement in his eyes. "I thought only men had that problem."

"What problem is that?"

"Not quite knowing where to look."

Her face heated, but she somehow found a quip to match his. "Funny, because I thought I was examining your stitches."

Ha! Since her glance had skipped right over the pucker of flesh partially visible above his waistband, that was about as close to a fib as she could get.

"Of course you were."

He knew. The man knew she'd been enjoying the view!

She plunked a metal tray beside him, instruments rattling

in protest. "Do you want those stitches out, or should I call the doctor?"

He reached for her wrist and tugged her forward. "I'd much prefer you do it."

Why now? Why was he flirting—and, yes, he was definitely flirting—with her in a public place, when he'd totally ignored her back at the apartment? She couldn't figure him out.

"Then let me get started." She was not up to playing word games with this man—now or ever. Not when his skills in that department far outranked hers, which were pretty much non-existent.

He let go of her, a slight frown marring his brow as he reached up to tuck back a lock of hair that had fallen over her cheek. "I'm sorry, Sophia. I keep forgetting you're from a different world."

A different world. As in the poor little orphan girl no one had wanted? Not even him?

There were times he seemed to be attracted to her. But it was probably just because there was no one else. He was stuck here in Brazil for a couple more weeks, and she was available—you couldn't get much more available than sharing an apartment. Except he hadn't been interested enough to actually go further than a kiss. Not without falling asleep.

Why that had bothered her so much, she wasn't sure.

"You're right," she said. "We are from different worlds. Better for us both to remember that."

He leaned back and studied her face, his own features shifting from lazy amusement to closed and shuttered in a few brief seconds. He nodded. "Point taken. Okay, let's get this over with."

Her heart in her stomach, she sluiced alcohol onto a piece of gauze and carefully wiped down his shoulder, deciding to go from easy to hard. Sliding her fingers across his abdomen was definitely going to be the more difficult of the two areas. She took the tweezers and carefully gripped the first knotted suture and pulled it taut, snipping it close to the incision line and sliding it free of his skin. Doing the same for the next five stitches, she kept her attention focused on the task at hand, snipping and dropping each section of suture material into the basin. When all the stitches were out, she examined the site, then wiped it down one more time with a fresh piece of gauze.

"I want to put a couple pieces of tape across it to make sure your movements don't pull anything open."

"It should be closed by now."

"Humor me." She gave him a smile, although it was a little shakier than she liked. Cutting two pieces of surgical tape, she laid them perpendicular to the direction of his incision, pulling them snug to absorb some of the stress that came with moving his arm.

"You know that'll come off the first time it gets wet, don't you?"

She ignored him and took a deep breath before facing the stitches on his abdomen. Damn. She so didn't want to undo his pants, but with part of the sutures hidden beneath his waistband there wasn't a choice.

"I need you to—"

"Got it." He undid the button and edged the zipper down an inch or two. He peeled one side away until the rest of the incision came into view. "Will that do?"

"Perfect." Also perfect was the fact that he had on a pair of black briefs.

When her gloved hand lightly touched him, his abdominal muscles contracted, and he drew in a hissed breath. But when she looked up, he gave her a tight smile. "Tickles."

If only that was all she felt when she touched him. But, no, it was a whole lot more complicated than that, and she wasn't quite sure how to deal with it other than to just hurry and finish what she was doing. Following the same sequence, she sanitized the area and reached for the tweezers again, noting the muscles were still rigid against her fingers. Still tickling?

Was he afraid she'd nick him with the scissors? She wasn't about to ask so she went to work, snipping the stitches one by one from the surgical site.

"Are you hanging in there?"

"Just finish up, will you?"

She glanced up to see his jaw was as stiff as his abs, the skin pulled tight over his cheekbones. Was she hurting him?

She was being as careful as possible. Still, she slowed her movements, just in case. "Only a few more to go."

He didn't answer, just waited until she tugged the last stitch free and dropped it into the basin. "There. All done."

His muscles went slack all at once, backbone curving as he leaned forward, forearms resting along his thighs. He drew a long shaky breath, then let it out with a muffled curse.

Something was wrong. He hadn't even given her a chance to pass over the site with more rubbing alcohol.

Alarmed, she touched his shoulder. "Lucas, are you okay?"

"Just give me a minute, will you?"

"Why? Are you in pain?" Maybe something was going on with the repair the surgeon had done on his liver. "Let me see—"

"Dammit, Sophia." He shook off her hand. "I'm trying to do the right thing here."

"I don't understand. Did I hurt you?"

"Yes, that's exactly it. It hurts. But not in the way you think." He finally looked up, and the heat blazing in his eyes made her breath catch in her throat. "And if you say one more word in the next thirty seconds I swear I'm going to lay you down on this exam table and show you exactly what I mean by that."

She couldn't keep her eyes from shooting down to a certain area of his anatomy to see if he was saying what she thought he was.

Oh! How had she missed *that*?

Despite his seated position, the seam of his slacks bulged

in a way that could only mean one thing. Within seconds, a certain part of her had an equal and opposite reaction, going soft and liquid, preparing to receive whatever he had to give. And if that meant being sprawled beneath him on that table then so be it.

A shiver went over her, starting at her head and rippling all the way down to her toes.

She opened her mouth to speak, praying she made it before her thirty seconds were up.

The sound hadn't even exited her throat when the exam-room door swung wide and a male voice behind her said, "Dr. Carvalho, sorry to bother you. Someone said you were in here. I think we have something that might interest you." There was a second or two of silence that seemed to stretch to eternity. "Am I interrupting something?"

Sophia's mouth snapped shut like a clam that suddenly realized the world was a much more dangerous place than it expected.

Lucas never took his eyes off her. "Nurse Limeira was just taking out my stitches. I'll be right with you."

The second the door closed behind the departing doctor, Lucas slid off the table coming within inches of touching her. "Were you about to say something to me?"

She shook her head, allowing her silence to speak for her.

Cupping her cheek, his thumb whispered across her lower lip. It gave a fatal tremble that gave her away.

"I think you're lying. The question is whether it's for your benefit or for mine." He gave her a slow, devastating grin as he dropped his hand and took a step back. "You may think you dodged a bullet here, Sophia. But one day very soon either your luck is going to run out or my good intentions are going to fail me. When either of those things happen…honey, make no mistake. It won't be on a hard metal table or done in a rush. And most important of all, there'll be no interruptions."

# CHAPTER NINE

LUCAS TRIED TO keep his mind on the procedure from his perch high above the operating room.

Dr. Guilherme Lima sat beside him in the observation area. "I figured you'd want to see the new technique in action." Young and fresh-faced, the other doctor glanced over at him. "Also, your brother called a few minutes ago and wanted me to check in on you. He'd tried to call Sophia, but couldn't get an answer."

He hadn't heard her cellphone ring. Then again, he didn't think she'd had her purse with her when she'd followed him into the exam room to remove his stitches. Ringtones hadn't exactly been at the forefront of his mind, however, because he could have sworn Sophia had been about to respond to the challenge he'd thrown down. If he were a betting man, he'd go all in that she had been going to call his bluff.

Only he hadn't been bluffing. He'd been so hard and ready in those endless moments as her hands had trailed over his body that he'd been prepared to grab her and do exactly what he'd threatened to do: lay her over that table and show her exactly what she did to him.

Had she been about to accept?

Just thinking about it made his flesh react all over again.

*Get your mind back on the surgery, Carvalho or everyone in this hospital is going to know exactly where things stand between you and Sophia.*

Hell, not even *he* knew where they stood. All he knew was that she was killing him. Just by looking at him.

And her touch...

Deadly. Just like a hemorrhagic fever that ripped through the body with little warning, taking no captives.

He was toast.

His mind wandered to her lips and the silky skin he'd stroked thirty minutes earlier.

He glanced at the doctor beside him. "If a child from one of the local orphanages came in with a cleft lip, who would do the repair? You?"

"An orphanage?" The man's brows went up. "That kind of thing is handled through one of the public hospitals in São Paulo. Why?"

"Just thinking." Aware the other man was now staring at him, he went on, "I do charity work from time to time."

Somehow he didn't feel as much of a sense of pride in saying those words as he might have at one time because now he had a living, breathing example of someone he might have worked on had she been born in Africa or Mexico.

The young surgeon turned to look at him. "I could put you in touch with someone, if you want to know how that kind of thing works here. I did an internship at the Hospital de Santa Maria a few years back."

A few years back. This kid didn't look like he was out of his twenties yet, much less had been practicing medicine for more than a year or two. Suddenly, at thirty-four, Lucas felt old and unsettled.

But he didn't want to be settled. That was the whole point of his travels. He never wanted to be tied down. Stuck in one spot.

Nope. That wasn't true. He was *afraid* to be tied down. There was a world of difference between those two concepts. Despite the stability his adoptive parents had provided, he'd never really felt a true sense of "place." He'd been ripped from the only home he'd ever known and placed in an orphanage. Then his new parents, even though they hadn't meant to, had taken the rest of his identity away from him, including his brother and his last name. Including Sophia, who he'd never gotten the chance to know. Not really.

Weirdly, he was jealous of his brother because he'd had what he himself hadn't.

That in itself made him feel like a jerk. He'd been given everything, and yet he was coveting the one thing his brother had that Lucas didn't: Sophia's affection.

Hell, he'd had the world handed to him on a silver platter, and he still wasn't satisfied.

What did that make him?

Greedy.

Was that what was behind the persistent salute one part of his body kept giving Sophia? Was he enough of an animal that he felt the need to "mark" her and claim her as his—just to show his brother that she would have chosen him over Marcos during their time at the orphanage?

If so, he didn't like that side of himself very much because it meant he wasn't really interested in Sophia as a person but in taking what his brother had.

He glanced over at the doctor whose attention was wholly on the breast reduction surgery being done in the room below. The surgeon was currently making impossibly tiny stitches along the bottom curve of the woman's breast. Lucas couldn't help but admire the skill it took to keep that up for hours on end. No quick stapling of skin here, the other doctor had told him. Plastic surgeons in Brazil felt there was a fine art to making small precise stitches that left a minimal scar.

That was one thing they could agree on. Lucas tended to dislike staples as well. But he'd told Sophia the truth when he'd said he wasn't interested in this side of plastic surgery.

"I think I would like the name of your contact at the public hospital, if the offer's still open."

"Of course." The other doctor pulled his smartphone from his pocket and scrolled through the screens. "What's your email, and I'll send it to you? Speaking of charity work, you know that Marcos opened a free clinic in one of the *favelas*, right?"

"No, I didn't. Which *favela*?"

"The one right down the hill."

The place he'd been born. And the place he'd been shot. Had Marcos been there that day? He'd never mentioned anything about a clinic or working down there. Not that there'd been much time to discuss anything before he'd headed for the States.

Lucas recited his email address, his eyes still on the meticulous procedure going on below them.

His memories of the shooting were coming back in drips and drabs—standing on a hill overlooking the *favela*, the dilapidated shacks that seemed to stretch endlessly into the distance. The sounds of shouting, the police running up the hill after a group of men. The shots. Falling to the ground.

Sophia's sweet smile as he'd recovered from his surgery.

His memories weren't the only improvements he saw. His muscles were responding to therapy as well, growing stronger over the last week. Soon he'd be able to drive again. Fly home. The police would be able to handle the investigation without any help from him, leaving him free to take up life where he'd left off.

He frowned. Why did that thought suddenly fill him with anything but relief? He should be glad to get out of this place. To get back to the States.

Sophia's face swam in his head, her features murky and indistinct as they wavered in and out of focus. For just a second he thought he saw the image of a little girl with dark, short-cropped hair and huge eyes superimposed over that picture. As soon as he blinked, however, it was gone. And no matter how hard he concentrated or tried to bring it back into view, just like his childhood with his father and brother, it was lost to him for ever.

"Why are we here?" Sophia had to raise her voice as she glanced around the doctor's waiting room, which was housed inside one of the largest public hospitals in Brazil. Half-broken toys were shoved in a corner, while every chair in the place was occupied by an adult with a child.

A shiver went over her. How different would her life have been had her parents been able to bring her to a place like this? Instead, they'd left her at the orphanage and let someone else deal with her disfigurement.

She scrubbed the thought away, leaning against a nearby wall and trying not to face the reality before her. The one time she'd glanced around the room she'd been struck by the chaotic activity, but even louder than the noise was the hope and fear etched on each adult's face, while the children did what kids did best. Laughed, cried, threw temper tantrums, totally unaware that there was something wrong with them. At least in the eyes of the world.

"This is what I do when I'm not at my hospital, working." Lucas leaned closer in order to be heard.

She gave him an incredulous look. "So, when you're not working, you're…working."

He shrugged. "I don't have anyone or anything tying me down. I figure it's one way to pass the time."

Nice to know that's how he felt about people like her. She'd merely been a way to pass someone's time.

A brush of fingers touched her wrist. "That's not true," he said, lowering his voice. "This is something I've always felt the need to do." Then his hand reached up and scrubbed at his arm. The spot where she knew the tattoo of his father was inked. "For him. For people like him who have no one to turn to."

She nodded. That she could understand.

Just as she started to say something else, a tiny girl crawled towards them, head down as she powered her way across the room. Around eight months old and clad only in a diaper, she was followed closely by a woman who had to be her mother. When the child lifted her head, Sophia saw that she had a bilateral cleft, a line running from each nostril down to her upper lip. Her mom murmured an apology and scooped the child up. When she started to move away, Sophia stopped her, leaning over to smile at the child, who immediately responded with a wide smile, the problem with her mouth doing nothing to dim the happiness in her eyes.

"She's beautiful. Is she yours?" She didn't know why she asked the question, maybe because her own folks hadn't been around to see her through surgery.

"Thank you. And, yes, she is." The woman spoke Portuguese, but her accent was different. Angolan, maybe? That might explain why the baby was a little older than most infants who had this type of surgery—although if her palate was cleft as well, that could be the reason, as those repairs were sometimes done later to give the bony plates time to grow.

Lucas brushed the backs of his knuckles over the baby's cheek, giving her a smile as well, although his eyes were sharp as he studied her. Seeing how he would approach the surgery maybe?

Just then the door to the back opened and a nurse appeared, clipboard in hand, and called a name. The woman in front of them smiled. "Well, that's for us. Wish us luck."

"Of course," Sophia murmured, not sure what else to say. But when the woman turned to leave, Sophia again reached out to stop her. The young mother turned back, and Sophia touched her own lip. "You're going to be so happy you had this done."

The woman's eyes widened. "You? You've had…"

"Yes. Many years ago." She hesitated then quickly dug into

her purse for a card. "If you need anyone to talk to, please call me."

The woman accepted the slip of paper then reached down and clasped Sophia's hand, giving it a squeeze. "Thank you so much."

With that, she turned and went to the door where the nurse stood, and the trio disappeared. Soon the woman's baby would have a whole new look, but more than that, her future would be much brighter than it would have been had she not had surgery.

Fingers threaded through hers, and she looked up in surprise as Lucas pressed their joined hands against the warmth of his leg. "That was nice of you."

"I always wonder if my parents would have made a different decision had they had the money or a good support system in place."

He frowned. "What do you mean, a different decision? I thought they passed away."

"No. Why would you think that?"

His hand tightened around hers. "I just assumed…"

Oh. She got it. She'd been raised in an orphanage, so therefore her parents must have been tragically killed in a car accident. Or died by some other means. Like his and Marcos's parents had.

She shook her head. "Not all children in orphanages are actually orphans. My parents are still very much alive." She shrugged. "It's no big deal. Some people just can't afford to raise a child—especially one with medical issues. So…they send them away instead."

# CHAPTER TEN

No big deal.

Lucas couldn't believe she'd actually used those words. Being abandoned by parents who were supposed to love you was a huge deal. His dad had been as poor as dirt and yet he'd done the best he could…had kept his boys by his side until the day he'd died.

He had a feeling that if she'd been talking about any other child she'd have been furious. Just like he was now. As he sat in the doctor's office, listening while the pediatric surgeon talked about the various patients he saw, his gut did a slow, angry burn.

He'd had an hour to digest the fact that Sophia wasn't an actual orphan before they'd been called back to the doctor's office.

No. She *was* an orphan. Just because her biological father and mother were still on this planet, it didn't make them parents. In any way, shape or form.

Did she still have contact with them? Were they lost to her the way Marcos had been to him for many of his formative years?

He hoped Sophia had washed her hands of them, hoped they never got to share a single one of her special milestones. They didn't deserve it.

She half turned towards him then touched his knee. It was then he realized the doctor had asked him a question.

"I'm sorry. I missed that."

"I asked where you practice." Older, with a slightly stooped posture, Dr. Figuereiro's eyes glimmered with a trace of humor and sharp intelligence.

Lucas forced himself to tune back into the conversation. The plastic surgeon had given up valuable time to speak with them. He didn't deserve to sit there while *his* damn mind wandered all over the place. "My actual medical practice is in California, but I travel to Africa and Mexico whenever possible."

"That must be very rewarding work."

It was, but Dr. Figuereiro's work must be rewarding as well. He nodded at the wall where photo after photo was tacked to a giant corkboard. There were so many images that they overlapped. "Are these all your patients?"

"Yes." He smiled as he swiveled his chair to glance at the wall. "These are my kids. It never fails to bring a lump to my throat whenever a parent sends me updates."

Sophia shifted next to him, and his heart cramped in his chest.

Some parents sent nothing at all. As soon as they left the office, he was going to ask her what happened. Had her parents abandoned her before or after the surgery?

Before. He would almost bet on it.

As casually as possible, he laid his hand on the back of her chair, needing to touch her but not willing to make it as obvious as holding her hand. Instead, he slid his fingers beneath her curtain of hair, where the doctor couldn't see, and used his thumb to stroke across the back of her neck. She sat up a bit straighter but didn't try to shift or pull away.

"We saw an older baby out in the waiting room," he said. "Do you often get them so late?"

The man pursed his lips. "When they can't get what they need in their own countries, they're forced to go elsewhere. We're only one of several places that accept cases like hers."

Sophia cleared her throat. "Your waiting room was packed earlier."

"It's like that every day. We deal with all kinds of craniofacial problems, not just cleft lips and palates."

His focus shifted to Sophia. "Your repair is excellent, by the way. How long ago was it done?"

Sophia shrugged. "I was a little older as well, about a year old. So thirty-three years or so ago."

"You had it done here in São Paulo?"

"Yes. I grew up at Saint Mary's over in the *Dutra* area."

"I've worked on kids from that home for many years." Dr. Figuereiro pulled his glasses down from the top of his head and perched them on his nose. He glanced at her over the top of them. "Would you be offended if I took a look?"

"No, of course not."

Standing and coming around to their side of the desk, he took hold of Sophia's hand, signaling her to get up and forcing Lucas to drop his arm from around her shoulders.

Once she was on her feet, the doctor peered closely at her lip, tucking his hand beneath her chin and turning her face to different angles. Lucas was fine until the man touched the scar itself then his gut tightened, a ball of some strange emotion turning round and round until everything inside him was all jumbled up. Sophia, on the other hand, seemed unfazed by the intimate touch.

Yet when *he'd* touched it, she'd tensed immediately, claiming he made her feel self-conscious about it. But why? He did the exact same type of surgery all the time, so why was she so nonchalant about someone else touching her?

"Thirty-three years… I think I may have done this repair." He let go of her and gazed up at the ceiling, as if doing some quick calculations in his head. He glanced at Lucas. "Which technique do you use when dealing with unilateral clefts?"

"A variation of Millard's rotation."

"Yes, I was beginning to use Millard's right about the time

your young lady was having her surgery done. She had a good outcome. I'm glad."

Lucas's brain ceased to function after the "your young lady" comment.

Sophia quickly shook her head. "Oh, we're not together. I'm helping Dr. Carvalho recover from surgery." She added, "In a professional capacity only."

The surgeon glanced from one to the other with a quirk of his brow. "Interesting." He patted her on the shoulder. "Well, thank you for letting me look."

Sophia retook her seat. "If you did the surgery on me, I'm forever grateful. Most people don't even notice my scar."

Was it his imagination or had her emphasis on the word "most" carried a slightly caustic inflection?

Dr. Figuereiro waved off her thanks. "It's what I'm here for. Although I don't think I have many more years of surgery left in me. I'm about at the age where it's time to pass the baton on to the next man in line."

"What'll happen to your patients?" Lucas asked. "Are there other doctors willing to take on those from lower socioeconomic levels?"

If his father had found a doctor as caring as this one, he might still be alive. It made Lucas all the more aware of how different Sophia's life could have been had she not gotten a top-notch surgeon like Dr. Figuereiro.

"Are there others who are willing? I hope so. It takes someone who's in it for the right reasons." He smiled. "Interested in the job?"

Something in his chest leaped at the thought before he forced the emotion back. He laughed instead, pretending he didn't know if the doctor was serious or not. "I bet you don't get many surgeons from other countries."

"To practice medicine, you mean?" He shook his head. "Not many. Most doctors working with NGOs head straight for the Amazon. Or Africa. With all the hospitals around here, São Paulo isn't exactly an exotic destination for medical teams. Why?"

"Just curious." He noted that Sophia avoided his glance and he didn't bother sliding his hand onto the back of her chair again. He certainly didn't want the good doctor to think there was anything going on between them, especially as he had no idea if Dr. Figuereiro and Marcos knew each other. The last thing he needed was for something to get back to his brother and set off a chain reaction that would be difficult to explain away.

Although Lucas certainly hadn't been worried about Marcos's reaction when he'd threatened to lay Sophia on the exam table and do her right there in the hospital. Of all the moronic things to have done, that was pretty much at the top of the list.

But he was thinking rationally now.

And he was going to do everything in his power to make sure he *kept* thinking with a clear head, no matter what crazy impulses his nervous system might send out. Like sticking around for a while? Definitely not a workable plan.

He stood, making sure to take it slow and easy as he reached across the desk to shake the good doc's hand. "Well, thank you for your time. You still have some folks waiting out there."

"My pleasure." The other doctor clasped his hand in a firm, unwavering grip, then stood as well. "Come back some time when we have time to exchange ideas on technique. Or if you get the urge to extend your visit indefinitely."

Indefinitely.

No. That wasn't happening. He couldn't see himself doing what Dr. Figuereiro did: work on someone like Sophia and then thirty years later still be in the same location. Even in the States he'd already practiced in two different cities and had volunteered in more than six countries. And even now something inside him was itching to move on to something new.

*You wouldn't want those roots to suddenly start growing, right?*

He decided to go with a noncommittal reply. "If I decide to, you'll be the first to know. How's that?"

"I won't hold my breath. How's that?" Another smile accompanied the words, and the doctor came around the desk as Sophia also got to her feet. He took hold of her shoulders then kissed her on the cheek in standard São Paulo fashion. "And you don't be a stranger either, young lady. I still have room on my cork board for another picture or two if you'd care to send one in."

She smiled. "I just might do that. Thank you again for having us." She paused. "Do you have a card? I'd like to give you a call some time."

To talk about her surgery?

Dr. Figueureiro went back around his desk and pulled open one of the battered side drawers. "If you ever want to come down the hill from that fancy hospital, I might be able to use another nurse. Or whoever takes over the practice might need one." He cast another sly glance in Lucas's direction.

Color seeped into Sophia's face right on cue as the doctor passed a card across the space. She accepted it, hurriedly stuffing it into her handbag.

Lucas was sure that was the last thing Sophia wanted, to work with someone who'd kissed her and then fallen asleep, someone who'd threatened to seduce her in a hospital room. Yeah. No wonder she'd turned red.

Once outside the office, they headed to her car. As they got in, Lucas pulled the seat belt across his shoulder, very thankful it wasn't his injured one. The lower part of the mechanism, however, was a different story. It crossed directly over where his stitches had been, and although the skin might have healed, it was still pretty sore. He glanced sideways to where she was twisting the key in the ignition. "Sorry about that, Sophia. I don't know why he thought there was something going on."

She didn't even look his way. "I can't imagine."

"Is something wrong?" She'd barely said two words the whole visit, other than asking for the doctor's card.

"Nope." She sat there for a moment, her fingers wrapped around the steering wheel. "I'm thinking about going home tomorrow, if you think you can handle things from here. I'll still come by and pick you up for your physical therapy appointments, and I can bring meals by if you need me to. But you seem to be pretty self-sufficient at this point."

All he heard was that she was going home.

Leaving.

His throat squeezed shut for several seconds before he forced it to relax so he could breathe normally.

What the hell was with that? Why did he care if she stayed or if she left? After all, he'd been "leaving" one place or another his entire life.

So why was hearing it from Sophia—who was not a permanent fixture in his life in any sense of the word—making him want to pretend to be a whole lot sicker than he was?

He had no idea. Maybe it was the crazy thought Dr. Figueriro had planted in his mind. His wandering heart was starting to kick into gear again with a new and exciting opportunity. But coming here to do anything would be a big mistake. That doctor's patients didn't need a temporary fixture. They needed someone they could count on to be there to see them through the hard times—tragic times. And to show those kids that someone really did care.

He didn't do that on his volunteer trips, and had never felt bad about it. But this was different. This was a community that saw too little stability—he, more than anyone, should understand that.

He forced his mind back to Sophia and her comment about leaving, noticing she hadn't made any move to pull out of the parking space and into traffic. Drawing a deep breath, he managed to say, "If that's what you think is best, that's what you should do."

"You'll be okay?"

"Absolutely." He kept his voice light, forcing into it a lazy amusement that he didn't feel at all.

"I'll leave you my cellphone number." She finally looked at him. "You can call me if you want or need anything."

Call her. If he wanted anything. Needed anything.

No way. No how.

He was not even going to think about the ramifications of that statement. He wouldn't call her, because if he did, it would be for one thing. To take her in his arms and drag her down the hallway of his brother's apartment until they were both sprawled across that huge king-sized bed of his.

What Lucas wanted and what he should have were two entirely different things, however. Maybe Sophia had finally wised up and realized the last place she should be was in the same house as him. Especially after what he'd nearly done in that hospital room. He couldn't promise her it wouldn't happen again. Because it would. Maybe not today, maybe not tomorrow. But soon.

That thought should shock him back to reality, but it didn't. It made the anticipation of kissing her—touching her—that much sharper.

Only one thing was stopping him from doing all the things he'd dreamed of doing to her, and that was Sophia herself. He didn't want to hurt her, but he knew if he slept with her there was a very real chance that he could. That he *would*. If that happened, Marcos would pummel him into the ground, and Lucas would stand there and let him do his worst—because he wouldn't be doing anything that Lucas wouldn't be doing to himself.

Sophia was sweet. Innocent. She didn't deserve to have someone screw around with her affections. Someone who had no intention of sticking around and making things permanent.

So he wouldn't call her. She was doing absolutely the right thing in running as far away from him as she could get.

But as much as he might believe that in his heart of hearts, at this moment it was the last thing Lucas wanted her to do.

# CHAPTER ELEVEN

SHE DIDN'T WANT to go home today.

But asking Lucas to eat lunch at one of the city's famed *rodízios* was pretty pitiful as far as delaying tactics went. Maybe she hadn't expected him to capitulate to the idea of her leaving quite so easily. He had. Hadn't even blinked when she'd suggested moving out.

Sitting across from her in the steakhouse's dimly lit interior, her dining companion glanced around the place.

Dark wooden tables contrasted with the many white-suited servers, who traveled from table to table, each man laden with a different cut of meat, some on wheeling carts, other types carried on wide sword-like skewers.

"So how does this work exactly?" Lucas asked.

"How is it that you've never been to a *rodízio*? Your parents never took you to one? Not once?"

"We lived in the States for most of my life." He shrugged. "Maybe they just never had the opportunity."

Sophia had thought him one of the lucky ones to have been adopted. But maybe she'd been wrong. His adoptive father was Brazilian, so it was hard to understand how he could speak Portuguese but not know how to order meat.

She tapped a wooden placard that sat in the middle of the table and showed him how to turn the knob that flipped a tab from red to green. "Green means you want them to bring meat to your table. Red means to stop. The word *rodízio* basically means 'making the rounds,' which is what the servers are doing. We normally try to have several different cuts on our plates before switching the sign to red. Then once you're ready to start again, you turn it back to green."

"No side dishes?"

She nodded towards the middle of the room where there was a long buffet table. "There's salad and vegetables over there, but most people come here for the meat."

"And how do you know which cut is which?"

She laughed. "Well, I can't help you with that, because I don't know the names in English. I can tell you what I like, and you can taste it and see if it appeals to you."

His fingers tightened on the knob for several seconds, eyes narrowing as he studied her face. "Oh, I'm pretty sure it would."

"You never know. Everyone has different tastes."

He leaned forward, his gaze unwavering. "I'm sure your taste would suit me just fine."

She sucked down a quick breath, suddenly aware that he'd taken her words the wrong way. She hadn't meant them to be risqué. But if he offered to taste her, she was going to be in big trouble, because she wasn't sure she'd be able to resist him.

Now, more than ever, she needed to keep her wits about her. "Um, let's turn it to green, shall we?"

"Let's." He flipped the lever and gave her a slow wicked smile. "Green for go."

Thankfully this place was efficient, so almost as soon as the card had been changed, a waiter came over with one of the shiny rotisserie skewers. "Filet mignon, *senhor*?"

Lucas nodded. "Now, *that* cut I understand, it's the same in both languages."

Sophia indicated she would accept a couple of slices as well. Once the server had carved them and deftly slid the cuts onto their side plates, she picked up her knife and transferred a piece to her dinner plate, slicing through her meat without looking up. Placing the bite in her mouth, she let the buttery tenderness melt on her tongue.

Lucas's eyes widened as he bit into his own meat, and she could practically hear his taste buds cheering.

Unable to hold back a smile, she said, "Good, isn't it? No one does grilled meat like Brazilians." Maybe that sounded a little arrogant, but it was true.

He swallowed, brows lifting. "Seems you've been holding out on me, Sophia."

"Are you complaining about my cooking?"

"Your cooking is…delicious."

Another server arrived just in time to stop the blush she could feel hovering on the edges of her face.

"Are those what I think they are?" he asked, staring at the thinner skewer, which was laden with chicken hearts.

"Yes. They're really good." She nodded to the waiter, who slid three of the grilled hearts onto her plate.

"I think I'll pass." He thanked the waiter but declined. "Besides, I'll get more enjoyment from watching you eat them."

There were times Sophia could almost believe he was Brazilian despite his accent, but there were other moments when it was obvious his link with his homeland had been severed—or at least worn to a hair-thin thread. It made her sad. It also made her aware that playing word games with someone like him was very dangerous, no matter how much fun it seemed at the time.

"Maybe you should try something before you dismiss it out of hand. I bet Marcos is eating all sorts of American foods." She cut off a tiny portion of one of the hearts.

His mouth tightened. "I bet he is. He's probably devouring everything in sight."

Shock flashed through her system. She'd caught hints of anger from time to time in Lucas's attitude when he talked about his brother, but it made no sense. "You make him sound like a bad person. He's not, you know."

He sat back. "I know he's not."

"Then why do you seem to—?"

"He had to take care of me constantly when we were kids." He shrugged. "I'm sure it was a huge relief once I was gone, and he didn't need to worry about me any more. He didn't have to give up his shoes, his food, his blankets. His *life*. My adoption was the best thing that could have happened to him."

She stared at him. Was that really what he thought? That Marcos had viewed him as some kind of burden? Tears pricked at her eyes. "Lucas, your brother grieved terribly when you went away. He already blamed himself for your father's death, and then when you left, he...well, he didn't speak to anyone for months. He kept that picture—the one that's on his television stand—under his pillow and refused to let anyone near it. One of the cafeteria workers heard about it and bought a frame with her own money. Marcos has never taken the picture out of it as far as I know."

"I just assumed he'd be..." He dragged a hand through his hair.

"Well, you were wrong. About him. Maybe even about Brazil."

Forcing herself to take a deep breath, she picked up the fork with the chicken heart and held it out to him. "You were born here, Lucas. I know it may not feel like you belong, but you have this country's blood flowing through your veins. Give it a chance."

From the set of his jaw she wondered if he was going to refuse, but then he took the fork from her and put the piece of meat in his mouth. He chewed. Swallowed.

He handed the fork back and gave her a half-smile. "Different. Not bad. Certainly not what I expected. And thank you for what you said. About Marcos. Someone told me he has a free clinic in one of the *favelas*. Any chance I could see it?"

"Of course. I go down there with him all the time, I'm sure

he'd be happy for you to visit. I'll set it up." She paused. "You need to talk to him, Lucas. Tell him what you told me."

"Maybe. Someday."

A gentle sizzle went up her spine at his words. He hadn't dismissed her suggestion out of hand. And he'd grudgingly said the chicken heart wasn't bad, it was just different. He even wanted to venture into the *favela*. Maybe she was wrong. Maybe that link hadn't been sliced completely through after all.

When he reached across the table and picked up her hand, she tilted her head in question.

"There was a little girl at the doctor's office today who looked like you."

"There was?"

He nodded. "She was about four years old. Beautiful, with these huge brown eyes that seemed to see right through you. Just like you did when…" He paused, frowning, his hand tightening around hers.

Sophia's heart picked up speed, thudding louder and louder until she was sure the whole restaurant could hear it. "Like I did when what?"

"When you looked at me in the orphanage." His eyes came up and speared hers. "I just had a quick flash of your face go through my head. Did you meet my brother and me at the orphanage that first day?"

She licked her lips, then nodded.

"You held Marcos's hand but not mine." His voice was soft, as if he was lost in some distant memory. "In fact, after that first glance you acted like I didn't exist."

Only because he'd frightened her. He'd been…too perfect. But then she'd let her guard down and included him into her world, and soon the three of them had done everything together. At least until Lucas had left. Then had come the pain.

And if she wasn't careful, if she let her guard down again,

history would repeat itself because he wasn't likely to stay this time, either. "We were all pretty close, from what I remember."

She flicked the little sign to green, unwilling to continue down this path. "I still need to finish packing. Are you ready for the grilled pineapple? It's what we normally finish the meal with."

His lips tightened. "Yes. I know you're anxious to get back to your place."

If he only knew how wrong he was. She just needed to get away from him, because she was so close to giving in to the little kernel of need that was quivering inside her, getting ready to burst open at any second like a piece of popcorn bombarded by microwaves.

Lucas might as well be giving off tons of the stuff, because she felt warm and fidgety whenever he was around. And she had no idea how to make it stop, other than to just remove herself from the vicinity.

Fifteen minutes later they walked out of the restaurant. Sophia handed her parking ticket to the attendant outside, who radioed the number to someone else. Lucas's fingers curled around hers. "Thanks for all you did for me this week. I couldn't have done it without you."

"I think you'd have found a way. I didn't do all that much."

Other than let him kiss her. Undoing his pants as he'd slept. Getting an eyeful the next morning.

And hearing him say a little girl looked like her.

He'd called her beautiful. Twice now. It spun her heart round and round in her chest. "I'm glad I was there."

"I'm glad you were, too." The hand holding hers exerted slight pressure, turning her towards him. "Are you sure you have to—?"

"*Moça?* Your car is here."

The voice to her right made her tense. Before she could pull her hand free and give the man a tip, Lucas beat her to it, pressing a bill into the man's palm with his free hand. *"Obrigado."*

He then walked her round her car and opened her door, only releasing her when she slid into her seat. Going to the other side, he climbed in beside her.

Despite the lunch-hour traffic, they made it back to Marcos's apartment within fifteen minutes, and she punched the button on the box out front, waiting until the entry gate slid open. She then found the apartment's assigned parking space and pulled her little car into it. "Speaking of Marcos, have you heard from him in the last couple of days?"

"No. Although I'm not really expecting him to call. Not after the way he sounded the last time I talked to him."

Yes. He'd sounded in love. Happy.

Sophia was glad for him. But things would have been a whole lot less complicated if he hadn't gone traipsing off to the United States. He'd have been the one dealing with Lucas, not her.

They rode up in the elevator in silence, and the longer it dragged on, the more uncomfortable she got. Surely one of them could come up with a topic of conversation that would fill the next few minutes. Then she'd be packed and on her way. She'd be home in an hour.

Why did that thought not fill her with relief? Once they left the elevator, Lucas took the key out of his pocket and inserted it in the door. The second she passed through it, she started to hurry back to the bedroom, only to stop when she heard her name.

She turned toward him. "Yes?"

"Don't leave without saying goodbye."

She blinked in surprise. Why did those words have a ring of finality to them? It wasn't like either of them was leaving the country. Oh, yes, of course. Lucas *was* leaving, as soon as he got the all-clear from the doctor. "I won't."

Going into her room and shutting the door, she sank onto the bed and stared at her suitcase. She did not want to toss her things into it and walk away from him.

*You're not walking away. You're driving. And you'll only be fifteen minutes away from him in case of an emergency. Besides, this was your idea.*

She might as well have been going two thousand miles, though, because once she moved out nothing would be the same.

The same as what, exactly?

No more intimacy like they'd had on the couch. She'd been so close to stretching out beside him and sleeping next to him that night. It had only been the fear of damaging the stitches in his side that had made her go back to her room.

It scared her how right it had felt to kiss him. To crawl onto his lap and want to devour him whole.

Not a smart move, unless she was willing to settle for a short fling.

Grimacing, she got off the bed and picked up the nearest item of clothing, tossing it into the suitcase. Then another... and another.

Who cared if everything had a million wrinkles? They'd just match the rest of her. On the outside she was bright and bubbly, full of optimism towards life. But inside it was a different story. She had trouble forming attachments with other people. Long-term relationships were next to impossible. Because of her parents? Maybe.

Not even the two men who'd been her lovers once she reached adulthood had scratched beneath the surface. She'd liked them well enough, and sex had been pleasant but it hadn't gone beyond that. Neither of them had stuck around for very long. Marcos was her only lasting friendship.

Which was why Lucas scared her so much. She'd never experienced anything like that molten kiss on the couch. It had taken her by storm, transforming into a dangerous, churning vortex that threatened to suck her into its depths. Besides, he hadn't even tried to talk her out of leaving.

And if he did?

Swallowing, she latched one side of her overnight case before realizing she'd left her straightening iron in the other room. Opening the door carefully, she eased into the hallway and scurried for the bathroom, hoping she didn't run into him on the way. As soon as she got that last item packed she was out of there.

Lucas was in the living room, pouring himself a stiff drink, when he heard a noise behind him. A throat clearing.

Forcing himself not to spin around, he set the decanter back on the tray at the bar and capped it. He lifted the glass and took a healthy swallow of the fiery liquid before finally turning to face her.

"Are you off?"

"Yes." She licked her bottom lip, curling it in slightly as her teeth came down to meet it, drawing his attention to them. "You asked me not to leave without saying goodbye."

He took another drink, and the burn of the liquid washed across his epiglottis then flowed into his stomach a few seconds later. "So say it."

"I'm sorry?"

What was wrong with him? It wasn't like she was walking away from a twenty-year marriage, so why was there a part inside him that was taking this personally? Acting like she couldn't stand to be around him?

He moved towards her, hearing her rough intake of breath as he did. Instead of stepping back, though, she held her ground, her chin lifting in order to continue meeting his gaze.

Lowering his voice, his fingers clenched the drink. "Say goodbye."

He waited for the word, expecting her to hurl it at him and then turn on her heel and walk away. Instead, she watched him as if trying to figure something out.

Unable to help himself, he reached up and touched the side of his whiskey glass to her jaw, dragging it slowly down the length of it until it rested on the delicate point of her chin. Her lips parted and he brushed the rim of the glass across her top lip and then the full bottom one, using the slightest pressure to open her mouth even further.

She still made no move to leave.

He took her hand and lifted it, curling it around the tumbler. "Take a drink."

She hesitated and then obediently tipped it, taking a small sip of liquid, her mouth touching the glass where his had, her throat moving as she swallowed.

A spear of raw desire went through his gut, the point lodging somewhere deep inside him. There was no way he was going to pull it back out. Not yet.

"Stay one more night. Just one."

The fingers of his injured arm curved around her nape, the movement jarring his shoulder, but he ignored the pain, wanting nothing more than to banish the fantasies he'd had about her once and for all.

He only knew one way to do that. Experience them for real. All of them. She'd let him kiss her. Would she let him do more than that?

She licked her lips. "Okay."

Lucas took the whiskey glass from her, tossing the rest of its contents down his throat before letting the tumbler drop to the thick area rug beneath his feet and leaving it there.

The last time he'd kissed her he'd fallen asleep. Well, this time, even if he wound up flat on his back, there was no way his eyes were shutting—not even to blink. Not until he'd drunk as deeply of Sophia as he had of that whiskey. Not until her heat washed over him and through him, obliterating every other thought.

Then, and only then, would he let her go.

# CHAPTER TWELVE

A FEW MINUTES ago she'd wondered what she'd do if he asked her not to leave. Well, now she knew.

Sophia ignored the glass he'd dropped a second ago, unable to look away from his smoldering gaze.

Warm hands came up and cupped her face. "I want you in this house. In my bedroom."

"Why?" She wasn't sure where the question had come from, but once it was out there it was too late to retract it. Why couldn't she simply accept that he wanted her? Even if it was just for a single night?

His eyes narrowed slightly. "Do either of us need a reason?"

Okay, that stung a bit, but not enough to make her back away, maybe because her knees were jelly at this point. "I guess not."

Maybe he sensed something in her voice, because his thumbs brushed over her cheekbones. "Sophia, if you haven't been able to tell how much I want you—have wanted you since I first laid eyes on you—then I've been hiding it better than I thought."

Since he'd first laid eyes on her. Those words sent a shiver rippling through her.

Because, like him, she'd wanted this for quite some time... probably more than she should have.

With that, she closed the gap between them and stood on tiptoe until her lips connected with his.

Lucas went totally still for a heartbeat or two, and she wondered if he might change his mind. Then, with a low groan, his hands tunneled deep into her hair as he stepped into the kiss, head turning sideways, mouth opening to fully take hers in a searing kiss.

Her neck arched beneath the force of it, but his palm was right there at the back of her head, supporting her, allowing him to move against her mouth as hard and as fast as he wanted.

And, *Deus*, she wanted it, too.

His arms were blocking her from reaching his shoulders, so she settled for wrapping her fingers around his forearms, needing desperately to hold onto something as his tongue entered her mouth in one rough thrust that took her breath away.

It was as if he'd finally thrown off the chains of control, and what it awoke within her was almost primal. Sophia's hips connected with his as she moved between his splayed legs, feeling him hard against her belly.

Her heels were high, but not high enough.

*Stilettos.*

The thought flashed through her head. She should have worn her highest heels, because she wanted that pressure lower.

As if reading her mind, his knees bent, one hand going to her butt and cupping it as his erection found the bone of her pelvis and pressed hard.

Oh! So close. So very close.

But still not quite there.

His fingers trailed down the back of her skirt until he reached the crook of her knee, wrapping tight around it. The pressure made her mouth water.

Then with one decisive tug her inner thigh slid up, tender flesh scraping along the hard muscles of his leg.

His mouth left hers, lips trailing over her cheekbone until he reached her ear. "Keep your leg right there. Don't move."

*No. No moving. Check.*

Her breath hissed in when his body gave a subtle shift that had his leg between hers, moving deeper until his thigh rested right where she needed him the most. *Yes!* The hand that had been supporting her knee abandoned it, his arm wrapping around her lower back instead as he hauled her fully against him.

He held perfectly still, his breath rasping against her ear as he suddenly contracted and released the muscles of his thigh in just that spot.

*Deus!*

He repeated the act. This time a moan worked its way up from her throat.

"Shh, Sophia…just feel."

She bit her lips as she held herself still and silent as he tensed against her over and over.

The experience was incredible, as if they, along with the world around them, had frozen in time, leaving only the rhythmic flick-flick of his flesh against hers. A light switch turning on-off…on-off. Her universe shrank down to that one tiny point on her body as she anticipated each sweet surge of energy just before it hit.

It was relentless. Her elevated thigh trembled against his leg, but she didn't move. Couldn't. Didn't dare.

Tighten. Release. Tighten… With each change a crank turned somewhere inside her and a spring wound tighter and tighter.

Her eyes fluttered shut, trying to combat the growing tension.

*Too soon. Not yet.*

Lucas's breathing changed, grew harsher, and she realized his erection was pressed hard against the curve of her hip.

Seeking release just as badly as she was.

*He wanted her. Needed her. Now.*

Like a flare going off inside her, she ignited, the force of the blast surging up and through her body, gaining momentum until the shock wave hit her vocal cords. Holding back was no longer an option. She cried out, clutching at his shoulders for all she was worth as wave after wave of pleasure spun her round and round like a loosed top.

Lucas's guttural groan of encouragement met her ear about the time his mouth clamped over hers, kissing her in a fury, absorbing all the nonsensical sounds she continued to make, his teeth and tongue echoing everything she was feeling.

*Oh, God...oh, God...oh, God.*

He gripped the back of her knee, maybe realizing she was in very real danger of collapsing to the floor in a heap, then gently allowed her foot to slide back to the floor before wrapping both arms around her. He lifted his head, murmuring to her as the dizzying rotation slowed, along with her racing heart.

The humiliating realization hit her. He'd barely touched her. Had simply flexed his muscles—literally—and sent her into the stratosphere.

"I… You…" She tried to find the words to say, but nothing was as it should be.

He nuzzled her cheek, totally unaware of the conflict raging within her. "*I* am not done yet. Not by a long shot. Neither are you. That was just the appetizer."

"It was?"

He moved to her ear, his teeth nipping her lobe, sending a shiver through her. "I told you when this day came it wouldn't be on a metal table, and it wouldn't be done in a rush." He chuckled. "This was the only way I could keep the last part of that promise. If I'd have been inside you a second ago, it would have been all over. And the last thing I want is for… *this* to be over."

Anticipation slid through her veins, his growled words erasing her doubts. He didn't think she was too eager. He'd *wanted* her to climax—had intended to push her over the edge. Because he hadn't been able to trust himself not to join her.

She reached up and wrapped her arms around his neck, suddenly very glad it wasn't over either. Her bravado came back, at least a tiny portion of it. "So if it's not going to be on a metal table, then what kind of table did you have in mind? Wooden?" Her glance went to the dining room where the huge mahogany table stretched long and wide.

"Uh-uh." A hungry gleam came to his eyes. "Not this time."

*There was going to be a next time?*

Why not? Right now she'd give him just about anything. Including as many "next times" as he wanted.

He went on. "I don't want you sliding away from me. I want you sliding *on* me. All the way down. Just like I imagined it."

Her heart stuttered. The man's words painted a picture that was all too clear. And that was one portrait she wanted to be in. Right now.

"My room," she whispered.

"Mine." His palms slid down her arms until he'd captured her hands. "If I could pick you up, there'd be no doubt where you'd end up. Or who'd be on top. I'd like nothing better than to feel you sink deep into the mattress, just before I sink deep into you."

*Meu Deus do céu.*

Still gripping her by one wrist, he towed her into Marcos's bedroom, not bothering to close the door behind him. Why should he? No one was home.

*No interruptions.*

The third part of his promise.

Her nipples tightened, breasts aching. He was right. He couldn't be on top because of his side and shoulder, so she'd be doing most of the work. That was absolutely fine by her. As inexperienced as she was in the art of seduction—and she was just beginning to realize how shallow her previous wading pools had been—she could probably figure out what went where and when. But since she was evidently heading this thing up, maybe she should be allowed to call a few of the shots.

She reached out and gripped a handful of his T-shirt with her free hand just before he reached the bed, stopping him. When he turned towards her with a concerned frown, she smiled. "Don't worry, Lucas. You're going to get your fun. But it's my turn now."

With that she tugged free of his grip on her wrist.

One brow went up. "I think you've had your turn," he pointed out.

She laughed, knowing exactly what he was referring to. "That's where you're wrong. You liked seeing me like that, making me lose control. That was all about you. This part is for me."

With that she slid her hands under his T-shirt, allowing her thumbs to snag on the hem and avoiding his injured side, while inching the fabric up his torso and smoothing her palms over the warmth of his skin.

His breath hissed in. "This is not my idea of fun."

"Sure it is." Wow, maybe he was right. Being uninhibited had its good points. The nubs of masculine nipples passed beneath her fingertips, and she paused. "Lift your arms."

"Sophia." The warning tone didn't deter her one bit.

"I'm just taking your shirt off. I've done it before, remember?"

He did as she asked, and she tugged the piece of clothing over his head. Once it was on the floor, she reached up and kissed the lower part of his jaw, loving the way the stubble felt on her lips, shivering as she remembered the way it had scraped her tender flesh as he'd slid his cheek along hers in the living room.

His hand came up and tangled in her hair, but when he directed her towards his mouth and started to lean down, she pressed her lips to his shoulder instead, inching her way down his body. The pounding of his heart beneath his chest wall met her open mouth at one point, inciting her to continue her quest.

"Sophia…" This time her name was a whispered plea.

She reached the nipple she'd touched a moment earlier and flicked her tongue across it. His breath shuddered in on a strangled groan. When she closed around the tight flesh, his reaction was instantaneous, his hand tightening in her hair. She thought for a moment he was going to drag her away from him, but then he bit out a low curse and pressed her closer instead.

Need spurted through her, and she suddenly knew exactly how Lucas had felt as he'd sent her into oblivion a few minutes ago. His obvious pleasure fueled her own, a vicious cycle that was anything but vicious.

Moving to his other nipple, she hoped to distract him long enough to…

There.

She found the button to his pants and managed to slide it free. Her fingers went to the tab, this time knowing full well what lay beneath it.

Maybe they wouldn't make it to the bed at all. Maybe she'd simply wind her leg around him the way she'd done in the living room and take him that way.

*Zi-i-i-p.* The most beautiful sound in the world.

Lucas tried to take a step back, but she followed him, her lips never leaving their chosen spot, her fingers squeezing between the edges of his pants and finding him hard and ready. She applied more suction, hoping he could feel it all the way down there, like she had during that last violent kiss.

On cue, his erection jumped beneath her hand. *Oh, yes.* This was definitely her idea of fun.

She'd never known what a huge turn-on it was to have a man stand there while you were free to roam his body…explore every inch of him.

And she meant to do exactly that. With her mouth.

Decision made, she ran her tongue down the warm flesh

of his chest, continuing down his stomach, feeling the bump, bump, bump as she cruised down his abdomen, like three speed bumps that warned her to slow down...warned her of danger ahead.

What if she liked danger?

Because she certainly liked what was ahead.

She tugged his briefs down over his swollen flesh, baring him to her eyes.

*Almost there.*

She sank to her knees and opened her mouth wide, just as a gurgled sound came from above her. The hand still embedded in her hair tugged sharply enough to get her attention.

"No." He dragged her back upright. "If this is going to end, that's not where I want to finish it." Power-walking backwards to the bed, he sat on it, looking hotter than she'd imagined possible with his fly open and his penis straining above the black elastic of his underwear.

"Take off your clothes," he murmured. "Starting with your blouse."

The woman had almost made him come, and she'd barely even touched him. Just a couple of squeezes with her fingers, and he'd been almost there. Then, seeing those red lips part, wet and round, as she'd got ready to go down on him had sent lust crashing through his skull. He'd wanted her to do it, had started to close his eyes in ecstasy, but what he'd told her was the truth.

He wanted to sink into her depths and wonder if he was going to survive the experience. And he wanted that to happen with her sitting on top of him, where he could see every nuance of that expressive face as he brought her to another peak. And he would. Whatever it took to hold off his demons until then, he'd do.

Sex had never been a clawing, rabid creature that strained to break free. Until today.

Even as the thought came and went, her fingers skated down the length of her silky, bronze-colored top, flicking open one button after another. She tugged it free of the waistband of her narrow black skirt until she revealed a lacy bra—red.

Fire-engine red, five-alarm red.

It looked as hot as he felt.

He swallowed as the blouse dropped to the floor.

When she reached behind her back, he stopped her. "Come here."

She licked her lips and hesitated, so he repeated the command, his voice lowering to coax her forward. "Sophia, come here."

She moved towards him, and when she was within reach he slid his hands behind her back, relishing the soft, smooth skin beneath his fingers. He tugged her a few steps closer. The bed was high, the perfect height for all kinds of things. Had Marcos bought it with this type of encounter in mind?

Screw Marcos. He had nothing to do with this.

But the bed made him change his mind. Having Sophia sitting on top of him wasn't how this was going to play out. Not with the precarious state he was in. He needed to be in control of how fast, how deep, or he was done for.

He leaned forward and inhaled the intoxicating scent coming off her skin, her arousal hitting his system like nothing he'd ever experienced. His nose swept to the side, grazing the pucker of the rosy nipple just visible through the wispy lace fabric.

"Lucas, please." She braced her hands on his shoulders and tried to ease him back on the bed.

"Uh-uh. My turn," he reminded her. It felt so good to say that, felt wonderful to have her body right here where he could touch, taste, see every tiny mark, lick across anything he wanted to. As if to demonstrate, he pressed the tip of his tongue to the underside of the nipple in front of him, pushing up, then flicking across it.

She moaned, fingers tightening on his shoulders and pressing closer.

Yes. He liked to make her do that. Hoped to make her do a whole lot more.

His fingers crept under her skirt, walking slowly up the backs of her thighs until he found the lower edge of her panties, following the line around. He swallowed at the moist heat coming from her center, knew exactly how it would feel to drive home. And he wanted to. Ached to. Needed to.

He dragged her underwear down her legs as he continued to lap over her nipple with broad, firm strokes, the tip so very hard against his lips, his tongue.

"Step out."

As soon as she did so, she started to hike up her skirt and climb onto the bed, but he stopped her. Standing to his feet, he ignored her soft, disappointed murmur. Not much longer. But he needed a condom. Hoped his brother at least had something in one of these drawers. But, first, one more thing.

He moved behind her and planted his hand between her shoulder blades, his thumb rubbing back and forth with sweeping strokes. "Bend over the bed for me."

She glanced back at him in confusion.

"Like this," he said, applying easy pressure with his palm and watching as she bent to his will, just as he'd bent to hers earlier.

And, yes, it was so very good. But it was about to get better. "Stay there, Sophia. Just for a minute."

She whimpered, sounding as turned on as he felt. He shed the rest of his clothing and yanked open a drawer or two.

A blue box winked up at him. Success!

Tearing open the first packet he could get his hands on and dropping the box on the floor, he sheathed himself then moved behind her, inching her skirt up the backs of her thighs, until she stood exposed. Her heels just added to the sensual image.

He leaned over her, positioning himself against her slick

heat, gripping her hips, his legs trembling with the effort of holding back. "Ready?"

"Yes." Her butt inched higher, a glorious, beautiful offering. One he could resist no longer.

He entered her in one quick thrust, hearing the wind rush from her lungs as her body sank into the plush surface of the mattress. Forcing himself to suck down a couple of deep breaths when all he wanted to do was pump like a wild man, he put his mouth to her ear. "Are you okay?"

"Mmm. Yes." She pushed back against him, her hips rotating as if trying to force him to move.

He wanted to. Hell, he wasn't sure he could avoid it. But he desperately wanted her to go with him.

Letting go of one of her hips, he pushed his hand between her body and the mattress, sliding it down the softness of her belly until he reached the narrow strip of hair between her legs.

Damn, he'd thought the heat coming off her panties was hot. That had been nothing compared to this. She was a furnace, searing him inside and out.

He touched the spot he knew would do the most good then angled his hips and began moving in short, controlled bursts.

She matched his tempo, burying her face in the mattress, her hands clenching and unclenching the coverlet as she panted, trying to force him to go deeper. She was close, her legs widening to give him better access. Access that he immediately took advantage of as he continued to use his body and fingers, fighting his own release every step of the way. She was gorgeous, the long length of her spine stretched over the bed, the swell of her hips moving back and forth to the rhythm he'd chosen.

"Oh! Oh!" Her body stiffened, and like a jockey approaching the finish line he leaned forward, urging her on even as his own adrenaline shot through his veins. It hit, her and then him, the strong contractions of her body causing him to crest almost immediately. Her fierce moan ripped through him, as everything turned inside out and he pressed his face to the side of her neck as he rode both of their climaxes out to the very end.

He slowed, the muscles in his legs trembling as he tried not to rest all his weight on her, not that his injured side would allow him to collapse fully on top of her.

His hands followed her arms until he reached her fingers, then threaded his own through them. He kissed the side of her neck, allowing his eyes to close as he tried to slow his breathing and regain his sense of the here and now.

*Here:* his brother's bedroom…his brother's condom…his brother's friend.

*Now:* probably the biggest mistake of his life…and there was absolutely no way to fix it.

As his sweat began to dry to a sticky film, reality crept in, its sharp talons tearing through the ecstasy he'd felt seconds earlier and revealing the sinister truth hidden behind the haze of lust.

*What the hell?*

He'd just had the best sex of his whole damn life, so what was he doing, overanalyzing everything?

He didn't believe in steady relationships, but that's not what this was. It was simply a one-time event that was anything but simple. It would probably never happen again.

Something he was already regretting.

But how could he ask for more of the same? How could he tell a woman whose parents had thrown her away that he only wanted her for a little while—that when he was through, he'd do exactly what they'd done and leave her behind without a second glance?

# CHAPTER THIRTEEN

*DID HE WANT a next time or didn't he?*

Sophia stood beside the bed, her blouse hanging off one shoulder. She'd jerked awake in shock this morning as she'd realized where she was. What she'd done. Each and every second of their time together replayed through her head.

She'd scooted out of bed, intent on getting away as fast as possible. Why was she still here? She could be already out of here.

Just through the doorway lay her overnight bag, and freedom. She tugged her shirt over her shoulder, and did up a couple of the buttons before she stopped again.

Leaving would be the smart thing.

Which was why she'd slept with him in the first place, right? Because it had been smart?

*Deus.* It might not have been wise, but it had been good. Really good. Better than anything she'd done in her entire life.

She'd always played it safe—safe job, safe friends…safe men. She'd never really explored her sensual side. Not that she'd even thought she had much of one, until now.

Who would even know? Not Marcos. He was in the States. And Lucas was only here for another week or two at the most, so there wasn't much chance that he'd blab to anyone, right?

Her legs trembled just thinking about the possibilities. She smoothed her skirt down over her thighs, realizing something was missing.

Her panties! *Deus*, she'd almost forgotten he'd taken them off, leaving her skirt on. Her glance skated around the edge of the bed, expecting to see them lying on the floor. She could put off making a firm decision until she found them.

That was if she could get up the courage to ask him straight out if he wanted her to stay for a few more days. Once he was gone, life could go back to normal. But until then she could live on the wild side. Be uninhibited. Just like Lucas was.

*Look for the panties* then *think!*

A spilled box of condoms reminded her in all too graphic terms what had happened here last night.

When he'd bent her over that bed...

She closed her eyes and took a deep breath as a wave of lust crashed over her. Then another.

"Where are you going?"

The low question made her jump, her eyelids coming apart in a flash and turning her into a chicken. "I was just getting ready to take a shower before, um, going home."

*So much for asking him about a repeat performance.*

Lucas sat up, still naked and sporting a morning erection that made all kinds of crazy thoughts whisk through her head. Like crawling back into bed and running her fingers through that gloriously mussed hair until he begged for mercy. Then she'd finish him off.

"What's the rush?" he said. "We can have breakfast and talk about last night."

Talk. Okay, she'd definitely not thought this through very well. She'd been counting on action to carry the day. Besides, if he wanted her to stay, he'd say something. Like he had last night.

She gave a little wave of her hand. "Last night was great. We've both been under a lot of pressure recently. And pressure eventually needs to find an outlet. A pressure valve. Sex is a known stress reliever. *I* certainly feel better, how about you?"

Wow, that was brilliant. It even sounded pretty believable, considering the words had tumbled out at around a hundred miles per hour.

*Smooth, Sophia, very smooth.*

"A pressure valve." His eyes narrowed, and he swung his legs over the side of the bed, still making no effort to cover himself. "That's what this was?"

She concentrated on her panties. If Lucas wanted her to leave, she really should take them with her. After all, what if Marcos came home and found them? She tilted her head sideways and tried to see past the line of darkness beneath the bed. Her underwear was red, the carpet white, how hard could it be to spot them?

"I think so." Her voice was still pretty steady, even though her heart was pounding at an alarming rate. "We're practically strangers, so how could it be anything else?"

Wow, maybe she was more sophisticated than she'd thought.

Instead of smiling with relief, the edges of his mouth tightened, turning white. "You make a habit of having sex with strangers?"

Oops. Something had just zigged when it should have zagged. "No, of course not."

"Just with me. A stranger."

Yikes.

"Well, it was just one night and…" She shrugged. Forced her eyes to keep scanning the floor for her errant underwear. She was tempted to go down on her hands and knees and peer under the bed, except she didn't have any panties on, and he was still so…so *up*.

"So if it was *more* than one night, that would make us… what, exactly?"

More than one night?

Her head came up, and she stared at him. "Are you asking me to stay longer? And do more of what we did last night?"

Before she realized what he was going to do, he'd snagged

her wrist and tugged her between his splayed legs. Warm hands went to the backs of her knees and began gliding upwards.

"I was going to discuss this over breakfast, but the answer is yes to both questions. I want you to stay. And I want to do more of what we did last night. Much more." His slow smile burned away any last doubt she might have harbored. "But first I want to make one thing perfectly clear."

"Wh-what's that?" she squeaked, her heart rate already spiking into the hundreds.

Using the hand that lay just below the bare flesh of her butt to hold her in place, he reached beneath his pillow and pulled out her panties, letting them dangle precariously off one finger. "You and I, Sophia, are *anything* but strangers."

"So this is it?"

After a few suspicious glances and one confrontation they stood in the heart of the *favela* where a red-bricked shack lay deserted—no sign to indicate it was a clinic. Sophia had needed to reassure a couple of men who'd blocked their path that they meant no harm. Luckily they knew her—they just didn't know him. The second she'd told them Lucas was Marcos's brother, they'd stood aside. Word had traveled fast, because people came out of their homes, a few of them waving.

"Yes. This is it."

Sophia adjusted her dark tank top, glancing down as if to make sure the small red mark he'd left on her right breast this morning wasn't showing. It wasn't, but she'd know it was there...would serve as a reminder of what they'd done. When he'd awoken to find her eyes on him, her shirt hanging open to reveal the entire right cup of her lacy red bra, he'd wanted her all over again. Then she'd mentioned home...had called him a stranger, and anger had spurted through his system. He'd needed to show her exactly how well he knew her. Starting with the silky flesh beneath that bra. The way she'd squirmed, moaning as he'd sucked her flesh into his mouth, lapped over it with his tongue afterwards, had driven him crazy.

His body had reacted all over again.

So his brother wasn't a stranger to her. But *he* was?

*Not the time, Carvalho.*

Sophia put a key into the lock on a door that looked like it could be kicked in by a small child. Pushing it open as far as it would go, she flipped a cardboard sign on the inside of the door so that it read *Aberto*, then motioned him inside.

It could have been the setting of any one of his charity trips, but this was his home country, and from what he could remember, this was *his* favela. A dirt floor made of the ubiquitous red clay that covered much of Sao Paulo was clean swept and the unpainted walls were raw bricks of the same color. A clay tile roof topped it off. Maybe the colors had been chosen to match the ground. Everything had the same muddy red tones.

He glanced around. "Where are your supplies?"

Sophia nodded at a folding table propped against one wall and two white plastic chairs next to it. "That's it. We don't leave medicines here. Keeping anything of value invites a break-in."

She went over to the table and turned it on its side, opening and locking the legs in place.

"Here, let me help."

"No need. I can do it."

He started to insist then bit back the words. Forcing her to accept his help was what Marcos would have done. And Lucas had strived his whole life to never make anyone feel as guilty and suffocated as he had while under his brother's watchful care.

But Sophia had said his brother hadn't resented doing any of the things he remembered him doing.

Instead, Marcos had grieved.

Maybe she was right. He should talk to him once he got back.

He glanced at the sign on the door. "Are we seeing patients today?"

"Might as well now that we're here, don't you think?" Her movements seemed quick. Jerky. She adjusted her shirt again. Maybe she wasn't as okay with this whole setup as he'd thought.

He caught her arm. "Hey. Stop for a second." Looking into her eyes, he tried to read behind the warm brown irises. "Are you okay with staying at the house?"

"By the house, you mean your room, I'm assuming?"

Okay, he wasn't going to get into the fact that it wasn't actually his room. "Yes. Are you having second thoughts?"

"After this morning? Hardly."

Relief swept over him, just as there was the sound of a throat clearing from the doorway. Lucas let go of her and turned to find an elderly man with a young child standing there. The man eyed him, then turned to Sophia. *"Onde está Dr. Pinheiro?"*

She smiled at the newcomer. "You know Marcos doesn't like to be called that, Senhor Silvano, especially by someone who knew his father. And he's traveling right now." Sweeping a hand in Lucas's direction, she went on. "This is his brother, Lucas. He's a doctor, too."

Old wizened brows crept toward the heavens. "Lucas? Little Lucas Pinheiro?"

He stiffened at the name. "It's Lucas Carvalho now but, yes, I'm Marcos's brother."

The little girl headed for Sophia, who swept her into her arms, planting a kiss on her dusty cheek. "How's my little angel today?"

"Fine."

Sophia carried the child to the other side of the room, in a not-so-subtle attempt to give Lucas and the old man some privacy.

"You've never been here before," the man said.

Actually, he had. Just in time to be shot by a couple of thugs who evidently lived somewhere in the *favela*. But he wasn't about to say it. "No, sir. I live in the States."

He noted that the man kept one hand hidden behind his back, and a sick thumping set to work inside Lucas's head.

*It wasn't a gun.*

He decided to tackle the obvious. "What can I help you with?"

The man pursed his lips, studying him for a moment. "You think you can pull a meat fork out of my back without breaking it—or killin' me? Wife wouldn't like it if I ruined it."

*What?* The man had a heavy accent and there were more teeth missing than present, but surely he hadn't just said... "Could you repeat that?"

"A fork, son. I have a fork stuck in my back." He proceeded to shuffle his feet to the left, turning his body. Lo and behold, the glint of twin metal tines topped with a wooden handle appeared from beneath the man's thin button-up shirt, along with a large red stain.

Lucas moved closer immediately. "How did this happen?"

The man gave an embarrassed shrug. "I didn't like the wife's dinner. She didn't like me saying so."

*Holy hell!*

"She stabbed you with a meat fork?"

He chuckled and glanced over his shoulder. "Actually, she was all worked up, and I backed away from her as quickly as I could. The sink was full of dishes. If I didn't know better, I'd think she planted it there on purpose. Good thing the clinic opened up or I'd have had to ask her to pull it out. And with the mood she's in...well, I'd rather not take any chances."

Lucas could honestly say he'd never pulled a fork out of a man's back. Ever. Luckily, the tines weren't terribly long, and it looked like they'd just hit the fleshy part on his side. But he might need a tetanus shot, if he wasn't current.

"Soph? Do you think you could keep your little friend occupied for a while?"

"Why?" She turned his way, eyes widening as she saw the problem. "Oh. Um, yes. We'll just go outside for a short walk. Call if you need me."

As she started to scoot past him, he caught a quick glimpse of red where her tank top had slipped to reveal a sliver of her current bra of choice.

Hmm. Red must be her favorite color. That was okay, it was quickly becoming his favorite as well. He couldn't hold back a smile as he turned to the task of righting Mr. Silvano's wrong.

When it came down to it, whether it involved sharp forks or bright red bras, men were pretty much at the mercy of the fairer sex. And the weapons they wielded could be downright lethal.

# CHAPTER FOURTEEN

*"PRECISO AJUDA!"*

The cry for help came at the same time as the alarm on a heart-rate monitor went off down the hallway. Sophia jumped from her station as Sonia, Sílvio Airton's daughter, came skidding out of the room at the end of the corridor, waving to her.

Oh, no! Sílvio had improved enough that he was scheduled to go home later this morning. She'd just been writing up his discharge papers.

Hurrying down the corridor and entering his room, she took one look at the monitor and saw the classic wiggly line that signaled V-fib, a potentially fatal arrhythmia.

Jesse, her swollen belly showing she hadn't yet given birth, stood close by, her hand over her mouth, tears spilling down her cheeks.

*Deus!*

Sophia urged everyone back, knowing more personnel would arrive within a minute, along with a crash cart. Until then she moved to the head of the bed and quickly assessed her patient. Grabbing a bag valve mask and fitting it over Sílvio's mouth, she squeezed the device at regular intervals, getting off around three pushes of air before another nurse arrived with the crash cart, followed by a third, who asked the frantic relatives to step outside with her. Relief swept over her as she called out orders to other members of the team as they arrived, thankful Sílvio's family wouldn't have to witness the frenzy as the resuscitation attempts swung into full gear. By the time a doctor arrived thirty seconds later, CPR was already in progress.

*Come on, Sílvio, fight!*

A nurse lubricated the defibrillator paddles and charged them up, handing them over to the doctor when he asked for them.

"Clear!" Everyone stepped back as he pressed the paddles to the patient's chest and activated the trigger. Sílvio's muscles contracted as the charge went through him. Sophia sent up a silent prayer as everyone stopped to look at the cardiac monitor, waiting to see if his heart would restart itself.

"Still in V-fib," she said, stomach tightening.

"Again, charged to three hundred," called the doctor.

The nurse upped the charge of electricity to be delivered and as soon as it reached the desired level, the doctor attempted conversion again. A second of asystole crossed the monitor after the electricity was delivered, and everyone held their breath, hoping the heart's natural pacemaker would reboot itself and send lifesaving blood pumping through the Sílvio's tired body once again.

Instead, the flatline persisted, and Sophia sucked down a quick breath as everyone jumped back to action. Defibrillation was useless against asystole. Sophia intubated him and reattached the bag valve mask, while another nurse began chest compressions.

Forty-five minutes later the room looked like a battleground with used equipment littering every surface. All to no avail.

The doctor shook his head. "Let's call it."

Although she cared for all her patients, there were some who tugged at Sophia's heartstrings no matter how objective she tried to be. Sílvio was one of those patients. Letting go of his bag valve mask and taking a step back made her eyes burn, even though she knew the doctor was right. There was nothing more to be done. His body had just been too tired to keep fighting.

Limbs trembling as the rush of adrenaline began to subside, she concentrated on taking long steadying breaths as the doctor called out the time of death and the recording nurse wrote it on the chart.

Looking down at her patient's weathered face, Sophia hoped that somewhere he knew how hard they'd fought for him. How hard his family had fought for him.

She hoped he knew how much he'd be missed.

Her throat contracted and, unbidden, Lucas's face swam into focus.

*Not the time, Sophia.*

The team went to work disassembling the equipment as someone went out to inform the family. Sonia and Jesse would want some time alone with him to say their goodbyes, and she wanted the scene to look as peaceful as possible.

She brushed her hand across the thin grey tufts of Sílvio's hair, before removing his intubation tube and gently swabbing his mouth clean.

The doctor, maybe noticing how shaky she was, laid a hand on her shoulder. "We did what we could, Sophia."

She blinked hard. "I know. He didn't even get to hold his grandbaby." That probably didn't make much sense, as the doctor didn't know about any of that. "He was just...nice, you know?"

"Yes, he was." One more squeeze, and he slid out of the room and on to his next patient.

The team filed out one at a time, Sophia being the last to leave. When she finally exited and saw who was waiting at her desk, the burning in her eyes increased.

Lucas stood at the end of the hallway, hands propped low on his hips, looking sexy and alive. Somehow it didn't seem right. Not after what she'd just been through. Her steps slowed as she glanced at the clock, surprised to see that technically she was already off duty.

Damn. She hoped to hell he didn't want to dissect their decision to keep sleeping together, because she just wasn't up to it right now.

Especially as she could almost feel the mark he'd left on her tingling to life.

Because despite the fact that things between them were fun and the sex was out of this world, she realized that when it came time for Lucas to go, she was going to miss him. And she didn't *want* to miss him. Wanted things to remain light and uncomplicated.

Could anything really remain uncomplicated with this man? He was complex and impossible to understand...and, God, she was glad he was there.

Pulling even with him, she tilted her head to look at him. Eyes swimming with sympathy, he gazed back at her. "I'm sorry about your patient."

"You heard." She wasn't surprised. News traveled like wildfire on the ward. Then again, with Sonia and Jesse standing in the hallway, their fear and anguish obvious, it wasn't hard to realize what was going on in that room.

"I asked someone." He reached out to brush a strand of damp hair off her brow. "Do you want to go somewhere?"

Nothing about their situation. Just an intuitive knowledge that she needed to get away.

She closed her eyes and started to wipe the back of her hand across her brow, only to realize she still had her surgical gloves on. She stared at them for several long seconds. Somehow taking them off seemed so...final.

As if he knew what she was thinking, Lucas took one of her hands and peeled the glove off, and then the other, rolling one into the other like a pair of socks. "Come on. Let me take you somewhere for some coffee or a hot meal."

She nodded, unable to do anything else, still not sure why

he was there, but it didn't matter. Signing off her shift and collecting her purse, she murmured goodbye to one of the other nurses. As they walked towards the exit, she was all too aware of the warm, firm hand beneath her elbow. "I parked on the other side of the hospital."

"Leave it. We'll take a taxi."

"Are you sure? They're hideously expensive."

"Less than they are in California. I took one to the hospital today."

She'd dropped him off after their brief run to the *favela*, telling him she'd be back to get him for his therapy session—hadn't stopped to wonder how he'd arrived. "I'm sorry I didn't make it back in time."

"Don't worry about it. I already cancelled today's session."

"But you shouldn't. You need to—"

"Take you someplace quiet. It's not just about your patient. I need to talk to you." Wrapping an arm around her waist, he set her feet back in motion.

Something in her stomach leaped. Talk to her. About what? "It doesn't have anything to do with...you know what, does it?"

"No. It's about Marcos."

Her stomach squirmed again. "Is he all right? Maggie?"

"I'm assuming they're both fine, as I haven't heard from them." He gave her a smile that was half exasperation, half compassion. "Will you please keep walking? It's nothing bad. I promise."

Nothing bad. Well, that was something.

Fifteen minutes later the cab stopped at Ibirapueira Park in the middle of downtown São Paulo. She glanced at him in surprise. Sophia loved this place, came here whenever she got the chance. Although it was crowded on the weekends, it was a delight during the rest of the week. A green oasis in the middle of a city filled with concrete walls and choking pollution.

"Is this okay? I thought we could get some truck food and find a quiet place in the grass."

She smiled and touched his arm. "This is perfect, Lucas. Thank you so much."

It *was* perfect. Maybe a little too perfect.

They got out of the taxi and strolled into the park, bypassing the bike rental stand and the parking ticket vendor. The air was cool for this time of year, and Sophia sucked it down, the lush green grass and towering trees never failing to instill in her a sense of peace.

She glanced at Lucas who strolled next to her. "Are you sure you're up to this?"

"As long as you don't try any fancy moves, I think I'll be able to keep up."

Her stomach shimmied beneath her ribcage at the memory of just how well he'd been able to keep up last night... and this morning. Hard to believe that less than twelve hours had passed since then.

No, she was the one in danger of not keeping up.

The sensual games Lucas seemed so adept at were all new to her, which was why she'd agreed to his request to stay. She wanted to explore. To learn what her body was capable of. Maybe that's why both of her other relationships had fizzled out after only a few months. Neither of them had elicited the wild passion that Lucas brought to the surface.

They reached a fork in the road, and Lucas paused as if not sure which way to go. That's right. He wasn't familiar with the park. Or his birth culture, for that matter. "Let's go to the right. There's a nice place off the beaten path. We can pick up some food at one of the stands on the way, if you still want to eat."

"Sounds good to me."

Minutes later, Sophia carried several spicy meat kabobs, while Lucas held two chilled green coconuts, the tops removed with a single whack of a machete, leaving a small hole through which to stick a straw. They found a shady spot in the grass far enough from the pavement that they had a bit of privacy bu close enough to watch the daily activity in the park—whether it be runners pounding the pavement or riders rolling by on inline skates or bicycles.

Lucas toed his loafers off, enjoying the freedom that always came with ridding himself of his shoes. He leaned back on one elbow, careful to keep his side fairly straight, and took a sip of the coconut water. Crystal clear and slightly sweet, the icy liquid slid down his throat like a dream.

"Another thing I don't remember." He studied the fruit. "Although I'm sure I must have had one of these at some point in time."

"It's very Brazilian." She took a drink from her own coconut and then set it down on the grass beside her, handing him one of the kabobs.

Maybe it was, but Lucas didn't feel Brazilian. Which was why he'd wanted to talk to Sophia about Marcos. If anyone knew his brother, it was her. Maybe she could help him sort through some of his conflicting emotions regarding his birth parents and his brother. He wasn't sure now was a good time, though, after what she'd just gone through at the hospital. He'd seen the hint of moisture in her eyes as she'd talked about her patient. He glanced around, letting his feet sink into the thick grass. "It's beautiful here."

"It is." She nodded. "One of my favorite places in the entire world."

He couldn't imagine having a place like this—a spot he could actually call his favorite. A strange sensation spread through his chest as he wondered if this could become one of those special places he'd want to return to again and again. He glanced at the woman next to him. Sophia's dark hair glowed with health, her cheeks finally getting some color back in them after the crisis at the hospital. Even in scrubs, she looked beautiful.

Something inside her purse buzzed just as she'd put a bite

of meat in her mouth. She reached inside her bag and glanced at the readout, before handing it over to him.

Frowning, he tilted his head and she gave a couple of exaggerated chews to show she couldn't answer it then pointed at the readout.

*Marcos Pinheiro*, the screen read.

He pressed the talk button. "Hello?"

Silence. Then, "Who is this?" His brother's voice, true to form, bristled with suspicion.

"It's Lucas. Sophia's mouth is full at the moment, so she asked me to answer her phone."

There were several more seconds of silence before he realized his words could have been construed to something less than innocent. "We're at the park and got some food."

"Oh. Okay, good. So she's there with you."

Hadn't he just said that?

"She's right beside me. How are things there?"

"Pretty damn good. How about there? Your therapy going okay?"

He kept facing forward, not about to tell him that his therapy had just been upgraded to include a certain set of nocturnal exercises that got his heart pumping a mile a minute. Somehow he didn't think Marcos would approve, especially from his growled demand when he'd heard a man answering Sophia's phone. "Therapy's good. My stitches are out already."

"Any leads from the police?"

Why did Lucas get the feeling his brother had not called just to find out how he was doing? Especially as he'd called Sophia's cellphone. "Not yet."

"Well, I'm glad you're feeling okay." Marcos cleared his throat. "Er...what would you say if I told you I was thinking of running off to Vegas with Maggie?"

Vegas?

He was pretty sure the running-off part had nothing to do with playing the slot machines. Or maybe it did...marriage was the biggest damn gamble known to man. "That's awfully quick, isn't it?"

Sophia put her hand on his arm, her brows raised in question. He held up a finger, trying not to let his surprise at Marcos's words show on his face.

"Quick, maybe. But I've never been more certain of anything in my life."

"Wow."

What else could he say? Maggie seemed like a great woman, giving and compassionate. He'd even asked her out himself when they'd met at the medical convention a few weeks ago. He could see now how bad a match that would have been. No, he needed someone like...

He glanced at Sophia again, then looked away.

Nope, not even going there. He needed no one.

He quickly added, "Congratulations. I'm really happy for you both."

"Thanks. That means a lot to me."

Sophia tugged his arm again.

"Hold on for a second, Marcos, will you?"

He put his thumb over the receiver and held it for a second. "Marcos and Maggie are getting married."

Her mouth fell open. "Married. You're kidding!"

He wished he were. "No. Do you want to talk to him?"

"In a minute. Let me catch my breath."

Perfect. He put the phone back to his ear. "Okay, I'm back."

Marcos's voice was amused. "So what'd she say?"

"She says she's glad for you and hopes you'll have many happy years of wedded bliss."

The woman in question punched his arm hard enough to sting.

"Hmm...that doesn't sound like Sophia. She's always grumbling about my lack of fun."

Yeah, well, he didn't exactly want Marcos to know how much fun he and Sophia were currently having. In this man's bed, of all things. He made a sound he hoped sounded non-committal.

"So, anyway, we're planning on a Vegas wedding, and we want you and Sophia to join in via a video call." He chuckled. "We figure it's as close as we can get to having you and Soph here in person. And we want you as best man and Sophia as maid of honor. The wedding chapel advertises a huge screen where we can see you as we take our vows."

A video-conferencing type of thing? Was Marcos kidding? He rolled his eyes. "I don't know, Marcos. I have no idea what Sophia's schedule is like."

The last thing he wanted to do was sit in front of a computer screen and watch his brother throw away his freedom.

Only he didn't sound shackled. The opposite, in fact.

"Sophia has that hospital wrapped around her little finger. They'll let her off. Maggie is pretty firm on wanting this, Lucas. And I'm pretty firm on doing whatever it takes to make her happy. Besides, it's been a long time since I've been able to share an important moment with my brother."

Lucas's brain glitched, sending a wave of longing rolling out through his neurons, first hitting his ears, which responded with a dull roar. He blinked hard before those signals had a chance to reach his eyes. "Okay. I'll pass the phone to her so you can talk to her."

He handed the phone over, avoiding her eyes as she took it and put it to her ear.

What else could he do other than suck it up and sit through a half-hour ceremony? Okay, this wasn't a tragedy. So he and Sophia were sleeping together. As long as they didn't say anything, no one would have to know. Things could just continue like they were now.

Even as he thought it, the rigidity of his spine began to ease and the buzzing in his head receded.

What could go wrong, right?

As soon as she got off the phone, though, he knew something was indeed wrong. "Are you okay?"

She nodded. "I'm really happy for them. Really I am."

Brushing back a lock of hair that blew over her shoulder, he said, "I sense a 'but' in there somewhere."

She bit her lip and shook her head. "It's nothing."

Clearly it wasn't "nothing."

He leaned forward and put his fingers beneath her chin, tilting it so she was forced to look at him. "Tell me."

"I figured Marcos would get married one day, and I can't imagine anyone better for him than Maggie, it's just…"

He waited, sensing there was something trapped inside her. Some fear about Marcos getting married. "You think it's too soon?"

"No. No, it's perfect. *Maggie* is perfect. And I've wanted this for Marcos for a long time. I just didn't think he'd do it in the States."

Why that made a difference one way or the other, he had no idea. Then it hit him like a bolt of lightning. "You're afraid he'll stay. There in the States."

She nodded and pulled her chin from his grasp. "I know it's not fair, it's just that I've known Marcos my entire life."

That statement sent a fiery arrow right through the center of him. "You're afraid he'll leave you."

"Not in a romantic type of way, it's never been like that between us. But if he leaves…" She drew a deep, shaky breath. "If he leaves, it means that just like those first few years at the orphanage, I'll be all…"

Her words trailed away, but Lucas could hear the rest of the sentence clanging through his skull, the noise almost deafening.

He knew what she'd been about to say with almost a hundred percent certainty. If Marcos left and moved to the United States, then, just like her days at the orphanage, she'd be all… alone.

# CHAPTER FIFTEEN

"THERE ARE WORDS HERE."

Sophia traced the straight line of the medical symbol tattooed on Lucas's arm as she lay next to him in bed. Only it wasn't really a line at all. It was some kind of script.

After her almost-confession at the park, she'd leaped up, declaring that she was ready to leave. They'd gone back to the apartment, but when she'd tried to retreat to her room Lucas had taken her hand and pulled her against him, kissing her with a gentleness that had made her want to weep. He'd then led her back to the bedroom and proceeded to make love to her until she'd forgotten everything except what he made her feel.

Her body was still tingling from the encounter twenty minutes later.

"Hmm. Words where?" He tugged her leg until it was over his hip, thumb stroking her calf.

Flat on his back, and naked as the day he was born, she marveled at how he could do that. There wasn't a hint of embarrassment and because of how sure he was of himself, his confidence spilled over to her, allowing her to behave in ways she'd never dreamed possible. She felt wanton and happy tucked against his side, just as bare as he was.

"On your tattoo. Down this little line. I never noticed them before."

His thumb stopped its movement for a second before starting up again. "Yes, there are."

She squinted at the letters, trying to sound them out. *"Non Omnes Vagantes Deerant."* The words weren't English. Or Portuguese. "What does it mean?"

"It's Latin, adapted from Tolkien. It means 'Not all who wander have lost their way.'"

He dragged her on top of him with a suddenness that drove the wind from her lungs. "But the last thing I want to do right now is discuss Tolkien."

A laugh came up from her throat as she realized something was already stirring down below. The man really was insatiable. But that was all right because when she was with him, she felt pretty insatiable herself. "Okay, Dr. Carvalho, so what do you want to talk about?"

His thumb brushed the faint red mark still visible on her right breast. "I want to talk to you about this."

She went breathless. "What about it?"

Leaning up, he nipped her shoulder, then went a little lower, repeating the action, sending a shiver over her that worked its way south.

He reached her left breast, hovering over the spot that mirrored the mark on her opposite side. His tongue smoothed over her skin before his head came up. "How do you feel, Sophia, about men who bite?"

He wanted to watch.

Sophia had suggested they go together to rent formalwear for Marcos and Maggie's wedding, as it was a fairly common practice in Brazil. Seeing her in those dresses would be a mixture of torture and lust, but it was too late to back out now, even if he wanted to. Which he didn't.

Sophia had turned fiery red when the manager of the rental store had assumed they were a couple, then she'd tossed her head and given him a cheeky smile. "Do you want to see what I try on? I'll make it worth your while."

She'd already done that last night. And the night before.

Sophia was quickly becoming an addiction he just couldn't kick.

A stupid decision, but pretty much in line with every other choice he'd made lately. And hell if he didn't want to see her in that pair of killer shoes. She'd picked them up from her apartment on their way to the shop, tossing them into the back of the car, telling him those shoes had once brought Maggie a whole lot of luck.

He'd been too shocked to ask her exactly what kind of luck. Especially when her lips had curved in a secretive smile that had made his stomach tighten.

Yep, his rash decision to help her choose her outfit seemed more dangerous with every passing second.

The saleswoman measured him for a tuxedo, then led him to a red satin chair and asked him to have a seat. Feeling a little too much like a sheik or a wealthy pervert wanting his own private peep show, he sank into the chair.

It seemed to take for ever for Sophia to come out of that dressing room, but when she did...

God in heaven, when she did, it took everything in him to remain rooted in that chair. He made a point of propping an ankle nonchalantly on his knee and leaned back, although doing so set his abs on fire.

Dressed in a shiny green dress that criss-crossed over the front and revealed just a hint of cleavage, the rest of it fit her like a glove, coming to just above her knees. That left a long golden expanse of leg bare to his roving eyes until he reached the lucky shoes.

And they were every bit as mouthwatering as he'd feared. Lots of glittery straps held her foot in place and the heel was a mile high. When she turned round, the muscle in her calf stood out in sharp relief, and a sexy indentation ran along the side of her leg from just above her ankle to the bottom of her knee. Hell, he'd always been a sucker for a great pair of legs, and he knew from experience that Sophia's were strong and lithe and far too flexible for his peace of mind.

She spun back around, a smile on her face. "So? Is this the one?"

The one he wanted to peel off of her inch by inch? Oh, yeah. "I think so."

The saleslady stepped forward. "You don't want to see any others? We have many wonderful dresses. And your wife has a beautiful figure."

Didn't she, though? Hearing the woman refer to her as his wife made something in his gut slide sideways, though, and he hurried to make that sensation go away. "She's not my wife."

Sophia shifted her weight, a slight frown marring her brow.

What the hell? "We're not married at all," he clarified further. "Not to each other and not to anyone else."

Maybe Sophia was worried that the saleslady might think they were having an affair, or that they were sneaking off to one of the country's infamous motels—which he'd heard were not for sleeping. Neither were the "drive-ins", which had no movie projectors, no white screens and no concession stands. Just a row of open bays into which you drove your vehicle, a curtain swishing closed behind you. If you'd ever had a fantasy about doing it in your car—or were simply strapped for cash—that was the place to go. Both locales were made for one thing and one thing only: fast, hard sex.

Something he shouldn't be imagining right now. Especially not with Sophia standing there in that tantalizing outfit. He could just slide the dress up those delectable thighs like he'd done with her skirt that first night and have her climb on top.

The saleslady cleared her throat, not seeming at all upset by the fact that they weren't married. "Let me put her in something else. You won't be sorry."

Sophia shook her head and took a step back, her smile nowhere to be seen. "I think this one will be fine."

Somehow he'd ruined her mood. Had it been the marriage thing? Surely she knew there couldn't be anything more than casual sex between them. Not for the long haul. He just didn't do that. *Couldn't* do that.

His gut shifted again—an angrier tightening of his innards that set his teeth on edge. He didn't want to leave the store on bad terms with her, nor did he want to leave the country that way. He wanted the good memories of their time together to follow him home. Maybe part of that was due to some misplaced jealousy over his brother's relationship with her. Maybe Lucas wanted to own an inch or two of that prime real estate that was her heart. He wasn't sure of the exact reason, but it squeezed him until he gave in.

He lowered his voice to coaxing levels. "Come on, Soph. Just one more. Maybe something in..." He glanced at her hair. "Red."

He knew from experience her inky-black locks would look phenomenal flowing over the color, since he'd seen her in a bra that very shade. It would be hard pressed, though, to outdo the green she had on now, as it was nothing short of heartstopping. There was definitely nothing wrong with the way that dress hugged each and every curve of the woman's body.

She wavered for a moment before her face relaxed, and she nodded. "One more." She glanced at the saleslady. "In red, if you have something."

"Oh, yes, I have the perfect thing. Come with me."

Sophia had felt so sure about vamping it up in front of Lucas and having some fun with him. Until the saleswoman had mentioned the word "marriage." Lucas hadn't been able to set her straight fast enough. If she'd had any doubt that that's not how he felt about her—not how he'd *ever* feel about her—she need look no further than the consternation on his face.

So why was she here in a store dressing room, getting ready to put on the gown of a lifetime? She snorted. At least the thing wasn't white with a train and a veil. Who knew what kind of reaction that would have gotten? He'd have probably taken off at a sprint, injuries or no injuries.

She slid the silky red fabric over her arms, trying to decide how to get her head through the single shoulder strap that started out on the right and was supposed to go over her chest before fastening on the left in back. She finally just ducked and hoped for the best.

It worked. The dress whispered down her body like a dream, the full skirt stopping at knee level. It wasn't as revealing as the bandage-style dress she'd had on a few minutes ago, but the fabric swished over her hips, hinting at curves while not blatantly outlining them. If anything, it was sexier than the first one. She stared at her reflection. The gathered bodice clung to her breasts, the sweetheart neckline following the rounded tops perfectly then dipping in the middle. The red strap bisected her chest, providing a line that drew the eye from right to left, a set of four glittery rhinestones marking the spot where the fabric joined the dress in front and in back. Since her sandals also had a criss-cross webbing of straps punctuated with glittery dots of stones, it made the two items seem like a matched set.

It was perfect. The *dress* was perfect. But the last thing she wanted to do right now was go out and show it to Lucas.

She wasn't sure why. When the saleswoman popped her head into the room, her mouth fell open. "I knew this would suit you." She smiled. "I think your gentleman friend will be rethinking his earlier words."

Hardly. Lucas had made it perfectly clear that he wasn't interested in sticking around. She drew herself up, the thought lending her the courage necessary to smooth the dress over the fronts of her thighs and give the woman a sharp nod of her head. "No, he won't, and I don't want him to. But as he was the one who wanted to see this dress, see it he shall."

The saleswoman murmured for her to wait just a second or two and then reappeared with a pair of chandelier earrings and a wide silver cuff that she wrapped around the upper part of Sophia's left arm.

"This dress needs no necklace. Sit for just a second, please."

Sophia did as she asked, perching on the white tufted stool, while the woman quickly pinned her hair up in a messy bun, tugging a few strands down to dance around her shoulders.

Why was she taking the time to do this? If she had some weird urge to do a little bit of matchmaking, then the poor woman was wasting her time. There was no match to be made here.

Even if she herself wanted it, which she didn't.

The memory of Lucas and that baby at Dr. Figuereiro's office came to mind. The kindness in his eyes as he'd smiled at the child—no hint of shock at her deformity. Just acceptance of her as she was.

He'd make a perfect father. One who would love his child no matter what.

Unlike her own family?

She swallowed. *Forget it, Sophia. He's not interested. Not now, not ever.*

A shard of hurt lodged in her chest, its pain a sharp reminder that she was still alone, no matter how many people she surrounded herself with. No matter how chaotic her job was at times. At the heart of it she'd never really had anyone to walk through life with other than Marcos, and that was all about to change now that he was getting married. While she was ecstatic for him, it just made her sense of loneliness that much harder to bear. But no one needed to know that except her.

Within another two minutes she was on her feet and headed out the door of the dressing area, her chin held high and proud.

When she stepped through the curtain, Lucas froze, his

gaze trailing over her. Then his breath came through his teeth in a low whistle that told her what she already knew. The dress looked good.

He stood and moved toward her. *"Sophia, você é lindíssima."*

Beautiful. He'd called her beautiful. And the verb he'd used was the one that described permanence. Not a quick "you look beautiful today" or "you look beautiful in that dress" but "you *are* beautiful"…a state of being that endured.

He took her left hand and lifted it, applying slight pressure as he urged her to turn around.

The dress wasn't particularly low in back—it hit just beneath her shoulder blades—but with her hair up, it probably made it seem like there was more skin showing than there actually was.

Something brushed against one of the earrings, sending its heavy weight swinging back and forth against her neck. The sensation made a shiver go through her. As did the warm finger sliding down her spine, from the hair at her nape to the top of the dress. Her breath caught, and she noticed the saleswoman, standing at the dressing-room door, had a knowing smile on her face.

"Beautiful," he said again, slowly turning her around to face him. When his eyes met hers, they contained that same molten glow she was coming to recognize.

He wanted her.

Catching one of her loose strands of hair, he wound it around his fingertip, tugging slightly. "Your hair looks good up."

She licked her lips. "So you like this dress better than the other one?"

"I like you. In either dress." He leaned forward until his lips were against her ear. "*Out* of either dress."

His palm cradled the line of her jaw, his thumb going beneath her chin and tilting her head back.

He was going to kiss her.

She knew it with a certainty, and suddenly she didn't care who else was in the room. She wanted his kiss. Wanted his touch. Wanted to have an out-of-dress experience.

A thread of a song came from the dressing area, and Sophia nearly cursed aloud. Lucas pulled back, eyes narrowed on her face. She swallowed. "That's my phone. It's...um, in my purse."

"Do you want me to get it?" the saleslady asked, reminding them of her presence and bringing Sophia back to earth with a bump.

"Please." Right now, she didn't think her legs would hold her up long enough to make the trek to the dressing room.

Lucas released her and took a step back, and then another, shaking his head slightly as if trying to figure out what had happened.

Within another thirty seconds the saleslady handed her the purse. "I'll just be over there, if you need me." She motioned to a rack of dresses on the far wall.

"Thank you."

*Sophia, what were you thinking?*

Her phone rang again, cutting off in mid-tune this time, as whoever it was hung up. She dug around in her purse until her fingers closed around the hard plastic case. Pulling it out and glancing at the readout, she saw it was Lídia, another nurse at the hospital. She pressed redial and waited as the phone on the other end rang once...twice, then the woman answered.

"Sophia, where are you?" Her voice sounded weird. Scared, almost.

"I'm at a dress shop, why?" No reason to admit she was there with the patient she was supposed to be babysitting. One she'd been bonking every night for the past week. One for whom she'd just modeled some very sexy pieces and flashed a length of leg that should have been obscene.

"Haven't you heard the news?"

Her heart stuttered. "What news?"

"The subway—the red line near Palmeiras—derailed."
There was a pause. "It's terrible, Sophia. They're saying there
could be hundreds of casualties."

# CHAPTER SIXTEEN

SOPHIA GLANCED AT Lucas as the horror of the situation finally sank in.

His head was tilted to the side, and he stared back at her as if trying to figure out what was going on.

"Have the victims started arriving at the hospital yet?"

"No, the station is in chaos and the first responders are still in the tunnel, trying to get past the wreckage. Can you come back in? We're going to be overrun as soon as the ambulances start arriving."

"We're not far from the Palmeiras station. I have a doctor with me—maybe we can head over there and see if we can help. Once they start transporting patients, I'll come to the hospital. How many are going to be routed our way, do you know?"

"Not yet. It's rush hour. You know how tightly packed the subways are at this hour."

She did know. People jammed in until it was impossible to fit in one more. At times it felt like the trains swallowed mouthfuls of people and then belched them out again at successive stations. "I'll check it out and call as soon as I know something."

Lídia came back, "Okay, but please be careful."

"I will."

As soon as she punched the "end call" button she quickly

explained to Lucas what had happened. "I have to get over there now."

"*We* have to get over there. Like you said, I'm a doctor." He took out his wallet and peeled back some bills. "We'll be back."

The woman hesitated. "But if the dress is ruined..."

As soon as he added a few more notes, she nodded. "Don't worry about it. The dress is yours."

With no time to change back into street clothes, they hurried out of the store. When she started towards her car, Lucas stopped her, motioning toward a nearby taxi stand. "It'll be faster in one of those."

Sophia unstrapped her high heels and kicked them off her feet.

"Do you need me to run in and get your other shoes?"

"I have a pair of slip-ons in the car. I'll just grab them while you hail a cab."

By the time she'd yanked on the ballerina flats the taxi had pulled up beside her, and Lucas was out of the car, holding the door open.

She slid into the seat, and he got in beside her, motioning for the driver to be on his way.

"Does he know where we're going?"

"Yes. Evidently everyone knows what happened with the subway except us." She wasn't sure if the censure in his voice was aimed at her or at himself. But right now she didn't care. Adrenaline coursed through her system as she prepared for what was sure to be a wrenching scene. She needed to put everything out of her mind except the task at hand. People were counting on her to be at her professional best, and she owed it to them to show up with that attitude.

A warm hand reached out and gripped hers and she couldn't stop herself from leaning against Lucas, putting her head on his shoulder as she tried to draw from his strength. "All those people...trapped."

"We're going to get to them. I have credentials with Médicos Sem Fronteiras—Doctors Without Borders. They should let me in as well."

Traffic was at its crushing worst as it was every day at rush hour, but the driver was a whiz at getting in and out of the smallest places, sticking an arm out the window—hand wagging up and down—to signal whenever he wanted to move into another lane. The well-known gesture wasn't a request. It was a statement of intent: *I am coming over.*

Despite the driver's expertise, within two miles traffic had been reduced to a tangle of cars and snarling drivers, probably as a result of the subway accident. "It'll be faster to walk, Lucas. We're only a couple of blocks away."

She let go of his hand and started to fumble around in her purse for some money, only to have him beat her to it, handing the driver a fifty-*real* note with a murmur of thanks and a short "Keep the change."

Then they were out of the taxi and dashing between the stopped lines of traffic until they reached the sidewalk, where the distant jumble of police cars, ambulances, and fire trucks gave a grim prognostication of what they would find up ahead. The out-of-sync bursts of flashing lights only increased that feeling, like a deadly arrhythmia that was sweeping out of control.

She glanced over at Lucas. "I can run ahead if you need to slow down."

"I'm fine. Keep going."

If he was in pain, she couldn't tell. His face was a mask of determination as they continued to sprint the remaining blocks to the entrance to the subway station. Once there the crowd outside the doors pressed close, and she realized the police must be stopping people from entering. Names were being screamed out, and the sound of desperate pleading assailed her ears as relatives and friends tried to gain admittance. When the crowds grew too tight to move, Lucas grabbed her hand and edged towards the front, calmly using the size of his body to push his way through. Every stray bump of a stranger's elbow must have been agonizing for him, but he kept moving. "We're medical personnel, let us through."

Time after time, the rough statement parted the waters. When they got to the station door she saw she was right. About twenty military police were stationed in front of it, riot gear on, batons at the ready. When one of the officers glared at them when they took a step forward, Sophia yelled, "I'm from the hospital. I'm a nurse." She gestured at Lucas. "He's a doctor. We came to help."

The nearest officer motioned them forward. "I need to see some ID." If he had any thoughts about the way she was dressed, he said nothing.

Thank God she'd brought her purse. She grabbed her wallet and flipped it to the windows that held her residency card and her medical identification. Lucas flashed two different IDs as well.

It worked, because the officer scanned the documents then stepped aside. He looked her in the eye. "Rosángela Melo Medeiros, my mother, was probably on that train."

Oh, Lord. How it must hurt him to be stationed outside when all he probably wanted to do was rush inside and tear the place apart, looking for his mom. She touched his arm and repeated the woman's name. "Rosángela Melo Madeiros. I'll remember. If I see her or hear of her, I'll get word to you."

He gave a curt nod that betrayed nothing and yet said everything, then looked away, going back to the job at hand. If anyone could feel the desperation of those in the crowd, this man could. She prayed his mother was one of the lucky ones.

The escalators leading to the lower levels had been shut off, probably because of the danger below, and as she and Lucas hurried down the steps on foot, the passageway grew dimmer, the main overhead lighting switched to the emergency systems. At least there was no smoke coming up the passageway, but she did have to hold her dress bunched around her legs to keep the warm currents of air from blowing it up.

It was eerie to see the pale concrete block stairwells that led four levels underground so devoid of people. The screaming from outside hadn't followed them into the subway system itself, although she heard the distant whine of saws and other equipment. To Sophia, the lack of human voices seemed ominous, but it could just be that the train was too far inside the tunnel for much sound to make it out.

One of the first responders they met on the way down said they were working on getting the doors to the train open, and they hadn't fully assessed the number of injured, although those in the first couple of cars appeared to have borne the brunt of the impact. When she and Lucas finally reached the platform, empty stretchers were lined up in wait.

Sophia identified herself to one of the emergency workers, and he directed them to the person in charge, a burly man with a clipboard, just as the sounds of chaos from the tunnels finally reached them.

The guy pointed a pen at Lucas. "You're a doctor?"

"Yes. Reconstructive surgery, but I should be able to help."

"We're going to need all the help we can get. You up to going into that tunnel and doing triage?"

"Absolutely." Lucas glanced at Sophia. "We both are. Sophia's a trauma nurse."

The man's brow went up as he scanned her dress, obviously wondering what in the world she thought she was doing coming in like she was.

"André," he called to one of the men standing down on the tracks. Obviously the main power had been shut down or he'd have been electrocuted. "Take these two down to the train. They can help identify critical-needs patients."

As they made their way into the darkened tunnel, Lucas glanced at Sophia, glad she no longer wore the sky-high heels she'd had on at the dress shop. In the distance he could hear the sounds of machines at work...and screaming. His chest tightened, and the memory of Sophia feeding him that bite of meat came back to him, her voice telling him, "I know it may not feel like you belong here, but you have this country's blood flowing through your veins."

These were his people—and they were suffering. He quickened his step.

André spoke, having to yell to be heard over the noise. "They're trying to get the doors open. It's a mangled mess down there." Suddenly there was the sound of metal rending and then the volume of screaming increased with a suddenness that made Lucas pause. When a strange kind of rhythmic thud hit his ears, along with distant grunts, he realized what it was. The doors were open and people were leaping off the trains willy-nilly and onto the tracks. The thought sent a chill through him.

Sophia said the trains were packed to overflowing at rush hour. So if passengers started pouring off the trains, they'd have to come by the three of them to reach the station that lay behind them.

The shouts grew louder, mashing together into a single unit of sound. Closing in at a rapid pace. Lucas glanced back the way they'd come. They'd never make it to the platform before the first wave of passengers reached them. He could pray that everyone was filing out in an orderly fashion, but if he knew human nature they would be rushing towards safety. Heaven help anyone in their path.

He gripped Sophia's hand and hauled her towards him and shouted at the worker who was leading them into the bowels of the tunnel. "We need to get against one of the walls, so we don't get trampled."

Even as he said it, in the distance he saw shadows—bouncing forms that had no real shape, but there were a lot of them. Heading towards them at frightening speed. "Now!"

As if realizing what he meant, André's eyes widened then his head swiveled towards the back of the tunnel, just like Lucas's had done seconds earlier. Putting an arm around Sophia's waist, Lucas pulled her to the nearest concrete wall and pressed her into it, wrapping his body half around her so the crowds would reach him first. Then he braced his feet wide, made sure André had heeded his warning as well, and waited for the tsunami to hit.

Panicked eyes were the first thing he saw, all filled with the same desperate fear. Then something struck his shoulder and swept by him. Again and again, the deafening sounds of terror accompanied the slap of human flesh, the blows almost dislodging him several times and sending pain ricocheting through his injuries.

They'd promised to try to locate the police officer's mother. That hope was all but dead now. He tucked Sophia's head into his shoulder, desperate to keep her safe, as more and more people swept by, the frenetic pace slowing as the numbers grew, the mass—like an oil slick—spreading further and further out to the sides. Lucas squeezed as tight as he dared without crushing Sophia against the wall, and prayed it would be enough to keep them both from being trampled or worse. Because if one of them lost their balance and fell—or if one of the passengers caught Lucas's shoulder hard enough and spun him sideways and into the stream of bodies, it would be all over. One or both of them could die.

# CHAPTER SEVENTEEN

THEY WERE STILL ALIVE.

He lifted his head, trying to figure out how long they'd been standing there. Fifteen minutes? Longer? People were still moving past them, but the numbers were beginning to thin—the pace slowing, as those at the back of the line were evidently less frantic than those at the front.

His body felt like it had a couple of weeks ago right after his surgery. And he was pretty sure he'd be covered with bruises from head to toe. But he was still breathing. He glanced down at where Sophia stood with her arms curled over the back of her head. Touching one of her hands, he was relieved when she straightened from her position.

"Are you okay?" His voice was hoarse and he had to clear his throat and ask again in a louder voice.

Sophia nodded and turned her head sideways to look up at him. "A little scratched from the wall, but I think I'll live." Her eyes narrowed a bit as she studied him. "Did you get hit in the head?"

"I don't think so, why?"

"Your left eye is turning purple. I can't tell if it's injured or just dirt from the tunnel."

He scrubbed it against his shoulder, wincing as a dull ache went through the socket. Nope, he was going to have a shiner. Hell, he didn't remember getting hit that hard. "It'll be fine."

He glanced to the other side, where André had been, and found the spot empty.

A wave of nausea hit the pit of his stomach. His eyes swept the tracks where people still trickled by and spotted the worker standing with his arms outstretched as if guarding something.

Or someone.

"Stay here for a minute," he muttered to Sophia.

His relief at seeing the man ended when he noticed two people on the floor.

One of the figures was crouched beside someone else.

A child?

The crowds were sparse enough now that they were splitting down the middle and streaming on either side of André, keeping the tiny group safe for the moment. Lucas maneuvered his way towards them little by little, trying to be careful not to injure anyone else in the process.

Once there, he gave the man's shoulder a squeeze. "Good job."

The worker glanced at him, his cheek smeared with dirt. "I saw the two go down…wasn't sure I'd be able to make it to them in time."

"You probably saved their lives. If you can stand guard a few minutes longer, I'll take a look."

Not waiting for the other man to respond, he knelt beside the pair. The person on the floor was indeed a child…a girl around six years old, her eyes open and glassy-looking, a huge knot on the right side of her forehead. There was a shoe-shaped smudge on the white blouse of what looked like a school uniform.

A man's footprint.

Lucas's head filled with a buzzing sound, his vision turning red for a second or two. What was wrong with people?

Even as he thought it, he knew his anger wasn't entirely fair. He'd treated trample injuries from concert venues or in natural disasters before. Sometimes people were so tightly packed against one other that they were swept along without any real control over their movements. Those in front were propelled forward by those behind them, until the whole group moved as a single entity. If someone fell, there was often no way to stop and help them. He'd worked on facial lacerations from just such situations. Worse, it was a horrible way to die.

Thankfully, this girl wasn't dead. Or maimed. But she was injured.

Sophia knelt beside them as well, making him frown. "I thought I told you to stay where you were."

"I can think for myself." Her eyes were on the still figure of the little girl, and she reached down to brush her fingers across her hair. "Is she okay?"

"I was just checking her." He didn't have his medical kit or a way to test her pupillary reactions, but he was going to bet she had a head injury. Whether it was a simple concussion or a fracture could only be determined at a hospital. Leaning down, he peered at her eyes, carefully noting that neither pupil was blown, both appearing to be the same size.

When she groaned and started to move, Lucas murmured to her in what he hoped was a reassuring tone, asking her to lie still. He glanced at the woman, whose brown eyes were streaming with tears. "Are you her mother?"

The woman nodded. "I—I was holding her, but someone pushed me and she slid down. I couldn't find her."

Sophia touched her shoulder. "It's not your fault. We're here to help you both." She picked up the girl's hand and pressed it into her mother's. "Try to keep her calm while we make sure she's okay."

The mother, who'd seemed as stunned as the girl a minute or two ago, took a deep breath and nodded.

As if she knew exactly what he wanted her to do, Sophia took the girl's other hand, allowing Lucas to assess her without worrying about whether or not the child was going to twist away from his touch. Starting at her shoulders, he ran his hands down her arms, feeling for obvious fractures. So far so good. He wanted a backboard, though, to stabilize her neck and spine.

Her ribs felt intact as well, and he watched for any reaction to the steady pressure of his hands, but other than that moan she'd given a few seconds ago she was calm. Maybe a little too calm.

Her belly felt soft, another good sign. Despite the shoeprint on her shirt, maybe there'd been no real damage done.

Then he found it.

The second his fingers skated over her thigh through the fabric of her skirt, he felt a hard, uneven ridge that he immediately identified.

Bone.

It had missed coming through the girl's skin by just a hair. He caught Sophia's eye, and her brows lifted in question as if knowing he'd found something. "Hold her steady."

She didn't ask what was wrong, just nodded. Lucas tried not to think about how she seemed to anticipate his every move, about how well they worked together. He forced himself to concentrate on the job at hand instead.

The last thing he wanted to do was frighten the mother. Or the child, who could thrash around and push the bone through. If that happened, bacteria from the tunnel could enter the open wound, or the sharp edges of the bone could shred an artery. If either of those things happened, they were in big trouble.

"André," he called to the man still standing guard above them. "I need something to use as a splint. I'll hold your position, if you can find me something straight."

Lucas knew there were probably worse injuries on the trains themselves, and he wanted to get to those passengers as soon as possible, but he also needed to secure the girl's leg before he handed her off to the next batch of people.

Before the other man could answer, the first sign of help appeared in the tunnel. Several EMTs jogged toward the train, carrying stretchers. Must have been the ones they'd seen wait-ing on the platform. One of the medical workers stopped be-side them. "What have you got?"

The man didn't question Lucas's right to be there, just jumped in to help as if he were someone he worked with every day.

"Fractured right femur and possible head trauma."

"Right." The EMT squatted beside them. "Anything worse in the trains themselves?"

Lord, he hoped not. "I haven't been able to get down there yet."

"I'll stabilize her if you want to head over there, Doc," the guy said.

"Great." Lucas glanced at Sophia, not wanting to leave her.

"Go," she said. "I'll find you later."

He nodded then leaned over to kiss her, his hand grazing her cheek before standing to his feet. His glance touched the little girl on the ground. At least she had a mom to stand guard over her. One who'd refused to leave, even though she herself could have been trampled in the process.

He wondered what Sophia was thinking at this very second. Was she remembering her own parents, who'd abandoned her over an injury that was easily repaired? Who might have even left her in a tunnel very much like this one to fend for herself?

He didn't want to leave—wanted to be that guy who would stick around, who would be there for her no matter what.

He couldn't. Not now. Not in a few weeks when he'd have to head back home.

*She can take care of herself. She's done it her whole life.*

If that was supposed to make him feel better, it didn't. He climbed to his feet, addressing the medical worker. "Okay. I'll go see what I can do."

"Appreciate it," the EMT said.

He hurried down the tunnel, following another stretcher, the procession of empty ones filling him with foreboding about what he'd find when he got to the train. Then he forced every thought out of his head except for the job at hand. And prayed things were not going to be as bad as he feared. But when he arrived at the first twisted subway car, the smear of a bloody handprint on the window, accompanied by low moans from multiple directions, told him he was wrong.

It was going to be every bit as terrible as he'd feared. And worse.

Lucas glanced at his watch as he handed off his last patient to a waiting volunteer. Eight hours had passed and they were finally able to attend to the least injured of the victims.

One of the medical workers nodded to him as he passed by and Lucas lifted a hand in a quick wave. He'd been surprised at how easily he'd been accepted by everyone. Despite his accent, they'd worked beside him, accepting his recommendations for treatment without question. It made him feel... needed. Wanted.

He jumped from the car onto the tracks and leaned back to stretch his back, every muscle in his body stiff and sore.

He didn't know the exact number of fatalities but there were a lot. The dead had been laid out in rows side by side in one of three cars and covered with anything the workers could get their hands on. Including Lucas's shirt, which had been used to drape the face of a boy who was similar in age to the girl he'd treated in the tunnel. Only this boy's head injuries had been catastrophic. The only blessing was that death had probably been instantaneous. A hollow ache settled in his chest as he wondered if the child's parents had been killed as well. The scene had been so jumbled, appearing as if people had been thrown around the cars like rag dolls. No one was certain who belonged to whom. The terrible task of identifying the dead and injured would fall to frantic relatives.

Some would rejoice. Others would mourn.

Several of the patients he'd attended were extremely critical. Who knew if they'd even made it to the hospital.

He'd only seen Sophia twice during that time, but just in passing—there'd evidently been no opportunity for her to leave and go to the hospital, as she'd promised Lídia, she'd been needed here at the accident site. But in the last two hours he hadn't seen her at all. They were down to people with minor wounds, and now that he had time to take a breath, he found he missed her.

*That's just the exhaustion talking.*

He knew it was the case, but it didn't help fill the hole in his gut.

Hell. Maybe it was time for him to go home.

Not to Marcos's apartment, but home to the States, before whatever was going on with him got any further out of hand. Before he made a promise that he *couldn't* keep.

Moving gingerly down the tracks, he noted most of the people milling around now were official-looking folk with clipboards. Inspectors, probably, trying to assess the cause of the accident.

Further down, he spotted someone resting against the dirty concrete wall of the tunnel, a dark jacket wrapped around her, a strip of red cloth peeking out below it.

Sophia.

His chest cramped and he wasn't sure whether it was with relief or some other emotion. Someone had evidently loaned her a coat. For some reason, he wanted it to be *his* jacket she wore, even though he had nothing to give her at the moment. Not even a shirt. Was that how Marcos had felt when he'd handed over his own flip-flops and insisted he put them on? Had his brother felt this fierce protectiveness that seared his insides and coated his throat?

No, it wasn't the same at all.

He had no claim over Sophia. But it did make him realize something. Despite her parents' abandonment, there were people who would reach out to her. Sophia was strong, she'd proven that time and time again, but there was also a delicate vulnerability to her that tugged at him. Made him want to keep her far from anything that might hurt her. Judging from the coat she wore, he wasn't the only one touched by that side of her.

She saw him, and her eyes lit up, making another part of him ache.

Pushing away from the wall, she came towards him.

He put his arm around her waist, not sure if he was supporting her or if it was the other way around. "I thought you'd have left by now."

She shook her head. "I wanted to make sure there wasn't anything else I could do to help."

"I think we've done all we can." His fingers tightened, pulling her a bit closer, the feel of her softness molding to him like a balm in the midst of tragedy. "Let's go home."

Suddenly he knew that he wanted nothing more than to hold her. Kiss her. Erase the horror of what he'd seen, if only for a few short hours. He'd make no promises. And if she didn't want him after today, he'd back away for ever.

He was probably being selfish. But as he leaned down and dropped a kiss onto her temple, her warm scent obliterating the smell of fear and death, it was the only thing he wanted to do.

She tilted her head and allowed him to graze her lips with his. He had to fight not to deepen the contact. Not to press her against the wall of the tunnel and prove to himself that they were both here. Both alive and unharmed.

As if she could sense exactly what he was thinking, she murmured against his mouth, "Take me home, Lucas. Please."

# CHAPTER EIGHTEEN

SOPHIA SHUDDERED AS Lucas slowly unzipped her dress, his every move reflected in the bathroom mirror in front of them.

The expensive garment was covered in dirt and blood, as was her hair. Her skin. It was as if the misery and terror of a thousand people were ground into her soul and could never be washed away.

She reached down so she could pull the dress over her head, only to have him stop her with a murmur. "You did this for me when I couldn't do it for myself. It's time I did it for you."

He'd taken her clothes off many times over the last several days, but this felt different. Somber. Weightier. Maybe because of the tragedy.

The tenderness as his hands slid down her arms made her breath catch, and when he linked his fingers with hers, giving a gentle squeeze, her stomach twisted.

His gaze came up, meeting hers in the reflective surface. One of his eyes was indeed black and blue, and would probably be even worse tomorrow. It looked like he'd been in the fight of his life, rather than fighting for the lives of others.

He was strong and kind.

And she loved him.

She swallowed. *Deus*. She loved him.

She was supposed to have kept this light and fun. A quick fling while he was recovering from surgery.

It was supposed to be all about the sex.

When had that changed? During their time in the subway tunnel, when he'd cared for that little girl? Or had she been headed this way from the moment he'd strode towards her in a hospital gown?

It didn't matter. What did matter was that he was here with her now. Surely he couldn't touch her like he was and not feel *something*. It was on the tip of her tongue to ask, but she didn't, fearing if she was wrong he'd recoil in horror. She couldn't bear it if he turned away from her right now, when she needed him so very much.

Letting go of her hands, he tugged the dress up and over her head, leaving her in just her bra and panties.

He leaned down and kissed the side of her neck, his body moving in behind hers. She shivered as his heat enveloped her, warming a tiny portion of her heart, filling her with hope as she remembered the tender way he'd held her hand and led her from the tunnel—the soft press of his lips as he'd kissed her temple. How a few days ago he'd told her to say goodbye while sounding very much like he'd wanted her to stay.

He had to care at least a little, right?

"Stay here while I turn on the shower." He whispered the words against her ear, his teeth teasing her lobe.

It was obvious where this was headed. If she was going to salvage some portion of her heart, she needed to stop it now.

Only she didn't want to. She wanted to see if she could tell anything from the way he took her. Instead of walking into the shower enclosure, though, he opened the door to the bathroom and left.

Sophia frowned in confusion, until he returned with a square packet. Okay, so he was thinking more clearly than she was. She turned around, leaning a hip against the counter to watch him undo his belt, his shirt already long gone, left behind in the subway tunnel. The remnants of his gunshot wounds stood out against his tanned skin, making her chest ache. He'd been through so much since coming to Brazil.

"How are you feeling?" she asked.

"Sore. Tired."

"Then…?" she motioned toward the condom he'd tossed on the counter, wondering if she was wrong.

His lips curved. "Not that sore. Not that tired." His smile faded as his eyes ran over her. "The only thing I want right now is you, Sophia."

Her stomach clenched at the way he said it. Surely the intensity she heard in his voice meant something. He wanted her. *Her.* Some part of him had to care.

"I want you too, Lucas. I do."

He moved toward her and laid his hands on the countertop on either side of her hips. His cheeks slid along hers. "You have no idea what those words do to me."

Oh, yes, she did, if they were anything like what his had done to her.

She slid her arms under his and folded them over his back, holding him close and pressing a kiss to his shoulder, next to the scar from his surgery. The way his breath hissed in at her touch made her smile.

*She* did that to him. She tried it again, adding just the barest hint of her teeth this time.

Lucas stepped back with a grunt. "I need to get that shower running, or you're going to have to take me sweaty and filthy."

She'd take him any way she could get him, but she let him go. He undid his pants and rolled them down his hips, along with his briefs.

Whew. He was already hard. Ready.

She was ready, too. She reached back and started to undo her bra, only to stop when he slowly shook his head.

"Don't. I want that."

*Deus.* Lowering her hands and wrapping them around her waist, she waited as he switched on the water. When he came back, he had droplets clinging to his dark eyelashes, running down his strong chest. All she wanted to do was lap the moisture up with her tongue.

He didn't give her a chance. Crowding her back against the counter, his hand skimmed up her back until he reached the hair at her nape. Gathering it in his hand, he tugged her head back and held it there for a second or two as if to show her that she was completely at his mercy.

She was.

He enthralled her. Seduced her. Held her very heart in the palm of his hand.

He could do anything he wanted to her right now, and she'd let him.

His lips touched her chin. Swept along the line of her jaw. Edged down the side of her neck until he reached the joint where it met her shoulder. Lips became teeth as he pressed into her skin with enough force to wring a moan from her, a series of shudders racking her body.

He held on as his fingers reached up and flicked open the clasp to her bra. When he let the strapless garment drop to the floor, he finally came up and claimed her mouth in a searing kiss that left her reeling and clutching his arms for support.

Somewhere in the back of her head she was aware that her feet were slowly moving forward as Lucas continued to kiss her, as his tongue swept into her mouth and taunted her with long, slow strokes.

Then a warm stream of water cascaded over her head, making her gasp. Lucas pulled away with a smile, taking hold of her shoulders and turning her away from him. He leaned his chin on her shoulder for a second or two before reaching for a bottle of body wash on the rack in front of them. The feeling of being enveloped by him was made stronger when—his arms still around her—he tipped the container and squirted a generous amount onto one of his palms. Returning the soap to its spot, he slowly rubbed his hands together and placed them on either side of her belly, the lather making a sudsy trail across her skin as he inched his way up toward her breasts, hands circling ever higher.

"Your skin is soft. Like silk."

The firm, insistent press of a certain part of his anatomy against her lower back said she wasn't the only one affected by his touch. And even though she knew where he was headed, her breath still caught in her throat when his hands curved over her breasts, fingers brushing her nipples. Instead of lingering there, like she was aching for him to do, he moved higher, still smoothing the layer of suds across her body. Along her collarbone, up the line of her throat.

"I need more soap," he murmured, his chin never leaving its perch. The rush of warm air against her neck was heady. "Can you reach the bottle?"

She leaned forward, noting that he followed her movements with ease. Expecting him to hold out his hand, she was puzzled when his palms slid up and down her arms instead.

"Open the cap."

She did as he asked, fumbling a bit but finally managing to get the thing open. Still he remained where he was.

Did he want her to return the favor? She started to pour it into her hand, only to have him stop her. "Not there."

He wrapped his hand around hers and directed her to the spot just over her left breast. "Right here."

He wanted her to pour it over herself? Gulping when he let go of her hand, she tipped the bottle and let the liquid drizzle in a stream down her breast, practically melting when it ran over the tip of her nipple and continued down toward her stomach.

"Nice." His hand came up and worked the soap into the sensitive peak. "Now the other side."

She wasn't sure she could—felt drunk with the pleasure of what he was doing. And just as she started to turn the bottle he squeezed the nipple he was working on, causing the soap to dribble onto the floor, instead of hitting her body.

"Oh, Sophia. You missed." He bit the side of her neck, and

she almost dropped the bottle altogether. "You'll have to do better than that. Try again." The last two words were growled against her ear.

Her breath huffed in and out of her lungs, and she felt less confident with every second. But his fingers had eased up and were now stroking in soothing motions over her soapy breast. So she tried to do it in a hurry this time, only to have him do the same thing, fingers gripping the most sensitive part of her breast and sending a shock of electricity arching straight to her center.

"Ah!" The sound came out as a cry as her hand squeezed hard against the soap bottle and sent a jet of it shooting out into space.

He swore against her ear, his erection jerking against her back. "Hell." Reaching around, he took the container from her. "You, young lady, are sending all kinds of thoughts spinning through my head."

The soap turned in her direction and with quick, rhythmic squeezes Lucas sent spurts of the creamy white liquid against her breasts, her stomach, her inner thighs. The act was obscene and erotic all at once, and she immediately grasped what kind of thoughts he was talking about.

Yes! She wanted that. Wanted him on her. Marking her as his.

Twisting in his arms, her fingers swept down his sides until she found what she wanted. Hot and hard in her hands, she reveled in the feeling of power as a tremor went through him. She gave him a slow smile. "I need some of that soap, only *my* hands are full this time." She slid them in a long, slow stroke over his engorged flesh. "Right here."

His eyes blazed as he lowered the bottle and allowed it to flow over her hands, over his own skin. She stroked and squeezed, trying to drive him as crazy as he'd driven her seconds ago. Still holding him, she allowed the rush of water to wash away the suds.

A groan sounded above her, and when she glanced up, his eyes were closed, his head leaning back against the tiles.

Now was her chance.

Being as quiet as she could, she kept stroking him as she got to her knees in front of him. Her mouth watered. She'd barely gotten a chance to look at him during their time together, and had certainly not gotten to taste him.

Leaning forward, she opened her mouth and engulfed the head of his penis, hearing a sharp grunt above her, followed by the sound of her name.

His hands went to the back of her head, fingers tunneling into her hair. But instead of pulling her away like he had on other occasions, he pressed her closer. A thrill went through her as she willingly went down to the limit of her endurance and came back to gulp a quick breath of air before moving forward again.

She'd never done this to a man, and was surprised at how fierce her own pleasure was as she allowed her tongue to stroke down his length and swirl around him, trying to keep a steady rhythm going.

She heard him muttering above her, a combination of what she thought were English swear words and supplications as she continued to try to take him deeper and deeper. A few seconds later, his grip on her hair tightened, and he hauled her away from him, the popping sound as he left her mouth ringing through the space around them. He went down on his haunches in front of her and cupped her cheeks, then kissed her, long and deep, his tongue pressing into her mouth again and again as if he had to finish what she'd started.

She'd wanted to finish him. Was disappointed that he hadn't let her.

The feeling didn't last long, though, because as soon as his mouth left hers he dragged her to her feet and ripped open with his teeth the condom he'd brought into the shower. As soon as it was on, he turned her to face the shower wall. "Spread your legs for me."

*Deus.*

She shuffled her feet apart, her right cheek pressed tight against the tiles. And almost as soon as she did so he bent his knees and found her, pushing home in a rush.

"Hell. I've been thinking about this." He pulled out and thrust deep again, driving the air from her lungs. "Every second of every day. You drive me crazy."

How could he even form words? Her mind was a mush of rolling waves that carried her up high and then dropped her, before starting to climb once again.

Time and time again he pressed her into the wall, his lips at her ear, breath rough as he bathed her in incoherent sounds that she instinctively knew were meant for her alone.

She'd wanted him to mark her. Well, he was. With each pump of his flesh into her he was branding her as his, her body instinctively gripping each time he entered her as if to bind him to her.

One of his hands found her breast, while the other slid between the tile wall and her stomach before moving to the V between her legs, his thumb finding her most sensitive spot and stroking over it.

"Lucas."

"I'm right here." As if to prove it he moved deep. So deep. Pressing against some inner part of her as his thumb continued to move in tight circles. He didn't let up, and although it felt like his body was tense and still behind her, the pressure inside her static, there was a rhythmic push and release happening that drove her wild.

It was too much. Not enough.

His fingers kept moving below and above, then suddenly he clamped down on her nipple as well as the nub between her legs.

The shaft of pleasure was shattering in its intensity, spearing straight down with a single thrust that wrenched a scream from her. Her body went off all at once, fierce spasms taking her inner muscles by storm.

Lucas's shout hit her ears at almost the same time, his body moving frantically to keep up with hers, driving into her again and again.

When her brain finally re-engaged, she realized they were both on the shower floor, both on all fours. Lucas's body was around hers. In hers. Touching her inside and out.

She wanted this man. More than she'd wanted anything in her life.

*Please, want me, too, Lucas. Please.*

Something inside her broke on a sob that came out before she could stop it. He stiffened above her as another and then another came out, leaving her helpless to staunch the flow. She had no idea why she was crying, whether it was with happiness or grief, but Sophia knew one thing was true.

What had passed between them was irrevocable. There was no going back. And as that thought wormed its way into her mind, so did a sense of despair. She had given absolutely everything she had to give, and then he'd wrung even more from her. More than she'd ever dreamed possible.

Whatever happened between them after this didn't matter. Whether it was good or bad, it would change nothing.

Because she would never be the same ever again.

# CHAPTER NINETEEN

HE'D MADE HER CRY.

Sophia lay curled into him, one long, slim leg over his thigh, her slow, even breathing telling him she was asleep.

He'd tried to get her to talk to him, but she'd insisted it was nothing, just the aftermath of the subway accident, followed by what had happened between them in the shower.

It was normal, she'd insisted, as if she cried every time she made love.

That was a lie. She hadn't cried the other times they'd been together. And he sure as hell didn't want to think of her getting this emotional with someone else.

After turning off the shower, he'd somehow carried her to the bed, despite his injuries, and held her as she continued to cry until she'd finally been limp against him. Her sobs had given way to hiccups, which had remained long after her tears had stopped flowing.

His heart raged inside him. At first he'd thought he'd hurt her somehow by going too deep with his thrusts. That had changed as he'd realized the heartbroken sounds hadn't been from pain but had been due to something else entirely. He may not have hurt her physically but he sure as hell had done something to her emotionally.

He hadn't made her any promises, so it wasn't that. And she'd refused to discuss it. Had finally just fallen asleep with moisture still on her cheeks. He'd pressed her face to his shoulder, his hand stroking along the silky skin of her back as he'd tried to think about what his next move should be. He wanted to fix it—whatever "it" was—but had a feeling nothing he did would help.

*Dammit!* He'd never been at a loss for words before. Never felt so unsure about what he should do.

Lucas gently slipped from beneath her leg and got up, holding his breath as he prayed she wouldn't stir. Her hand reached out for a second...found his pillow and clutched it tight.

His throat spasmed as he watched her for a minute or two.

The urge to get back under the covers and gather her to him swept over him, the urge so strong he clenched his hands into tight fists to refrain from acting on it.

Breathing hard, he had no idea what was happening to him, but he had to get away from this bed right now.

Going into the bathroom, Lucas braced his hands on the marble countertop in the bathroom, staring at the fresh red scars on his shoulder and abdomen. When he moved his arm to look closer, his tattoo caught his eye. He ran his index finger down the black staff that lay at the heart of the rod of Asclepius symbol, remembering how Sophia had stroked across it just like that.

Everyone noticed his father's name and the words "Promises Kept" that he'd had inked onto his flesh. But like the faint scar on Sophia's lip, very few people ever saw the extra words he'd had inscribed down the length of the staff a few years ago, or they wrongly assumed the black Latin words were part of the ornate design.

Not Sophia. She'd seen them—had asked what they meant.

*Not all who wander have lost their way.*

The wording was slightly different from Tolkien's original quote, but Lucas had thought it fit him to a T—an explanation of his nomadic lifestyle.

Only right now Lucas wondered if he'd been lying to himself all along. Because a part of him felt untethered, aim-less…lost.

Being in Sophia's arms last night had felt strangely like coming home. He hadn't wanted to leave them. Ever.

Only he couldn't afford to stay.

He had commitments back in the States. And he couldn't pretend to be someone he wasn't. If he stuck around, he'd eventually hurt her. Again.

Dr. Figuereiro's offer popped into his mind. He immediately dismissed it. He never stayed in one place for more than a few years at a time—and that type of job required a commitment that was beyond him. Not that he'd ever tried it but, still, it wouldn't work. He'd eventually want to leave for parts unknown. And then he'd hurt a lot more people than just Sophia—those hundreds of photographs on the good doctor's wall were evidence of that.

*You need to leave. Now. While you still can.*

*Before you do something that will hurt her even more further down the line.*

Dressing quickly, he picked up his wallet and stuffed it into his back pocket. When he moved to the doorway, he caught sight of Sophia's dress lying crumpled on the floor. Once a vibrant red, the fabric was stained with dirt and blood from the rescue efforts at the subway. It was battered and bruised. Barely recognizable.

He glanced back at Sophia and wondered if what they'd done last night had left her feeling like that discarded dress. God, he hoped not.

The memory of peeling that garment off her body came back to him.

*You did this for me when I couldn't do it for myself. It's time I did it for you.*

Hadn't his brother done the same thing when they'd been kids? Helped him do things he hadn't been able to do for himself?

Was that why he had chosen to work with underprivileged children? Trying to pay Marcos back over and over for the sacrifices he'd made on his behalf?

Maybe it was time he actually did something for his brother. Like stand beside him as he took his marital vows?

He scooped up the dress and held it to his face for several long seconds. He might not be able to make things right with Sophia but he could at least try to fix one thing. With a heart full of lead he made his way to the front door, leaving his set of keys on the side table. He then let himself out of the house… and out of Sophia's life.

"He said to do whatever it took to make it right."

The dry cleaner handed Sophia the garment bag containing her dress. A dangerous prickling started behind her eyes, but she straightened her spine.

She would not allow herself to cry. Not right now.

Waking up to find Lucas gone had been just about the worst thing she could imagine. He'd left no note. No nothing. The second she'd seen his set of keys, though, she'd known. He had gone, and he wasn't coming back.

She'd been shocked when the cleaner had called the next day to say her dress was ready. Dress? She'd told the woman she must be mistaken, she hadn't taken anything in to be dry-cleaned. When the clerk had mentioned the color and said a gentleman with an American accent had brought it in, her heart had contracted. Maybe he'd left a note with the dress.

"D-did he say anything? The man who brought in the dress?"

"Just what I said. That he wanted me to do whatever it took to make it right. Money was no object."

Money was no object.

If anything should set her back on her feet, it was that. Lucas wanted to be back in the States, back at his practice where he had the kind of life most people only dreamed of.

She'd been a fool to even hope he might want to stay here in Brazil. Stay with her. He didn't love her. Had never even hinted that he felt anything for her but lust. He'd fulfilled his end of the bargain, giving her a few wildly sensual nights that she would never forget. It wasn't his fault that she'd fallen in love with him.

But if he didn't care at all, why had he bothered sending her dress to be fixed? Guilt?

No, he had nothing to feel guilty for, as she'd never confessed her feelings.

The dress wasn't the only thing that confused her. Lucas's lovemaking had seemed different that last night. Enough for her to hope that he might feel something for her, too.

She murmured her thanks to the dry cleaner and then made her way out of the shop, still trying to sort through her jumbled emotions.

Marcos's wedding was in a week, and he'd called that morning to make sure she'd still be able to video-call. No one had mentioned Lucas, and she wondered if his brother even knew that he was back in the States.

The one good thing that had come out of the accident was that she'd been at the hospital almost nonstop over the last couple of days. But now that more victims were being released, her hours would soon slack off again, which meant she'd have way too much time to think.

She needed to take a break. Do something to force her out of the funk she was sinking into. Lucas had only been in her life a short time. She refused to spend the rest of it reliving each and every word he'd said and trying to read something into it. It would have been better if he'd just faced her and told her flat out that he was done—that he was headed home. Instead, he'd slunk away without a word. That didn't sound like the supremely confident man she'd come to know over the last couple of weeks.

So why didn't she figure out a way to ask him once and for all why he'd left like he had? Maybe then she could move past this chapter.

The idea grew until she couldn't see beyond it.

The man owed her an explanation. And she intended to get it.

With her chin held high and the bag over her arm, she made a decision. If her dress could be fixed, so could she. She knew just what to do to start that process.

First, she was changing jobs. It was high time she started thinking about someone other than herself and the way she saw it, Dr. Figuereiro's office was the perfect place to do that. And, second, she was going to call in a favor from a friend. If anyone could figure out a way to make this happen, it was Marcos.

Why had he thought this was a good idea?

Standing beside Marcos and Maggie in the wedding chapel, Lucas fiddled with his bow tie. He didn't really have a choice. He'd taken Sophia's advice and talked to Marcos about their past. They'd settled quite a few issues—well, as much as anyone could hope for with a brother who hadn't been able to think about anything other than his bride-to-be.

Besides, if he'd told Marcos why he didn't want to stand beside him as his best man, he'd probably have more than just a black eye. And from what he'd heard, Sophia hadn't even hesitated about taking part in the ceremony, so maybe he'd made a mountain out of a molehill. Maybe she hadn't been affected at all.

Unlike him, who hadn't gotten much sleep since he'd left Brazil a week ago. Every time he nodded off, images of Sophia came and tormented him with hints of what might have been.

But it couldn't be. Not for him. There was no way he could

hold someone's happiness in his hands and be expected to keep it safe. He wasn't made that way.

Was he?

Marcos jabbed him with an elbow. "You okay?"

"Yeah. Sure." He yanked on his tie again, wondering if he'd ever get rid of this strangling sensation.

Probably not. Maybe he could just work longer hours, make more volunteer trips.

And risk hurting a patient because he was too tired to function?

No. That wasn't the answer.

Then what was?

If he knew, he'd be in a whole lot better shape than he was.

He forced his mind back to the task at hand and glanced at the happy couple. Maggie was beautiful in a cream lace dress that hugged her slender curves. His brother was obviously head over heels in love with her, if the protective arm around her waist and appreciative stares were anything to go by.

All Lucas wanted to do was get this wedding over with and get out of there. He hadn't really expected to lay eyes on Sophia ever again—and the thought of seeing her image on that enormous screen in front of them was twisting his gut into hard little knots.

And yet the thought of *not* seeing her made his throat clog with emotions he didn't understand.

The minister walked in and greeted them. "I understand we're going to place a video call to Brazil?"

"Yes, we'd like a close friend to take part in our wedding."

More than a close friend. At least, for Lucas. He felt more for her than he'd ever felt for anyone in his life.

Was this love?

He clenched his jaw. No. It couldn't be.

Then why was he suddenly so anxious to see her that

he could hardly breathe as they punched the numbers into the machine?

He stared at the screen as the phone on the other end buzzed twice. Three times. Four. Five. Out of the corner of his eye he saw Maggie glance at Marcos, who squeezed her hand.

"She'll be here," he said.

He sent Lucas a pointed look. Although he hadn't shared everything with his brother, he had confessed that a few things had happened that shouldn't have. His brother had put two and two together and come up with five: that Lucas had broken his childhood friend's heart, and if that was the case, Marcos was going to break him.

But he hadn't broken her heart. Right?

So why the hell had she been crying?

It couldn't have been heartbreak, because he'd been right there with her. Had spent most of the night with her. No, her tears had seemed to come from what had transpired between them in the shower. It's what had helped propel him out the door.

The minister clicked cancel after the tenth ring. "Do you want to go on without her, or should I try again?"

"Try again." There was an ominous rumble to his brother's voice as he glanced toward the back of the chapel at the doorway. Surely he wasn't thinking of skipping out.

Evidently the minister sensed something was wrong as well, looking a little nervous as he hit redial.

That was nothing compared to the rock in the pit of Lucas's stomach.

The phone rang again. Once. Twice.

The sound of running feet came from behind them, the clickety-clack of high heels unmistakable.

"Sorry I'm late."

Every ounce of air left Lucas's lungs as he swung round to find Sophia hurrying up the aisle of the small chapel.

She stopped for a second, and they stared at each other.

The woman was gorgeous. Cheeks flushed. Hair pulled up into soft curls on her head.

That red dress.

His throat tightened further. She'd gotten it from the cleaners. Had worn it, even after he'd left her without a word of explanation.

And she was here. In the States.

Sophia jerked her eyes from his and went over to Maggie, hugging her tight. "Sorry. The card key at the hotel was different than I'm used to. I couldn't figure out how to make it work."

Lucas hadn't been able to figure out how to make it work either. And he wished to hell he could.

He wanted her attention back. But she smiled at Maggie and then hugged Marcos. There was no smile for him.

Marcos grinned back at her. "We were getting a little worried about you, kiddo. I thought maybe there was a problem with the flight."

"No, it was great."

Maggie reached out and squeezed her hand, pulling Sophia next to her. "We're so happy you decided to come in person."

"I wouldn't miss it for the world." Sophia's smile faded as her glance skipped past Lucas.

He got her message, though. She wouldn't miss Marcos and Maggie's wedding, even if it meant facing him again.

And yet he'd been standing here aching to see her, the sensation so strong that he could barely talk.

*Because you love her, you idiot. And you threw away your one chance to be with her.*

He loved her.

Seeing her in the flesh made him realize just how much. She was selfless and compassionate, kind and sexy. And she really did take his damn breath away.

Forcing his voice from his chest took a superhuman effort. "Good to see you, Sophia. I see the dry cleaner called you."

"That's right," Maggie said. "Lucas told us about what happened."

"Yes. It was quite an… Quite an experience," Sophia murmured.

Even from a couple of yards away he could see the hot color that stained her cheeks.

The minister cleared his throat. "If we're ready, could everyone stand on the little yellow marks? I have another wedding in a half-hour."

They all shuffled into position forming an intimate little U, which unfortunately put Lucas directly across from Sophia.

No one had answered the obvious question that pulsed through his skull: how had Sophia gotten here? And why? He would have thought the last thing she'd want to do was face him after what he'd done.

Marcos reached out to clasp Maggie's hand, lifting it to his lips while Sophia smiled at the couple.

The orphanage had dubbed Lucas, Marcos and Sophia the Dynamic Trio.

It looked like his spot was no longer vacant. They now had Maggie to round out their little group.

Never in his life had Lucas felt so alone. So detached from everything he wanted out of life.

Maybe that's what refusing to put down roots did to you. Kept you from ever experiencing the true joy and pain of life. Yes, he'd avoided being hurt…avoided having those roots ripped up and his life torn apart. But at what cost? Those things were part of what made human beings who they were— times of pain making moments of joy that much sweeter.

As he gazed at Sophia, her image blurred suddenly and was replaced by that of a dark-haired girl with wide, trusting eyes. He peered deep inside his mind and tried to focus on the picture forming there.

Yes. He could see her. Her smile. Her laughter. Her tears.

When he came back to the present, she was still there. The same eyes. Same smile. He gulped. He'd seen those same tears.

He *knew* her. Had known her all his life. He'd just pushed away the memories, too afraid to walk down that road to the past.

And if he didn't tell her before she walked out of this chapel, he'd regret it for the rest of his life.

The short ceremony was a combination of tacky and charming, the way only Vegas weddings could be. But through it all Marcos's love for Maggie shone through.

And Lucas was more and more certain of his own love for Sophia.

Each time their eyes met, he wanted to stop the minister and tell her how sorry he was for leaving like he had. Tell her she'd been right about Marcos, about his ties with Brazil... about everything. He wanted to demand that she tell him if there was any chance for them. For him. Even though he had no idea what kind of life he could offer her.

The bride and groom's final kiss went on and on. When he glanced at Sophia, her head was down, and she stared at her toes, which he just noticed were housed in the same sexy shoes she'd been wearing the day they'd gone to the rental store. He was actually surprised she hadn't just shredded the dress or left it at the cleaners. But she hadn't. She'd worn it to the ceremony. That should tell him something, shouldn't it?

Marcos and Maggie finally parted, and from somewhere a shower of rice came down, hitting his skin with bitter little stings that seemed to taunt him.

Maggie laughed, blowing a kiss to Sophia. "Thank you so much for celebrating with us! We'll see you some time next week in Brazil."

Next week.

The realization came to him. This was it. The last time he would ever see Sophia, unless he did something about it.

Marcos grabbed his new bride's hand then paused beside him, murmuring in low tones. "You once gave me some very good advice about not being able to control everything in life. That if I loved Maggie, I should go after her. You were right." He slung an arm around her waist. "I'm handing back your own advice. If you care about her, don't let her walk away."

He then stepped back and slapped Lucas on the back. "Don't be a stranger, bro. I expect to see a whole lot more of you in the future."

With that, the couple dashed out of the chapel to the limousine that was waiting to spirit them away.

He glanced across the carpet to see Sophia's eyes on him. She motioned down at the dress. "Thanks for having it cleaned."

"You're welcome."

The minister opened his arms as if pronouncing a final blessing and hinting that they should be on their way. "Thank you for being a part of today's ceremony. We wish you and yours a very happy evening."

Sophia took a step back. Then another. She was leaving. Right now.

He cleared his throat as she started to turn away. "Wait." Glancing at the minister, he said, "Could you give us a minute?"

"A…minute?" Understanding dawned on his face, and he gave Lucas a knowing smile. "Of course. We still have a few moments before our next lucky couple arrives."

The man pressed something into his palm and when Lucas turned it over he saw it was a business card. "Call us when you're ready."

He had no idea if Sophia would even accept his apology, much less agree to marry him.

But he wanted her to do both. More than anything.

The minister withdrew, leaving him alone with her. Taking

a couple of steps forward, he hoped she could see the sincerity in his eyes. "I'm sorry for taking off like I did. It was wrong."

Sophia blinked at him. "I'm sorry I got emotional after... everything that happened."

"I thought I'd hurt you."

"You didn't at that moment. But I was afraid you would." She shrugged. "And you did."

The shot hit its mark and burrowed deep.

"Hell, Soph. I'm sorry. I've never been good at settling down in one place, and I..." He took a deep breath. "I don't know *how* to stick around. But I do know I love you, and I want to be with you. I want to go back to Brazil. With you, if you'll have me."

"You love me?"

He stepped even closer and touched his fingers to her cheek.

"I do. I saw you, Sophia. I finally remembered what you looked like as a little girl. You were beautiful. I knew you would be. Just like that child in Dr. Figuereiro's office." He shook his head. "It's taken me thirty years to be able to look back and accept being a poor, filthy kid from a *favela*. But I can see it clearly now."

His fingertips brushed down her jaw until he cupped her chin. "I'm thinking about taking Dr. Figuereiro up on his offer. But only if you think you could fall in love with me someday."

"Someday? It's too late for that, Lucas."

A flash of hurt went through him, its bite worse—much worse—than the shower of rice a few minutes ago. He swallowed. "Well, then, I guess this is—"

"*Deus.* You're so quick to leap to the worst possible conclusion. It's too late because I'm *already* in love with you. I came to the United States to demand an explanation. And to tell you the truth about how I feel."

He hardly dared believe...

"Are you sure?"

"Absolutely."

He pressed a fist against his forehead and held it there as he tried to press back the volatile emotions that were beating against his eyelids, streaming through his veins. When he finally drew a deep breath, he looked up at her. "Don't go anywhere."

"I'm right here." She smiled, using the same words he'd used on their last night together. The relief and love he saw reflected on her face slid through him with a warmth that reached all the way down to his bones. A sense of certainty filled him as he drew her close—bent to kiss her. It was finally safe to put down those roots. Because Sophia would be right there beside him, her already deep system of roots providing an anchor for his, giving him a sense of something he'd been searching for his whole life: a place to call his own.

Home.

# EPILOGUE

MARCOS GRABBED SOPHIA and swung her around the reception
area of the empty clinic.

"Hey! What's the big idea?"

"I would tell you, but I promised Maggie I'd let her break
the news. She's due here any minute."

Her brows went up. "News. What news?"

Lucas strolled out of the back, took one look at his brother's
arm and gave a fair imitation of a disapproving scowl. "I'm
willing to share most things, but my wife is not one of them."

Sophia brushed Marcos's fingers from her waist and
crossed over to her husband of three weeks. "You don't have
to share. I'm all yours. Besides, he says Maggie has...*news*."

Draping an arm over her shoulders, he drew her close.
"*News*, huh? Very mysterious."

"Isn't it, though?" She batted her eyes at him.

Marcos glared at them as if they were spouting gibberish.
"What's with you two?"

"Nothing," they said at the same time, then laughed.

After a whirlwind engagement, Lucas was settling into life
at the clinic with an ease that surprised her. Dr. Figuereiro was
still there and would be until Lucas finished all his certifica-
tions and licensing issues. They were looking at a year or a
year and a half before everything could be legally handed off.
But Lucas said he was fine with it. And Sophia was fine with
accompanying him on volunteer trips to wherever his heart

desired. There was no fear that he was suddenly going to get itchy feet and leave her, because she'd already told him she was sticking to him like glue. Her home was where he was.

The door opened, and the woman in question strolled in, holding something behind her back. She reached up to give Marcos a quick kiss on the mouth, and then looked up at him with narrowed eyes. "You told them, didn't you?"

"No, I..." He glanced at them. "Tell her I didn't say a word."

Sophia grinned. "He didn't. Really, he didn't."

"Okay, good, because I have something to show you."

She pulled her hand from behind her back and wiggled a sheet of paper. Sophia took it and stared at it for a second before the tiny image took shape.

"You're pregnant?"

She hooked her arms around Marcos's waist. "Yes, we are. Six weeks, to be exact."

"What the hell? They scooped us." The statement burst from Lucas, and it set off a fit of giggles that Sophia couldn't contain. The giggle turned into a laugh that swelled and grew until she couldn't breathe, couldn't talk, tears streaming down her face.

She finally gulped back the sound. "Sorry about that. Congratulations!" Another choked laugh emerged at the end of the sentence.

Maggie's brows drew together in a frown, while Marcos's mouth opened and closed like a landed fish. Maggie huffed out a breath. "Is this a Brazilian thing, because I don't see what's so funny?"

Biting her lip hard, Sophia finally got herself under control. Then she reached over and squeezed Lucas's hand. "Show them."

Shaking his head and still muttering to himself, he went behind the reception desk and retrieved his own piece of paper and came around to the other side.

He handed it to his brother, who stared down at the sheet. "You…you…?"

Maggie evidently realized what had happened, because she shook a finger at them before coming over and catching Sophia up in a quick hug. "You guys! You too?"

"Yes. Eight weeks. Why do you think we were in such a hurry to get married?"

They'd invited Sophia's parents to the simple ceremony—something that had taken some doing, since Lucas hadn't wanted them anywhere near her. Although there were still some old wounds that needed to heal, her folks had done what they felt best all those years ago—leaving her where she could get the government-funded care they couldn't afford. They'd hoped she'd be adopted and given a better life than what they could provide. That hadn't happened, and as time passed, they'd been too ashamed to ask the orphanage to return her to their care.

Lucas held a hand out to his brother, and Marcos grabbed it, pulling him into a tight embrace.

"Congratulations, bro."

"You too. We seem to be following in each other's footsteps."

It wasn't just marriage and the pregnancy they had in common. Lucas had joined his brother in providing free health care in the *favela* where they'd been born. They hoped to expand from one day a week to two days over the next year, recruiting more doctors to join in the effort.

"We do seem to be, don't we?" Marcos paused for a second before continuing. "Maybe it's not each other's footsteps we're following. Maybe it's the path Dad laid down for us. He was determined to give us a better life. And he did. Even if he never had a chance to witness it."

Lucas glanced at where their wives were exchanging plans for the future, and thought about the unlikely way he and his brother had found exactly what they were looking for. "You know, I wouldn't be so sure about Dad not witnessing it. I think he might just know."

\* \* \* \* \*

# *Special Offers*

Every month we put together collections and longer reads written by your favourite authors.

Here are some of next month's highlights— and don't miss our fabulous discount online!

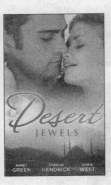

On sale 21st March

On sale 4th April

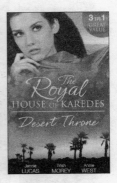

On sale 4th April

# *Save 20%*
## *on all Special Releases*